A Beach Wish

ALSO BY SHELLEY NOBLE

Lighthouse Beach

Christmas at Whisper Beach (novella)

The Beach at Painter's Cove

Forever Beach

Whisper Beach

A Newport Christmas Wedding (novella)

Breakwater Bay

Stargazey Nights (novella)

Stargazey Point

Holidays at Crescent Cove

Beach Colors

A Beach Wish

A Novel

Shelley Noble

This is a work of fiction. Names, characters, places, and incidents are products of the author's imagination or are used fictitiously and are not to be construed as real. Any resemblance to actual events, locales, organizations, or persons, living or dead, is entirely coincidental.

HarperCollins books may be purchased for educational, business, or sales promotional use. For information, please email the Special Markets Department at SPsales@harpercollins.com.

FIRST HARPERLUXE EDITION

ISBN: 978-0-06-291211-4

HarperLuxe™ is a trademark of HarperCollins Publishers.

Library of Congress Cataloging-in-Publication Data is available upon request.

19 20 21 22 23 LSC 10 9 8 7 6 5 4 3 2 1

To my children, Nick and Emma

A Beach Wish

Prologue

Zoe Bascombe graduated in marketing because, according to her family, she'd never make a real career out of music. What they'd meant was that she wouldn't climb a corporate ladder with hard work and smart investments—the only success they understood—but what she heard was, You don't have the talent to be a rock star.

She didn't want to be a rock star, she didn't want to be any kind of star, she wanted to write music. She'd studied piano—all well-heeled girls did—and tried her hand at composing; she even received a guitar one Christmas from her brother Chris. But when it came time to audition for Juilliard, she'd choked. She aced the entrance exam to Wharton. So . . .

After graduation, she landed a job at MAX4, a cutting-edge New York music event organizer, that put her close to music as she tackled exposure—marketing and physical; arranged transport for temperamental VIPs; synched schedules and herded staff members with less interest and ambition than her, hoping, praying, that somehow the climb up this corporate ladder would lead her to what she actually loved. Music.

And then she was downsized.

One day she was everybody's darling, the most requested project manager, the most indefatigable worker, the best packer—she never arrived anywhere with a wrinkle. Then . . .

"Due to a restructuring of the company . . ."

"It isn't your fault," she was assured by her superiors, all long-haired, jean-wearing corporate types. "We hate to see you go. But . . . seniority. You'll land on your feet. Hang in. Good luck."

There were tears. Not hers. She just gathered up her personal items and left, no closer to music than when she'd been doodling in the margins of her *Marketing*

Strategy textbook as she sat in class on the Wharton campus.

She spent three months looking for jobs by day and writing music and going to clubs by night.

It didn't take that long to know she couldn't afford to keep her apartment. So, leaving a month's rent with her two roommates, she returned home to live in her old room with her mother as her only companion.

Home. That day, home seemed like a failure, and family—like her revolving door of VIPs—was just a bunch of people to make happy and all too ready to complain about how you were doing your job.

Or they would have been if she hadn't walked into the kitchen three days later to find her mother dead on the floor.

A blood clot, they said. Jenny Bascombe had been living on borrowed time. Had known she was. And like the consummate organizer she was, she had planned her own funeral. Or in Jenny's case, the lack thereof.

She wanted her ashes spread on Wind Chime Beach, a place none of her family had ever heard of. She'd left it to Zoe to arrange transport.

Chapter 1

Zoe Bascombe shot both hands through her hair, leaving it in short, dark spikes. "I don't know why they're all angry at me."

She looked back at the porch steps where her family stood framed by her mother's perennial border. Her two eldest brothers, Errol and Robert, tall and blondish like their father, though Errol's hairline was beginning to recede. Their wives, suitably thin and coiffured. Their several children, fidgety with that glazed-eye look that said they'd been away from their iPhones too long.

There was also an aunt and two uncles on her father's side. No father—he had left them years ago for his new secretary. And her mother's attorney, the one person who looked back sympathetically at Zoe where she stood by the door of her SUV.

They were still in a state of angry denial. Zoe was, too.

Her youngest brother, Chris, also blond, the most handsome of the three and her only ally, opened the driver's door. "You better get going if you want to miss rush hour."

Zoe tried to smile. "It's always rush hour on Long Island."

"It'll be okay."

Easy for him to say. He didn't have to drive to the back of beyond with their mother's ashes strapped into the passenger seat. "Why—"

"Hush. Just go and find out. She must have had a reason. She always had a reason."

For everything, Zoe finished.

"I could go with you."

Zoe shook her head. "Just me. Like you said, she must have a reason."

"She trusted you to do it." He choked back a laugh. "Check out Errol. He looks like he'd happily toss her into the perennial border and be done with it."

"She'd be happy there," Zoe said. Her mother's garden was famous, appeared every spring in all the local magazines. "So why does she want to go to this Wind Chime place? She's never even been there. And why—"

"Just go. Call me when you get to the hotel."

"It will be late."

"Call me." He gave her a quick hug.

Zoe slid into the car.

Chris shut the door, smiled, and stepped back.

Zoe took a quick last look in her rearview mirror, where her family appeared as a perfectly framed photo for a bare second before dispersing out of frame. *Like an Etch A Sketch drawing turned upside down.*

Zoe could practically hear them wiping their hands of the situation.

She didn't look back again. She drove straight down the driveway and onto the street, cutting off life as she knew it in the blink of a turn signal.

It was a hot day and she turned on the air-conditioning. She'd rather lower the windows and let the air blast in to ruffle her hair—brunette like her mother's—but she was afraid of disturbing the simple celadon urn that her mother had bought for the purpose.

Putting the urn in the passenger seat had been Chris's idea. His idea of humor . . . Humor was Chris's way of coping. But Zoe knew it was because neither of them could stand the idea of their mom smothered in the darkness of a tote bag on the floor of the back seat.

Zoe glanced at the urn. "It's not like you're going to want to chat."

Was sarcasm a stage of grief? Because she'd been feeling really sarcastic lately.

"Why didn't you do something? Why didn't you tell us? Why didn't you let me help? Why?"

She didn't expect an answer and she didn't get one. Her mother wouldn't be answering ever again. She'd already said her last word on the subject—any subject.

Zoe sped up and passed under a light just as it turned red. She waited for a siren, that humiliating pull to the side of the road. A ticket. Or for lightning to strike. For a voice from the grave. Only there was no grave. Just the jar of the corporeal remains of Mrs. Jennifer Campbell Bascombe sitting on the seat beside her.

She reached for the radio, pulled her hand back. Her mother didn't really like music. Never let her or Chris play the car radio as kids. He was her closest brother, seven years older. Zoe had been the "surprise baby," not that anybody but her mother had seemed to welcome the surprise.

Zoe hummed under her breath. She needed air; she needed music. She needed to know why she was driving her mother out of state to be laid to rest with strangers.

In her own way, Jenny Bascombe had been a stranger. Not that she ever let it show. But now that

Zoe looked back on it—and she'd had plenty of time to do that in the past few days—there had been moments when her mother had seemed . . . remote.

Chris called it passive aggressive. Zoe wasn't so sure.

She merged onto the highway. Made her way into the left lane. The sooner she got there, wherever there was, the sooner she could . . . fill in the blank. Get back home? The boys were probably already putting up the "For Sale" sign on the midcentury ranch where they'd all grown up.

Look for a job? The will had been read. As always her mother had left no loopholes. She'd been wealthier than Zoe realized, and she'd divided her estate equally among her children except donations to a handful of her favorite charities. Now Zoe would have time to find the job she really wanted.

Not as a songwriter. That would seem like a betrayal. Still . . . a melodic line wove through her head, just a few notes; she'd been working on it before . . . but it had been silent since her mother's death. She'd thought it was lost forever.

"You might as well know. I brought my guitar. I found it in the attic when we were cleaning it out. It's in the back seat. Remember the Christmas Chris bought it for me? He wrapped it himself. He must have used two rolls of paper to get it all covered. I remember your face when he brought it out of hiding. I never knew if it was because it was a guitar or because he'd used the expensive wrapping paper." Zoe sighed. "I guess I'll never know now."

Why hadn't she talked to her mother more? After Chris left for college, and her father moved out, it had been just the two of them. She could tell her mother almost anything, but now it occurred to her that her mother had never talked about herself. She'd expressed concern over her rose bushes, wondered aloud if she should make petit fours or meringues for the Friends of the Library fund raiser. Deliberated over what to give the grandchildren for their birthdays. But nothing about *her.*

"Why was that, Mom?"

It didn't even feel odd, Zoe still doing the talking and her mother, if not listening, at least not interrupting. The way, Zoe realized, it had always been.

"Looks like it's just you and me . . . babe." She smiled. " 'Babe. I've got you, babe,' " she sang, knowing if her mother were hanging about in the afterlife, it would piss her off.

A song in a stack of old LPs on a turntable she and Chris had found in the attic one rainy Sunday afternoon.

They'd taken them downstairs and were singing along to Sonny and Cher—before, according to Chris, Cher had found Bob Mackie, all three of whom Zoe'd had to Google.

Their mother had burst into the bedroom, her face a livid red, her body shaking with wrath from her cultured pearl necklace to the razor cuffs of her linen slacks. She snatched the arm off the record, sending the needle scratching across the surface.

Without a word she gathered up the albums and the player, yanking the cord out of the socket without a thought, and left the room.

They never saw them again.

Actually, they never even mentioned them again. Only in their most outrageous moments did they dare recall even to each other the "S-and-C incident."

Now they would never know what had set her off. And at this moment nothing seemed more important than to know why their suburban garden-club mother had revealed that one brief glimpse into whatever was lurking deep inside her manicured façade.

Why hadn't Zoe realized it before now? There had always been a part of Jenny Bascombe that she didn't share. Maybe Zoe was about to find out what it was.

" 'I've got you, babe,' " Zoe sang at the top of her lungs, and burst into tears.

It took Zoe an hour just to get to the Whitestone Bridge, which would connect her to I-95 North, where the real trip would begin. She inched her way up the parkway, caught between Long Island rush hour commuters desperate to get home and island weekenders desperate to get to the beach. But she was wrapped in such a fog of looming disaster and nagging doubt that she'd hardly noticed.

Traffic didn't let up when she eased onto the highway and was met with another sea of cars. Where were all these people going? I-95 was a nightmare at the best of times. Today wasn't one of those. Maybe she should have flown somewhere and rented a car. But could you fly with . . . ? She didn't even want to think about it.

So she hunkered down for the long haul and did what she always did when she could snatch time to herself. Wrote lyrics in her head. Hummed a tune to go with them . . . the same elusive melody that kept pushing at her mind since she'd turned onto the highway . . . the one she thought she'd lost along with her mother. Would she forget her mother as easily as she'd forgotten that kernel of song?

She always forgot them if she didn't write them down. Which she couldn't do in traffic and she was too embarrassed to sing them into her phone's note recorder. Especially in front of her mother.

Get a grip. She can't hear you. She's gone. Maybe. Of course she was gone.

She tested the tune out loud, glanced at the urn. "You can blame Sonny and Cher." Though except for that one time, her mother had never discouraged her interest in music. Had driven her to her piano lesson once a week even though it was twenty minutes away. Of course, everything on Long Island was at least a twenty-minute drive.

Zoe had even caught her occasionally wearing earbuds while she gardened, though Zoe had assumed she was listening to a recorded book. Now she wondered. Had her mother been a closet heavy metal fan? Country-western? Bach?

Zoe's stomach growled. When she reached New Haven, she pulled into a drive-through. No way was she going to leave her mother unattended or take her inside a restaurant. She got a hamburger and a drink, texted Chris with an update, and ate as she drove.

Why had she agreed to do this? Nobody was happy with it. They tried to talk her out of it. She wanted to be talked out of it. But she knew she would do it. It was her mother's final request.

"I wish I could be happy about this," she told the urn. "I wish I understood."

Only a few times had Zoe glimpsed moments of the other woman she'd begun to suspect lived inside her mother. Perhaps only the vestiges of a younger self. She'd tried to imagine her mother as a sorority party girl, or a Cher groupie following the band, wearing strings of beads and waving incense. But she just couldn't.

Her mother had been . . . contained. Going about life as if it had been preordained, doing it with a smile, usually. She was never late for car pool, baked cookies for school birthdays, belonged to committees, spearheaded food drives, had the best perennial border in town.

She loved her children and her husband—until twelve years ago, when he left them for his secretary, Ashley, and he became, for all intents and purposes, "that lousy rat bastard." It was the only swear word Zoe had ever heard her mother say.

She doted on Zoe, something the boys said would keep her daughter from realizing her full potential. Maybe it had. But it had also kept her from missing her father, or feeling guilty that maybe somehow his leaving was her fault.

The silence stretched to an hour, then two. Connecticut passed into Rhode Island, Massachusetts, and at last New Hampshire. Zoe actually welcomed the usually irritating voice of "the girl"—she refused to give her GPS a name—when she said to turn off at the next exit.

She turned onto an access road. Gas stations, fast-food restaurants, drugstores, traffic lights. And more traffic lights.

One town melted into another as trees and houses gave way to more gas stations, fast food, then more towns, and more . . . This went on for another hour and Zoe wondered why "the girl" hadn't just kept her on the highway longer.

The sun began to set behind her. The fast food and gas stations fell away, leaving only trees and fields. The road became narrower, the trees denser, the houses sporadic. And it was rapidly becoming dark.

"Turn right in three-quarters of a mile."

"We must be getting closer," she told the urn. She made the turn onto an even smaller road, covered by low-hanging trees that managed to cut out what little light was left by the encroaching night. The few buildings that appeared in clearings in the trees were closed for the night—or forever. It was hard to tell. She began to doubt the reliability of her GPS.

It should be only another half hour to the inn where she'd reserved a room. She stretched her back, turned on her high beams only to have the light bounce back.

Fog. Great. A half hour? With the fog it could easily stretch into an hour.

"Turn right at the next—"

"What? Where—" She almost missed it. The small sign was practically covered over with underbrush.

Zoe turned right, straight into oblivion.

Well, actually, it was just a rutted road that might have been paved at one time, but had long ago lost most of its surface. Surely this wasn't the way to the spa. "Exclusive" was one thing, but "take your life in your hands to get there" was another.

She slowed, swerved to miss a huge rut only to hit another. The SUV lurched and Zoe automatically stuck out a hand to protect her passenger.

And came face-to-face with a tree. She slammed on the brakes. The road forked to either side; two signs appeared in the beam of her headlights. A weathered wooden one with an arrow pointing to the right fork and letters she could hardly make out. Except PRIVATE.

Okay, they wouldn't be going there. The other sign was in moderately better shape and announced TOWN to the left. She turned left.

This had to be the back way into town, the old road,

one of those GPS decisions to take her on the route with no tolls or no traffic jams or something.

The Solana Inn and Spa had a great website. Had looked very upscale. Modern, fêng shui'ed into the next century. Zoe had stayed in a lot of great hotels because of her work, but she would never personally consider staying in a place that expensive, that healthy, or that trendy, but she was glad she had this time.

A nice Jacuzzi tub, room service, and glass—or two—of white wine sounded really good.

"You really should ask before you make these decisions," she told the disembodied, now quiet, voice in her dashboard. "This is taking forever."

She eased the SUV ahead.

She was barely going ten miles an hour. Slow enough to see what appeared to be an abandoned shed by the side of the—and she used the term loosely—road.

She did see a light up ahead. One single light that didn't seem to be near the road, but off in the distance, as it winked in and out from behind the trees.

"Does this look right to you, Mom? I hope this isn't the product of some crazy Google search gone wrong. 'Top Ten Best Places to Spread Your Ashes,' and you didn't notice the post was from 2002."

Strange shapes appeared in and out of the darkness. Old wooden buildings? Houses? It was impossible to tell what they'd been originally. But they were definitely no longer in use. For a staggering nanosecond Zoe feared this might be the spa. And the website was just a ploy to lure unsuspecting young women into the clutches of—

The SUV hit a hole, and Zoe squeaked in true too-dumb-to-live heroine mode. She puffed her cheeks and blew out air.

"Please be going someplace. Someplace civilized."

But her GPS had grown dark; the voice, silent.

Heart hammering, she eased the car out of the pothole. Was it too late to turn around? Go home? Just admit to her brothers that they'd been right all along? Forsake her mother's last wishes?

She couldn't do it.

The road curved slightly and then widened onto a ghost town of shadowy debris that maybe had been buildings a long time and several storms ago. Then the one light in the woods winked out completely and didn't come back on. She was surrounded by total darkness and encroaching mist.

"That's it. I'm turning around." At least there was a road back there. There had to be a better way to the inn. She came to a stop, looked over her shoulder to start the turn.

An apparition stepped out of the shadows behind

her, unearthly tall with long white hair and a flowing robe. And by his side was an animal, a beast, not a dog or anything else from this world. *His familiar.* He raised his hand.

"Or not." Zoe floored the accelerator. The SUV shot forward, bouncing down the non-road like a cartoon car in the night. For better or worse, there was no going back now.

Chapter 2

Ten minutes—hours, eons—later, the SUV bumped onto pavement. Pavement, glorious pavement. Up ahead were lights, lots of lights, a whole town of them. And though it was late, places were open, and people strolled along the sidewalk. Music wafted out of bars. Ahead, the sign for Solana Inn and Spa rose from the lawn of a several-storied white clapboard inn, complete with turret that according to the website overlooked the sea.

"You have reached your destination."

"Great. Now you get chatty." Zoe pulled into the circular drive and stopped beneath the porte cochere, where wide steps led up to a porch bathed in light from hanging frosted globes.

Now, this was more like it. She unbuckled the urn from the seat belt and slipped it into a carryall, grabbed her purse, and turned over her keys to a strapping young man with a low ponytail wearing khaki pants and a white polo shirt with the hotel's name embroidered across the pocket.

"Welcome to Solana. May I help you with your luggage?"

"Just the computer case and bag in the back. Leave the other," she said, indicating the guitar case. She handed him two dollars, and clutching the carryall tightly against her side, she climbed the steps to the entrance.

The lobby was everything she'd pictured. Bright, clean, minimal, and pristine without appearing antiseptic or New Age. Music sounded from a doorway that led to the bar. And the band sounded pretty good. Always a plus.

The receptionist looked up from the screen of a sleek computer. She was young, a little younger than Zoe, late teens, early twenties and wholesome-looking. Her light blond hair was pulled back in a high ponytail, but the polo shirt and khakis of the outside staff had morphed into a flowing off-white gauze blouse and harem pants.

"Welcome to Solana."

Zoe smiled and handed over her credit card and driver's license.

"Ah, Ms. Bascombe. We were beginning to think you weren't coming."

"I was delayed a bit. Must have taken a wrong turn. Tell me the only way into town is not down a rutted road through a ghost town."

"Oh Lord. GPS, right?" The receptionist sighed. "We've been trying to get the state to put up a better sign and they did, only it's worse."

"You mean it's paved all the way here."

"Of course. But there are two turnoffs within a few yards of each other. You took the first one, right?"

"Evidently."

"It happens. Most people turn around and go back to the main road."

Zoe wrinkled her nose. "I meant to but . . ." *But I saw a ghost in the road and I freaked out and now I feel like a fool.*

The girl nodded but didn't look up while she was plugging in Zoe's information.

"Zoe. Life," the girl said, with what could only be called a wistful smile.

"Bascombe," Zoe said. "My last name is Bascombe."

The girl's smile broadened. "No. I mean, Zoe is the ancient Greek word for 'life.' It's a lucky name."

"Oh," Zoe said. She looked for the girl's name tag; it always paid to learn your contact's name—plus she liked knowing people's names. But nothing spoiled the pristine fabric of the gauze blouse.

The receptionist handed her a plastic key card. "We have you in Sea Light."

Zoe choked back a laugh. That had so many meanings and plays on words, she didn't even attempt a comment.

"On the third floor. It has one of our best views. The elevator is down the hall to your left, next to the stairs. And if you're hungry, the bar is open and the grill serves until eleven. We have both traditional fare as well as our spa specialties."

"Sounds good."

"I'll have your luggage sent to your room. Would you like to leave your tote here and I'll make sure it gets upstairs?"

Zoe clutched the straps of the bag. "That's okay. I'll just keep it with me."

"Well, bon appétit, then." The receptionist went back to her computer screen.

Zoe headed straight for the bar. As she reached the doorway, the singer moaned, "Jenny, oh, Jenny."

Zoe stopped, slightly unnerved. She recovered quickly; it was just a coincidence. Still . . . "Hey, Mom, they're playing your song," she said to the tote bag. Maybe she was losing her mind. But really, ghosts, the Sea Light room, and a local folksinger with her mother's name on his lips. It was too weird.

The bar was crowded, the lighting dim except for the small raised stage in the far corner where a spotlight cast an uneven glow over the performers. Four of them—a guitar, a fiddle, a bass, and a piano. Three of the musicians were pretty young, but the guitarist was an older dude with a long ponytail.

To the left of the stage was a large fireplace, now dark. At the back of the room, French doors opened onto a softly lit patio. Every table seemed to be occupied, as well as the couch and several easy chairs that made a comfortable niche in one corner. A long wooden bar ran across the opposite wall, where a muscular, bearded bartender served beers and cocktails with a grace that sat incongruously on his mountain-man appearance.

The guitarist crooned on. He had a good voice. *And a deep soul,* thought Zoe, and stepped into the room.

He looked up. "Jenny" cracked into a sharp note. His fingers froze and the guitar pick fell to the floor. He looked straight at Zoe. She took an involuntary step backward. The band played on without him.

Then he disappeared behind the heads of the crowd.

A moment later he stood, the pick retrieved, and joined in on the next verse, but his eyes were still on the doorway.

Zoe backed out of the room. In the lobby light, the spell was broken. But for a minute she'd felt . . .

Too many hours on the road. Too much heartbreak. Strange visions in the dark. Her mother's ashes resting close against her side.

The singer had recovered and was singing his "lonely sad song," followed by something about trembling leaves.

Maybe she wasn't that hungry, after all; maybe there was a fruit basket in her room. An apple would be fine, a granola bar.

She cast a last longing look as a waitress passed by carrying a tray of burgers and onion rings. But the band had geared up for another song, and no way could she face that penetrating stare or the man's gravelly, mournful voice.

As soon as Zoe reached her room, she took the urn out of the carryall and placed it on the dresser, a sleek dark wood and brass-handled affair. The urn's smooth curved surface, the delicate green glaze, fit right in with the décor.

She bit back a somewhat hysterical laugh. "If I'd thought ahead, I'd have brought a doily to put under you."

A fruit basket was sitting on the table. She found the mini fridge demurely hidden in the wardrobe, sighed with relief when she saw there were indeed mini bottles of—she took one out and looked at the label—organic Chardonnay.

She unscrewed the top and poured the contents into one of the two wineglasses that shared a tray with two water tumblers. These were just the sort of amenities she looked for when choosing accommodations for her VIPs. Of course she didn't have to do that anymore. She no longer had VIPs.

She took a sip of wine. Full bodied, yet smooth.

She walked over to the drapes and drew them aside, revealing glass doors that opened onto a small balcony. "Cool." She slid them open and stepped outside to a light breeze and a clear, star-studded sky. Below her, a lawn was surrounded by shadowed shrubs and flowers. Tiny pagoda-shaped lamps picked out a brick path that led into the landscape. She could smell the sea, hear waves in the distance punctuated by a gentle echo of the band that was still playing in the bar.

She yawned and gulped down half the wine in her

glass, then walked back inside. She briefly considered leaving the doors open to take advantage of the crisp ocean air and decided against it. She was from Long Island, after all. No telling what or who might climb in during the night. Psychopaths? Ghosts from her past—or her present?

She closed the doors and the drapes, downed the rest of her wine, and turned to face her mother. "Why are we here? We should have talked about this before—all of us. Together. Maybe I should have waited. The boys were all against it, even Chris. They're pretty angry.

"Why just me? Chris would have come, even though he's terribly hurt. They all are. You don't want friends and family to see you off? It doesn't make sense.

"What am I supposed to do? Why didn't you leave better instructions? You're the mistress of clarity, the organizer of organizations, the devil in everyone's details. Why were you so sloppy at the end?"

She raised her glass, realized it was empty. Marched over to the mini fridge and pulled out another little bottle. She wasn't much of a drinker and she was already feeling the effects of the first glass; at least tonight she might sleep. Maybe if she had tried drinking before bed the past few days, she wouldn't be in this state.

Of course she would be. She turned on the urn. "What am I going to do now that you're gone? You were my safety net, my refuge, you were always there for me. Always, even when I could see that it was inconvenient, that if you had been someone else and not my mother, you would have been annoyed that I bothered you. Why did you let me rely on you so much all these years?

"Why did you wait until you were gone to rely on me?

"Who were you?" Zoe stared at the urn, swaying slightly from the wine or possibly the image of her mother hiding inside waiting to be summoned. One good rub and she would appear like that old sitcom genie that popped out of a golden lamp. Though her mother wouldn't be caught dead in flowing chiffon with her navel showing. Of course *her* mother wouldn't have flaunted convention and refuse to be buried in the family plot—and yet she had.

Well, tomorrow Zoe would do her duty, find this Wind Chime Beach and spread the ashes. She'd go home and hope that someday her brothers would forgive her for fulfilling her mother's wishes instead of theirs.

She started to open another bottle of wine, opted for a granola bar from the basket instead. She sat on the bed, opened the package, and took a bite; she chewed while she texted the only brother still speaking to her. *Arrived at hotel. Safe for now.*

She took another bite.

Her phone pinged. *K.*

"K." Just one letter. The granola bar turned to gravel, and she spit it in the trash. She didn't bother to unpack but pulled a nightshirt out of her suitcase and took it into the bathroom to change. A stupid time for modesty; there was no one there but her.

She brushed her teeth and climbed into bed. She tried not to look at the urn sitting so alone on the dresser.

"I've got you, babe," she whispered.

And tomorrow, she would have to let her go.

It was after one when Eve Gordon peeked into the silent lobby of the Solana. Seeing it empty, she stepped inside. She always made a point to mingle with her guests, but not when she was dressed in a pair of stained, wet baggy jeans and an overlarge T-shirt. Being the proprietor of an upscale inn and spa didn't mean you didn't have to sometimes get down and get dirty.

She'd spent the past hour and a half uninstalling a plastic bag from the laundry pipes. How or why it got there still eluded her.

She smiled, tired but satisfied now that the bag had been successfully extricated without having to call a plumber. The lobby lights had been dimmed, leaving just enough light for late-returning guests to see their way across the lobby to the elevators. There was no one behind the reception desk, so their last guest must have arrived for the night. Eve fought the urge to check the registration list. Mel wouldn't leave her post early, even though Eve knew she was not happy about having to work a double shift.

Well, that was family for you. Noelle had been called out of town for a job interview. *Out of town.* It's what she'd always planned for her girls. Make a good home for them and give them the means to fly on their own. Harmony had flown to California and stayed. She had a good job and a growing family. Noelle had yet to settle, but she had her sights on New York, Boston, Chicago. Only Mel showed all the signs of sticking around—and for all the wrong reasons.

There was still work light in the bar, though the patrons and band would have departed an hour or so ago. She wandered inside. Mike McGill was standing behind the bar doing a final inventory for the night.

He looked up, nodded, and poured her a glass of Chardonnay. She perched on a barstool in front of him.

"Get the pipe cleared?"

Eve savored the crisp white wine. "Yes, a plastic bag. Go figure. Good crowd tonight?"

"Pretty good, but . . ."

Eve put down her glass. "But?"

"I'm not sure, but Lee was . . . Something happened during the last set. He just kind of looked out the door and stopped playing altogether. I was afraid he might be having a mini stroke or something."

"Is he okay?"

Mike frowned, rubbed a spot on the bar with a white cloth. "He seemed okay after that. But he had two bourbons when the set was over."

Eve shook her head. "He hardly ever drinks." *Anymore.*

"I know, but he closed the place down. I didn't want him driving home in his condition. So I put him to bed on the couch in the office. Hope that's okay."

"Of course. Thanks, Mike. I'll go check on him."

"I don't imagine he'll wake up before morning, but I took the keys to his truck." He reached beneath the bar and dropped a ring of keys on the bar in front of Eve.

She scooped them up and put them in her jeans pocket. "Thanks. I wonder what could have set him off."

Mike's large hand closed over hers and gave it a squeeze. "How many years have you been trying to figure out what makes your father tick?"

"Too many."

"So you probably won't figure it out tonight. Go, get some sleep. I'll close up. You have eleven folks signed up for the new session of Body Bliss first thing tomorrow. Though several of them were having a great time at the bar tonight so . . ." Mike wiggled his hand in the air.

Eve yawned. "Kira will whip them into blissful shape."

"I have no doubt."

Eve finished her wine and pushed the glass over to Mike. "Thanks," she said on another yawn. "See you tomorrow."

He raised his hand in farewell and went back to his inventory.

Eve headed across the lobby. She intended to call it a night, but as she passed the reception desk, she couldn't stop herself. She went behind the desk and into the office. Lying as if dead on the leather couch against the back wall, her father, Lee Gordon, once lead guitarist and singer of Night Chill, looked like any one of the old men who lived in town. *What are you dreaming, Dad? Of glory? Of fame? Of just getting through tomorrow?*

She lifted the edge of the cotton quilt that Mike had draped over him. Tucked it beneath his shoulder, not that he would notice. She kissed his cheek, sunken from years of hard living and scruffy from not shaving. A look that had driven his fans wild in his younger years. But tonight, with his mouth slightly open in sleep, it just made him look unkempt.

"Night, Dad," she whispered, and tiptoed out. She let herself out the side door and walked down the short path to the cottage where she lived with Mel, and Noelle when she was in town. The porch light was on. Either Mel was inside asleep or had been and gone.

Chapter 3

It was still dark when Zoe woke up. In her dream she was playing a lullaby on the baby grand in the living room. Her mother stood at her shoulder, singing. Singing? That couldn't be right. Zoe sat up in bed, disoriented, but not nearly as tired as she should be. She shot out of bed and padded across the shadowed room and pulled the cord to the drapes, then stepped back, blinking against the sudden, painful brightness.

Talk about your light-blocking curtains. It was dazzling outside. And later than she'd thought. She opened the glass doors, stepped onto the balcony, and stretched, letting the sun warm her face, breathing in the fresh morning air.

She peered over the balcony rail where, below her, a

swath of lawn spread out like a carpet—like a sea—like a . . . crescendo of green.

And flowers, and shrubs, and pampas grasses with their feathered tops riffling in the breeze. A path meandering down to a white sand beach. The waves a distant steady rhythm, intertwining with the breeze to create a smooth line above the staccato of human activity below her.

A perfect place for letting inspiration flow. And for saying good-bye.

She rested her elbows on the railing and watched a yoga class on the beach "greeting the sun." She tried to clear her own mind, think of nothing. Not music, not poetry, not family—not the duty that lay ahead.

What did it say that a woman wouldn't want to be buried near her children? Did it even matter? It wasn't like they were all going to rest eternally together. People moved on, joined other families, bought their own family plots. Her family didn't even visit the cemetery.

Somewhere below her, the quiet hum of conversation was punctuated by the clink of . . . silverware. The aroma of breakfast. That fast-food burger from her drive was a dim memory. She went inside and headed straight to the shower.

Twenty minutes later, armed with her laptop but

not the urn—which she'd replaced in the carryall and hidden in the closet behind her suitcase—Zoe went downstairs in search of sustenance.

She found it at the end of a short hallway: an airy restaurant with a patio eating area. She stopped at the "Please Wait to be Seated" sign, then opted for an outside table and followed the hostess—another wholesome-looking young woman—across the room.

She was seated at a table next to a bush heavy with red flowers, with a view of the lawn and a vee of blue ocean in the distance.

The hostess handed her a menu. "Enjoy your morning. Elena will be with you shortly. Would you care for coffee, tea, juice while you decide?"

"Coffee—please." The woman left and Zoe bent her head over the menu. She scanned past the "healthy living" part and went straight to the eggs, passed over the turkey bacon and meatless sausage to the locally raised real pork links, and was deliberating over sourdough, whole wheat toast, or a waffle with fresh fruit when the waitress returned with her coffee.

"Good morning, I'm Elena, and I'm happy to serve you."

Zoe decided to stick to eggs, sausage, and toast and gave her order. As soon as Elena smiled herself away,

Zoe took a sip of coffee, hesitated only long enough to savor the rich, heady roast, then pulled out her laptop. Which was ridiculous. She had no work to do here. None that needed a laptop. Not a calendar or a spreadsheet. Not one idea for a lyric, not even a bass line inspired by the waves.

She opened it anyway. She wasn't the only one with an open laptop on the table, and she wondered if any of the other guests were actually doing business or just gazing into the distance like she was.

And that's how the waitress found her when she returned with Zoe's breakfast.

"How do I get to the beach?" Zoe asked.

"You can take the path through the garden over there, or there is a direct elevator to the beach access road."

Zoe considered asking the girl if it was called Wind Chime Beach. It seemed just like something a chic spa would name their beach. But if it was, they might not like ashes being spread so close to where their clientele worked on their asanas and tans.

She closed her laptop and dug in. Her breakfast was delicious, every fried, eggy, porky morsel. She ate it all and agreed to a refill of the rich coffee. She reopened her laptop, but instead of writing, she sat back and watched a large orange-and-black monarch as it flitted among the flowers.

A shadow momentarily blocked out the sun. She looked up.

A tall, buxom, thirty-something woman dressed in yoga pants and a bright yellow off-the-shoulder tee was standing over her.

"I hate to bother you, but would you mind awfully if I sat in your extra chair? You look like you're working and I promise not to say a word, but I'm dying for a cup of coffee and they won't seat me until the rest of my party arrives." She made a goofy face and Zoe immediately liked her.

"Please." Zoe gestured to the empty chair. Actually, she wouldn't mind the company for a few minutes.

"Thanks. We had such a night and I don't know how I'll ever face Morning Mantra without some Joe."

Elena appeared to fill the newcomer's cup and topped off Zoe's. She would be buzzing to the beach before long.

The woman across from her took a sip of coffee and let out a long sigh. "Ah. Heaven. I'm Karen, by the way."

"Zoe."

"Which package are you doing?" Karen asked.

"I'm not. I have other business in town."

"Oh. And I interrupted. Sorry."

"Not at all." Zoe closed her laptop. "Are you doing a package?"

Karen nodded. "Soul Sister Weekend. I'm here with two friends. Hot stone massages, Jacuzzi, morning yoga, facials. It's really nice. Plus the food is really good here. The last place we went was all kale juice and nature walks. They have a real bar," Karen said. "The gin may be organic, but it has an alcohol content that you can count."

She leaned closer to Zoe. "Plus there are a lot of great places to eat and drink in town if you get tired of the hotel. Lots of places to hear music, but they have a pretty good house band here. The guitarist is an old dude, but he used to be semifamous back in the seventies. I've never heard of him, but he's a big deal around here."

"I think I heard him for a minute last night."

"And the spa really is wonderful. You should try some of the specialties while you're here," Karen added.

"They should hire you for PR," Zoe said, when she could get in a word.

"Not me. I'm a number cruncher. Inventory control for a national sporting goods manufacturer. What do you do?" Karen leaned over to sip her coffee; dark brown hair swung past her cheeks, cutting off her expression from Zoe's view.

Good question, thought Zoe. "Well, currently I . . . I'm in the music industry."

Karen put down her cup. "Wow. Like a musician? Do you perform? Are you on tour?"

Zoe swallowed. "Actually, I work at the event end."

"Like rock concerts?"

"And award ceremonies. Galas. Things like that."

"That's so exciting."

Zoe nodded. It had been a pain in the butt, but it had also been exciting and it had given her lots of opportunities to be around music. It just hadn't gotten her a gig writing it.

"Do you know any rock stars?"

"A few."

A woman, possibly the activity hostess, had been making her way around the tables, and she stopped at Zoe's. She was fortyish, maybe a little older, but tall and fit, with wavy reddish-blond hair, and seemed slightly familiar. The mark of a good hostess.

"Good morning, Karen. You must be Zoe Bascombe. I'm Eve Gordon, the proprietor of Solana. So glad you made it in last night. Mel said you took the old turn into town."

"Nice to meet you. It was an adventure."

"Oh, I love adventures," Karen said. "Though I don't have too many. What happened?"

"Just a little fog. And a few potholes."

"We'll be sure to give better directions at the end of your stay. The highway is two minutes away."

"Good to know."

"Zoe says she's here on business," Karen said. "But I've been trying to talk her into joining us for one of the packages. I know, you could meet us for Body Bliss tomorrow morning."

Eve laughed. "We'll be glad to accommodate you if you decide to stay. Anything you need, please just ask." She moved on to the next table of patrons. It was a nice touch—not too much, no hard sell, and she hadn't stayed long enough to incur an awkward silence.

"Isn't she the sweetest? The spa is family run. Everyone is really friendly and seems to like their jobs." Karen's eyes rolled upward. "Unlike someplace I could name."

"A particular sporting goods office, for one?"

"The stories I could tell. Oh, there's Elaine and Brandy." She waved at the two women who had just stepped into the sunlight. Zoe felt a jolt of envy. Three friends having a fun weekend away. Until recently, Zoe would have considered a weekend alone in her apartment with time to do laundry a fun weekend away. But not today.

The women hurried over, and Zoe slipped her laptop into its case.

Introductions were made. Elaine curvy, with curly light brown hair, and Brandy, thin and muscular, definitely the athlete of the three.

Zoe stood. "You guys sit down. I have to get going. So nice to meet you."

"We aren't running you off, are we?" Elaine asked.

"No. I'm here on business and it's way past time I got to it."

"Thanks for the seat, it was nice meeting you," Karen said. "Maybe we'll see you tonight at the bar."

"Maybe," Zoe said, and headed inside.

Maybe she would meet them at the bar tonight. Maybe she'd stay for a few extra days. Do one of the packages. That would be a change, a weekend in a hotel, where she did nothing but get pampered instead of taking care of everyone else. The idea was growing on her.

But first she needed to find Wind Chime Beach and do her duty to her mother. Then she could take a few days for herself before she had to get back to her life.

The thought stopped her midstep. And just what was her life? Would she return to Manhattan and make the rounds of event planners, land another hair-tearing job as an event coordinator? At least MAX4 had been big on music. She might end up organizing corporate think tank weekends. Or worse.

Besides, she'd given up her apartment. She couldn't go back home, not by herself. Chris would take her in. But she couldn't camp out at his place while she looked for a job. Chris was an actor, but even he'd had the good sense to hook up with a real estate developer, Timothy. They lived in a beautiful apartment on the Upper West Side. She wouldn't intrude.

She rode up the elevator in a fog more debilitating than the one she'd driven through the night before.

The maid had already been. The bed was made; there were fresh flowers on the dresser. The whole room smelled clean and peaceful, and she would have been happy just to relax there, except for what she knew was waiting for her in the closet.

She forced herself to take out the carryall and carefully placed the urn back on the dresser. "I'm not taking you with me. This is purely a recce. And the idea of searching through town for this Wind Chime Beach—a place that, by the way, isn't even mentioned on the town website—with you slung over my shoulder is just too depressing.

"Last chance to change your mind. Are you sure this is what you want? Won't you be lonely spread everywhere, drifting around on the sand or the ocean with . . . no one to talk to?"

She stopped, horrified. She was the one doing all the talking. Her mother had left days ago. She wasn't coming back.

Zoe pushed her fingers through her hair. "I suppose I should do some kind of ceremony? A prayer?"

She didn't know any.

A song? Music had once lit a fire inside her, made her feel vibrant. But it had been a private feeling. She didn't really perform in public. Certainly not for her family. Music was *her* life, not her mother's.

Now she was afraid that fire had been doused—killed by her own inattention.

She grabbed her purse and went downstairs. She stopped by the desk on her way out and was surprised to see the same girl as the night before.

"Doing double duty?" Zoe asked her.

"Huh?" The girl looked up. "Oh, hi. Yeah, the person who usually does the morning shift called in sick. And my sister Noelle is in New York interviewing for a job, so I have to stay here until the afternoon shift comes on."

"Instead of going to the beach?"

The girl grinned. "Yeah."

"Well, I'm looking for a beach, too."

"Oh, you just go right down the path out back to the stone steps. There are umbrellas, and lounges, and towels and showers, everything you'll need. Even a juice bar." She leaned over the counter and said conspiratorially, "You have to smuggle in your own vodka."

Zoe laughed. "Good to know." Could this possibly be the beach where she was supposed to spread her mother's ashes? "Actually, I'm looking for a specific place called Wind Chime Beach."

The girl frowned. "Wind Chime . . . I don't think I know of a beach . . . Well, there is Wind Chime House."

"That must be it."

"But it's just an old house that used to be a hippie commune."

"A hippie commune?"

"Yeah."

"And people still live there?"

"Oh, sure. Floret and Henry and a couple old dudes who retired and came back to live there. And Eli and his uncle David live there. He's kind of the caretaker. He's really a photographer, but . . . well, it's a long story. And Eli; he's like my best friend."

"They won't mind if I visit them?"

"Oh, no, it was a pretty big deal in its day. People are always coming to visit and reminisce or to see where their parents or grandparents used to live. Only don't mention that you're staying here."

"Why?"

She leaned over the counter. "It's not our fault. Floret and my great-grandmother have been at it for years. Nobody knows why, at least not that they tell me. It would be funny, if it didn't upset Mom so much. How did you hear about it?"

"My mother." It slipped out without Zoe thinking.

"Wow! My mother was raised there. Maybe yours hung out there, too. Maybe they know each other."

Zoe shook her head. "I doubt it. I'm not sure my mother was ever here. She was raised in Long Island with a string of pearls around her neck. Her linen pants didn't dare wrinkle. I never saw her let anything 'hang out.' "

The girl laughed. "She doesn't sound like the type to live in a commune."

"No," Zoe said automatically. So why would her mother want to come here? "Does this commune have a beach?"

"It does. It abuts ours." She rolled her eyes. "Mom's been trying to buy it forever. But Floret and Henry won't sell."

"So I can just walk from your beach to theirs?" It still sounded a little too public for what Zoe had to do.

"Not really." The receptionist made a face. "It's barricaded. We, actually my great-grandma, built a jetty across the sand to keep our people from wandering too close, and they put up a sign not to climb on the rocks because it was dangerous. But it's really because their people like to sunbathe nude. I don't know what the big deal is—our people are *practically* nude." She slapped her hand to her mouth.

Zoe laughed. It had been a while.

"I'm Mel."

"Let me guess. Short for Melody."

"Have you ever heard anything so dorky?"

"Zoe?"

Mel laughed.

"I think Mel is a great name."

"Thanks."

"So if I want to get to this Wind Chime Beach, how would I go about it?"

"Oh. Just go right out the door. Two blocks, then on the next block you'll see two white houses, then a smaller cottage with one of those little wishing wells out front. That's the Kellys' house. They own the local diner if you get in the mood for good and greasy. You just go down their driveway. Their house is on your left and Little Woods will be on your right. You go all the way to the end. And you'll see it."

"Well, thanks, Mel. I think I'll go over now and take a look.

A faint flush spread over Mel's face. "Sorry. I talk too much. Everyone says so."

"I don't think so," Zoe said. "I've enjoyed talking to you."

"Thanks."

Zoe started out the door, but as she opened it, a man stepped in.

"Oh, excuse me."

"I beg your pard—" He stopped cold and Zoe recognized the off-key singer from the bar.

She smiled perfunctorily and tried to slide past him. He didn't move; his expression didn't change. He stood blocking her way, staring at her in a way that made a chill run up her spine.

"I'm so sorry." She ducked under his arm and fled.

Lee Gordon stared after the girl who'd just left the inn. So he wasn't losing his mind. *She was here.* She couldn't be here. Why had he drunk that bourbon last night? He couldn't do that shit anymore. Not booze, not drugs, not women, not any of it.

So why was it coming back now? He spun around, marched over to the reception desk where his youngest granddaughter was minding the store.

"Hi, Granddad, how was breakfast?"

"Huh? Good and greasy."

"What are you gonna do if Kelly ever goes organic?"

"Starve, I guess. Who was that?"

"The woman who just left?"

Girl. She was just a girl. "Yeah."

"One of our guests. Why?"

He pulled himself together. "No reason. Where's your mother?"

"In the office. Granddad, what's the matter?"

"Nothing."

Eve stepped out of the office. "I thought I heard your voice. I guess you went to the diner for breakfast instead of enjoying our four-star fare."

"Of course I did. Who is that woman that just left here?"

Eve raised her eyebrows. "Now I'm clairvoyant?" She looked at Mel.

"It was Zoe. Ms. Bascombe."

"Bascombe." Lee spat out the name.

"Yeah," Mel said, and bit her lip. "Why are you angry?"

"I'm not angry. Where was she going?"

Mel looked uncertainly at Eve.

Oh Lord, thought Eve. Her father had his "turns,"

as her grandmother called them. It came from his years of fast living. They were all used to it, but he'd never been interested in a guest before. And certainly not so aggressively.

"Well, girl?"

Eve bristled. "Who are you calling 'girl'?"

"My granddaughter."

"Yeah, well, you sound like some up-country redneck. She has a name."

Her father's eyes locked with hers in a standoff that catapulted her back to an earlier time. A time when Lee Gordon was still doing the music circuit, when his moods were mercurial and extreme. Eve had loved him with all her heart, loved and feared him, because you never knew when he'd become the crazy man she didn't recognize.

"Mel, then. What's this Zoe person doing here?"

"She's a guest, Dad," Eve said. "Just a guest, here to have a nice weekend."

"She was going to the beach," Mel said, her voice tentative.

"She can get to the beach out back."

"She was asking about a beach called Wind Chime. I sent her down to Floret and Henry's since you can't get to their beach from ours." She shot her grandfather a defiant look.

Eve stiffened.

But instead of his usual outburst, her father softened. "Sorry, Mellie. I'm just a grumpy old man."

"Probably Kelly's sausage," Eve said.

"Probably," Lee said. "Well, I'll see you." He turned toward the door.

"Where are you going?"

"Home. I'll be back for the early set." He saluted Mel, nodded to Eve, and strode out the door.

"That was weird," Mel said as soon as he was gone.

"It was," Eve agreed.

"Why do you think he was so upset? It wasn't sausages."

Eve shook her head. "Granddad has a lot of . . ."

Mel rolled her eyes. "Issues."

"Yes. Things set him off that don't bother the rest of us. I've never been able to figure him out."

"Just have to love him the way he is," Mel said.

"How did I get such a wise daughter?" Eve knew in that split second she shouldn't have said it. She could see Mel gearing up for battle. Eve cut her off before she could begin. "And that's why it's important for you to go to college. So you can continue to make wise choices."

"You don't understand."

Oh, but she did. She'd been young and headstrong

once. And gotten herself pregnant at the end of her senior year. Of course there had never been a mother in the world who could convince her children that she knew exactly what they were feeling. And that it was her job to make sure her children didn't make the same mistakes she had.

She'd never even known her own mother.

Would she have listened to her advice if she had? It was just one of the many things she'd never know.

As far as her father was concerned . . . he never even tried to give advice. He'd been too busy wrestling with his own demons. She'd never known what he was thinking, and she didn't know now. Was she wrong to be concerned?

He wasn't a violent man. Never had been. Not toward others. His anger and bitterness always turned inward, destroying himself and, unintentionally, those around him. She thought he'd mellowed, gotten over his disappointments in life. But she'd seen something in him just now that frightened her.

And it had been set off by Zoe Bascombe.

Chapter 4

Okay, that was just weird, Zoe thought as she walked down the sidewalk away from the inn. She stopped at the corner to regroup and take a look around. The town was as charming in daylight as it had been busy the night before. A jumble of row houses and stand-alones had been built, or repurposed, as the business district. Not an empty storefront that she could see.

Successful and busy.

She had to wait for several cars to pass, then crossed the street. She walked past a boutique that displayed colorful beachwear. Next to it, the window mannequins were clothed in basic black and designer labels. An antiques store, a gourmet deli, a cigar store, a pub featuring live music. That was tempting—would have been tempting, under ordinary circumstances. In Manhattan, she sat in with the house band at her favorite bar at least once a week when she wasn't traveling.

She came to Kelly's Diner—presumably the same Kelly whose driveway she'd be using—wedged between a store named Babykins, Infant Couture and a beach accessories shop. At the end of the block a bookstore named Book Nook was housed in a white frame cottage.

Usually with some time off, she'd have peered in the windows, gone inside to browse. She was always looking for little gifts for her co-workers or her family, or bargains for herself. But today she wasn't tempted. Between her doorway confrontation with that old rocker and the duty that lay ahead of her, she had no patience for shopping.

The day was warm—there wasn't a breeze to temper the high-riding sun—and she stood at the curb wishing she'd stopped at the deli for a bottle of water.

Kitty-cornered from where she stood, a quaint white clapboard church was shaded by two giant trees. A glass-covered sign welcomed all to their services. Zoe's family had never been very religious, though there was something about the ritual of it all that appealed to Zoe. And the music. Churches might get some things wrong, but they sure knew how to do music.

But not for her, not today anyway. Today she was looking for a beach. She crossed the street before she could change her mind. She was suddenly anxious to get this trip over with. And at the same time dreading what she might find—or not find. *Please don't make me have to go back to hand the ashes over to Errol like he had demanded before I left.*

She passed a big white house on the corner that had been converted into offices. Then another large house, also painted white. A third house was a little stone cottage with the white wishing well in front that Mel had told her about. It looked out of place next to the stately old homes.

Beyond it was the undeveloped lot Mel called Little Woods. Zoe turned down the drive, hugging the far side, where the trees sheltered her from the sun and, to be truthful, where she could avoid any confrontations with the homeowners. The drive was paved as far as the Kellys' garage; then the pavement gave way to cracking and heaving, before giving way to a stony, rutted car path.

It was a pleasant walk in spite of whatever might be facing her at the end, but foremost in her mind was *Don't tell them I'm staying at the inn.* Floret and Mel's great-grandmother were adversaries. She fervently hoped she wasn't going to be welcomed with a shotgun and the feuding Hatfields. Or would it be the McCoys?

Still, she wasn't prepared for the sight that met her at the end of the drive. The yard was an open space of knee-high weeds and hard dirt, with a rusted station wagon—probably left over from the hippie era—sitting idle off to one side. Straight ahead, a few straggly shrubs tangled against a sagging picket fence across the front of a three-story leaning tower of dilapidation.

Wind Chime House. The name was painted on a white wooden sign on the gate.

She had reached her destination.

Eve leaned back in her desk chair and rubbed her scalp. Curiosity had driven her to the office computer. Not just curiosity, but unease. Her father's agitation had settled in her. And she didn't like it.

She'd spent a childhood trying to hold him to the earth, to family, to her.

She didn't miss her mother, most of the time. She'd never known her, so she didn't really see how she could miss her. Maybe it was just the idea of a mother that left a little piece of Eve always longing.

Being brought up at the commune, she'd lived around other kids whose parents weren't married and some who were raising their kids on their own. Those were the days when people "hooked up," long before the hookups of today. Strangers who passed—and made love—in the night. No one missed their other parent; some didn't even know who they were. And didn't care.

Until they went to school in town.

School had been hard. The town kids made fun of the commune kids, and the parents disapproved of their lifestyle, their clothes, their morals—their otherness. So they'd stuck together. There had been six or seven of them in the early days, but gradually they'd all moved away, except Eve.

Eve had lived with her grandmother at the commune until she was thirteen. It was a lonely time. Her father was usually away on tour. Her grandmother was busy building her real estate empire; meetings and travel kept her away almost as often as Eve's father. It fell on Floret and Henry to nurture Eve as best they could, though they had no children themselves.

Eve loved them for it. Henry was a scientist who taught her about the stars and the mysteries of the universe. Floret was a mystery unto herself, but she loved plants and animals and Eve, and knew how to make hurt go away, of knees and stomachs and hearts.

Then one day, Hannah—or Granna, as Eve called her—had returned home. There was an argument with Floret, then Granna came and told her to pack her things. They'd moved into town that very afternoon. No explanation.

It was because of the fight. But Eve didn't learn that until much later. And to this day she'd never learned what the fight was about.

That was the beginning of the end for the commune. Hippies looking for a life where they could flourish in peace were replaced by yuppies looking for weekend houses where they could chill, which Hannah Gordon was happy to sell them. There hadn't been a new kid at the commune until David Merrick returned eight years ago to raise his nephew Eli.

A godsend for David, a rejuvenation for Floret and Henry, but the beginning of the unraveling of Eve's plans for Mel.

Eli was a nice boy, in love with Mel, and God knew she was nuts in love with him. But they were so young. Had seen nothing of the world. Had no way to provide for themselves except by working at the inn.

Eve had made the inn her dream. She'd had no choice.

But Mel and Eli had options—if only they'd take

them. In another month they would both go off to their respective colleges. Problem solved. Right now, she had another possible situation on her hands.

Eve leaned on her elbows, pressed her templed fingers to her lips, and peered at the computer screen. Zoe Bascombe had made a reservation online. Her driver's license and credit card were on file. Her answer to the website's "How did you hear about Solana?" was "Other." The reply box had been left blank.

She Googled Zoe's name, drummed her fingers on the desk. She didn't usually do this kind of background check on her guests, not unless their credit was questionable. This morning, however, she pushed away her sense of intrusion and refined her search. And was surprised at the number of hits that appeared. LinkedIn, Facebook, Instagram, Snapchat—the list went on.

She clicked on Zoe's Facebook profile. Zoe Bascombe. New York City. Great Neck. UPenn–The Wharton School. The usual young-woman social posts: party photos, beach, horseback riding, snowboarding. Loves music.

Eve sucked in her breath. Nothing odd about that. Most young people liked music, and Zoe worked for an event firm—*a firm that catered to music business clients.* A good job for a young woman.

She kept searching. Parents: George and Jennifer

Bascombe. *Jenny?* Eve's mother was named Jenny. Jenny Campbell. It was a common enough name.

George Bascombe was a prominent Long Island attorney. Jennifer was a member of the Great Neck Garden Club, a string of charities.

Eve's fingers hovered over the computer mouse, trembling slightly. She clicked on Images.

A head shot of George Bascombe. George shaking hands with city officials. George and his wife, Jennifer, at a hospital fund-raising ball. George and Jenny Bascombe accepting a check for the Make It Better Organization.

Eve clicked to enlarge the grainy photo. Zeroed in on Jenny. She was turned in profile, but even so, Eve could see the resemblance to Zoe. She clicked back on Zoe's Facebook photos, scrolled past the friends and activities and food and parties and found one of Zoe and her mother—and stopped.

The photo was in color. The two women, mother and daughter, were strikingly similar. No mistaking them for anything but mother and daughter. The eye color was amazingly the same, and unusual. Almost a lilac blue.

There were no photos of Eve's own mother, but she'd seen those eyes before. On her own daughter Mel.

But eye color didn't mean anything. A coincidence.

She kept scrolling back and back, until she came to a Throwback Thursday photo: *Me getting ready for Julia's Sweet Sixteen. Straight hair. Ha-ha.* The hair was dark, had obviously just been blow-dried or flat-ironed. But it wasn't the hair that had arrested Eve's attention.

It was the face.

They could have been sisters, Zoe and Mel. It was uncanny. And it wasn't coincidence.

Zoe stood where she was, waiting to see a sign of life, but no one appeared to greet her. Actually, the place looked deserted.

So now what—did she dare open the gate and walk inside?

She took a few steps over the trampled weeds and gingerly lifted the latch. Hesitated. Hippies were peace loving, right? She opened the gate and stepped inside.

Like Dorothy opening the door to the land of Oz.

Inside the sagging fence were no trampled weeds, no dried-out grass or hard-packed dirt. Just color. The house, unpainted eyesore that it was, was surrounded by flowers. Reds, blues, yellows, oranges, and lavenders not laid out by design, but growing randomly, as if someone had cast handfuls of seed into the wind. Above them, giant yellow sunflowers swayed on their stems like drunken sentinels.

Jenny Bascombe might have been appalled at the craziness of the planting, but she would have loved the color.

And the scent. One whiff dissolved into another against a pervasive smell of lavender . . . *blue, dilly dilly.* A lullaby her mother used to sing.

"Hello?" she called tentatively. Getting no response, she walked down the flagstone path toward the house. "Hello? Is anyone here?"

Someone was there. From behind her they let out a frightening "Ma-a-a-a-a." The voice didn't sound human.

And it wasn't.

It was a beast, a little beast, galloping toward her.

Zoe looked wildly around. She was cut off from retreat. Her only hope was the house. She sprinted up the walk, took the wooden steps to the porch two at a time, and banged on the door.

"Hello!" she called, her voice rising in panic.

"I'm out here."

She turned around, looking for the source of the voice and keeping a wary eye on the animal that had stopped at the bottom of the steps and was eyeing her curiously.

It wasn't a dog, she realized with relief. It was a . . . goat? Must be—goats were the new "cute" pets. This was definitely a goat, brown flecked with white hairs. An old goat? She chuckled in spite of her racing pulse. "You old goat."

The goat lifted a hoof onto the front step.

Zoe backed up. "Sorry, sorry. I didn't mean it. You're a lovely goat."

"Dulcie! You cut that out." The voice, high and lilting, came not from inside the house but from behind a large vegetable garden fenced in with chicken wire. The goat turned toward the voice and so did Zoe.

A large sun hat appeared from behind a row of tall bean plants. A floral gardening glove waved. "Over here. Now, Dulcie, you let the lady come on down."

After a beady-eyed look toward Zoe, the goat trotted over to the garden.

Zoe slowly went down the steps to the yard. But she didn't venture farther. The gardener's hat was bobbing along behind the top of the staked plants toward the end of the row where Dulcie waited outside the mesh fence.

The gardener came out into the open, reached back to close the gate, and putting a protective or perhaps controlling hand on the goat, she came to meet her.

Zoe guessed the gardener was a *she* from her high voice and diminutive size. Her face was completely hidden by the floppy, wide brim of her hat, revealing only a long gray braid that draped over one shoulder. Baggy overalls were rolled to just below the knee. The shoes were old, scuffed leather work boots.

She stopped when she was several feet away from Zoe and pushed the hat back, revealing a sun-wrinkled face and a welcoming smile.

The smile broadened. "My sweet Lord. You've come back—"

Dulcie butted her side, and she staggered several steps.

"Oh," the gardener said, and righted herself. Her head tilted one way then the other. "You're not . . . Oh my . . ."

Oh dear, thought Zoe. "I'm just visiting," she said, smiling reassuringly to show that she wasn't trespassing.

"Well . . . So glad you've come . . . ." The woman started forward. Stopped again. Frowned at Zoe and shook her head before resuming her trajectory, the goat trotting placidly by her side.

Zoe braced herself for another run to the porch.

"You have a beautiful garden," she said, keeping one eye on the goat.

The woman turned her head to look. "Yes," she said dreamily.

Well, thought Zoe. Mel had said this had once been

a hippie commune. Maybe the old folks were still getting high.

"I came to see your beach," Zoe prompted.

"Ah." The woman turned and looked over her other shoulder.

Zoe followed her gaze beyond the vegetable garden to a grassy half-mowed lawn that sloped down to a white beach and the sea. Farther to the right, she could see the back of the Solana Inn and Spa and the patio where she'd just breakfasted. The inn's perfectly manicured vibrant green lawn sloped down to a longer white beach. The two beaches met at a rock jetty that sliced through the stretch of sand.

Dividing one from the other.

Zoe could see people on the inn's beach lying beneath the bright colorful umbrellas placed there for the use of the guests. There was no one sunbathing—nude or otherwise—on this side of the jetty. The beach was completely empty.

"I'm Floret."

"Zoe," said Zoe.

"Life."

"Yes," Zoe said, hardly taken aback by this second recognition of her name's meaning. She was beginning to think that there was more to this town than she had anticipated.

"Well, there is the beach." Floret made a vague gesture with her hand, still clothed in its gardening glove.

"It's beautiful."

"We're not selling," Floret said pleasantly.

"I don't blame you," Zoe said, somewhat bewildered by Floret's lack of vehemence.

"Oh."

"But why is it called Wind Chime Beach? I don't see any wind chimes."

Floret smiled her vague smile. "Because there aren't any."

Zoe nodded solemnly. "Did there used to be? The house is called Wind Chime, too, isn't it?" Surely, this couldn't be the special place where her mother wanted to be laid to eternal rest. A tourist town, a dilapidated house, with a nutty old lady in charge of a beach that had no wind chimes? Zoe forced another smile. It was weird how Floret looked at a place before pointing it out, as if she were checking to make sure everything was really there.

"It's because of the wind chimes."

"But . . ." Zoe had come on a fool's errand. She couldn't leave her mother here.

"The wind chimes are in the woods."

"The woods," Zoe repeated mechanically. This was maddening. She quickly looked around, saw a cluster of trees on the far side of the old house. Actually, except for the yard and the beach, they were surrounded by woods.

"You can hear them sometimes . . . when the wind blows . . . in winter when the trees are bare."

"On the beach?"

"Oh, not on the beach."

Zoe clenched her hands behind her back to keep from pulling her hair out. This poor woman couldn't be living here alone. Surely there was someone who was more "in touch" who could give Zoe some straight answers. A man. Mel had said Floret and . . . Henry. That was his name. She looked back toward the house. "Is Hen—?"

"Only on Wind Chime Beach."

Zoe stopped, her question cut off. "There's a different beach called Wind Chime?" she asked gently.

"Oh, yes." Floret broke into a happy, reminiscent smile. "Only now we call it Old Beach. It's lovely, magical." She frowned, another mercurial change in her demeanor. "But no one goes there anymore."

"Why?"

"The stairs."

Stairs? Stares? This vague creature could mean either.

"They rotted out after Gloria, I think her name was."

"Gloria?"

"The hurricane. I believe it was Gloria."

"I see."

"Is that why you came? To remember? It was always your favorite place. Yours and—"

Dulcie bleated, a grating sound that hurt Zoe's ears.

Floret merely turned her smile on the goat. "You're absolutely right, my dear."

Definitely two tokes short of a doobie.

"Well . . . yes," Zoe agreed. "To remember . . . in a way. Would you mind terribly if I just took a look? At the beach. I'll be very careful. No lawsuits or anything."

Her little assurances fell flat. Floret's eyes widened . . . with fright? Insult? Anger?

"I promise. I'll just look and come right back. I won't touch anything. Just look."

Floret looked toward the trees on the far side of the house. Her gloved handed lifted slowly. "Over there."

"Thank you. Thank you so much." Zoe hurried toward the woods before Floret could change her mind or Dulcie decided to follow her.

The path was easy enough to find, overgrown with weeds but trampled down by foot traffic. Odd, considering Floret had said no one ever went there anymore, though Zoe imagined the path might lead anywhere.

She didn't stop until she was out of sight of the house. Beneath the trees, the sun was almost totally blocked except for dapples of light that slipped through the heavy foliage.

She was enveloped in total stillness. No breeze ruffled the trees and Zoe became overly aware of her own footfalls, a rhythmic stuttering on the underbrush. They were answered by the underlying hush of unseen waves and the counterpoint of a bird call, the scurry of animals in the brush.

It *was* magical. And a little frightening.

And then she heard something different, like a knife against a champagne glass before a toast. She stopped. But there was nothing. She waited, then started walking again; she'd seen a wedge of blue ahead and a thrill of anticipation hurried her steps. Anticipation and dread. Worse than before her failed Juilliard audition.

Was this the place? Was she really going to send her mother, what was left of her, into the wide-open space of sand and surf? One storm and she would be cast into the open sea.

No, she couldn't. All sounds and thoughts vanished except the pounding of her own heart. Zoe stood still, clenched and unclenched her fingers, slowed her breath and her heartbeat, giving herself time to bolster her resolve—trying to master the sheer terror of the final good-bye.

She took the final steps into the sunlight. Only she

wasn't at the beach but standing on a ledge at a set of rotted wooden steps that led downward and out of sight.

She gingerly eased forward and looked over. A secluded crescent of sand, as white as any she'd seen, lay below. Probably once a charming assignation place, it was now cluttered by large pieces of driftwood, seaweed, and other detritus—a plastic bag, several cans and bottles left by man or by waves.

She shook herself, trying to dispel the melancholy and sense of disappointment that suddenly overcame her.

None of this made sense. Why here? If *here* was where she was supposed to be. It was lonely enough for privacy. She could even say a few words, to float away like her mother on the wind. But this was not how she'd envisioned her mother's last resting place.

"Why are you doing this?" she asked, forgetting that she was quite alone.

She reached for the splintered handrail of the stairs. They didn't look stable, but it wasn't very far down. If they wouldn't hold her, she could probably jump down to the beach without major injury.

Then how would you get back up?

She put her foot on the first wooden step. Tested her weight. It held. Tried the second step. For a perilous moment it sagged; she grasped the handrail tighter, getting a splinter for her effort.

Another step, then another. She'd almost reached the bottom when the wood gave way. She grabbed the rail with both hands. adding several more splinters. Here she stayed, half standing, half crouching, and clinging on for dear life. What had she been thinking?

Slowly, she released one foot, stretched it toward the sand. She could almost reach, but not without losing her precarious balance on the wood.

What the hell? She pulled her foot back, then swung her body forward and jumped. She landed on the sand with a thud, sinking down several inches, huffed out a relieved breath, then looked at her palms in dismay.

She spent the next few seconds picking out the biggest slivers of wood. The rest would have to be extricated when she was back at the hotel with her tweezers and travel sewing kit.

She looked back at the steps and the trees that formed a curtain in a semicircle behind the beach, closing off the outer world. Very private. And to her relief she saw that the woods actually sloped off to each side until they met the sand. The undergrowth was thick, but she'd surely be able to find a way back to the path without having to risk the stairs again.

She turned toward the water, lifted her face to the sun. A breeze ruffled the air.

And she heard it, a tinkling of glass. A soft solo,

joined by another and another until the sound disappeared into the woods.

She waited, but the breeze had died as quickly as it had begun, and so had the sound. But she found its origin. A nearby tree branch bent in an arc over the sand. And from it, little rectangles of glass, orange and blue and purple, hung by thin threads from a medallion of tin.

Wind chimes.

They were still now, quiet, but almost alive, as if waiting, waiting, waiting for the next breeze.

Zoe wanted to capture that image in words, in notes, but she couldn't seem to move. She was waiting, too. And she was ready when she felt the first murmur of breeze in her hair, heard the first clear ring, and she laughed silently as the woods filled with the sound of the chimes.

Good one, Mom. I don't know how you found out about this place or why, but I get it.

Her throat burned and she didn't fight back the tears that filled her eyes. This was the place where she would have to finally let go.

"Hey! You shouldn't be down there!"

Zoe shrieked. She looked frantically around and came to a stop when she saw a man standing at the top of the stairs, feet squared, body poised aggressively forward.

"Jeez, you scared me."

"I beg your pardon."

Zoe's eyes narrowed. *Was that a hint of sarcasm?* "Floret said it was okay."

"Floret made a mistake. It's very dangerous, and if you used these stairs going down, don't use them trying to get back up."

"What do you suggest?"

She thought he growled. Then he moved away.

"Hey, wait a minute. You can't leave me down here. Hey!"

But the man had disappeared.

To hell with it. She'd made it down; she could get back up again. She was nothing if not resilient. Besides, now that she was finally here, she wasn't quite ready to leave.

One thing she knew, she'd have to sneak back when no one was about or they'd have her arrested for sure, either for trespassing or for going against whatever private burial code she was about to violate.

Finally, she knew what she had to do. Her mother would lie in rest here among the wind chimes.

But not on a beach strewn with garbage. She walked over to the largest piece of driftwood, which someone had obviously used as a bench. A battered plastic bag was caught beneath it, a soda can lay on its side in the sand.

Zoe started to pick it up but a piece of glass, half hidden by the sand, arrested her attention. She dug it out and held it up to the light. It was flat and colored yellow, smooth on three edges and jagged on the fourth. A nylon string was still attached through a little hole at its top.

She knew where it had come from. Broken off in a storm perhaps, it had come to rest in the sand. She leaned over and placed it on the log. She wouldn't throw it away. Maybe its other half was waiting to be found.

"Now what are you doing?"

The voice was so close that she whirled around, tripped over the log, and fell on her butt in the sand.

Chapter 5

"Jeez, what is it with you?" Zoe looked back at the man standing on the other side of the fallen limb. He looked very tall, though that could just be a trick of perspective. Darkish hair, faded jeans, faded T-shirt. Holey sneakers. Kind of good-looking.

Possibly dangerous. In a stalking psychopath way. And she was sprawled on her butt in the sand.

He leaned over and stuck out his hand.

She scooted back.

"What?" he asked. "You want help getting up the hill or not?"

She looked at his hand, took it, and he pulled her to her feet.

"Ow." She pulled her hand away.

"Are you hurt?"

"I picked up a few splinters on the way down."

"It could be worse. You could have fallen, really hurt yourself. You might not have been found for weeks."

"Oh, give me a break. You would have heard me yelling."

"I might, but I might just leave you down here for being stupid." His lip twitched and Zoe wondered if it was the beginning of a smile or a sneer of disdain.

She saw movement in the trees above them. There was someone else up there. "How did you know I was down here?"

"Floret told Henry and Henry told me."

"Is that him?" she asked, motioning back toward the trees.

The man turned to look. "Where? I don't see anyone."

"He was there, in the trees." But the lurker had stepped out of sight. Was he on his way down to the beach? Should she be afraid?

"Probably just a hiker. Now come on, you're trespassing. Don't make me call the cops."

"I thought Floret owned Wind Chime?"

"She does, but she doesn't always know what's best."

"That is so condescending."

"Nope, it's the truth. And you need to go."

The breeze made a preemptive strike, setting off the chime behind her head. It was joined by another and another until they echoed through the woods.

They both stopped, listening as the sound ebbed and flowed and died away.

"That's beautiful," Zoe said, half to herself.

"It is." He gestured to a bank of shrubs. "This way, please." It was said in a ludicrous tone, as if he were seating her at a restaurant or the theater.

She couldn't tell whether he was messing with her or was just naturally a pompous ass. She decided not to argue. She let him hold on to her elbow as they traversed the sand. She didn't comment on how it reminded her of a felon being taken into custody. She supposed, in a way, she *was* trespassing. She'd told Floret she had just come to look.

He guided her to the far edge of the beach where a scree of large rocks led to a crevice between the trees and a gnarled mass of bared roots. The man, who still hadn't bothered to introduce himself, slipped ahead, stepped onto one of the roots and then another until he'd climbed to solid ground.

He reached back to help her, but Zoe defiantly and stupidly refused to take his hand. She stepped onto the same root and saw immediately why he'd offered—albeit silently—to help; her legs were shorter than his.

She looked quickly around for a handhold. Reached for another root and, in spite of the pain in her palms, pulled herself up until the root was holding her weight.

That's what being stubborn got you if you were Zoe Bascombe. The splinters were probably driven like stakes into her palms.

He waited for her on the path where it forked in several directions.

He gestured toward the center fork and Zoe took it. She knew immediately it wasn't the way she had come. She slowed. Her heart was beginning to stutter with wariness.

"Shortcut." Then he smiled. "You could probably outrun me, if I get fresh. Which I won't." He finished with that outstretched "after you" hand gesture again.

He was definitely messing with her. He was rather charming in a sarcastic way. But . . . serial killers were always said to be charming.

She was acutely aware of him walking several steps behind her. Then she became aware of something else. A tiny refraction of light, a pinpoint of color appearing in the branches ahead of her.

And another off to the left. Barely visible. They were everywhere she looked. These little bits of discovery. Hanging from branches high and low, one made of coral shells was close enough to touch. A little farther away, bronze tubes hung like a waterfall from a leafless branch. Some were only silhouettes in the play of light and dark; some were broken and hanging by a single thread.

And she thought of the broken glass she'd discovered on the sand and felt an overwhelming urge to find its home. She stopped, turning slowly, just taking it all in, waiting for the next breeze to set the chimes off again.

He prodded her forward. She staggered a bit, then took a couple of steps. Stopped again as she heard a distant note, a faint ting of sound behind her. Felt the first ruffle of a breeze.

"It's starting," she whispered.

"Will you please—"

"Shhh." It was coming closer, carried on the breeze. And suddenly she was surrounded by . . . fairy sound. It whirled around her ears, talking to her, then moved on as it made its way through the woods, gradually retreating as softly as it had come.

The man had stopped. He was listening, too. It made her like him better.

They stood not two feet apart until the breeze had gone, the leaves were still, and the sound a mere memory. A memory she was trying intently to keep in her head.

"Can we go now?"

It was gone. Even the memory.

"Sorry," she said, and started up the path, faster this time. For a second she'd been swept up in something magical; now she felt somehow vulnerable and unprotected. Like a newborn, or Spider-Man without his web.

But safe. She had come to the right place. She didn't know how or why her mother knew of this place, but it would be the perfect place to spend eternity.

She followed without protest behind him. And was both relieved and disappointed when they reached the sunlight and the untended outer yard of Wind Chime House.

She started to open the gate to the house, but the man stopped her.

"Main Street is that way, down the drive."

"I wanted to thank Floret."

"Floret's busy right now."

"Okay, that's it." He'd wrecked her mood and was acting like a jerk. "What's the deal here? I thought hippies were all embracing, *mi casa, su casa* kind of people, put your feet in the circle and chant 'ohm' kind of people. At least Floret was friendly. You're downright"—she searched for a word that wasn't four letters—"off-putting."

He laughed. "And you've got an attitude."

"What's wrong with that?"

He didn't answer right away.

"Well?"

"Well, I'm thinking."

"Don't strain anything."

He raised both eyebrows. "Really, you can't do better than that?"

She blushed. It had been the most childish thing to say. Something she would never have lowered herself to say to her own brothers.

She'd discovered a door into her mother and to music that she hadn't expected. And he was throwing her out.

Well, she hadn't come this far to give up. She'd seen where giving up led her. She wouldn't let it happen to her mother's memory. As hard as it would be, she knew she couldn't go back now. Her eyes filled. She blinked desperately; she'd made enough of a fool of herself already.

"You can do that on cue?"

She shook her head.

"Dammit, stop it."

She nodded and hurried blindly down the drive.

A booming voice yelled, "David, go after her."

His name was David. Zoe broke into a run.

She heard an expletive, then feet pounding behind her. "Wait a minute."

She didn't stop.

He caught up and jogged alongside her.

"I'm leaving," she said.

"Henry wants to talk to you."

Henry? Of Henry and Floret. Was he going to threaten her, too? She didn't slow down but risked a glance over her shoulder. Saw the figure standing on the porch.

Oh, holy hell. Literally. It was a man. Tall, really tall, with long white hair. Long flowing robe. Her apparition in the fog. And by his side, Dulcie, the beady-eyed goat.

"Thanks anyway, sorry to have bothered you," Zoe mumbled, and fled down the drive to the street.

David crossed his arms and watched her. "Don't mention it," he muttered under his breath. Just what they needed, some oversensitive nitwit full of neuroses standing in the middle of the woods like a nutcase. *Weird. Just weird.* And why on earth did Henry want to see her? Why not say that to begin with? He could have invited her in to tea, rather than trying to scare her away.

He turned and walked back to the house, where Henry stood on the porch like Noah waiting for the animals. The only animals left at Wind Chime were a few chickens, a couple of stray dogs, a handful of feral cats, and Dulcinea, who was giving him the evil eye. As far as David was concerned, she could go to the petting zoo anytime. And the sooner the better.

He walked up the steps.

"She wouldn't stay?"

"I never got that far. I think I scared her."

"Perhaps." Henry stepped aside to let him pass. It was all very solemn, whatever was going on. David didn't have a clue; he usually didn't with Henry and Floret, but they were good people, with kind hearts and generous spirits, and he was thankful for them.

The two of them went inside, leaving Dulcie standing guard over the porch. Floret was on the back veranda, setting out drinks and cookies. Midmorning elevenses in the British tradition, though as far as he knew Floret had never been farther than North Carolina in her life. But Floret was like that, picking up things she read and incorporating them into her life. Not to put on airs, but to have a good time.

He smiled and took his place at the table.

"Tea or lemonade?" Floret asked, as if nothing had sent her and Henry into a tailspin just a few minutes ago, and sent him running to stop the interloper from getting close to the ravaged piece of sand they were suddenly out of the blue calling Wind Chime Beach.

It had always been the Old Beach as long as he could remember.

"Lemonade, thanks." David reached for a cookie. "These are safe right?"

Floret smiled seraphically. "Of course. It's elevenses."

Of course, David thought. Her marijuana-laced baking only came out when the day's work was done and she and Henry took one of their flights of fancy or wherever they went together.

David sometimes envied them their specialness. His parents had had it; he'd never found it. He was afraid Eli thought he had found it in Mel Gordon, but David could see only rough waters ahead for those two. Much too young and unshaped by the world. People might have been able to live blissfully that way once, but not in these times, when you needed every tool you could get to survive.

Henry stood with his back to them, his hands clasped behind him, staring out to the sea. David sat back and munched his cookie while he tried to find some of the inner calm that the sound of the waves was bringing to Henry.

A few minutes ago both Henry and Floret had coursed with inner energy, reactive energy. Which was odd. They got lots of visitors; they came and went, sometimes pitching a tent in the yard or moving in to the house; sometimes they moved in and stayed. Henry and Floret were never surprised, always welcoming, never questioned why.

So what was it about this young woman that had thrown them off-kilter?

It hadn't lasted long; they seemed perfectly fine now. Or was that resignation? The energy emanating from them was definitely different than usual.

She'd seemed like a flake to him. Picking up trash like some ecology nut. Then stopping to listen to the chimes. Well, that was understandable. They always stopped him, too. A lot of people wouldn't really notice. Wouldn't be moved by them. Understand the fragility of—

Anyway, he would have picked up the trash if he'd known it was down there. No one ever went there anymore.

Floret finished pouring tea for herself and Henry and sat down.

Henry turned from his ruminations and joined them. "She's afraid of us," he said, as if they were in the middle of a conversation.

Henry often began that way. David was used to it. In fact, he'd never known Henry to be any other way, and he'd known him for over thirty years, since David was four and he and his brother, Andy, and their parents had come to live at Wind Chime. Henry, the physicist turned dropout, and his lovely botanist hippie partner for life, Floret, and the other members of the commune had made them welcome and kept them safe.

"You sent me to stop her."

Floret put down her cup and folded her hands. "Don't be silly. She can't be stopped. She couldn't then and she won't now."

David shook his head. "Floret, give us poor Earthlings some context."

She pursed her lips at him. But she was trying to suppress a smile.

"Oh, I'm very much here now. But I was confused then. I looked up and for a moment, time fell away. It really did. I confess it was a little frightening to go all at once like that instead of gradually slipping from one state to another. If it hadn't been for Dulcie I might have said something I shouldn't, I was that shocked to see her."

"A goat saved you from a cosmic faux pas?" David said patiently.

"Why, yes. I saw her—the girl—and naturally I thought—at first. Impossible, of course. I don't know what came over me. And then Dulcie let out a warning bray and butted me and everything was normal again."

"She's not Jenny." Henry sat down and reached for a cookie.

"Who's Jenny?" David asked.

"Well, I know that. Her name is Zoe." Floret frowned. "But . . ."

"No buts," Henry said, sounding uncharacteristically harsh.

David leaned forward. "Who's Jenny? What's this all about?"

"It's a long story, many decades old."

David settled back to hear what saga Henry was about to unfold. He was disappointed.

"More recently, about six months ago, to be precise," Henry continued. "We received a letter from an old friend.

"It was accompanied by a package. The letter asked us to give it to the person who came looking for Wind Chime Beach and to welcome her."

"And to keep her safe," Floret added.

"Safe?" David repeated. "Is she in some kind of trouble? Is this going to be dangerous?"

"No, it was just a benediction we all said sometimes, back in the day, to nurture each other and keep our spirits safe."

Well, thank God for that, David thought. Then something niggled deep in his memory.

"Ah, you remember," Henry said, and smiled.

He did remember. *They'll keep you safe.*

"At first we didn't know what to make of it," Floret added. "A lot of people *could* be asking about it, the beach. It was a very special place in its day. Many found love there." She smiled at Henry.

He nodded. "And sometimes more than they bargained for."

The two of them got those faraway looks they often got when thinking about life, and David waited patiently for the moment to pass and for them to come back.

"But this friend was very dear to our hearts," Henry said.

"Very dear," Floret echoed. "And of course we would welcome her, whenever she came," she said, rousing herself. "But I wasn't expecting, I had no idea. She looks just like Jenny."

"Obviously her daughter," Henry said.

"Who exactly is Jenny?" David asked.

The sound of the front screen door banging shut and a backpack being dumped on the floor stopped the conversation.

"We're out here, Eli," Floret called.

Footsteps thudded across the wooden floor and David's nephew exploded onto the veranda. That was the only way to describe the energy of an eighteen-year-old. He lived a life of high energy tempered only slightly by having spent the past eight years living with Henry and Floret at Wind Chime.

He snatched a cookie and stood looking at the adults while he munched.

"What's up? You all look a little mind-blown."

"Well, we are rather," Floret explained.

"Have anything to do with the girl who was running down the drive like her life depended on it?"

David bit back a smile. She talked tough, but it was all façade. He was glad he'd scared her away. Whatever or whoever she was, she was bound to cause trouble if Henry's and Floret's reactions were anything to judge by.

"Did Dulcie try to bite her? She really needs to get some manners."

"No," Floret said. "David . . ."

"Uncle David bit her?"

"No, of course not," Floret said, in all seriousness.

"You scared her away." Eli shook his head and took another cookie. "What did ya do? Ask her on a date?"

"Very funny. I just escorted her off the property."

Suddenly serious, Eli pulled up a wicker chair and sat down. "You don't think she's a spy, do you?"

"No," Henry said. "She's . . ." He seemed stuck for a word. "A Pandora, I'm afraid."

"Pandora, like 'open the box and free the evil of the world' Pandora?"

Floret patted Eli's hand. "Not evil, just discomfort and maybe some unhappiness, but in the end, it will be . . ."

They all sat up, but she trailed off.

"But first," Henry said, "we must decide how to proceed."

Eli looked at David, gave him his they're-at-it-again eye roll. "You three'll figure it out. I gotta get cleaned up."

"Going out?" David asked.

"Ye-es. Do you mind?"

David shook his head. "With Mel?"

"You might as well get used to it. We're soul mates. Thanks for the cookies." He leaned over and kissed Floret's cheek, then trotted out of the room.

They were all silent as they listened to him bound up the stairs to the second floor.

"Not to worry," Floret said. "It will all work out. It always does."

David started to say, *He's only eighteen*, but they'd heard it all before. "So is there something you want me to do to help with this Wind Chime Beach situation? Those stairs are beyond repair. I could tear them down, but I don't think she'll be back. I was pretty firm about what happens to trespassers."

"She'll be back," Henry said. "We've been expecting her."

Eve stood in the shade of the oak tree outside her grandmother's white frame house. Looking at it, you'd never know that it contained not only her grandmother's home, but the inner workings of her small but consolidated real estate empire. Hannah Gordon owned a third of the buildings in town and at eighty-eight showed no signs of backing off.

She was respected by the locals, not always liked, but she'd been the only mother Eve had ever known. Granna and Floret. They'd both been mothers to her until "the fight" that ended their deep friendship and began the struggle for the Wind Chime property.

Eve knew she had to go inside. The old woman would be home. She did most of her work from there these days. Arthritis was slowing her down. Surgery had renewed her eyesight, but she despised having to wear her state-of-the-art hearing aids in public. It was a sign of weakness, and Hannah Gordon did not show weakness.

Eve's insides were churning like a teenager being sent to the principal's office. But it had to be done. She had to know.

She couldn't go to Floret. Eve was never totally sure about the state of Floret's mind, and she didn't want to expose her to Hannah's wrath if Hannah found out they had been discussing the past.

And Eve didn't dare ask her father. The few times she'd tried to ask him about her mother, he retreated inside himself to the dark place that so often controlled his life—and hers. He'd obviously recognized something in Zoe Bascombe that reminded him of Eve's mother. Eve had learned early on not to ask. She wouldn't press him now.

But there was no mistaking it. Zoe Bascombe's mother was Jenny Campbell. And that made her Eve's half sister. It had to be that. All the doppelgangers in the world couldn't be more alike than the teenage photos of Mel and Zoe. Eve had printed out both photos, and they were in her shoulder bag. Evidence. Let Hannah try to deny the resemblance.

Her grandmother had always said Eve took after her father, but Eve knew there was part of her mother inside her. She knew it because sometimes she felt different from her family, not worse or better, just different. She held on to those feelings, cherishing them, savoring the knowledge, secretly, something only for her. Then life would take over, and she would forget for a while that a part of her was living in the world somewhere else.

She took a fortifying breath, then strode up the driveway, across the grass, and up the steps to the rectangular porch cut into the side of the front façade. She slowed to peer in the living room window. No one was there. Hannah was probably at her computer in the dining room, which she'd converted into a home office.

Eve knocked on the door, opened it, and stuck her head inside. "Granna? You here?"

There was no answer, but she could hear sounds coming from the office.

Eve went in and closed the door behind her. No going back now. She walked through the living room, where a breeze lifted the organza curtains of the open windows—no central air for Hannah Gordon. Across the old oriental area rug, past the dark Victorian furniture, and through the archway into the office and into a total contrast of white state-of-the-art electronics—computers, fax machines, and printers. Her grandmother sat behind her desk, almost hidden by the screen of her desktop.

"Granna. Granna!" Eve repeated.

Hannah looked up, a vague expression on her face.

"Turn on your hearing aids."

Hannah scowled at her, but turned them on. "What brings you here at this time of day?" Her voice was surprisingly light, only slightly raspy with age. She'd let her hair go white and kept it short, because she was convinced it made her look younger. Eve never understood that logic, but there was a lot about her grandmother she didn't understand and was pretty sure she never would.

Eve came around the desk until she was standing at Hannah's shoulder, pulled out the two photos, and set them down side by side on the desk in front of her grandmother.

Hannah pushed them with her index fingers until they were perfectly aligned. "What's this?"

"You tell me."

Her grandmother pursed her lips; she didn't like games and obviously thought this was one. "It's pictures of Mel. I remember this blouse—she was ten or twelve, right? I don't remember this." She pointed to the photo of Zoe Bascombe. "Her hair is darker. It must have been one of those spray-on deals because she would never do something like that to her lovely hair."

Eve swallowed. Her mouth was so dry she was afraid to speak. She licked her lips, but it did absolutely no good. Her grandmother was watching her, a slight frown on her face, and Eve thought, *She has such great skin for a woman her age.*

"Eve?"

Eve pointed to the photo nearest to her. "This is Mel." She pointed to the next. "This is Zoe Bascombe at sixteen."

Her grandmother stilled, barely noticeable, but Eve had spent a lifetime trying to read between the lines of her family. And that infinitesimal moment of reaction telegraphed all she needed to know. "Who is she, Hannah?"

"Hannah now, is it? I don't know who it is—why should I? Just some girl who looks a little like Mel. Where did you come up with this?"

"On an internet search."

Her grandmother sighed, a mixture of resignation and disgust. They'd been here before. Eve looking for pictures of her mother, asking questions and getting nothing except, "Best forgotten. You don't want to upset your father, do you?"

Eve didn't. Life was dark and frightening when her father had one of his "spells," and she'd always backed off, finally trained herself not to ask, not to wonder. But this was a total slap in the face. It couldn't be coincidence.

"Well?" prompted Hannah, with a slight impatience. "I'm in the middle of something, here."

Eve pulled herself together. "It's from a Google search I did on one of my guests. Something I don't normally do, but Dad had such a strange reaction to her that it made me curious. And lo and behold . . .. Want to know who her mother is?"

"Not really."

"It's a woman named Jenny Bascombe, née Campbell."

"Two very common names. Must be thousands of them."

"But not with a daughter the spitting image of Mel."

Hannah pushed the photos onto the floor. "What are you doing? You're just going to upset everyone."

"I'm already upset. So is Dad."

"You didn't tell him this crock of bull, did you?"

"I didn't have to."

"Let it drop. This girl is no more related to you than Sam Hill."

Eve crossed her arms over her chest, put them down again. "I don't believe you. I'm forty-eight years old and you've never told me the truth about my mother. I want to know. Now."

"Go home, do something useful."

"No. You tell me or I'm going to ask Zoe Bascombe."

Her grandmother closed her eyes. "I told you. She was young. She got pregnant. Her parents took her away. We adopted you. End of story."

It was all Eve ever got. But now it wasn't enough. She'd never asked out loud if her mother had loved her. She'd left and hadn't come back, hadn't called, hadn't written.

"I need to know more than that."

"Why? Because of this Bascombe woman? Send her packing. We don't need the aggravation."

"She was asking about Wind Chime Beach."

Her grandmother's hand hovered above the keyboard, but she dropped it to her lap. She slumped back with a long sigh, and for a split second Eve was afraid she'd killed her.

"Granna, are you okay? Granna?" She turned the chair to face her.

Hannah's eyes opened. "Of course I'm fine." But her voice sounded weak.

"You're scaring me."

"Go back to the inn, Eve. You're making too much out of this. Leave it alone."

It was over, for today anyway. Her grandmother had spoken, and nobody ever won against Hannah Gordon when she'd made a stand.

"Did I tell you I'm thinking about buying the Kelly place?"

It took Eve a minute to catch up. "They're selling?"

"Not yet, but they will."

"They won't. They love that cottage and Jim can walk to the diner and back every day."

"Not if the diner is closed down."

"He's never said anything about closing."

Hannah smiled briefly, showing a row of white, capped teeth. "I understand that there have been some serious safety and sanitary violations."

"Bull." Eve narrowed her eyes at her grandmother. "I never heard . . ." It hit Eve in one great tidal wave of understanding and disappointment. Hannah was warning her to back off. "The whole town will fight you if you try to sabotage their favorite diner."

Hannah shrugged. "I'm just a citizen trying to do my duty."

Eve didn't think her grandmother cared that people feared and despised her. And her explanation didn't fool Eve, nor anybody else, once they'd heard what she was up to. "You want the easement on their property so that Henry and Floret won't have access to the street."

"Perhaps. Is there anything else?"

Eve reached down to pick up the photos, but a thin, bony hand stopped her.

"Leave them."

Eve pulled her hand back and left without a word, without her habitual kiss on the cheek. Down the hall, out the front door, and into the noonday heat.

It wasn't until she was on the street that the first tear fell. Tears of anger, not hurt. Those tears had dried up a long time ago.

Chapter 6

Zoe didn't go back to the inn immediately, but wandered through town, alternating between trying to recapture the sound of the wind chimes and wondering how she'd gotten here. It bothered and intrigued her that her mother had chosen this place to rest. It was so uncharacteristic of the suburban woman she knew.

How did her mother even know about Wind Chime? She knew her way around social media okay, but Zoe, who spent a good part of her life online, had scoured the internet for information on the beach. Nothing had popped up. It was virtually unknown.

Had she been here at some point in her life? She'd certainly never mentioned it, at least not to Zoe. And when would she have come here? Her mother wasn't a traveler. And she would never consider a girls' weekend away or a vacation without her children. Plus she hated the beach.

Zoe stopped in the deli and got a bottle of water. She was hungry, but too restless to stop at one of the town's cafés.

What was she going to do? What if she went back and explained things to Henry and Floret? They might refuse and then where would she be. She couldn't sneak around like some thief. Her mother deserved better than that. Besides, she refused to dump her mother's ashes on a beach that was littered with debris and trash.

She wanted to call Chris for advice, but it wasn't fair to put him between her and Errol and Robert. If her mother had wanted Chris to do this she would have asked him, not Zoe. But she'd asked Zoe. Because she knew Zoe wouldn't say no?

How could she?

She found herself standing in front of the corner bookstore, clutching an empty water bottle in her hand. She absently perused the titles in the window.

There were several bestsellers, one of which she'd already read. A whole bunch of political nonfiction, a book of local poetry. One half of the window was taken up by a large display. A coffee table–type book of photography, surrounded by stacks of the same title. It was opened to show two full-page color photographs of . . .

Zoe leaned into the glass to get a closer look.

Wind chimes. Beautiful in their simplicity. Nuanced in sun and shadow, translucence and darkness, intriguing.

On the front cover, *LIGHT* was spelled out in amber letters across a dark mountain landscape. And the photographer was David Merrick.

David Merrick. David. Wind chimes. The man from the commune? He was a photographer? She tilted her head to see the spine of the book and the publisher. A major art publisher. Interesting.

She went inside and bought it.

When she came out again, she saw Mel from the inn, head bent, striding down the sidewalk. It took a second for Zoe to recognize her; she'd changed out of her gauze uniform and into jean shorts and a pink camisole T-shirt, and her ponytail had been tied up in an unconstructed bun on the top of her head.

Even from where she stood, Zoe could tell Mel was upset and that they were on a collision course. Should Zoe smile as they passed and keep walking? Duck back into the store and avoid her?

Mel stopped at the corner and wiped the back of her hand across her eyes.

Zoe ran to catch up. "Mel?"

Mel stopped, turned, sniffed. "What?"

"Are you okay?"

Mel wiped her hand on her shorts. Looked away, nodded, shook her head.

Now what? It would be easy to walk away. Really, it was none of her business and she had problems of her own. Zoe had spent a lot of her job being a sympathetic shoulder, even when she didn't feel very sympathetic. But she was a problem solver, at least in her professional life. And there was something about Mel . . .

Stay out of it, Zoe told herself. "Can I help?" she asked.

Mel sniffed and walked a few steps toward her. "Why are you here?"

Taken aback, Zoe shrugged. "Buying a book." She held up the copy of *LIGHT.*

"No. I mean here in town."

Zoe shrugged. "Just visiting."

"Why did you ask about Wind Chime House?"

Zoe's stomach plummeted. Had Floret called the inn and complained?

"My mother sent—told me about it."

"Why?"

To bring her . . . She'd almost thought "home." But her mother had been born and raised on Long Island. "I don't know."

Mel wiped her face with both hands. "Didn't you ask her?"

"No."

"Why?"

I didn't have the chance. Why, oh, why had she stopped Mel in the first place? Zoe thought of the urn sitting unguarded in her hotel room. Had the maid found it? Reported a suspicious-looking vase in the closet? Had she looked inside? A thousand disastrous possibilities flashed in her mind.

If she was smart, she'd say sorry, go straight back to the inn, and check out. She could register in a hotel down the road and try to sneak back to Wind Chime Beach.

But for some reason she was drawn to Mel.

"You know, like when somebody says they'll be in New York, and you say 'make sure to get to Rockefeller Center'?"

Mel looked up and gave her a piercing look that was unsettling and at the same time strangely familiar.

"Wind Chime is not Rockefeller Center."

"Of course not, that was just an example."

"Then why are Mom and Granddad fighting about it?"

"About Wind Chime?"

"About you asking about it."

So that was it. "Did I get you in trouble? I'm sorry. I had no idea . . . Do you want me to talk to your mom?"

"No. It doesn't matter. It's really Granddad who got upset."

"The man I ran into as I was leaving?"

Mel nodded. "He got angry and yelled at me, then Mom yelled at him and went into the office and closed the door."

"I am so sorry. It was all innocent. I'll tell your mom it wasn't your fault for telling me."

"It doesn't matter, she was already mad at me. Everybody is." Her head suddenly snapped toward the street as a big silver Cadillac drove past. "Shit. That's Granna, my great-grandma. Do you think she saw me? She'll know where I'm going. I am so screwed . . . Shit." She pulled away from Mel. "Don't tell Mom you saw me or where I was going."

"No problem," Zoe said. She had no idea where Mel was going, except in the opposite direction of the Cadillac. And quite frankly she was more interested in the Cadillac, especially when it turned into the drive that she'd just left.

David and Henry had just finished rehanging one of the freshly painted shutters and were considering an afternoon beer when David saw a late-model Cadillac coming up the drive. He knew who it was; everyone in town recognized that symbol of wealth and power. He was just surprised. Hannah Gordon didn't venture this way much.

"Here comes trouble," he said to Henry.

Henry looked up. "It was inevitable," he said, and went into the house.

David was used to Floret's and Henry's cryptic statements, which the two of them seemed to understand without explanation, but which left most everyone else, including David, in the dark, even after all these years. But today's talk of reappearances and inevitability followed by the unexpected visit of their arch enemy—though Henry and Floret would deny that they felt any animosity toward Hannah—sent a ripple of unease up his spine.

A minute later, Hannah came to a stop inches from where David was standing. He wasn't sure if it was malice or just that she was old as the hills and should have had her driver's license revoked a decade ago. Still, he refused to give her any satisfaction by jumping out of the way.

And how stupid was that? It wasn't his fight. He didn't even know what it was about, except that Hannah wanted their land. Hannah was voracious that way. Hell, Hannah wanted everyone's land.

But in this case it was more than greed. She and Floret had had a falling-out years ago. When he was still a boy, much too young to remember, much less understand why.

He opened the car door and held it for her like an obedient lackey. He knew that made her think she had the upper hand. But he put his faith in Henry. "Good morning, Hannah."

"David." The old woman eased herself from the car, nodded minutely to him, not even bothering to look him in the eye. "Where are they?"

"*They* being?"

"Don't be cute with me. I'm not in the mood. Where are Henry and Floret?"

"I imagine they're in the house."

He followed her inside. She was wearing a navy blue pants suit. Her cap of white hair clutched her head like a helmet.

Dressed for business—or war, David thought. He sometimes thought he could remember a time when she had lived here and worn a long floral dress. He could find no vestige of that memory in the woman who preceded him into the house.

Henry was waiting in the foyer when Hannah stormed through the door.

It was funny, David thought. How the old woman

could come in like a whirlwind on sheer determination. She had to be close to ninety, tall still, but frail-looking, and so thin that it didn't seem she'd be able to balance on all that height.

She marched straight over to Henry.

"Welcome," Henry said, as if she were some young truth seeker. "To what do we owe the pleasure—calling a truce?"

"When hell freezes over." The old woman scowled and looked around. "This place looks shabbier than the last time I was here."

Henry smiled. "Then you should come more often, and you wouldn't notice it so much."

Hannah turned her scowl on him.

God, she was a bitter old woman. David knew she'd lost a son in the war; her surviving son, Lee, was a local music legend, though a bit of a recluse. She had two daughters living nearby. She had several grandchildren, one of whom was Eve Gordon, and great-grandchildren, and owned a good portion of the town. She should be enjoying her twilight years. And yet she seemed miserable.

David shuddered.

Henry beamed. "Have a seat, Hannah."

"Where is Floret?"

"Making tea."

Without a word, Hannah turned and tottered toward the kitchen. It was as if being in the house was suddenly draining her strength. David and Henry both hurried after her. Whether to protect Floret or aid Hannah if she fell, David didn't have a clue.

Floret was just pouring water into the teapot, and the aroma of chamomile filled the air around them.

"Don't bother," Hannah said. "I won't be staying that long." She looked around and walked over to the old farm table, but instead of sitting down, she leaned on both hands on a chair back. "I'm here to warn you that you may be getting a visitor."

Henry smiled as if he had no interest in her information.

David had to stop himself from reacting. Maybe the old broad was really a witch like some people said. How on earth could she have known? Though Henry and Floret hadn't been surprised at all. Floret had even sent their visitor down to Wind Chime Beach. Though with Floret you never really knew if she was being lucid or off in a fog, which David had come to suspect had to do more with teas and brownies than loss of brain cells.

"Already came," said Henry, and pulled out a chair for Hannah to sit down.

"Damn." She sank into the chair, but straightened

so quickly David wasn't sure that he'd actually seen the split second of defeat before she gathered her armor again.

Floret brought the teapot to the table, followed by a plate of the same cookies they'd been eating earlier out on the veranda.

Hannah eyed them suspiciously.

"They're honey cardamom. Your favorite."

"Who says they're my favorite."

Floret gave Hannah her most vacuous smile. "They've always been your favorite. Have you forgotten?"

David smoothed his face, preventing the grin that was threatening to burst out. Score one for Floret. The old girl wasn't as dense as people sometimes thought. Then again . . . sometimes she was.

Hannah didn't bother to answer, and she didn't take a cookie or reach for the cup of tea Floret had poured her.

"Will you please sit down, Henry? You're very distracting hovering like that in—that dress."

"Was I hovering?"

"You look ridiculous in that getup."

Henry looked down at his white caftan. "This getup is what I choose to wear. You used to not complain—in fact you used to say that—"

"I know what I used to say. Sit down. I need you to pay attention."

Henry stood over her for a few seconds looking benign. He was anything but. David used to think he was a magician, that he could tame animals and soothe people merely by looking at them.

He walked around the table, seated Floret with the formality of a butler, and sat down opposite Hannah.

Hannah turned her hard, dark eyes on David. She probably wanted him to leave, so he sat in the free chair and reached for a cookie he didn't want.

The energy between Hannah and Henry arced across the table. David glanced at Floret, feeling a gulf of space—possibly outer space—between her and the other two. What on earth would she say if given the opportunity, and would it play into Hannah's hands? Because Hannah never came without an ulterior motive.

For a lunatic moment, David considered going to get Dulcie to keep Floret from bursting out with nonsense.

"What did you tell her?" Hannah demanded.

Henry reached for a cookie. "What was there to tell?"

"You know I really hate it when you do that."

"What is that, Hannah?"

"When you answer a question with another question."

"There are only questions."

Hannah banged her knobby fist on the table. It wasn't very effective, and she didn't usually make those kinds of mistakes in her constant display of one-upmanship. She must be rattled.

"Just don't talk to her. And don't let Floret say a word; she'll spill the beans, for sure."

Floret was staring into the middle distance, but at the mention of her name she turned to Hannah and said dreamily, "She was lovely, she looked just like Jenny, at first I thought she was Jenny."

David froze. What was going on here? And why was everyone so concerned about a wandering tourist who wanted to see the beach? And who the hell was Jenny?

Hannah groaned. "Give me patience."

"Not to worry," Henry said. "David chased her off."

David shrugged. He wasn't about to show any other reaction. And he certainly wasn't going to describe what happened, especially not to Hannah Gordon.

He really hated the way she treated her once-closest friends. All over some slight years ago, and now over money and property—and power.

Hannah gobbled up real estate like a hen on corn. She wanted Wind Chime for God knew what. Ostensibly so the inn could use the beach that abutted their property. Eve just wanted use of the beach, which Floret would have gladly shared if Hannah hadn't gummed up the works with her unrelenting bitterness.

She couldn't be satisfied just leasing the beach. She had to own the entire property.

She'd probably raze the house to build banquet pavilions or something equally distasteful, but not if he could help it. This was Floret and Henry's home. And his and Eli's.

David had grown up here. He had returned eight years ago, when his brother and sister-in-law were killed in an accident and he became the guardian of ten-year-old Eli. He was only twenty-seven then and clueless about how to raise a grieving boy. But he knew who would. Eli had thrived living with Henry and Floret and the other few hippies who had returned to live here in their retirement. And living here gave David the freedom to accept an occasional assignment that required travel.

Hannah would have to walk over him to get her hands on Wind Chime House.

While David had wandered off on the path of memory, the tension around the table had grown, most of it emanating from Hannah Gordon.

She pushed her chair back and stood, looking more awkward than powerful, and for just a second David found himself feeling sorry for her.

Hannah raised a crooked finger. "Don't talk to her again."

"Hannah," said Henry patiently. "Will you never learn that some things are inescapable?"

"Let me tell you what's inescapable. If you encourage that little bitch, I'll make sure you lose this place. I will stop at nothing. Do you understand?"

Henry smiled.

David knew it would infuriate Hannah.

"You know, Hannah. Sometimes I see the girl in you. And I truly don't know what happened to make you so not your true self."

Hannah cut a vicious look toward Floret, but it was wasted on Floret, whose attention was rapt on her life partner.

"Do not cross me in this." Hannah turned and, looking much older than when she'd arrived, walked determinedly to the door. A look from Henry, and David rushed to see her to her car. But she stopped him at the kitchen door.

"I know the way, don't bother to see me out."

He returned to the kitchen and watched from the window until he saw the Cadillac drive away. Then he turned to Floret and Henry.

"What's going on here?"

"All in good time, my boy. Shall we finish our tea? Then we'll get the rest of those shutters hung."

Mel ducked into the trees just as the silver Cadillac came down the drive from Wind Chime House and turned onto the road. She'd doubled back through the woods or else she'd be sitting in that car right now, being treated like some idiot who didn't have a mind of her own. But she'd jumped into the trees without hesitating a second. It was an automatic reaction, something she had perfected over the past few months. It was like the whole world was against her—her and Eli. She hated the sneaking and hiding. But it didn't seem like she had a choice. In anything.

She peered out from behind the tree until she was sure the car was gone, then sank back against the rough bark and let out a huge sigh of relief. It wasn't fair. Why did she have to hide from her whole family just to see her best friend?

Was that why her great-grandmother had gone to Wind Chime? To tell David not to let Eli see her anymore? Threaten would be more like it. Mel didn't get why they didn't like him. Well, they did like him, except for Granna. And it seemed as if she didn't like anybody.

What if she'd come to threaten Floret and Henry

because Mel was seeing Eli? If she did something to those two to make them lose their home, Mel would never forgive her great-grandmother.

And Eli would never forgive *her*. Her eyes stung just thinking about the things that could go wrong. Her mother was already on her case.

They didn't understand. Her mom, since her dad left, was finished looking for love, and David Merrick had never wanted it in the first place. At least that's what Eli said. Who didn't want love? That was crazy.

No wonder they were all against her and Eli being in love. But why were they mad because Zoe Bascombe had asked about Wind Chime Beach? No one had ever told Mel not to mention the commune. People were always visiting it.

Now, just because this girl—woman really, but she seemed more like Mel than her mother or sisters—had asked, everyone was arguing. Well, Mel was a woman, too. Eighteen in three months. Eighteen, then she'd be legal and no one could boss her around anymore.

The thought made her giddy and sad. And frightened. If they couldn't tell her what to do, would they still take care of her? Could she still come to Sunday dinners, and what about Christmas and birthdays?

Would she be estranged from her mom? Her mother had never had a mother. Not a real mom. Granna and

Floret had taken care of her when she was young. Then she had taken care of herself. Mel knew that Granna had bought the inn for her, but she'd made it work all on her own.

Mel could do that. Turn something into a way to live. She wasn't sure what yet. Maybe the inn, except that already belonged to her mother. But something.

"Gotcha!"

Mel jumped about a hundred feet. And turned into Eli's arms. "You scared me. Where did you come from?"

"I saw you walking back from town and was coming out to meet you, but I had to wait until Hannah left. Did you see her? Cripes! There was such a scene." He pulled her closer. Kissed her.

She gave in to the feelings of safety and love and wanting to be with him forever. The other stuff went out of her head—almost.

She pushed him away just a little bit so she could see his face. "What was she doing here?"

"I don't know. They all went into the kitchen. And I couldn't really hear without putting my ear to the door. No way was I going to take the chance of your great-grandma catching me. That would be the end of everything."

Mel sighed. "What are we going to do?"

Eli grinned and she loved him all the way to her

toes. He pulled the backpack off his shoulder and held it up. “Everything we need for a getaway picnic.” He frowned. “One thing I did hear was that someone came to the house today asking about our beach.”

Mel grabbed his arm. It was muscular, not built like some guys, just hard and strong.

“The woman from the hotel. She was asking about our beach? I thought it was called Old Beach. It’s really called Wind Chime Beach?”

“First I ever heard of it. I was just coming back from town when I saw her running down the driveway like ghosts were after her.” Eli laughed. “It wasn’t a ghost; it was Uncle David.”

“He was chasing her away?”

“I think so. Henry called her Pandora.”

“Pandora? Why?”

Eli shrugged. “Floret said not to worry, but you know Floret, she wouldn’t worry.”

“Do you think something bad is going to happen?”

“Nah. I hope not. I don’t think so.”

“But if it does?”

“It won’t.”

But if it did, Mel knew it would be all her fault.

Chapter 7

Zoe tossed her bookstore package onto the bed and headed for the bathroom and her sewing kit. She spent the next ten minutes digging slivers out of her palms and dousing them with an antibacterial cream. Then she took her new book to the balcony where she stretched out on the chaise and opened to the backflap of the jacket.

And there was the face of the man who had thrown her off the Wind Chime property.

He looked very dashing in the photo, artistic with sensitive brown eyes looking back at the camera. The sarcasm she'd borne the brunt of today was nowhere to be seen.

False advertising, she thought. *A lie.* She turned the

book over and flipped through the first pages until she got to the title page.

There was a preface that she didn't read, written by someone whose name she didn't recognize. The first photo page appeared without warning. She'd been expecting a table of contents or at least an author's note.

But it just started. And the first photograph was . . . a beach? She peered more closely. A desert? It was sand, contoured into dunes, the heat visibly rising from its surface. There was no description, nothing to tell the reader what they were seeing.

After the desert photo, there was a close-up of something that might be an orchid. She'd seen curved petals like that at the New York Botanical Garden, but she couldn't be sure.

It was a little annoying not to have a clue, not to know what you were looking at. Then came the two pages of wind chimes. They were the first of several wind chime photos, as she was to discover. Sometimes hanging from a branch, sometimes hidden among the trees like *Where's Waldo?,* sometimes so close that you couldn't really tell what they were.

They were spread throughout the book, seemingly without rhyme or reason. Waterfalls, deserts, rock formations, tree bark, waves, hummingbirds—and always wind chimes. Some photos were powerful, others so delicate that she was afraid to breathe on the page.

There were no descriptions, no explanations, no poetic sayings, not even an index at the end.

There were also no people.

Intentional? Or a window into the photographer?

Poignant, quiet, angry, accepting. Woven together into a wordless story.

The guy could take pictures. She'd been sucked into them in the same way she was with a beautiful song, a symphony, or when the wind chimes today had passed through her world and opened a new one.

There was something about David Merrick's photos. Beautiful—but solitary.

She knew how that felt.

Zoe closed the book.

It was a sunny day, high clouds floating through a blue sky. A heady breeze blew cooler than the air around it. Below her on the lawn, a yoga class was just ending. Spirits renewed, the participants would soon be sunbathing on the hotel beach, drinking healthy drinks or spiking them with liquor concealed inside their beach bags.

All in all, a nice day's work on their psyches and their tans. And suddenly she wanted to be down there with them. Not here alone, hands raw, heart sore, holding on to her mother even after her mom was clearly gone. Fulfilling the wishes of the dead and not enjoying life.

Was it selfish to want some fun when she was here to mourn?

The only time she ever stayed at a hotel was when she was working. Making sure important people got where they needed to be, ate what they wanted to eat when they wanted to eat it. Always grabbing sustenance on the run, her cell phone on the table of some canteen or fast-food joint so she could hear it if someone needed her ASAP. Sometimes she didn't even get to the concerts until it was time to pick up her group and shuttle them to some fancy party.

It was hard not to think that maybe her mother had sent her here on purpose. Not because she was efficient, or because they had some special mother-daughter bond, but because she thought her daughter had something to learn.

Which was ridiculous. Her mother's instructions had been written months before, when Zoe had been on a career path to the stars. Rock stars, at least.

Maybe it was the spa's good energy, or the crazy people at the commune, Mel and her boy troubles, or the enigmatic, sarcastic photographer, but something felt different. A sense of freedom with no schedule to keep to, no one demanding her time, her energy, her skills. And with it was the awakening feeling that there was no hurry.

And the sudden knowledge that at Wind Chime Beach, her mother would find peace.

It might take some work to convince Henry and Floret, but she wouldn't go creeping about like some thief. She'd clean up the beach, spread the ashes with love, sing and carry on and send her mom out in style. Maybe the people at the commune would join her.

It might take time. And guess what? She had time. She'd spend a few days at the spa, try a package, lie out at the hotel beach. She even had a swimsuit hidden beneath a stack of folded underwear in the top drawer of the dresser. She always took her swimsuit when she traveled, though she barely ever got a full hour at a pool. And though she certainly hadn't planned to swim while she was here, she'd packed it out of habit. Now she was glad she had.

She'd listen to some music, not at the bar downstairs, but at one of the other restaurants or pubs in town that advertised live music. If she got drunk enough, she might even sit in with one of the bands if they were amenable. Hell, she even had an instrument sitting in the back seat of her SUV.

Soon enough she would be back on the job market. But for now . . .

She turned back into the room, marched over to the phone, and booked her room for another five days, then turned to the urn.

"There's been a snag. It could take a few days. Hope you're not in a hurry."

She moved closer, ran her finger along the cool, hard contour of the urn. "I found Wind Chime Beach. I heard the chimes. I get it. The peace, the magic, the specialness. I just don't understand why you of all people got it. You were never fanciful, you couldn't even come up with an idea for a Halloween costume. You never gathered us all in the car and took off on an adventure. You never even went to a beach, because you said it made your hair frizz. But I get it. What I don't get is how you got it. And it's really important to me."

There was no answer from the urn. There never would be.

The phone rang and her first thought was that Chris was calling at last. But it was the house phone.

"Hello?"

"Hi, Zoe?"

"Yes?"

"This is Karen. We met this morning at breakfast. We're all headed downstairs to the bar for happy hour; they have great appetizers. Would you like to meet us there?"

"I—" She stopped her usual autoreply, that she'd love to, but she was just too busy. She wasn't too busy. "Sure. I'd love to."

"Great, about fifteen minutes? See you."

Karen ended the call. Zoe changed into slacks and a silk tee, dumped essentials into her shoulder purse, then stopped at the urn.

"I'm going out with the girls." And she swore her mom said, "Text me when you get home."

Zoe met them in the lobby.

"Hope you don't mind eating here tonight," Karen said, and they went into the bar. "Elaine has something going with the fiddle player."

Brandy rolled her eyes. "At least there won't be any jokes about embouchure this trip."

"It was the clarinetist in a New Orleans jazz band last time," Karen explained.

"Hey," Elaine said, and gave Karen a playful punch. "I'm legally divorced after the longest-running court case of the century. The ex finally took the kids for the weekend—God forbid they should interfere with his golf game. The last time they came back, Robbie said he wasn't going anymore, all they did was sit in the golf cart for two days running."

The hostess showed them to a table near the bandstand.

Elaine pulled out a chair and sat. "Hopefully he'll do something fun with them this weekend."

"How many kids do you have?" Zoe asked.

"Three. In rapid succession." Elaine sighed. "Lots of fights. Lots of unprotected makeup sex. Not a good start or finish to a marriage that was hopeless from the beginning."

"I guess not," said Zoe, and sat down.

They ordered drinks, then headed for the hot buffet bar where they loaded plates with wings, sausages, quesadilla wedges, and a pile of other happy-hour food—all organic. Brandy was the only one who ended up with more hummus and crudités than fried meats, but she seemed perfectly happy. And she was definitely in better shape than her friends—or Zoe, for that matter.

The bar began to fill up. They ordered another round of drinks and decided to have dinner. Zoe was stuffed but she thought, what the hell, she hadn't had lunch. Actually, she'd been neglecting meals for weeks now. Her clothes were loose and she'd been out of breath just running down someone's driveway this afternoon. It was a long driveway, but still.

Maybe she'd join the others in some yoga tomorrow. Who was she kidding? The closest she'd come to yoga in the past few months was a hot pretzel from a vendor on Fifth Ave.

But tonight was about socializing and laughing—something else she hadn't done much of lately. Brandy kept them in stitches with stories about her recent honeymoon. Her new husband was an ex-basketball player, now an announcer with a sports television affiliate in Philadelphia.

The three friends ordered another round of drinks but Zoe knew better—she didn't want to be the one staggering through the lobby toward her room. The other three were obviously big drinkers and eaters, even Brandy, who was still munching carrot sticks and hummus along with her Moscow Mule.

The band began to set up, and Zoe began to think about going upstairs. She'd caught the eye of the guitarist several times as he climbed back and forth among the amps. She supposed that angry look was part of his persona. It had probably been sexy a few decades ago. But the "bad boy" appeal was nonexistent in this old guy. It just made him look unpleasant.

And angry at her.

"I really have to do some work." She started to stand.

"You're kidding, right?" Karen said. "The night is young."

"Sorry. But I'm behind as it is." Behind in getting her life together, maybe. Mainly, she just didn't want any more weirdness from the bandstand.

"Let me get the tab," she said on impulse, and took the check the waitress had been adding to throughout the evening.

"No," Brandy said. "We go dutch all the way."

The guitarist was still staring at her and it was beginning to creep her out. "No, really. My treat." Zoe backed away, nearly hitting a passing waitress.

"Then tomorrow we treat you," Karen said.

"Meet us on the beach after morning classes," Brandy said.

Elaine merely waved distractedly in her direction. She was already in full flirtation mode with the fiddler.

Zoe hurried to the bar where the bartender was talking to the woman she'd met that morning, the proprietress, Eve. Mel's mother, who was mad at Mel for telling Zoe about Wind Chime House, and who Mel had asked Zoe not to tell that she'd seen her that afternoon. She was too tired to confront their family idiosyncrasies tonight.

"Making it an early evening?" the bartender asked as he took her credit card.

"Work to do." She smiled her too-busy-to-talk-now smile.

People usually got the message. Eve didn't.

"Do you have business locally?"

"No. Actually I'm, uh, working remotely." Just a

little white lie. Just reshuffle the words and you had "I'm not remotely working."

"We have pretty good Wi-Fi here," the bartender said.

Zoe smiled. Signed the check, adding a big tip, something her mother taught her. *Always tip big the first time, and they'll treat you right after that.* Though now that she thought about it, how did her mother know that? She never paid for anything. First it was their dad, then the men who would never become her second or any other kind of husband but who still continued to woo her year after year.

"Night." Zoe turned toward the door just as the band started to play.

"Jenny," crooned the singer, as if calling Zoe back. But Zoe barely slowed down. Eve's penetrating gaze on her back propelled her through the door.

Eve watched Zoe Bascombe hurry from the room. The girl was definitely spooked. She knew. She must know. That must be the reason she'd come here. Not to visit the spa or the beach like the other guests, but to return to Wind Chime Beach. Her mother must have sent her. Her mother—and Eve's mother.

Did Lee know? From the way he'd been acting he must have a suspicion that Zoe's mother was Jenny Campbell. Why else start the set with his "signature" song. He usually didn't sing it until the end of the evening. Saving the best for last, but in his case, ending his day with what tortured him most, even after all these years.

There could be no mistake. Eve had a half sister. They didn't know about each other—at least Eve hadn't known. And Zoe still seemed clueless, just spooked.

Was it fear or knowledge that made her act so furtively? Was she checking Eve out? Why not just ask Eve if they had the same mother? And why come here now? What did she want?

Eve stopped herself, horrified at her own suspicions. She'd spent years undoing the mistrust of people that exuded from her grandmother, and which Hannah had wittingly or unwittingly taught Eve to expect in life. It hadn't always been that way. When they'd lived at Wind Chime with Floret and Henry and the others, Eve had seen the good in people every day. Had trusted them, depended on them, loved them.

Her grandmother had always had an edge, a strain of mistrust. She was born and raised nearby. The family had worked hard just to survive. Then she'd lost a husband and a son. Her daughters had married local boys who turned out to be lazy and angry, ready to blame everyone but themselves for their lack of success. And they blamed Hannah for not doing more for them, when she'd actually been very generous. Over and over and over she loaned them money she knew she would never see again; then one day she stopped.

The daughters cried and cajoled and when she didn't cave, they turned their backs on her. Hannah knew they were just waiting for her to die so they could claim their part of her self-made empire.

But not Eve. Eve loved her like a mother, even as she watched her grandmother turn from bitter to toxic to destructive. And she loved her anyway.

And then there was Eve's father, whose own heartache had hardened Hannah's. And they'd spread that hardness to Eve. Floret and Henry had been the antidote to the poison that spread around her. Until the "fight" that tore them apart. Even after that, Eve had stayed close to them. Usually without Hannah's knowledge.

Hannah had bought the inn for Eve and turned it over to her. Eve had made good. She had a legacy to leave her own daughters, who were all hardworking and caring people.

And never once would Hannah tell Eve about her mother.

Sometimes the "Hannah streak," as middle daughter Noelle called it, would try to wriggle its way into

Eve's psyche, like just now with Zoe Bascombe. And when it did, it had to be dealt with ruthlessly.

There was no place for anger or bitterness in Eve's life. It would be the death of her and the Solana.

People came to her to get in touch with their inner feelings, to learn to accept life the way it was, to find solace, or peace, or help through a crisis. And she was there to give them a haven in which to do that.

Without judgment.

Tonight she had an awful feeling that Zoe Bascombe wasn't here to enrich her own life, but to unravel Eve's.

"Deep thoughts," Mike intoned softly.

Eve jumped, not realizing he'd leaned all the way across the bar to whisper in her ear. "What?"

He frowned at her, jerked his head toward the door to the storeroom. Eve slid off the barstool and went around the bar, waited while he told Gary, the barman, to take over for him, and then let him trundle her through the door.

As it shut behind him, Lee's sonorous, sad voice became an indistinct hum.

Mike turned her around and took her by the shoulders. "What's up?"

At first Eve just shook her head. The whole thing was too strange. Her father was acting crazy, her grandmother was being secretive, and a woman had checked into her inn asking about a local commune.

It sounded ridiculous.

"Out with it."

"Zoe Bascombe." She stuck after the name.

"What about her?"

Eve shook her head again. She could tell Mike anything, everything. He was more than a bartender, a right-hand man. He was her best friend. Had always been her best friend from the first time he'd chosen her for his tug-of-war team on the school playground. He was a town boy; she'd been one of the "hippie brats." He was always there for her and she took him for granted.

He'd been there at her hippie wedding ceremony to Walter Flannigan and kept her going when Walter left them for the promise of wealth in the oil fields of Alaska. Had stood by her when the call came that Walter had died on the job.

They were on-again, off-again lovers. Friends with benefits who led their own lives.

"I think she's my half sister," Eve blurted out.

"Whoa."

"Possibly," she qualified.

"Huh. Did she say so?"

Eve shook her head. "I looked her up. Her mother's

name is Jenny Bascombe, née Campbell. My mother is Jenny Campbell."

"There must be a lot of Jenny Campbells out there."

"That's what I tried telling myself, but then . . . I found this." She unfolded the copies of the two photos of Zoe and Mel she'd made as soon as she returned to the hotel and had been carrying around all day.

Mike took them, moved over to the desk, and turned on the work lamp. Set the two photos down side by side. Let out a low whistle.

Eve leaned against his back. "This is Mel." She pointed to the one on the right. "And that is Zoe at sixteen. They're practically identical except for the hair color."

"Huh."

"You don't seem surprised." Not getting a response, she asked, "Do you think it's just a coincidence?"

"No. I noticed it before."

"What? When?"

"Last night. She checked in late and took a look in at the bar. For a second I thought she *was* Mel. Something about the way she moved, or tilted her head. I didn't think that much about it until Lee started acting so crazy." He shrugged. "You weren't the only one watching her tonight."

"Lee? Do you think he suspects?"

"How could he not? But whether he's willing to confront it is a whole 'nother other."

"Oh God." Eve covered her face with her hands.

He pulled her hands away. "What are you going to do about it?"

"I don't know."

"Well, if you need moral support, you know I'm here."

"I know, thanks."

"But right now, as your bartender, I need to get back to work."

"Thanks, you always make me feel sane when I get nutty."

"Aw, get on now." He turned off the desk lamp and opened the door. Lee's song hit them like a blow to the solar plexus. It was a new verse, one that Eve had never heard before, and one she knew had just been written.

"I saw you last night in a dream
You were young, but I wasn't
You wanted to stay but I scared you away . . ."

Eve slammed the door against his words.

"You're going to have to face him," Mike said.

Eve nodded. "And he's going to have to face her."

Chapter 8

Mike turned Eve around to face him. “Why? He had an affair when he was just a kid, and I for one am glad he did.” He smiled, that lopsided half smile, half grimace, goofy and loving and all Mike.

Eve loved him for it and for all the support he’d given her over the years. “Because he’s obviously upset by her.”

“She’ll be gone soon.” He frowned. “She’s here on business, I think she said. How long is she registered for?”

“Two nights.” So far, Eve thought. But she couldn’t let Zoe Bascombe go before letting her know she had a sister, if only half. And for Eve . . . Well, it meant the world to her. Even if they had nothing in common but a mother.

Only a mother? That was major. Zoe could tell her so much.

"I'm going to ask her to stay on."

Mike snorted. "First you'll have to tell her the news. Unless you think she already knows." He gave her a gentle shake. "Think this one down the road a bit."

Eve nodded. He was right. She didn't know Zoe Bascombe. It wouldn't be fair to spring this on her. She didn't know where it might lead. She'd all but given up the possibility of having a half sister or brother somewhere—until she'd seen those photos. And if she had a half sister, she might have a whole half family out there. Was she ready to go there after all these years?

"I'll be mindful."

"You always are." Mike kissed her forehead. "Take the rest of the night off. Who's on night duty?"

"Ernie Wilson."

"Good. I'll close up." Mike opened the door a crack. The band had started on a new song. Mike ushered her out. "Sleep well." He went back to the bar and Eve headed for the side door and home.

The cottage was lit up and for a moment Eve hoped Mel would actually be there instead of out with Eli. But it was Noelle, home earlier than expected. She was curled up on the couch, a bowl of popcorn on the coffee table next to her, a movie streaming on her open laptop. She was fast asleep.

Eve tiptoed past and went into the kitchen, made herself a cup of tea. Kept one ear out for Mel's return or for Noelle to rouse. Why was Noelle home so early, and why was Mel so late?

She sat until her tea grew cold, poured it out and rinsed the cup, and then with nothing left to do but worry, she went to bed.

But not to sleep.

Her brain was a jumble of moving parts, none of which made sense and all of which were in trouble of accelerating out of control. She'd known at an early age that you couldn't control most things. If she could, she'd have had one of those nuclear families the kids in town had. A father who went to work in the morning and came home at night in time for dinner. She'd have a mother to shop with for school clothes and sing her to sleep.

Her father had sung her to sleep, *Lavender's blue, dilly dilly* . . . But he was usually gone. Then Floret did, or sometimes even Henry tried, though he couldn't, as everyone knew, "carry a tune in a bucket," which never made sense to her, because he chanted the most beautiful sounds that weren't words but that were better than words.

Hannah didn't sing. She didn't try, or maybe she just didn't like singing. Maybe because it had taken her only living son away from her. Or brought Eve's mother to Wind Chime in the first place.

Eve turned over, tried to empty her mind, heard the movie go silent, then Noelle go off to bed. She hadn't even checked to see if Mel had come home. Was that an omen? Good or bad? *There is no good or bad . . . just things we don't understand.*

Eve wasn't sure she still believed that. She rolled to her back, moved to her side and drew up her knees. Finally she took her phone out of the bedside table drawer and looked at the time. One o'clock.

Mel had been upset this morning when she'd left the inn. Eve didn't blame her.

She'd just been doing her job, helping guests and being friendly. As she pointed out to both of them before she left.

She was right. Eve and Lee had been reacting to the appearance of Zoe Bascombe. Mel had done everything right and she'd caught flak. An innocent bystander. And suddenly a constant reminder. At least to Eve.

She needed to talk to Mel. Actually both—all three—of her daughters. But to Mel first. Not about

Zoe but about Eli. She had to make sure they wouldn't do anything stupid before Eve could sort out her own suddenly volatile existence.

That had to be dealt with first; then she could deal with all the issues at once, Mel and Eli, Noelle and her career, and even Harmony and her growing family.

She'd never been prone to putting off things that needed to be said, done, or at least discussed, but tonight . . . For the first time in a long time, she wasn't sure of herself, of what she wanted, or if she was even right.

And she wouldn't be until she found out the truth about Zoe Bascombe.

She pulled the pillow over her head. Threw it off again.

She had a half sister. What did that even mean, half sister?

For nearly fifty years Eve had been an only child. So what if Zoe's mother might also be Eve's? They shared a mother, but family? Memories? Kinship? They had no common background, loves, fears, nothing.

Eve heard the front door open and close. Mel was home. She went straight to her room.

Eve's eyes closed.

She had a half sister.

David paced the floor of his room at Wind Chime. Heard Henry go downstairs for his late-night snack. David was tempted to join him, but he didn't want to be standing in the foyer like an irate parent when Eli finally returned. It was after one, but Eli had turned eighteen two months ago. He was an adult. But he was still thinking and acting like a kid.

He had his big exam for the pre-semester science program on Sunday and he needed his sleep. He'd been looking forward to it for months, ever since Henry had seen it in an alumni magazine.

He'd studied like crazy, but now he seemed distracted. And David knew why.

Mel Gordon. Wherever Eli was tonight, Mel Gordon would be with him.

David stopped at the window, leaned on the sill. Where were they? Not at Mel's house. Eve would have sent Eli home hours ago. She was no more happy about this than he was.

Not that he had anything against Mel. She was a good kid. A little impulsive, which wasn't a totally bad thing. Had a good heart. But at seventeen, she was still kind of clueless. Immature for her age. Didn't seem to have any drive.

They might be happy together one day. But not yet.

The world was a tough place and getting tougher by the day. Wind Chime was a haven—that's why David had brought Eli here. But maybe it hadn't prepared him for surviving in a world gone crazy.

And what would happen when David left? Which he had to do soon. He couldn't make a living without working in the field. He needed outside assignments to fill the coffers. Not just the occasional book and travel page.

He needed new material. And he needed to breathe, to feel the exhilaration of discovery, of fear, of triumph. He'd been able to keep working because he had Henry and Floret to look after Eli while he was gone. But they couldn't anymore.

Eli was a man. He'd be away at school. He loved them but he wouldn't obey them. And they would never impose rules on him. It wasn't their way.

David saw him before he heard him, walking up the drive in the moonlight. He looked as if he didn't have a care in the world.

Yeah, David remembered those days when his biggest decision was whether to crawl another foot out on a ledge for the perfect shot or play it safe and be satisfied with the shots he already had. It was always the ledge. But it was his ledge, his life, and no one would be hurt if he made the wrong decision.

He went downstairs and was caught standing in the foyer when Eli came through the front door.

"Oh, man," Eli said, and slowly closed the door. "I'm a little late."

David couldn't even think of anything to say. *What do you think you're doing? Are you being responsible? Are you having sex?* Of course they were. *Are you taking precautions?* In the midst of unbridled teenage lust? He doubted it. *Who's going to support you if she gets pregnant? Do you think in your wildest dreams they'll ever let you marry her?*

"Where were you?" God, he sounded like an old fart.

"Just around. Hanging out. We lost track of time."

"Who is we?"

Eli shoved his hands in his jeans pockets.

"Mel?"

"So? You sound just like Mel's mother. It's because of that stupid feud, isn't it? That's so last century."

"It has nothing to do with any feud. It has to do with your future—and Mel's."

"Mel wants to get married."

David had been expecting this, was waiting for it, but hearing it out loud . . . He pulled himself together. "What about university, the pre-semester science program? The entrance exam is this weekend." David clamped down on his next thought.

"I don't know."

Well, David did. He knew that he had a responsibility to his brother to raise his child the best he could. And not going to school to marry a girl, neither of them with any way to support themselves, was no future.

"Our future is together."

"It may be, but right now—"

"What do you know? You don't even know what it's like to be in love."

Eli was right. David had never found one person who meant more to him than photography and freedom.

Henry stepped out of the kitchen, holding a bowl of yogurt and granola. Eli brushed past him and ran up the stairs.

David followed more slowly. Eli was teetering on a life decision, and David had made a hash of trying to help. Like he usually did.

"The future is the future," Henry said, and putting his free hand on David's shoulder, they walked up the flight of stairs together.

Noelle was up and sitting at the table staring into her coffee mug when Eve wandered into the kitchen the next morning.

"Hey," she said. "Coffee's fresh."

Eve nodded, got another mug down from the cabinet.

She had a headache from lack of sleep, from stress, from worry, and from the recognition that her world was about to change drastically and not knowing what it would do to her family.

She sat down across from Noelle.

"Guess you're wondering why I'm home two days early."

"You're always welcome."

"I didn't get the job."

"I kinda figured that might be the case. What happened?"

Noelle toyed with her mug. "I don't know. I thought I did a great interview. They said they were impressed with my résumé. I hit it off with the HR guy. But at the end of the day, they called and said I wouldn't need to come back for the next round."

"That sucks, but there are other jobs."

"Just not in graphic arts."

"Hey," Eve said, taking her coffee and moving around to sit next to her middle daughter. "You've been out of school for two months. It's not a race."

"I know. It's just . . ." Her mouth twisted, and Eve gave her shoulders a squeeze. "I really liked this company."

Eve knew. And she knew how stupid it would be to say that everything would work out. She said it anyway.

"I know. It's just really disappointing. Guess I better take over some hours at the inn."

"Take a few days, regroup, and reorder your job search. We can spot you a few tofu burgers while you get back up to speed."

"Thanks."

Mel appeared in the doorway; her hair was a rat's nest. She walked straight to the coffeepot without looking at either of them.

Eve tried not to ask the question. So she formed it as a statement. "I heard you come in last night."

Mel shrugged and started to take her coffee out of the room.

"Aren't you going to say hello to your sister?"

"Hi. Guess you didn't get the job."

"Mel," Eve began.

"So much for your fancy college education."

Eve's mouth dropped open. "Mel, what's gotten into you? If this is what hanging out with Eli Merrick is doing to your—"

"Why does everyone hate Eli?"

"OMG, are we still beating that dead horse?" Noelle asked.

Eve cringed. Whoever thought raising girls was easier than boys was living in an alternate reality.

"You're just jealous because you're old."

"I'm twenty-four."

"And can't even get a job."

"Okay, Mel, that's enough. You're not being fair, or kind." The last thing Eve wanted to do was intervene, but you don't kick someone when she's down even if she is your sister and will forgive you.

"Oh, sure, Noelle goes to college, so she's Miss Wonderful. But what good did it do her or Harmony? She spent four years and thousands of dollars to move to California, just to teach, then marry some dude and start popping out babies. She could have done that here. Noelle can't even get a job. At least I know what I want."

Noelle stood and leaned over the table. "Just shut up. You are such a bitch. And you don't know shit. And if you think you can live around here, mooning over Eli Merrick and mooching off Mom, you should get a life."

"Look who's talking. I've got a life. And Eli wants to marry me."

"No!" The word exploded from Eve's mouth before she could stop it. "Look, honey, we all like Eli, and if you still want to get married in a year or so, that's great. But first you need to—"

"Get an education," Mel said in a high-pitched voice that grated on Eve's already stretched-thin nerves.

"Have you been possessed?" Noelle asked in her most sarcastic voice. "Night of the whiny, entitled teenager?"

"We'll discuss this later," Eve said, trying to defuse an already volatile conversation; she wasn't feeling up to the job of mediator.

"I'm marrying Eli," Mel said. She glared at Eve.

Eve smoothed her face. Took slow breaths. Willed herself to stay calm for her daughters' sake, when her own life was about to blow up.

"I'm just saying that marriage and education aren't mutually exclusive."

"You don't want me to get married because you never married Dad."

"You don't even remember him," Noelle broke in.

"I would have if he hadn't died."

Noelle rolled her eyes, growled in exasperation, and walked away. "He didn't just die. He left us. He might not have planned on coming back. We'll never know."

"Both of you stop it," Eve said. "I loved your father." She'd never gone to college because she'd loved him too well, and too often. Harmony had been born eight months after she graduated from high school. No college, no travel to foreign countries. All the plans she'd made had fallen by the wayside. She didn't begrudge the loss; she had her girls and Walter Flannigan for a good twelve years before he left. And then he died. And Eve became a widow with three little girls and no degree.

Hannah bought her the inn and gave her enough money to get started. Eve had run the inn and gone to night school in business management, worked like crazy to give her girls better options. And she'd be damned if she let Mel throw her chance away.

"He was a good man. We were married in every way but a piece of paper from the courthouse. Those things weren't so important in those days."

"Well, they're important to me. And we're getting married."

Eve sat back in her chair. She was just too tired to argue this morning.

"You can't stop me."

"Just shut up, Mel. Can't you see you're upsetting Mom?"

"She can't stop me."

And something in Eve just snapped. It wasn't because of Mel, or Noelle, or even her long-dead husband. She pushed away from the table and stood up. "As long as you live in my house, I can."

"Your house? I thought it was our house."

"Well, now you know." Eve whirled around, stormed out of the kitchen and out of the house.

Mel stared after her mom. Paralyzed. She'd never seen her so angry. Her mom didn't get angry. At least, she never yelled.

Noelle was staring at the back door. She looked like she might cry.

"Noe?"

Her sister turned on her. "See what you've done," Noelle said, glaring at her.

Mel crumpled inside. "Everybody hates me."

"You really don't get it, do you? Not everything is about you."

"Obviously. It's about how wonderful you and Harmony are."

"Don't be such a bitch. You know that's not true."

Mel pushed past her, knocking into her as she passed.

"Where the hell do you think you're going?" Noelle demanded, following her into the living room.

"To my room."

"You're on reception this morning."

"You do it. You owe me one."

Mel slammed her bedroom door.

"Fine," Noelle yelled from the other side. "Be selfish."

"Eff you," Mel yelled back. She brushed away angry tears. She was being a bitch but she couldn't help it. Everything was falling apart and she just wanted to be happy. "I hate you all."

Eve had gone out the back and down the path several hundred feet before she stopped for breath. What had she just done? She never lost her cool and she'd just given her youngest an ultimatum. That was not her.

But she wouldn't go back and apologize. Because right now, she didn't feel like relenting. She'd worked her butt off, for some of the right reasons—at least what she thought were the right reasons—but a lot just to "make good."

What a stupid phrase. What was "making good"? How did you know when you achieved it? It was about as stupid a concept as half sister. Both were meaningless.

She'd let the girls stew a bit. She'd left them in total silence. She doubted if it lasted long. They were probably back at each other's throats before Eve got to the sidewalk. One thing about the Gordons, they were stubborn—and they knew how to hold a grudge even if they suffered for it.

She'd hoped this trait wouldn't show itself in her girls. But she wasn't surprised, and she wasn't altogether unhappy about it. Stubbornness got you through when everything else failed. She had every reason to know.

It was the rare moments like these, when everyone was feeling the need to lash out at the same time, that Eve was tempted to let them all sink or swim. Take off to parts unknown and let them fend for themselves. She'd always wanted to travel. Had managed to go a few places when she was on the high school soccer team.

But for the past fifteen years she'd worked nonstop, efficiently and diligently, and with love in her heart—it was a spa, after all. But more recently, she realized, she was working out of sheer habit.

She'd managed to walk away from her cottage without looking back. Were they watching her from the window? Bonding over her as the common enemy? "She's turning out just like Granna." Or had they already dismissed her? And were eating toast and honey and streaming the latest Netflix series?

She marched up the path toward the inn but turned onto the walkway that led to the street.

Mike's house was three blocks from Main Street, set back on a wooded lot on the banks of one of the tributaries that ran into the river and eventually to the sea. She just went there automatically, not wondering if he'd be awake, not caring if he had company. He was a popular guy, and though they were pretty close, she didn't have—or want—exclusivity.

She stopped outside the frame craftsman-style house, looked around for an unfamiliar car. Only Mike's beat-up old Jeep was parked at the side of the house, but that didn't mean that he was alone.

Why had she even come here? She could probably just sneak away before she was tempted to whine out the whole story to him, her long-suffering friend. Of course, he'd poured out some of his stuff to her over the years. They were a good team.

So why did she feel like she was taking advantage of him? She turned to go.

"Hey. You made the walk. Now come make the coffee."

She turned and smiled at Mike waving from his doorway, as burly as a spring bear. But much more good-natured.

She walked back to his door, said thanks with down-cast eyes, and slipped past him.

"Oh, brother," he said, before closing the door on the world.

Chapter 9

Zoe spent the morning pacing in her room. She practiced several scenarios for talking to Henry and Floret, most of which began with first stopping to listen to the chimes and hoping for inspiration. They'd been playing through her head all night as she slept. Even when she woke she thought she could hear them wafting up from the beach, but that beach was on the other side of Wind Chime House. It would be impossible.

The sound was really coming from inside her.

But what she would do after hearing the chimes was sketchier. Walk up to the house and declare her intentions of spreading her mother's ashes on Wind Chime Beach? Ease into it by—and that's where she got stumped. How did you ease into something like that? Better just to blurt it out.

Really, how could they say no? They were obviously living the hippie dream. They'd totally understand. As long as David Merrick didn't get involved. Though, surely, he was just trying to protect them and his wind chimes.

She'd have to somehow convince them that she meant no harm.

She couldn't put it off any longer. She'd just go and hope for the best. She grabbed her purse and strode to the elevator with the best of intentions. Well, maybe she should have breakfast first. Breakfast was the key to a productive day. And she planned to have both.

But not at the inn. She'd seen the diner on her way to Wind Chime yesterday. It would be faster than the inn. Then she'd go straight to the commune.

She peeked down the hall before she stepped out of the elevator on the ground floor, then tucked her head in preparation for scooting past the reception desk.

She didn't get far.

"Hey! Wait."

She didn't look around but kept going. She heard the receptionist come from behind the desk.

"Good God, Mel. What did you do to your hair? Mom's gonna kill you. No wonder you crept out of the cottage without saying good-bye."

A hand clamped around Zoe's arm and spun her around.

A woman about Zoe's age, with light brown hair that waved past her shoulders, stared open-mouthed at her. "Oh, I'm so sorry. I thought you were my sister."

Right, she'd called Zoe "Mel." A case of mistaken identity.

"Your hair looks great, really. It's just . . ."

"It wouldn't work on Mel at all," Zoe said, pulling herself together.

"Right. I'm really sorry. It's just we had sort of a misunderstanding and— I'm Noelle, Mel's sister."

"Nice to meet you." Zoe began to ease away.

"It's weird," Noelle said. "For a minute . . . Well, I'm really, really sorry. It's a great style. Perfect for your face."

"Thanks. Listen, I've got to run."

Noelle nodded. "Have a nice day," she said, as Zoe hurried through the lobby door to the street.

Leave it to Zoe to find the nuttiest family in town. She enjoyed interesting characters as much as the next person, but this was getting beyond weird.

She stopped at Kelly's Diner. It was pretty busy, so she sat at the counter between an old guy who hunched over his coffee cup like it was the dead of winter and a hipster couple who kept asking questions about which was the best beach.

According to Jim, the short, happy-with-his-own-food man behind the counter, there were several. He mentioned a few, none of which were named Wind Chime.

The breakfast was good and greasy enough to rival any self-respecting Long Island diner. And Jim, who turned out to be the Mr. Kelly who owned the driveway to Wind Chime House, was a jovial conversationalist as he moved from customer to food pass-through, filled coffee cups, and gave directions in an efficient but unhurried way, adding additional stains to his white apron as he went.

Zoe turned down a second cup. And, metaphorically girded for battle with a stack of pancakes and a side of bacon, she continued on her way to Wind Chime.

She had second thoughts as she reached the drive, second thoughts that grew into big, fat cowardice as she neared the house. But she'd come too far to give in to nerves now.

She hadn't made contingency plans for running into David Merrick, who was hammering new pickets onto the sagging fence. If you asked Zoe, he should pull it all down and start over. But nobody asked her. He didn't even notice her arrival. Bent over his work, shirtless, his bronzed skin glistening in the sun, he looked more like a manual laborer than the creator of those amazing photographs.

There was no way to get to Henry and Floret without passing by him. She strode ahead. He straightened and turned around just as Dulcie appeared from the woods and galloped toward her.

Zoe froze.

"Dulcie," David said.

The goat did a funny hop and trotted over to him.

Zoe scooted toward the gate with her hand outstretched, as if that could ward off attacking goats.

"Do you think I could talk to Henry and Floret this morning?"

"Sure. They're expecting you."

"What? How can they be expecting me? What did you tell them?"

"Not a thing. They already knew you'd be back. They've been waiting for you to show up. Evidently for weeks. I didn't realize that until after you left yesterday."

"That's crazy. No one knew I was coming here. I didn't even know I was coming here until yesterday. I only came back today to—to—" She didn't think he needed to know why she was really here—not after all his crazy talk about expecting her.

"To talk to Henry and Floret. Come on." David shoved the hammer he'd been holding into the loop of his jeans and started toward the gate, Dulcie by his side.

He grabbed a T-shirt off one of the pickets, then leaned past her to pull the gate open. Dulcie took the opportunity to lunge at Zoe.

Zoe threw herself behind David in a cowardly attempt to hold him in front of her as a goat shield, realized she was grasping bare skin, and jumped away. "Sorry, I . . ."

"She's friendly once you get to know her." David pulled the shirt over his head. "Too friendly, a-pain-in-the-butt friendly. Aren't you, Dulcie?"

The goat bumped her head against his leg, and he shut the gate against her indignant bleating.

"Why doesn't she have horns?"

David gave her a sideways look. "Wishful thinking?"

Zoe tried not to smile, but couldn't quite pull it off.

"Floret liberated her from Barry Jenkins, a local farmer, right after he disbudded her. It's a common practice among dairy goats."

"Does it hurt?" Zoe asked, momentarily distracted and feeling a sudden sympathy for Dulcie.

"I have no idea, but Floret called Barry a barbarian and took the goat. Just so you know, Henry ended up paying him fifty bucks on the sly. That was years ago." David turned toward the house and called out, "Company!"

The door opened and the tallest man Zoe had ever seen stepped onto the porch.

"She's here," David said, and a chill ran up Zoe's spine. Had he mimicked Jack Nicholson's line from *The Shining* on purpose?

There was no doubt in her mind now. Henry was her ghost. And Dulcie the terrifying demon from hell. She was such an idiot. They must have been taking an evening walk in the fog. *Perfectly normal. Right.*

Zoe climbed the steps and stopped in front of him. He was definitely tall, but not as tall as he'd appeared in the fog or even yesterday. In the daylight and up close he was not scary at all. Not yet anyway.

He was wearing a long blue-and-white-striped caftan. Today his long white hair was pulled back in a ponytail. There was a sense of calm about him that was seductive.

"Welcome. Come in." His voice was lighter than Zoe had expected. She'd imagined him as a bass, but his greeting came out in a round, smooth baritone. He turned to precede them, and Zoe saw there was a daisy stuck in the band of his hair.

It was dark and cool inside. She followed him down

a short corridor hung with handwoven tapestries, past a door that led to a country kitchen that smelled slightly of an herb Zoe thought she recognized.

The hall ended in a staircase and opened on the left to a large room filled with light and crammed with comfortable-looking overstuffed furniture. Each piece was covered in a different floral pattern in a combination of colors that would rival even Jenny Bascombe's perennial border.

Beyond that room was an enclosed porch that overlooked the sea. This was a long-established and well-loved home, Zoe could feel it. And she felt like an interloper.

"Have a seat," Henry said.

Zoe sat on the couch, trying to look comfortable and competent at the same time, failing at both.

David sat in a chair across from her.

She frowned at him. She hadn't planned for him to be around when she made her announcement, or rather, her request. She should never have decided to play this by ear.

He leaned back in the chair and crossed a foot over one knee. A move that said he wasn't going anywhere.

Zoe swallowed.

Henry left the room.

What the hell?

He soon returned with a tray of glasses and what appeared to be iced tea, followed by Floret carrying a plate of cookies. Today she had foregone her gardening overalls for a long dress printed with smiling owls.

Henry poured tea. Floret passed the cookies, and David Merrick sat staring out to sea.

After a nerve-racking display of manners, Henry sat in the big wing chair placed diagonally to Zoe. Floret sat down on the couch next to her. Even though she perched on the edge of the cushion, her feet didn't quite reach the floor.

"I have a confession to make," Zoe began. "I'm not just a sightseer. I have a reason for being here."

"Oh, we know, dear. You don't have to explain," Floret said, leaning over to pat her hand. She turned it over and looked at Zoe's palm. "Good heavens."

"It's nothing, just some splinters." Zoe pulled her hand away. She was losing her train of thought.

She clasped her hands in her lap, took a breath. "I came because . . ." Her voice gave out and she realized that so far she hadn't actually said the words out loud. She reached for the glass of tea, took a sip. It was light and naturally sweet. She gripped the glass in both hands—she couldn't say it.

Henry took the glass from her and placed it on the table. "It's all right, Zoe. We know why you've come; we've been waiting."

Zoe eyed him warily, then cut a look toward Floret, but they both looked perfectly benign. Maybe she was the one who was batshit crazy.

"I . . ." She looked across at David, who seemed a thousand miles away. Or maybe he just didn't want to participate in this crazy scene. Then why didn't he leave? She certainly had no desire for an audience.

Henry laughed, a mellifluous sound that reminded her of the wind chimes. "Not to worry, you're safe here. We're not cult leaders."

Zoe blushed.

"Not even psychics, though Floret can read tarot cards."

"And tea leaves," Floret added.

"Then how did you know I was coming? How do you know why I came?" The questions just flew out of her mouth. She couldn't have stopped them if she'd tried.

"She sent us a letter."

"Who?" blurted Zoe.

Floret leaned toward her. "Jenny, of course. She said you'd be coming and . . ." Her words trailed off and she looked over David's shoulder so intently that Zoe looked, too. There was nothing there that hadn't been there before.

"She sent you something," Henry said. "She asked us to keep it until you arrived, but you ran off so quickly yesterday, I didn't have a chance to give it to you." Henry stood and left the room.

No one moved or spoke until he returned holding a flat brown-wrapped package. He moved the platter of cookies and placed the package on the table, then retrieved a penknife from a nearby writing table and handed it to Zoe.

Zoe just stared at the package. It had all the trademark neatness and tape overkill that were—had been—her mother's.

"When? When did she send this?"

Henry looked at Floret. "Months ago. She sent us a letter along with it, asking us to keep it. That you would be here . . ."

"Sooner or later, I believe were her words," Floret said. "I didn't expect it to be so soon. When I first saw you, I thought . . . But it's no matter."

"It looks rather difficult to open," Henry said. "Would you like me to take off the outer wrappings?"

Zoe nodded; she was shaking so much she didn't

think she could even close her fingers around the little knife, much less use it without doing more injury to her hands.

It only took a few graceful swipes to reveal a box, about the size of a shirt gift box. Henry handed it to her.

She placed it in her lap, afraid to open it. She wanted to think this was some kind of game, a con, maybe, but for what reason? And how did they know all this? She pulled the top off. Whatever was inside was covered with tissue paper. She peeled it back to find a layer of bubble wrap.

She touched it, her smile wavering from reminiscence to grief. It was so her mother, this overkill of protection. She unrolled the bubble wrap and finally came to the object. Lifted it out. No reason to try to be private. They seemed to know everything already. Maybe they already knew what it was.

She held up a delicate piece of hammered bronze, formed into the shape of a heart. The action set off a cascade of clear sound as five smaller glass hearts danced on thin silver threads. *Wind chimes.*

Panic chased wonder into Zoe's throat. "I don't understand. She wants me to hang these at the beach?"

Floret nodded, and touched the metal heart, a gesture as soft as a caress. Zoe could see all the wrinkles in her face now. A tear ran down her cheek. "That's exactly what she wants."

Wanted. What she wanted. "But why? How did she know about this place? Did you know her? What am I doing here?"

Zoe darted a look to David, possibly the only sane person in the room. But he was now staring at the plate of cookies.

"You've brought her home," Floret said, still fingering the heart.

Home? "Home? She's from Long Island."

Henry exhaled, a sound somewhere between a sigh and a song. "The heart can have many homes."

They were all totally bonkers. "I have to go." Zoe tried to get up but a small, gentle hand on her arm prevented her.

Floret.

Henry leaned over the table and brushed the last piece of tissue paper from the box. A white legal-size envelope was taped to the bottom. Across the front, Zoe's name was written in her mother's neat copperplate hand.

Zoe's fingers were trembling so much, she couldn't even pull the tape away. Henry took the envelope from the box, used his penknife to slit it open. When he handed it to her, she swore there were tears in his eyes, or maybe the tears were in her own eyes.

It took two tries but at last the letter was open in her hands. Was she going to read this in front of them all? Shouldn't she take it back to the hotel so she could be alone?

Dear Dilly. Her mother's pet name for her. It had soothed her as a child; it soothed her now.

You were my life, Zoe. I knew you would be. And you've never disappointed me. I'm so proud of you. Something I could never feel about myself.

Your mother is and has always been a coward. And because I couldn't stand up for what I wanted, I made some tragic, tragic mistakes.

I'm going to try to rectify some of them now that I am obviously dead. I know you will fulfill my wishes about my remains. But there are other things I wish, I need, you to do.

It's a long story and Henry and Floret can tell it better than I ever could.

Zoe looked up at Henry and Floret. Henry smiled encouragingly, but Floret had succumbed to her own tears and sat statue-still as they streamed down her sunken cheeks.

What mistakes, Mom? You didn't make mistakes. You were a great mother.

I hope you and the boys know I love you all with my entire being. A mother couldn't have had better children. And I hope I did well enough that you know this.

"You did," Zoe said. "Always."

But I didn't do so well for another. In fact, I made an unforgivable choice. I'm afraid it's too late to rectify what I did, but I hope with all my heart that you will try to do it for me.

Zoe shook her head. She didn't understand.

Henry handed her a large white handkerchief, which she took and wiped her eyes and nose.

Look closely at my wind chimes, which I hope you will hang in the glen above Wind Chime Beach. All my children together at last.

Zoe frowned. There were five little hearts. What the hell was happening here? *You had four children, Mom. Me and Chris and Robert and Errol.*

There is one whom I never acknowledged in life except in my heart. But she never left my heart and

I hope you can see your way to letting her know, since I can't.

You are among my dearest friends. They will guide you through and see you safe.

The same words Floret had spoken to her less than twenty-four hours ago. Zoe reached the end of the page and moved to the next.

You have a sister. Her name is Eve. You've probably met her by now. She runs the local inn. I was certain that one day you would find your way there. I don't know how many years have passed or if it has only been days. I wish I could see my two daughters together. I should have insisted on it. Maybe I will before I die, but just in case, I wanted you to know.

"Eve? At the inn?"

Floret smiled but didn't answer.

Zoe found her place, kept reading.

The world is a hard place. You wouldn't think to look at me or to know me that my heart was broken early on and I've been broken ever since. So I'll just lay it out as briefly as I can and leave Floret and Henry to fill in the rest.

When I was young I met my soul mate. Are you laughing, dear Dilly, to hear your suburban mom say things like 'soul mate'? Sometimes I thought you guessed at the things I tried to hide, refused to accept. But perhaps that was just my hope.

I was a coward. I've always been a coward. I gave in to my parents and gave away the child we had created, Eve. She was adopted by his family.

But I didn't leave her in spirit and I tried to stay in touch with her; wrote her so many letters. At first I was just desperate for news of her. Later I wanted to share so many motherly things with her. Things I shared with you. At first it nearly drove me crazy because I never got a reply. Year after year I wrote, only to get no reply. But then I began to wonder and then to hope she never received them, because if she had and she never tried to get in touch with me, and if that was her choice, it would break my heart beyond repair.

Please let her know that I loved her and it ripped a part of my heart out when I had to leave her. Let her know I'm so proud of her, I came to her high school graduation, I wanted so much to tell her how proud I was and how much I loved her, but I didn't want to cause a scene. Hannah and Lee must hate me so much.

I am so proud of you both. And I'm more afraid of what I must say now, than I have ever been in my life. I saw Eve's father once after I was taken away. It was years later. He was still angry. And so was I because our bond was stronger than ever even after all the years apart.

He was performing at the coliseum. I went and was let backstage. The rest, as they say, is history. And you became my beloved surprise baby. Lee Gordon is your biological father. I never told him about you. I'd caused him too much heartache as it was.

I'd lost one daughter and I refused to have the other stigmatized by my weakness. You became my precious secret.

My wonderful, precious secret.

I told no one. I suspect George knew. We weren't so happy in those days as we had been. But he was a good father to you in spite of it all. And I hope I was a good mother.

So there you have it. My confession of a life not

in my control. I hope you will forgive me and grow to love your sister as I have loved the both of you. Introduce her to her half brothers, and beg her to forgive me, though I expect it won't matter much to anyone.

I hope the two of you can be friends and sisters, my beautiful daughters.

Love,
Mom

"Love, Mom"? What the hell? You drop a bombshell like that and then end it with "Love, Mom"? She might as well have finished with a smiley face.

Lee Gordon was her father. Could it be true, that bitter old man? No, George Bascombe was her father—the same father who had left his family for another woman and another family.

Eve Gordon was her sister. Her sister. And Eve's children . . .

"No." Zoe pushed herself up using the table for support. "No."

Floret smiled up at her. "There is so much she wants you to know."

Wanted. Wanted me to know. She's gone.

Zoe looked wildly around. She had to get out. Henry

and Floret's acceptance and serenity were suffocating her. And David Merrick's indifference was humiliating.

She wanted—needed—to know everything.

But Henry stood. "We'll tell you everything we remember, and you can catch us up on the rest, but later. First, you need to see Eve and tell her about the letter. She's been waiting a long time to hear those words."

Chapter 10

Eve came back from Mike's feeling a bit calmer and determined to confront both Noelle and Mel about their futures. She was still undecided about how much to tell them about her suspicions about Zoe Bascombe, but when she entered the cottage she was granted a mini reprieve. No one was there.

She changed clothes and hurried over to the office.

Noelle was waiting for her. She jumped up from the desk chair. "I thought you'd never get back. Are you still upset?"

"No. But we need to have a family sit-down and figure things out."

"Don't worry, things will work out. I'll get a job. You said yourself it's early days yet. But . . ."

"I know you will. But what?"

"The strangest thing happened after you left."

"With Mel?"

"No. She went to her room, then I heard her leave a few minutes later. It's something that happened a couple of hours after that. I came out to the lobby to see if you or Mel were here. And I saw, or thought I saw, Mel. She'd cut her hair and dyed it. I thought maybe when she left this morning, she'd gone out and done it out of spite just to be rebellious, you know?"

Eve nodded, but she had a dreaded idea of where this was going.

"And I went right up to her and told her so."

"And?"

"It wasn't Mel. It was one of the guests. I apologized the best I could, but, Mom, I was sure it was Mel. From the back she looked just like her and then when she turned around, for a split second she still looked like Mel. Then the image went away and she was just this nice-looking young woman whom I'd never seen before."

"Zoe Bascombe," Eve said.

Noelle bit her upper lip, something she'd always done when she was impatient. "So . . . ?"

"She does look a little like—" Oh hell, best just to

come out and say it. Eve shut the door. "I think she might be my half sister."

Noelle's mouth dropped open. "Wow. You have a half sister? Why didn't you tell us?"

"I didn't know."

"It's like one of those reality shows. That's so cool. And it means we have an aunt who actually might like us. That's fantastic." She frowned. "Wait. What do you mean she *might* be? Aren't you sure? Is that why she's here? To look for you? I swear it's just like TV. Did you Google her?" Noelle sat back down in the desk chair and pulled up the internet.

"Of course I Googled her. We have the same mother. Jenny Bascombe née Campbell. At least, the names are the same. And between her resemblance to Mel and the way your grandfather has been acting . . ."

"Granddad recognized her?"

"Actually, I think maybe Granddad thought she *was* Jenny Bascombe, come back to haunt him."

"Yikes."

Eve reached into her pocket and pulled out the two photos of Mel and a younger Zoe. She unfolded them and placed them on the desk.

"Holy cow," Noelle said. "They could be sisters. Have you talked to her? Does she know?"

"I have no idea, though why else come here?"

"Well, ask her."

"I will, I'm just waiting for the right time. And, Noelle, let's just keep this between us for now."

"You'd better go after her, David," Henry said as he watched Zoe Bascombe walk away from the house.

"Me? And do what?" David hadn't wanted to be a part of this disclosure thing. If he'd known what was about to go down, he would have refused. No, he wouldn't. He didn't refuse Floret or Henry anything. They never asked for anything he couldn't or wasn't willing to give.

But this seemed too intimate for him to go bungling into.

"Just make sure she gets back to the inn safely. I don't think she was prepared for all this news at once. Strange that Jenny never told her anything."

"Aw, jeez."

"And take her this," Floret said, coming to stand beside him. She handed him a small jar. "It's for her hands. Some of those cuts looked angry."

"They're splinters from the beach stairs."

"I did tell her they were rotten," Floret said. "Well, this salve will heal them nicely."

David took the jar. Dulcie of course wanted to go with him, and he had to wait at the gate for Floret to come get her before he could run after the departing Zoe.

He caught up to her at the end of the drive.

"Go away."

"Gladly," he said. "But Henry is worried about you."

"Tell him I'm fine."

"And Floret sent this. It's for your hands." He thrust the jar toward her.

She cut him a sideways glance and took the jar. "Tell her—"

"You're fine. Yeah. I get it. If you're going to be defensive, why don't I just walk quietly by your side and make sure you don't walk into a bus?"

She didn't bother to answer, and two silent blocks later they stopped on the sidewalk in front of the inn. He felt only a ripple of satisfied amusement when she tripped on the first step. He made an automatic grab for her arm but stopped himself just in time to avoid getting reamed for his concern.

As soon as she was up the stairs, he wiped his hands of the whole situation and decided to treat himself to lunch at Kelly's. He strode down the street thinking about what he would order. You could tell the days of the week by the diner's specials. They'd been pretty much the same since he'd returned to Wind Chime House almost eight years ago, dragging along a grieving, sullen, mad-at-the-world ten-year-old.

Eli had come a long way in those last years, mainly due to Henry's and Floret's nurturing. Henry taught him to see the inner workings of the world; Floret wrapped him in a safe haven of unconditional love.

At the time David hadn't had a clue about raising a child, or life, for that matter. Actually, he was still pretty much clueless. People made things so complicated.

He paused at the diner door to glance back at the inn. Zoe Bascombe stood on the porch where he'd left her, looking like part of the décor. Well, if she was still standing there when he finished his lunch, he'd call the desk and have someone take her inside.

He'd barely walked through the door before Jim Kelly called him over to the counter. He sat down, and Jim leaned over the counter until the edge created a crater across his stomach.

He lowered his voice. "Just what's been going on over at your place?"

"Not much," David said. "Started repairing the fence this morning."

"You know what I mean."

"Actually, I don't." No way Jim could have heard about their visit from Zoe Bascombe that morning.

And he knew for a fact she hadn't stopped by the diner on her way back to the hotel, so . . .

"Well, it must be something. Hannah Gordon's on my case to sell her the right-of-way back to their house."

"Again? Aw, Jim, you know she gets out her tentacles whenever the market is slow. She'll crawl off when something more interesting comes up for sale."

"This time she offered to buy me out completely."

A cup of coffee appeared at his elbow. "Thanks, Leeann," he said to the waitress, who grimaced from behind Jim's back. He must have been on a tear all morning.

"What do you mean, completely?"

"My whole property—house, land, everything. Lock, stock, and barrel. And she offered a pretty decent deal. Why would she do that unless Henry and Floret had done something recently to set her off again?"

That was a distinct possibility considering what had happened in the past two days.

"I've been seeing Eli and Mel Gordon hanging out a lot together. You don't think she's dragged them into the feud? Awful old woman," Jim said.

"I don't know why she would care about those two. We're all on the same page with that one. They're too young to settle down; they're both going to college. In fact, Eli is leaving in a few weeks to do a pre-semester science program."

"Good for him. Still and all." Jim shook his head and snatched the menu out of the hovering Leeann's hand. "That old witch is gonna get her comeuppance one day." He handed David the menu.

"I'll have the special," David said.

Zoe stood on the inn's porch trying to regroup. An impossible task, since her whole life had just been blown to smithereens. Her father wasn't her father; it was that . . . that . . . dissolute-looking guitarist.

And what the hell was she going to do now? She'd fled Wind Chime so fast she'd never even asked Henry and Floret about the ashes. Though, having gotten a good dose of them today, she imagined they already knew why she was here.

They hadn't asked her one question. Because her mother had told them what to do. Not trusting in Zoe's ability to get the job done? She pushed that niggle of doubt away. Her bugaboo, doubt. It hadn't been just nerves or stage fright or even out-and-out fear that had paralyzed her at her Juilliard audition. It was her doubt in herself.

She'd had a pampered childhood on Long Island; had never really failed at anything until then, not anything she'd really cared about. She'd never really tried to achieve anything that important before.

Her one break out of the flight pattern of her life and . . .

"Ms. Bascombe? Are you all right?"

Zoe jumped and might have yelped. She was so rattled that she wasn't sure. All she saw was the valet from the first night standing inches from her.

"Yes, thank you. Just thinking."

He opened the front door for her.

She stepped into the lobby, right into Eve Gordon. *Gordon.* Zoe Gordon. She licked incredibly dry lips.

For the longest time, neither of them moved.

"Ms. Bascombe?"

Zoe just looked at her. "We need to talk."

"I know," Eve said serenely. "My mother was Jenny Campbell, who married your father and became Jenny Bascombe. We're half sisters, aren't we?"

"Rather more than that," Zoe said, and laughed. She clamped her hand over her mouth trying to stop herself. She couldn't stop. She shook her head.

Eve frowned, but Zoe was seeing her through a fractured lens of disbelief and hysteria, and it made her sister—*her sister*—look unreal.

"I don't understand. More than half?"

Zoe gulped in air. She felt so odd, like maybe she

was going to faint, though she'd never fainted in her life.

She nodded, kept nodding. Gulped in air. "More. Sisters. We're sisters. Whole sisters."

Eve stilled, suddenly coming back into focus. "Noelle!"

The young woman who had mistaken Zoe for Mel stuck her head out of the office door. "Oh." She grinned. Why was she grinning? Zoe tried to breathe. This meant her father wasn't her father, for over twenty-five years. . .

"Can you watch the desk for a while?"

Noelle had started forward, but she stopped. "Sure. Take your time." She smiled broadly at Zoe and went back into the office.

She knew? Did they all know? What was happening here?

Zoe was being led down the hall. But instead of stopping at the elevator to Zoe's room, Eve kept going, out the side door, down a short brick path to a cottage surrounded by grass. Zoe thought it was a pretty cottage.

Eve opened the door. It seemed to Zoe that she was like a dream person. A sleepwalker. A good song title. "Dream Person, Sleepwalker."

A glass of water was thrust into her hand, and she drank half of it before putting it down on the coffee table in front of the couch where she was sitting.

She glanced up at Eve, who was standing over her. She didn't look like her—their—mother. Must take after her . . . their father, Lee Gordon. No. It just wasn't possible, there must be a mistake, and yet . . .

"Did she send you? Is she coming here?"

God, how did Zoe answer that one? How did you tell someone who hadn't seen her mother in her entire life that her mother was dead?

"Never mind. I get it. She doesn't want to see me." The blunt resignation in Eve's statement threatened to break Zoe's heart, and it was only going to get worse.

"It isn't that."

"She doesn't know you're here?"

"Not exactly, but she wanted me to come. She couldn't come, but she told me to." She paused, waiting for Eve to ask, but Eve stayed silent.

It was hard to watch a woman, her sister, old enough to be her mother, so tentatively eager, so dreading the answer. And knowing she was about to destroy that last flame of hope. Trying to feel what Eve must feel, what she was going to feel, the inevitability of it all. Eve's mother had never seen her perform in the school play, come to her dance recital, track meet, or Sweet Sixteen. Just one graduation ceremony in her daughter's whole life, and she hadn't even made herself known.

Zoe couldn't begin to understand how that must

feel. Her mother—their mother—had come to everything any of her children did.

But not for Eve. Except for her graduation. Zoe touched her purse where the letter was concealed.

"She couldn't come. Not the way you would want."

"Why? You came. Is she sick? Too busy?"

What could Zoe say? She'd been so shocked and in denial herself she didn't think ahead. Jenny would have.

"She doesn't want to see me."

"She wanted to." Zoe had the letter to prove it. But now it was too late. Why hadn't she stayed in touch with her daughter? Jenny Bascombe would have never let someone tell her what she could do or not do. She always found a way. But not when it came to Eve. And Zoe, for that matter. They'd all been living a lie.

Cheesy maybe. But it didn't stop it from hurting.

"She couldn't come. My—our—mother is dead." There, she'd said it. It was a relief, but at that moment the warmth seeped out of the room.

Eve started, swayed for a perilous moment, while Zoe sat watching, unable to help her. Eve stuck out her hand—*Sleepwalker sleepwalking*—found the arm of a chair and eased herself down onto the cushion.

"I'm sorry, Eve." It was such a stupid thing to say. She hadn't done anything wrong, she hadn't even known about Eve, none of them had.

She meant sorry for everything. *For our loss, for the years you didn't have a mother, and neither of us had a sister.* But it wouldn't make a difference.

Eve stared into her hands and Zoe stared at her.

She and Eve didn't look at all alike. Zoe had always taken after her mother. Eve was taller and larger boned than Jenny. She had lighter hair than Zoe but maybe not Jenny. For as long as Zoe could remember, her mother had dyed her hair. But the immaculate pants and tunic that Eve wore were spot on and though the necklace of silver and turquoise wasn't Jenny's trademark pearls, there was no mistaking the traits that Eve and Jenny shared. And Eve was the owner of a high-end inn and spa. Successful, self-assured, organized.

Their mother would have liked that. It's what she liked about Zoe. Zoe was all those things, except for the music. Zoe hadn't made it in music, but she'd certainly done all right in the event-planning business. Her mother had never stopped her from studying music, but she didn't encourage her either. And now she was beginning to understand that, too.

Maybe her mother had been right all along.

Had running the inn been Eve's first choice for her life? Or had she had other dreams, like Zoe?

There was so much she wanted to know.

"I never even got to meet her, to ask her."

"She loved you." Zoe snapped her mouth shut. Why had she blurted that out? It was true, according to the letter, at least.

She opened her purse, looked inside. The letter was still there, slightly crumpled where she'd shoved it hastily out of sight before leaving the commune.

"What happened? Was it an accident? Was she sick?"

"Look, before we get any further, I think you should read this. It was waiting for me at Floret and Henry's. She'd sent it months ago. She didn't know she was going to die. Or maybe she suspected. I don't know. She sent it because—" Because, organized as usual, Jenny wanted to make sure her life was in order even at the very end.

Zoe thrust the letter at Eve.

Eve stared at it. The navy and off-white swirls of the chair's upholstery seemed to move like the air around her, while her eyes stayed riveted on the paper she held by the very edge.

Then she began to read.

Zoe watched her, looking for the first sign of recognition, of anger or denial. Something that would make her world make sense again. How could her mother have kept this from her all these years? Did her father know? Either of them? She felt the laugh bubbling up again and quickly drank some more water. Put the glass down with a clunk.

Eve didn't seem to notice; her eyes flicked from left to right as she read. She paused every now and then, and Zoe wondered what word had stayed her attention.

She had a sister.

She watched Eve as she read. Perfectly still, her face showed no emotion as one tear after the other fell onto the paper. Finally, she looked up.

"She loved you," Zoe said. She moved from the couch to sit on the arm of Eve's chair. Then slid down to squeeze onto the cushion next to her. Her sister.

"She loved me," said Eve. And Zoe let her own tears flow. Really, there was no way to stop them.

Eve read the letter again, then went to make tea, and Zoe went to use her bathroom. She splashed water on her face until her mascara ran, then tried to rub the smudges off with a tissue. It only made it worse.

She looked around for a bottle of makeup remover, baby oil, even hand lotion. She'd never seen so much stuff packed into such a tiny room.

It was a hectic, wild mess. Beauty and hair products were balanced on the windowsill, the side of the tub, the back of the toilet. Zoe was amazed that they could get in and out of the room without setting off an avalanche of bottles.

She found lavender hand cream on the sink by the soap pump. It was good enough; she rubbed a drop under her eyes and blotted it off. She looked better, but the scent set off memories that surprised her. *Lavender's blue, dilly dilly.* It was her mother's favorite scent, and hers. And evidently Eve Gordon's, too.

She tossed the tissue into a wicker wastepaper basket already half-filled with papers and cotton balls.

It made her smile for a second. It was hard to reconcile this bathroom with the minimalist Zen-like feeling of the inn. And it was so not like Jenny Bascombe. Her bathroom had been immaculate at all times. She was the only person Zoe knew who could get out of a tub and not drip water on the floor. At home Zoe had her own huge bathroom. They all did, even her father—her George Bascombe father.

Did he know about Eve and about Zoe?

She flushed hot. All these years had he known and only waited for Chris, his real son, to graduate from high school before suing for divorce? Or had it been after that that Jenny, feeling free at last, told him, and . . . ? It was useless to speculate.

"Are you okay in there?" Eve asked through the door.

Zoe opened the door. "Yes. I wasn't snooping or anything, just amazed at how much stuff you have."

"It kind of sneaks up on you. Noelle graduated from college, so she's home while she's looking for a job. And

Mel, she's our free spirit, and her surroundings reflect that. Most of my toiletries are in the cabinet."

Zoe smiled. Why was she not surprised?

She followed Eve back to the living room where a pottery teapot and two handmade-looking mugs were placed on a wooden tray. Zoe sat while Eve poured the tea. It was the first time she'd been calm enough to notice her surroundings. A combination of pastels and rich, deep jewel tones. A floor-to-ceiling bookcase crammed with books and what looked like souvenirs from many travels. The walls shared space with posters of the Eiffel Tower, the Grand Canyon, and tropical islands.

"Have you been to all these places?"

Eve glanced up. "None of them. But someday . . ." She handed Zoe one of the mugs. "So, what do we do now?"

Mel sat on the driftwood log fingering a broken piece of glass someone had placed there. The sea and sand had smoothed the edges like a piece of sea glass. But it wasn't sea glass. It belonged in the trees behind the beach. Old Beach. Her and Eli's beach, that suddenly everyone was calling Wind Chime Beach.

Mel liked that name, if Zoe hadn't been the one to

name it. She wished she'd never come to the inn. It seemed like everything was all messed up because of her asking about the beach. Why did she need to know where it was?

It was Mel and Eli's beach. No one else ever came. She bet people didn't even know about it. She wished he was here. But he said he had to study before he left tomorrow to take some test to get him in the early science program at the university. If he got in, he'd have to leave at the beginning of August. That so sucked.

At least for her. She knew he wanted to go. She should want him to do what he wanted. But she didn't. And that was so lame.

Sometimes Mel didn't get herself at all. Maybe she was just a selfish bitch like Noelle said. She didn't get Noelle either, or Harmony. She thought she got Eli. They'd been best friends forever. Now everyone was against them.

She wished he would take a break from studying and come down, only he didn't know she was there.

She'd been sitting for hours, and she was hungry and thirsty. Floret was probably baking something, but she didn't want to go to the house and interrupt Eli. She'd promised not to. David might be there and not let her in.

She heard a noise on the path above her and stood

up. Maybe Eli—no. It was probably David. He must have seen her cut through the woods. It was like he had special radar to keep her and Eli from being together. She might be able to slip beneath the steps without him seeing her.

She and Eli had made a little nest there. *Our first home,* Eli said. But that had been at the beginning of summer. She darted across the sand and practically dove inside.

It was dark beneath the stairs, like a cocoon. It could sometimes get a little stinky after a storm, but today it was dry. There was an old crate that had washed up that they used as a table, plus a hurricane lamp and a sleeping bag, because really, who wanted to lie in the sand. Especially when you were having sex.

Sex. Her mother would kill her. It wasn't her fault that *her* mother hadn't taken precautions and had abandoned her.

Well, Mel would never give up her baby. When she had one. Which she wasn't going to do until she and Eli were settled and making money—somehow.

She wanted to stay home with her babies. And Eli wanted to be a scientist. Maybe he could teach in the high school or something.

She reached over and pulled the sleeping bag out from its storage sack. Spread it out. And stretched out on top. She heard someone step on the wooden steps. David wouldn't do that. Everyone knew they weren't safe. She held still. Heard nothing.

Whoever it was must have changed his mind. Mel sighed and curled up on her side. Closed her eyes. She wished Eli was there.

She counted the waves rolling onto the shore, listened for the moment when the wind set off the chimes.

And was startled by a noise much closer. Maybe Eli had decided to take a break, after all. She started to sit up but before she could get upright, she was knocked back down. The sleeping bag was yanked out from under her.

"No!" she cried, and grabbed it in both hands.

"Ma-a-a-a!" Dulcie dropped the bag and butted Mel's shoulder. It sent her rolling onto the ground.

"Dulcie! You dumb goat. You scared me. You're not supposed to be down here."

Dulcie just kept butting her, trying to roll her off the sleeping bag.

Mel laughed. "Stop it, you're tickling me. Go away. I'm not in the mood to play."

Ignoring her, Dulcie chomped down on the sleeping bag and tugged it toward the opening. Mel grabbed hold of it. "No, you don't. You'll wreck it. Let go. Let go, Dulcie."

Dulcie pulled. Mel pulled back. And they might

have stayed that way in a hopeless tug-of-war if Floret's voice hadn't called out, "Dulcinea? Where have you gone a roamin'?"

Dulcie lifted her head, dropped the sleeping bag, and backed out onto the sand.

"What are you doing down there, sweet one? Looking for lost love?" A pause while Mel imagined Floret smiling down on Dulcie as if she were a fairy-tale unicorn and not just some dumb goat. Sometimes Floret could be a little nutty.

Mel waited while Dulcie scampered behind the rocks and up to the path, making that stupid noise she always made to Floret. And Floret answering her, as if they were having a conversation.

They weren't. People couldn't converse with animals. Well, maybe horse whisperers. And maybe Floret.

Mel waited until she was sure they were gone, then stuffed the sleeping bag into its sack and crawled out. She couldn't put it off any longer. She'd have to go home. She'd make a sandwich and go to her room before Noelle or her mom got back.

She could sneak out later and meet Eli before he left. But what if he didn't want to meet her? What if he decided not to come back at all?

Chapter 11

For the next two hours, Zoe told Eve about her mother. It was a slippery slope, trying to balance things that would give Eve a picture of their mother, without making her feel slighted or that Zoe was somehow bragging. She told her about the perennial border and her prizewinning roses, about her committee work and her charity organizations. The good things.

She didn't tell her about the times her mother seemed remote, less than sympathetic when her children complained about some real or imagined slight. Zoe needed to process that more for herself before she shared.

She did tell Eve about finding the Sonny and Cher record and her mother's reaction. They both laughed, then cried a little.

"The poor woman" was all Eve said.

They were both soggy with tears and exhausted with emotional excess when Zoe said, "Now what? You know about her life with me, but do you know what happened before that? Henry said he would tell me but I needed to show you the letter first."

"I'm not sure," Eve said. "No one talks about it, not even Floret and Henry. Hannah, that's my—our—grandmother, Dad's mother. But we all call her Granna, you know, Grandma Hannah, Granna."

Zoe nodded, remembering the Cadillac and Mel's reaction to it.

"You'll meet her. She's sort of amazing. She can be tough, but she started out with nothing and ended up a millionaire from local real estate.

"We used to live at Wind Chime until I was about thirteen. Hannah traveled a lot in those days, was busy building her empire, so Floret and Henry became my surrogate parents."

"So why did you leave?"

"All I know is Hannah and Floret and Henry had a big fight. I remember it so vividly even today, because people didn't have screaming fights in those days, not at Wind Chime, anyway." She shrugged.

"Didn't you ask?"

"Oh, sure, but Hannah said terrible things about my mother, so I just stopped. I asked Floret, but you may have noticed she's rather fluid about which sphere she inhabits. She doesn't like confrontation. So she merely removes herself from the situation."

"Lucky her," Zoe said under her breath. "And Henry?"

"I think there was probably some . . . You know, it was the free-love era. Word has it the three of them may have loved freely. Together."

Zoe smiled. "Cool."

"Yeah, but then it all exploded and they've been enemies ever since. Well, at least Hannah has been. Henry and Floret just keep on keepin' on, I believe the phrase is. I think I need to process some of this before we ask Henry and Floret about the past. Can you wait until the morning?"

Zoe nodded. "Right now I just need to eat. I know that sounds so pedestrian, but I ate early this morning. And we missed lunch. And I'm feeling a little shaky."

"Want some company? It'll have to be the bar, since my cupboard is bare. It usually is. But it's early enough there won't be too many people there."

"Sounds like a plan."

They carried the tea things to the kitchen and went out the side door. "I wonder what happened to the letters," Eve said, and locked the door.

As they walked across the lobby, Zoe heard piano music coming from the bar. She stopped.

"Don't worry," Eve said, taking her arm. "It's too early for the band. Probably just one of the guests, and we'll get rid of them if it bothers you."

Zoe shook her head, and cocked her head, listening. "It can't be."

"What?" Eve said, and looked around the room.

"That's my song. I wrote that song. How is that even possible?" Zoe hurried across the tiled floor, Eve right behind her.

The bar was dimly lit and the sun coming through the French doors turned the two people at the piano into silhouette.

"Dilly!" The pianist swiveled his legs around the bench and made a beeline toward her.

"Dilly?" Eve said beside her.

"Chris?" Zoe said.

"Hey, baby sister." Chris wrapped her in a hug that lifted her off the ground. She loved the bigness of his hugs; he was only a few inches taller than she was and slight and wiry, but his hugs could encompass her whole world.

He put her down. "Surprised to see me?"

"Yes, what are you doing here?"

"I thought you might need some moral support."

"What about your play? Don't you have a matinee?"

"Another story. But you're in luck. I was noodling around at the piano waiting for you, and . . ." He lowered his voice. "Lee Gordon came in. Can you imagine? He toured with Night Chill, great group, a little before our time, but one of the classic rock bands. He came over and he liked what he heard. Hey, Lee," he said louder. "Come meet my sister, the composer and lyricist."

He turned to the man who had been leaning on the baby grand but now stood facing the three others—but only for an instant.

"You!" he spat, and strode past them out the door.

"What the—" Chris looked from Eve to Zoe. "Sorry. I don't know what set him off."

"We do," Zoe said.

"You do? Did you recognize him?"

Zoe laughed. Not a happy laugh.

"He's my father," Eve said.

"Wow."

"Chris, meet your half sister, Eve."

Chris's eyes narrowed. He glanced toward the door then back to Zoe. "Say again? You mean Lee Gordon and our mother? They, uh . . ."

Zoe tried to nod or shrug or something, but she seemed incapable of moving.

"They did," Eve said.

"No shit. You're like our half sister?"

"Yes."

"So am I," Zoe said.

He beetled his eyebrows. "Okay, lost me. She's my half sister and you're . . ." He looked at Zoe, and she could tell he was already thinking ahead.

"Promise you won't freak out."

"I'm an actor. It's what I do best. Hit me with it."

"Lee Gordon is my father, too."

Eve stepped back. "I'll leave you two alone."

"No!" Zoe grabbed Eve's arm. "Please?"

"Wait," said Chris. "You can't leave now. How is that even possible? You gotta give me context, Dil."

"I will, but I have to eat."

Chris spun a full 360-degree pirouette, stopping at the bartender who was leaning on his elbows at the bar, watching them intently. "Hey, Mike!"

"Have a seat," the bartender called back. "That table near the window where it's quiet. I'll bring menus."

Zoe held on to Chris's arm with both hands like she had as a kid anytime she felt insecure. And realized that she expected him to support her in this as in everything. God, she hoped she was right.

Chris veered toward the piano and snagged his drink from the top.

They sat down, Zoe to Chris's right and Eve facing him. Chris took a sip and put his glass down. "Now, *répétez, s'il vous plaît.*"

Zoe just sat there gripping the sides of the table.

He looked to Eve, but she looked away.

"Okay, let me prime the pump, then. Our mother, Jenny Bascombe, got it on with Lee Gordon at least twice and, if I'm not mistaken, several years apart."

Eve snorted a laugh.

"Damn." Chris leaned back in his chair then leaned forward again. "How long have you known this?"

Zoe could hear the hurt in his voice, and she quickly blurted, "Just since this morning. I swear."

Chris turned on Eve. "Did you tell her?"

"She told me."

"Okay, I'm having a hard time processing this."

"It's true. I'm not your full sister," Zoe said. "I feel like I am, but we're only half. Not yours, not Errol's, not Robert's."

"Are you sure? Where did you get this?"

Zoe fumbled in her bag. Realized the letter wasn't there. Had she left it at the cottage? Eve reached into her own pocket, pulled it out, and smoothed it against the table before handing it to Chris. "I didn't want to leave it in the cottage for anyone to find."

Chris reached into his shirt pocket and retrieved a

pair of reading glasses. All her brothers wore reading glasses. She didn't.

The "otherness" of her sent her into a nosedive. What if he hated her? What if they all did? Where would she go? Who would she be?

He pulled the table lamp closer and began to read while Zoe and Eve watched. Zoe was afraid to look away even long enough to see Eve's reaction. He seemed to be spending way too much time with the first page, but finally he turned to the second without looking up. When he reached the end, he carefully folded the letter up, placed it on the table, and covered it with his hand.

He looked at the two women, blew out a long exhale. Pushed his hand through his hair. Sandy and wavy, not like hers.

"So you're both Gordons," he said to Eve.

"So it appears."

"You sure I'm not . . . ?" He let the rest of his thought trail off.

"Not as far as I know. Though"—Eve broke into a smile—"you'd fit right in."

"Well, that's something. I'm not sure what, but hey. Hey," he said louder, "I have a half sister. And a bunch of other halves, too, I bet."

"Chris. I'm only your half sister, too," Zoe said tentatively.

"Nah, you'll always be my one-and-a-half sister."

He always knew the right thing to say. She wanted to throw her arms around him and cling there forever, but she didn't.

"You're not upset?"

"Upset? No. But I am in need of another drink."

Another drink appeared on the table next to him, along with glasses of white wine for Eve and Zoe.

"Man, you and I could take this on the road," he told Mike. "You got great timing."

"He gets a little silly when he's nervous," Zoe explained.

"I'm not nervous, I'm effing out-of-this-world gobsmacked, and probably after another drink or two, I'll be happy as a clam. And walking like one, too." He turned the full wattage of his charm-laced smile on all of them.

"To our mother . . ." He raised his glass to Zoe and Eve. "I always suspected she had a secret life. Though I gotta admit, I never expected this."

"I don't think Errol and Robert will be amused."

"No," he said, immediately sober. "Not at all. But we'll cross that bridge."

Mike cleared his throat.

"Sorry, what shall we eat?" Chris said, opening his menu.

When the bar began to fill up, Eve suggested they retire to someplace quieter. She still had a million questions to ask Zoe about her mother, but she could tell Zoe was feeling overwhelmed.

She was glad Chris had shown up. He could be a big help in reassuring Zoe that she was still a Bascombe, still loved, still had a place with them. Something Eve had been given all her childhood with Floret, Hannah, Henry, and the others. But not with her mother.

Now it was their turn to do the same for Zoe.

Eve wasn't sure about the other two brothers. From what little Chris and Zoe had said, they sounded like a couple of stuffed shirts, though stuffed shirts could be loyal, too, she supposed.

They stopped at the desk to find Chris a room for the night. The inn was booked but they usually held a couple of rooms in case of last-minute favors. And if any situation called for a favor, it was this one.

"It doesn't have a view except of the garden, I'm afraid," Eve said.

"Not a problem," Chris said, and took his key card.

They retrieved his suitcase from behind the reception desk.

"That's an awfully big suitcase for an overnight," Zoe said suspiciously.

Chris shrugged and smiled, though not with the warmth and insouciance that Eve was already beginning to recognize.

"Show closed."

"Oh, no," Zoe said. "I'm so sorry. When?" She turned to Eve. "It was really good, too."

"Just one of those things," Chris said. "Good reviews, decent box office, but the theater was booked with another show. The producers meant to move if the signs were right. I guess they weren't right. C'est la vie."

"I'm so sorry. And they just closed down?"

"Oh, hell, Dil. It's been down for several weeks."

"Why didn't you tell me?"

"And have the brothers offer me a job at their respective firms? Thanks, but no thanks."

"So do you have to get back for auditions? Can you stay and see where Mom . . . ?" Zoe glanced at Eve. "We could hang out for a while and get to know . . . all this."

"Sure, Dil. No problem."

"Why do you call her Dil?" Eve asked, already knowing the answer.

"Short for Dilly. Our mother always sang that song 'Lavender's Blue' to her when she was little: before bed, in the bath, when she fell down. In other words, all the time. It drove us all crazy."

"And to get their revenge, they called me Silly Dilly."

"I didn't," Chris said, with mock outrage. "Well, I did, then I just changed to Dil. Not to worry, I call her Zoe most of the time, and always in public." He frowned. "Not that that's much better."

Zoe punched his arm. "I'll have you know that Zoe means 'life.' "

"No kidding."

"My father, our father, used to sing it to me when he was home from tour," Eve said.

"Egad, zooks," Chris said. "How weird is that? I mean in a good way."

"When he was gone I used to make Floret sing it to me."

"Who's Floret?" Chris asked.

"You'll meet her tomorrow," Zoe said. "If you can stay and want to go see Wind Chime Beach."

"So you found it. Of course I'll stay."

"Maybe Timothy will come up and you can make it a long weekend."

"Tim's in Chicago."

Eve thought she detected a sudden coolness in his voice. Roommate? Boyfriend? Husband?

"Oh. When will he be back?"

"Actually, he's thinking about moving there. He's

in pretty deep with this development firm there. Big projects, big bucks." Chris ended with a shrug.

"Would you go, too?"

"Somehow I don't see myself at Steppenwolf."

Eve blinked. Of course. Not the novel or the band, but the theater company. From what she'd heard about the Chicago theater company, Chris wouldn't fit in with them at all.

Zoe seemed at a loss for words, so Eve stepped in.

"The band will be coming in any minute, and if you're not ready to confront Lee Gordon for a second time today, I suggest . . ."

"Let's go," said Chris. "You too, Eve. You don't mind me calling you Eve? You are my sister."

"Please do, but I should give you two some alone time. Why don't we meet after breakfast tomorrow? Give us all a chance to assimilate the changes."

"Didn't you ever try to find us?" Chris asked.

"I didn't even know about you. I don't even remember my mother. She gave me up." Eve's voice cracked, surprising her. "When I was little I asked about my mother. Every time I mentioned her, they all got so crazy, I just stopped. Hannah was and still is so filled with hate. And Dad was, well, Hannah wouldn't even let me mention her in his presence. Floret and Henry always danced around the answer—maybe they were afraid. I don't know.

"I just sort of pushed her out of my mind. We didn't have Google then. And I had several mothers and extended family to keep me busy and give me love and after a while she just faded away. Then Zoe came and I found an old photo and she and my daughter Mel looked so much alike—"

"And the rest, as they say," Chris said, "is history. Our history."

"Oh, Chris, I do love you." Zoe threw her arms around him.

"I think I love you, too," said Eve, and fought not to burst into a full-blown blubber.

"So let's meet in the morning," Zoe said, "and we'll go down to the commune and—"

"Commune?" Chris asked.

"Commune," Zoe said. "Henry said he would tell me the whole story once I showed Eve the letter. I'm sure he'll include you, Chris."

"Sure you don't want a nightcap?"

"Not for me," Eve said. "I'm pretty wiped out and I still have to close out tonight's books."

"How 'bout you, Dil, what now?" Chris asked.

"Right now, I think I have to go to bed."

"Lord, girl, it's not even eight o'clock."

"I know, but I'm beat. How about a cup of tea in your room while you unpack? I want to hear about what happened to the show."

Chris rolled his eyes as Eve imagined all brothers might do. And she liked him for it.

"Okay, tea, then bed for you. Then maybe I'll take a walk around the town. Got any nightlife here, Eve?"

"Something for everyone."

"Gotcha. Night, Eve, sister mine." He gave Eve a peck on the cheek.

Eve wished they would hurry and leave. She was tottering on the brink of a total meltdown and she didn't want to embarrass herself.

Zoe touched her arm. "See you in the morning?"

Eve nodded.

Zoe gave her a hug. Not a quick, friendly, see-you-later hug, but a long, sisterly hug. Then she took Chris's arm and the two of them walked toward the elevator.

They moved in step like a couple of dancers, Eve thought. Comfortable, sure of each other.

"I got you, Dil," Chris sang.

"I got you, Chris," Zoe sang back.

They stepped into the elevator and stuck their heads out long enough to sing, "And we got you, Eve," before the doors closed.

"I've got you, too," Eve said quietly. "I've got you."

She walked past the empty reception desk and into the office. The night clerk, Ivo Branch, was sitting on the couch eating a sandwich and streaming a movie on his laptop. He jumped up when she entered.

"My shift ended an hour ago and I didn't want to bother you . . ." He trailed off.

"Mel didn't show up?"

He shook his head. "She probably forgot, no biggie. I just got hungry." He closed his laptop and began wrapping up his sandwich. "You want me to watch the desk? I have something on later, but . . ."

"No, you go on, and thanks for staying. Be sure to add the extra time to your hours. I'll take it from here."

He shoved everything into his backpack and was gone with a "have a nice night," leaving a faint odor of tuna in the air.

Eve lit a candle. Not her favorite, tuna fish.

She'd barely sat down at the desk before the door opened.

She swiveled her chair around. "It's about time you showed—" And stopped. Her father stood in the doorway.

He seemed unsteady on his feet, and at first she thought he was drunk. God knows she had vivid memories of those times when he'd come home in the middle of the night, out of his mind with booze and bitterness. Eve didn't know which was more frightening, the alcohol or the emotions it unleashed.

"Come in," Eve said. "Is the band here?"

"No. Not yet."

She swallowed, or would have if her saliva hadn't fled, leaving her mouth as dry as sand.

He just stood there looking at her. And for a moment she thought he might just back up and close the door as if nothing had happened, but finally he took one step forward just enough to close the door.

"She's Jenny's daughter, isn't she?"

Eve wanted to say, Who are you talking about? She was so not ready for this conversation, fight, explosion, whatever might happen right now. She wanted to savor her newfound status. Wanted to put off confronting her father or her grandmother about all the years they kept her in darkness. But it would just postpone the inevitable.

"Yes."

"I could tell the minute I saw her. She walked into the bar. Why did she come here?"

"Why don't you ask her?"

Eve watched her father's fists tighten, release, tighten. Ready to lash out, hit something. She wasn't afraid. Not for herself, anyway. The only things she'd ever seen him hit were a wall, a tree, or a table, hard enough to send magazines sliding to the floor.

"Sit down. You'll give yourself a heart attack." Her voice sounded cold, as if she didn't care what happened to him. As if she didn't care about him. She did. She loved him, but right now he was the last person she wanted to see. And she didn't want to be the one to tell him that Jenny Bascombe, née Campbell, was dead.

He eyed her suspiciously, but finally lowered himself onto the couch. His long legs set at a perfect right angle to the floor. His back straight. But his head was bent. "Whatever you got to say, better say it. I've got to do a sound check in a minute."

In her mind she could hear Noelle saying, "Yeah, well, sound check this," and almost smiled. Her one daughter who never cut him any slack.

"So you gonna answer me? Did Jenny send her? What does she want?"

Eve took a breath and jumped off the cliff. "She wants to meet her father."

Lee's head jerked up. He narrowed his eyes. He hadn't shaved, probably in several days, but at least he didn't smell like bourbon.

She could see the confusion and the slow grasp of understanding transform his expression. He shook his head, as if that was enough.

"She's your daughter. Zoe Bascombe is your daughter, too."

"No."

Lee unfolded himself from the couch but didn't quite make it to his feet. He fell back onto the seat. "No."

Eve waited for him to riffle through the rolodex of his life.

"It's not possible."

Eve gave him a nudge. "Remember one little night backstage at Nassau Coliseum in the summer of eighty-eight? Jenny came back after the show. Must have been a big surprise after all that time, huh?"

His expression changed in a moment of recognition, and again into a sad, reminiscent smile that made Eve want to stop. To just take him in her arms and tell him to forget it. That she'd send Zoe on her way and to forget she'd ever come.

But Eve was too selfish for that. She wanted to know everything Zoe could tell her about her mother. She wanted to get to know her sister and her half brothers. She wanted her girls to know their aunt and uncles.

"Remember that night, Dad? She'd seen the ad and bought a ticket."

"I remember." His voice was so distant, Eve wasn't sure if he was speaking to her or to himself.

"You must have been glad to see her. Really glad."

"Don't use that tone of voice about your mother."

Eve flinched. "Then tell me the truth."

"The truth? She was the only woman I ever loved. She walked out on me. Gave you up. That's the truth."

"It didn't stop you from having one more go, though, did it?"

"Don't be vulgar."

"Did it?"

"No. And then she walked out again. But she can forget about walking back into our lives now. No more chances. And I don't believe that girl is my daughter. So if she's thinking about getting money out of me, she can forget it. They won't get anything from me or your grandmother. Not one dime."

"You arrogant bastard. You think after all this time she would suddenly need something from you?" Eve said. "What on earth could you give her but a bucketful of bitterness?"

He flinched.

"God, you're just like Hannah. You two are so poisoned. I used to think it was because of what my mother did, but I think you did it to each other.

"Well, you can stop worrying. Jenny will never want anything from you again. She's dead. That's why Zoe's here."

Lee sat for a long time, not speaking. Eve didn't

back down, though she was longing to comfort him like always. Maybe she should have left well enough alone. "Dad."

"Jenny has been dead to me for a long time. I don't want anything more to do with her or her daughter."

"Does that include me, Dad?"

He opened his mouth. Closed it.

"What did you do with the letters?"

He just stared at her.

"What did you do with them? Read them? Burn them? Throw them away so I couldn't see them?"

"What the hell are you talking about?"

"The letters my mother sent me."

"She never sent you any letters. She never wrote at all. Is that what this girl told you? That your mother wrote to you? She made it up. Lies, just like her mother's lies."

"Bullshit." Eve fumbled in her pocket for the letter. Thrust it at him. "Read it. But so help me, if you try to tear it up, I'll kill you."

His eyes rounded; his jaw went slack. He mechanically reached for the letter, but his eyes never left hers, as if searching for the lie that would save him. He wouldn't find it within her.

Slowly he unfolded the paper.

Read.

His eyes rested on the second page for a long time.

Eve tensed, alert for the moment his temper would erupt, ready to snatch the letter from his hands if he lashed out and tried to destroy it.

At length he ran his finger over a line at the bottom. "Mom," he said, barely audible, a thin creaky sound far from the silver voice of rock 'n' roll.

He looked up. "She came to your graduation? Why didn't she— She never said. No. It can't be true. It's just like her to lie. Your mother was a liar, Eve. It's time you dealt with it."

He sounded so certain that for a brief instant Eve almost believed him. But why would her mother lie, knowing she would be dead by the time Eve saw the letter? Learned the truth?

"What happened to the letters, Dad?"

Lee thrust the one he was holding back at her and stood.

She took it quickly before his rage erupted.

"What did you do with them? Why didn't you let me see them?"

"I don't know anything about any damn letters. There were none. Not a letter, not a postcard, not a phone call, nothing ever, until she walked into my dressing room eighteen years later—and I fell for her lies all over again."

She heard the grief in his voice. She didn't want to hurt him, push him into that dark place where he'd spent so much of his life. But she had to know.

"Promise me there were no letters," she said.

The only answer she got was the door closing behind him.

Chapter 12

Lee made one stop before he left the inn. The bar, just long enough to see Mike, though he couldn't stop himself from glancing at the bottles behind the bartender's head. "Tell the band to cover for me." Then he turned and got the hell out of the inn.

He didn't know where he was going. Right now he didn't give a shit. He just needed to get away. From it all. The people, the memories, the need to have a drink, down some pills, get high, get forgetful. Any way he could.

But that wasn't his MO. Hell, he wouldn't be done with this until he rubbed it in, wallowed in it, made himself sick over it. The betrayal. The bitch betrayed him. Twice. Devil's spawn.

He stumbled at the curb. She'd been a seductress

in an innocent girl's body. She'd sworn her undying love. Forever. To her forever was just a summer, but to him— Dammit, he was singing his own song like it was real.

It was real, all right. He was a poor excuse for a man, for a father. He stopped as it came flooding back to him in a rage of anger, not for the past—that he kept somewhere else and never let it out—but for tonight. He could see Eve's face even now. He'd hurt her. Said things—but what had he said? He could never remember when the rage overtook him. He should go back. Tell her. Tell her what?

A horn blared and he jumped out of the way just as some fancy four-wheel drive screeched to a halt. "You crazy old man—"

He flipped them off and kept going across the street. Tomorrow, he'd apologize tomorrow. He'd just go home now. Sit in the dark, try not to think. But home was the other way.

Down the drive. He could see the lights ahead. It had been a long tour. He was tired, strung out on his own misery. Hannah said, *You should quit. It's killing you. No,* she said, *She's killing you.* Hannah couldn't forgive. Never could.

His mother had kept him going. All the times when

he wanted to end it all, she'd kept him going. But she was a poison, just the same. No understanding Hannah. She brought him Eve, *Your first child,* as if he was going to bring home bastard babies from every one-night stand he ever had. Not if he could help it. She meant he'd meet somebody and settle down. Have a family.

She was wrong. He belonged to Jenny Campbell. Forever. And Eve. God, how he must have let her down. He was despicable. A has-been. Look at him. Just some broken-down old rocker nobody remembered. Not even himself.

He tripped in the dark. When had it gotten dark? Since he'd left the drive. And gone into the woods. No. Not here. He didn't want to come here. But already it was pulling him. Singing him a lullaby, though the air was still and the chimes were quiet.

So quiet that he could hear her singing on the beach—"Lavender's blue . . ."—and he would rush to her and make love to her and promise her forever. No one was singing tonight.

But someone was on the beach. He stopped at the stairs and looked down. Two people on a blanket or something. Wrapped up together like some—

He grabbed the stair rail, remembered just in time

that it was rotten, stole down the path, trying not to make a sound. Wanting to surprise them, scare the shit out of them for trespassing.

It didn't matter. They were so hot and heavy, he could have been Big Foot crashing through the brush and they wouldn't have noticed.

He slid down the rocks at the far side of the beach, stood a moment at the bottom to pull his keychain flashlight out of his jeans. It served him well on nights when it was too dark and he was too tired and heartsick to see the lock in his own front door.

He strode across the sand and turned it on. They tore apart, sitting up like a couple of damn jack-in-the-boxes.

"Get the hell off my beach." He roared it so loud that it almost made him laugh, until the light hit the girl full in the face and he saw that it was his granddaughter Mel.

"Get away from him."

She scrambled away, and Lee jerked his flashlight to the boy. He didn't have to. He pretty much knew who it would be. Eli Merrick.

The little shit lumbered to his feet. Pretty clumsy for a skinny kid. Probably his feet were asleep from messing with his granddaughter.

"Sir."

"Don't even start."

He jabbed his finger at Mel.

The girl jutted out her chin. "You can't stop us. We love each other."

Lee growled. He heard himself. It scared him. It scared them. Well, good. "Aren't you supposed to be on the desk tonight?"

Her mouth fell open. "Shit. I forgot."

"Then you'd better get the lead out."

She looked to Eli. Lee felt like smacking them both.

"Go on. It's okay."

She went toward the stairs, and Lee almost yelled at her to stop until he saw her pull her backpack from beneath them. Damn, they came here all the time. Lee swore he could beat the crap out of both of them.

He wouldn't though. He drew the line at that.

He flicked his head at her and she ran off. He turned to Eli.

"It's not her fault," Eli said.

"I'm telling you this once. You get that girl pregnant, you're gonna have to figure out how to take care of them yourself."

"I'm not—"

"Don't even start with me. You'll be stuck with the consequences. If you think Eve or Floret will take care of you, you can forget that, too. Hannah will make sure it doesn't happen." Lee stopped to take a searing breath. "You don't want to cross her."

"I—"

"Get out of here. And don't let me catch you down here again."

The kid just stared back at him. Lee fought the urge to throttle him. But he didn't, and finally the kid grabbed his backpack and trudged across the beach and out of sight.

Lee stood for a long time. Then he felt the wind across his face, and he knew what would come next. He dropped to the sand and covered his ears with his hands.

Zoe was the first one downstairs the next morning. The young woman who had mistaken her for Mel was at the desk. *Noelle.* She waved and smiled until Zoe knew she had to go over and introduce herself.

She looked more like Eve than Mel did. The reddish-blond hair was the same, slightly wavy, only longer and parted on the side.

"I've been dying to meet you since yesterday. I hope you don't mind. Mom told me. I think it's so cool. To have an aunt, I mean. The only other relatives even near my own age are my cousins. Not a brain between them and . . . ugh. Never mind. Are you going to stay for a while? Maybe for a long time. Mom would love that. Especially since Mel is going to college, if she doesn't do something stupid first, and I'm looking for a job and—"

"What kind of job?" Zoe broke in, attempting to stanch the unending stream of enthusiasm.

"Graphic arts." Noelle made a face. "I know. I should have gone into business, but I like art, what can I say?"

Zoe could relate. "Well, I say good for you. Where are you applying?"

"Wherever." She sighed. "Not that I'm having much success. Most people are looking for someone with experience and I only had one local-ish internship in college." She shrugged. "I needed to help out at the inn over the summers."

Zoe nodded. "So where do you want to be?"

"Anywhere interesting. I interviewed in Boston a couple of weeks ago." She named a big marketing firm Zoe was familiar with. "I made it through a couple of rounds."

"With a big company like that you might have to start out with an internship."

"Yeah, I'm beginning to realize that."

"Think you'd ever be interested in moving to New York?"

"Would I ever. Actually, I was just there." She shrugged. "Same story. They liked me, just not enough to hire me."

This is when Zoe Bascombe, scheduler of travel dates, mover of VIPs, organizer of promo drop dates, looked at her niece, and said, "Why don't you show me some of your work later. Maybe we can zero in on some appropriate avenues to pursue."

"Oh, man, would you? That would be so incredible."

"I see you've met Noelle."

Zoe turned to find Eve standing beside her. "Yep."

"Zoe's going to help me find a job," Noelle said. "I mean, point me in the right direction."

"Just give advice," Zoe amended. "If it's okay with you. I'm not even sure I can help." She got her first good look at her sister. Her sister. Eve looked like she hadn't slept much.

Unlike Zoe, who had zonked out as soon as she'd left Chris. She'd gone straight upstairs, turned on the television, and the next thing she knew a Sunday morning church service was flickering on the screen.

"Fine by me, I'm no help at all. Do you want to have breakfast? Floret said she'd have muffins and real coffee if we just wanted to come straight there, but if you'd rather have something else, we can eat first."

"Coffee and muffins work," Zoe said. "Chris is coming, too, if that's okay with you. And he never eats breakfast at all."

"He's part of the family. Speaking of whom. Here he comes."

Chris stepped out of the elevator and sauntered toward the lobby.

"How late were you out last night?"

"The better question is, how early was I back this morning? There is some amazing music in this town."

"We have our share," Eve said.

"We're going over to Wind Chime House if you're up for it," Zoe said.

"Wouldn't miss it. After coffee."

Zoe him took by the arm. "They'll give you coffee there."

"Or there are several places on the way," Eve said.

Chris slowly turned his head, giving them a deadpan face.

Zoe smiled.

Noelle laughed. "Please, please tell me he's my uncle."

Chris flourished one of his most ridiculous bows. Straightened up with a groan, and Eve and Zoe hustled him out the door.

"Okay, I'm a little slow this morning," Chris

said, edging himself between Zoe and Eve as they walked down Main Street. "But give me the lowdown on Wind Chime. Are there going to be a bunch of old dudes with ponytails wearing bell-bottoms and greeting us with peace signs and a joint?"

Eve shook her head. "You actually lived with him for how many years?"

"He grows on you," Zoe said. "Actually, he's the best."

Chris gave Eve a Cheshire cat smile.

"I can see that," Eve said.

Zoe was incredibly glad that she'd asked Chris to come with them. She and Eve were both so nervous that they could hardly stay contained, so she just gave in to Chris's antics and before long they turned down the drive to Wind Chime House.

"Floret and Henry, right?" Chris asked as he jumped to miss a pothole.

"Yes." Eve stopped. "Maybe I should give you a brief history before we get there."

"Good idea," said Chris, and turned to give her his full attention.

"Floret inherited the house from her mother when she was a little girl. It was uninhabited for years until one day she and Henry came to live here, bringing an assorted group of flower children with them. I was raised here by my grandmother and dad, who you met yesterday. And Hannah—well, maybe you won't have to have the pleasure."

"Moly. That bad?"

"Depends. She raised me and got me started when I wanted to buy the inn, but she's been carrying on a feud with Floret and Henry for years. We lived here until I was thirteen. It was a great place to grow up, lots of kids, people coming and going, peace, love, happiness. Now it's just Floret and Henry and David, who's raising his nephew, Eli, who is in love with Mel. And a few old-timers that come and go."

She shook herself. "Then one day there was a shouting match. All the shouting was on my grandmother's side. No one else ever raised their voices on the commune. She packed us up and we moved into town. She's always refused to talk about it. No one seems to know why it started. I doubt if they remember at this point. It's just a habit. But it came to a head a few years ago when I suggested that I wanted to lease their beach for hotel use."

"To keep out the nude sunbathers," Zoe said with a smile.

"Talking to my kids, huh? They think it's hysterical that old people would get out on the beach without their clothes. But it was a little off-putting to my guests. Anyway, we had come to an agreement until

Hannah got wind of it. The next day she had a backhoe come in with a load of rocks and built 'the wall' as the locals call it."

"And you all just caved?" asked Chris.

"Wait until you meet Hannah, and you'll understand."

"Sounds ominous."

"And that's about it, though there's bound to be more on the horizon."

They started walking again and soon came to the house.

Chris stopped to survey the vista. "Whoa. I'm loving this visual. Is that the border-wall beach over there?"

"One and the same," Eve said, and pushed open the gate. It moved more easily than it had the day before, Zoe noticed. The whole fence was standing a little straighter, the new pickets shining like capped teeth in an old mouth.

"Oh, and there's Dulcie," Zoe said as they stepped into the yard, and the goat raced toward them. Chris did a flying leap back through the gate and pushed it shut.

"And how embarrassing is that?" Chris asked. "And *what* is that?" He lifted his chin in Dulcie's direction. Dulcie gave Eve and Zoe a welcoming butt, then zeroed in on Chris.

"You might as well come in and say your hellos," Henry called from the porch. "She's not violent, just a little needy."

Chris raised an eyebrow but opened the gate. Dulcie gamboled and butted and pushed Chris the rest of the way into the yard.

"Needy and obnoxious," Chris said, and joined the others, Dulcie trotting along by his side.

"You've made a friend," said Henry as they reached the porch steps.

"Great," Chris said. "You're my favorite goat. Now go away." He climbed the steps and stuck out his hand. "Chris Bascombe, Zoe's brother. Oh, and Eve's, too. Hope you don't mind me—ignore the pun—butting in."

Henry smiled in his all-will-be-well way, and Zoe immediately felt better. And to think she'd thought he was some kind of evil spirit with his familiar just three nights ago in the fog. So much had happened since then.

"Floret has muffins and coffee out on the porch," Henry said, ushering them inside.

Chris caused a bit of a pileup when he stopped in the vestibule. "Wow," he said. "I get it. Wind chime."

Zoe looked around. She hadn't seen them on her first visit. She'd been too stressed and uncertain to notice her surroundings until she got to the tapestries, but the walls of the vestibule were filled with David Merrick's photographs.

"You'll meet the artist later," Henry said. "He's around here somewhere."

Hopefully not listening to her family history, Zoe thought. It was bound to be shattering. She glanced at Eve, who was as pale as Henry the night of the fog. Zoe gave her a quick smile; she'd been so busy thinking about herself that she hadn't considered what Eve must be going through.

Floret waved to them from the archway. She was wearing a long dress, soft and flowing, its pattern of blues and greens and yellows seeming to mix with the ocean and sky behind her. Her hair was loose, almost to her waist, and held back by two nacre clips.

"Come in, come in," she said in her high, tinkling voice.

"Enchanting," Chris said under his breath, and nudged Zoe and Eve ahead.

It took some time and choreography to get them all situated around the porch table with muffins and fruit and coffee served in mismatched china.

"Our history," Floret explained as she passed the cups around. "Each piece has its own memory."

"Like guests at every meal," said Chris.

Floret beamed at him. Another kindred spirit.

Zoe normally would enjoy the interchange. Chris was amazingly adaptable and easily entertained. "A cheap date," he often told her. "Everything amuses me."

But today she was too tense to enjoy his enjoyment. She wanted it over. Whatever new thing she was about to learn. And she knew Eve did, too. She could feel the energy humming through her sister. *Her sister.*

Henry passed by the back of her chair, briefly laid his hand on Eve's shoulder, and Zoe could see her visibly relax.

They were so strange, these two old hippies. Strange and out of touch and yet in touch with something special. Zoe liked them. But she wished they would just get to it.

And once they got past their first cups of strong pressed coffee, they did.

Henry's voice caught them by surprise, changing from conversational to storyteller without transition.

"Eve."

Eve jumped.

"Your mother—and Zoe's . . . and Chris's here—was a joy. Not your typical groupie, not a groupie at all. Just a young girl who went to a concert and fell in love. And Lee. He was transformed . . . for a while. He brought her back here after his tour. He and Hannah and his sisters had been living here for quite a while.

His brother had been killed in the war a few years before and Hannah was desperate to keep Lee from getting called up.

"He'd always been deep. Talented, but flawed. As are we all, but in Lee's case, it was like a little hole to darkness that hadn't been completely closed, nor fully opened to release that darkness completely and be done. So it always dogged him, even that summer when happiness ruled the days." There was something in his voice that foreshadowed a much sadder story and Zoe braced herself. They all knew how it ended, just not how it got there.

"Summer was at its zenith, full and fecund . . ."

"Like now," Floret added in her dreamy way. "Only . . ."

"Only in the past," Henry said.

"I sometimes get confused," she told Chris for some reason. "It's the brownies."

Chris nodded. Zoe wondered if he had any idea what Floret was talking about. She sure as heck didn't.

Floret chuckled. "You gave me such a start that day, Zoe. At first I thought Jenny had come home. You look so much like her." She paused. Looked out at the sea. "And she has at last."

A chill ran up Zoe's spine.

A look passed between Floret and Henry and he continued. "A halcyon summer. Then one day Jenny's parents came. None of us ever knew how they found her. If Jenny had contacted them. They just appeared one day and took her away."

"Just like that?" Eve blurted out. "She just walked away?"

"So it appeared. But, Eve, no one truly knows what is in someone else's soul."

Eve let out a slow, tortured breath. And Zoe breathed right along with her.

"It caught us all, especially Lee, by surprise. He was distraught, as you can imagine. To have no warning. With no reason that we could see. We didn't know about the baby until later. Lee went back on the road, tried to drown his sorrows in drugs and alcohol and music. It nearly killed him."

"He didn't go after her?" Eve asked.

"He never said. It was Hannah who found out that Jenny was pregnant and she arranged to adopt you, Eve."

"Hannah?" Eve shook her head.

Confusion? Heartbreak? Sadness? Zoe could see it all in her sister's reaction. *Her sister.*

"One day she borrowed a neighbor's car and drove off. That night she returned with you. Our new little newborn. Everyone here became your family. Your name was Eve. 'To breathe, to live.' Jenny named you that. Don't doubt what you meant to her."

Eve broke down. Zoe didn't bother to hide her own tears. Chris sniffed and blinked and finally pulled out his handkerchief.

"Then why didn't you tell me about the letters?"

Neither Henry nor Floret spoke. They were the only dry-eyed ones in the room. They'd had many years to come to terms with what had happened. But why hadn't they done anything? Tried to find Jenny? At least told Eve about the letters Jenny had written her?

"Why?" Eve asked.

"We didn't receive any letters until the one she sent several months ago telling us to expect Zoe."

Eve fumbled in the pocket of her slacks. "But Jenny says here that she wrote, but I never answered her letters. I never got any."

Henry and Floret exchanged looks, but it wasn't hard for Zoe to see where this was going.

"Hannah." Eve stood, nearly knocking over her chair. She started toward the front door but Henry was there before her.

"Don't go in anger. You don't know the whole story."

"Then tell me."

"I can't."

"Oh my God. She threatened you, didn't she. Didn't she?"

"Eve. She always threatens us. It makes no difference. We'll never change. We just don't know any more of the story than you. We were just happy to have you with us."

Floret had moved beside Henry, and they formed a calming wall between Eve and the door. But it didn't last.

"I'll never forgive her."

"Oh, Eve." Floret stretched out her arms, beseeching like one of those poor children in an alms poster.

Eve swept past her, ran down the hall and out the front door.

Henry and Floret both closed their eyes, and Zoe thought they must be praying or sending their strength along with her or whatever old flower children did. Because when they opened them again, peace had filled the room.

"Storm ahead," Floret said. And handed the muffin plate to Chris.

That was an understatement, thought Zoe, until a clap of thunder startled her from her chair. There really was a storm coming.

"Maybe we'd better—" Chris began.

"It will pass," Henry said. At the same time a wall

of raindrops assaulted the windows. Progressed like an army of foot soldiers across the roof.

The front door opened and shut. "Jeez Louise," said David Merrick from just inside the doorway. "Oh, sorry. Don't let me interrupt."

"Not at all," Henry said. "Coffee's still hot."

David dripped into the room. He and Chris were introduced, shook hands. Floret handed David a cup and he sat down in Eve's vacated seat.

"Did you see Eve?" Zoe asked.

He shook his head. "Was she here?"

Zoe nodded.

He started to stand. "Should I—?"

"No," said Henry. "If it has to be done, best that it's done quickly."

"'That tears shall drown the wind,'" Chris mumbled.

"Exactly," said Henry.

"Aw, crap," said David, and reached for a muffin.

Chapter 13

Silence fell around the table, while the rain pounded about them, and David finished his muffin and started another one.

Then, as suddenly as it had begun, the storm ended. The sun came out with a vengeance, its heat beating into the room as the air grew heavy with residual humidity.

"Wow," Chris said. "Beach weather again." He stood abruptly. "Thanks for having us. But I think we should be going."

Zoe frowned at him. She had a hundred questions, wanted to hear stories about their mother in her younger years, about her first coming to Wind Chime, about her and Lee Gordon, and maybe understand what made her run away. Was it really Jenny's parents?

Had they forced her to go home? The Campbells were really sweet, doted on their grandchildren. Zoe couldn't imagine them dragging a heartbroken, pregnant Jenny away. Eve was their grandchild, too.

Maybe they had just been doing what they thought best. But she wanted to know.

She started to tell Chris to go ahead without her, but Henry stood, too.

"I'm glad you're here," he said to Chris. "You and Zoe are part of the family now."

Chris nodded gravely. "Thank you. It's an honor."

Everyone turned to looked at Zoe. She stood and realized her legs were shaky. Chris took her elbow. And Henry walked them to the door.

"Thank you. I'll . . . I'd . . ."

"Come back anytime. All will be well."

And then somehow they were down the steps and standing in the yard. Chris kept moving her toward the gate.

"What's the hurry? Don't you want to see Wind Chime Beach? The woods when the breeze blows—"

"Yes," Chris said, looking behind them. "But right now you look like underdone pastry. You barely touched your coffee and that poor muffin was nothing but crumbs. Not one bite made it to your mouth. And

I know for a fact there's a big cheeseburger and a Coke with your name on it at that diner I saw in town."

Zoe's hand went to her cheek.

"Yeah," Chris said. "Shock, or something. I recommend protein and sugar before you pass out and I have to haul you over my shoulder and cart you off to the closest divan."

Zoe smiled. He was absolutely right. She'd be lucky if she made it as far as the street. And he used just the right amount of sympathy and silliness to keep her from being offended.

She squeezed his arm. "I'm so glad you came."

"Yeah," he said. "Now, let's get out of here. Dulcie the goat cometh."

They made it to the other side of the gate just as Dulcie butted the pickets.

"No wonder they have to make repairs," Chris said, and stuck his tongue out at Dulcie. She lifted her head and let out a grating noise.

"Love at first sight. I knew it."

They walked arm in arm down the drive, the puddles left by the rain already receding into the porous ground.

"What was all that about doing stuff quickly and tears in the wind?" Zoe asked.

"Shakespeare. Butchered, but the bard nonetheless. Fancy that old dude knowing the Scottish play."

"Which play is that?"

"Didn't you go to school?"

"Business."

"Oh, right. It's the play whose name you can't say."

"Oh," Zoe said, remembering. "Mac—"

"Jeez, don't say it!"

"Sorry." They'd reached the street and Chris had managed to take her mind off the meeting they'd just had and what they'd learned. There would be time to hear every tidbit. But for now, she could use the time to get used to her new family.

"So what's on your agenda?" Zoe asked once they'd been seated in a booth at Kelly's.

Chris looked over the edge of the oversized menu. "Audition? Give up my life and move to Chicago where I'll freeze my tail off while waiting for Timothy to build apartment complexes that I'll never be able to afford to live in?"

They ordered New Hampshire burgers and two Cokes.

"Seems kinda 'rock and a hard place' to me. A long-distance relationship, maybe?"

Chris shrugged.

"Chris?"

"It's that age-old question. The thea-tah or the relationship. Ne'er the twain, etcetera."

Zoe blew out air. "Sounds pretty bad."

"I'm leaning toward the theater. That can't be good."

"Not for happily ever after?"

"Not sure that was ever in the cards."

"Does Timothy know?"

"Frankly, I'm not sure he cares."

"I'm so sorry."

Chris huffed out a sigh. "The sad part is I'm not sure I do either."

"Are you in a hurry to get back?"

Chris leaned back while the waitress deposited plates and glasses on the table.

"Only if my agent calls. Now eat."

Eve didn't bother to knock but walked right into her grandmother's house. She'd tried to talk herself into slowing down, taking time to get control of her anger and sense of betrayal. Just to stop by the inn and change out of her rain-soaked clothes.

It was a losing battle. There had been letters. Many of them, according to her mother's letter to Zoe.

Why had she never seen any of them? If Floret and Henry only knew about one letter, what had happened to the others? They wouldn't lie. Her grandmother would. She'd do just about anything to protect what was hers, including her family.

Had she shown them to her father? Surely he would have said something, if only in a drug-hazed, whining stupor. He denied knowing about them.

Hannah had to have intercepted them. It was the only word for it. Which meant chances were, she still had them.

If Eve was feeling magnanimous, she would think that maybe Hannah had been saving them for her until she was older and had just forgotten. Yeah, what fool who knew Hannah would believe that? But Hannah might have kept them for the day she might need them. To use against someone else. Eve? Her father?

Well, that day had come. Just not in the way Hannah had expected.

Eve marched across the parlor, defiantly leaving wet footprints on the expensive carpet, and went straight to her grandmother's desk.

Now she hesitated. Searching someone else's desk was something her grandmother might do. But not Eve. No. She'd wait and—

The door to the kitchen creaked open and Hannah came through carrying a mug of tea with the string of the tea bag hanging over the side.

With all the money she'd made in her life, Hannah

Gordon was still just a working-class girl from the poor side of town. And she had made them all pay.

"Good Lord, girl, you nearly scared me to death. What is it now? Your father was over last night. Got me out of bed to carry on about Melanie and that boy from the commune."

"Melody, Hannah. Her name is Melody."

"You should do something about that situation before it's too late. Or you'll find yourself taking care of her little mistake."

"Like you took care of Jenny Bascombe's?"

"Show some respect. You were everything to me."

"I've been hearing that a lot lately. But I have to wonder. Was I really? Or was I just a pawn in your stupid power struggle with Henry and Floret?"

The mug Hannah had been holding crashed to the floor. Hot tea splashed onto Eve's ankles.

They stared at each other while Eve tried not to rub off the burning liquid on her pants leg.

Then Hannah bent down, picked up the pieces of pottery and dropped them in the wastepaper basket by her desk, leaving the spilled tea pooling on the hardwood floor.

She sat behind her desk and began scrolling through a page on her computer screen like nothing had happened, probably waiting for Eve to give up and slink away. She had many times before, mainly when she'd asked about her mother.

Not this time. Eve reached in her pocket for the envelope and letter that was beginning to show signs of wear. She held it up, ignoring the burning tingling of her skin where the tea had splashed.

Hannah didn't look up.

Eve stuck it under her nose.

"And what is this?" Hannah said dismissively, uninterested.

Eve pulled the letter out of Hannah's reach.

"It's from my mother to Zoe. It was waiting for her at Wind Chime House."

Her grandmother recoiled. But Eve knew it was just in preparation for a strike.

"Let me see it."

Eve shook her head. "I don't trust you. But listen to this." She read the part about Jenny's letters to Eve. "Year after year she wrote me, but she never heard back. Because I never got those letters. Not one. You never read me a letter from my mother when I was too young to read them myself. Never handed me an envelope addressed to Eve Gordon. What did you do with them, Hannah? Run to the mailbox every day to make sure you were always the first one to see the mail? Did you throw them in the trash? Burn them in the Franklin stove? Did you show them to my father? Or did you open them and read them yourself, gloating over your cleverness at keeping us apart?"

Hannah heaved a sigh. "They're in the drawer of the credenza," she said in the same way she might say, "The napkins are in the cupboard."

Eve stared. In the drawer, all these years? So close. She whirled around, practically lunged at the old curved credenza against the wall.

She yanked open the first drawer she reached. Rummaged through it with spasmodic fingers.

"The middle one in the back corner."

Eve stumbled over to the middle drawer. It was locked.

"Give me the key."

Her grandmother looked out the window.

"Give it to me or I swear I'll take an axe to it."

"Oh, Eve, don't be so dramatic." Hannah reached bony fingers inside her blouse and pulled out a key on a chain.

"You wear it around your neck? It's been almost fifty years."

"Just since that girl came to town." Hannah carefully unclasped the chain and let the key slide down into her palm.

Eve tried to breathe. She was so close to going over

the edge, she would gladly do her grandmother bodily harm.

Hannah held out her hand, fingers open. The key sat right in the middle of her palm, looking like a relic from a fantasy tale.

Eve reached out her own hand, slowly, so that she wouldn't react if Hannah suddenly snatched hers out of reach. She didn't breathe until the key was between her fingers and she'd turned back to the credenza drawer.

It was one of those old, thick brass keys, the keyhole big and loose-fitting. Even so, it took several tries before she felt the latch give and she pulled the drawer open with both hands.

She found them almost immediately. A stack of envelopes, tied up with a lavender ribbon. It seemed like the final slap. A mean-spirited, vindictive joke. *Lavender's blue, dilly dilly . . .*

She pulled the ribbon off, turned them over. The first envelope hadn't been opened. Nor the second or the third. Just as tightly sealed as the day they'd been sent.

She looked up. "You never read them?"

Hannah shrugged.

"Why? What if she wanted to come back? What if she needed us?"

"She gave up that right when she left."

"What is wrong with you? People break up all the time. Break up and sometimes get back together. Live happily ever after. You made sure that wouldn't happen, didn't you?"

"She broke my son's heart. The only son I have left. She didn't deserve a second chance."

Eve clapped her hand over her mouth. She didn't know if she was going to be sick, or yell a string of obscenities at the woman who had raised her. Raised and loved. But at what cost to them all?

Hannah's expression didn't change, but she seemed to have grown smaller during the last few seconds, as if the holes left inside her by so much loss, by such unswerving bitterness, were finally no longer able to support themselves, had imploded, sucking the life out of her very soul.

Eve cared about souls. She nurtured them. But she couldn't care about Hannah's right now. Right now, she only wanted to get home and read the letters she'd been waiting for for her entire life.

Noelle was at the reception desk when Zoe and Chris returned to the hotel.

"So much for sneaking past," Chris said as he waved and nodded.

Noelle came out from behind the desk. "Where is Mom?"

"She had something to do," Zoe said. "She should be back soon."

"What's going on? Why is everyone being so secretive?"

"We aren't," Chris said. "We're going to the beach. Do we need a special card or anything?"

Noelle shook her head. "Just your room key. Take the elevator down to G. It will let you off on the level below here and right on the path, but you'll need your key card to get back in."

"Gotcha," Chris said, and steered Zoe toward the elevator.

Twenty minutes later they had requisitioned two chaise lounges, ordered nonalcoholic Morning Mai Tais—there were two mini bottles of organic vodka rolled up in Chris's towel—and were lying side by side, eyes protected by designer sunglasses, their faces slathered in sunblock provided by a cute cabana boy.

"Now this is the life," Chris said.

"Hmmm," said Zoe.

"Stop it."

"What?"

"Stop thinking. It's keeping me awake."

"I can't help it. Everything is just so . . . Maybe we should check to see if Eve is back."

"No."

"But she's my sister." She hadn't quite gotten used to saying the words yet.

"And my half sister," said Chris. "She's made it for forty-something years without you organizing her life. I think she can manage for another couple of hours."

"I feel responsible."

"Look. Eve will do whatever she is doing and when she gets back and is ready for company, we'll be all relaxed and ready to lend our shoulders. Trust me."

"I hate it when you say trust me—I usually get in trouble."

"Not today, so come on. I declare this afternoon a Moratorium on Moroseness. You're going to get some sun while I'm checking my e-mails and pretending to look for work."

"I'll try."

"Zoe, you're still here!"

Zoe slid her sunglasses to the tip of her nose. Karen, Elaine, and Brandy stood in a row at the end of her chaise. She sat up. "Hey, guys. I'm here. I didn't know if *you* were."

"We're leaving this afternoon, but we wanted to say

good-bye," said Elaine, eyeing Chris, who had taken off his sunglasses.

"Well, it was wonderful meeting you all."

"Looks like you're having a great time," Elaine said.

"I . . . Oh, this is my brother Chris." She introduced the three women.

"You should give us your e-mail," Karen said. "We loved it here and are planning to come back for our next girls' weekend. Maybe we can meet up." She fished in an oversized orange-striped beach bag and pulled out a crumpled notebook with a pen attached by a ribbon to the wire spiral.

Zoe quickly wrote down her e-mail addy. "Have a safe trip," she said.

"Thanks, enjoy your stay."

"Who were they?" Chris asked as the three women wove their way up the beach. They'd definitely been partaking of a hidden stash of alcohol that afternoon.

"Some women I met. We had happy hour together at the bar downstairs. It was fun." She frowned.

"What's the matter?"

"Nothing. I just realized it was the first time in a long time I've actually sat at a bar just to have fun."

"Something you should do more often. I'm an expert."

Something about his statement made Zoe a little sad. Of her three brothers, she was closest to Chris. He was really the only one she'd lived with for any length of time and they'd always been simpatico. She wished he would find success and happiness. Hell, she wished the same for herself.

She slipped her sunglasses back on. There would be time for success and happiness when all this was sorted out.

Eve awoke with a start. Blinked against the lamplight. And bolted upright. She had fallen asleep. She'd come to Mike's to read the letters in peace.

She took in the bottle of wine, half empty, the letters spread out on the coffee table before her. Mike had made it himself from an old fallen tree.

A door opened. The sound of footsteps across the oak floor.

Eve hurriedly checked the time on the cable box. It was almost ten o'clock. Mike must be home. Crap, what if he wasn't alone?

She didn't ordinarily take advantage of their open relationship. But she'd been so upset, she hadn't even thought to ask him if she could use his house. Hadn't even told her daughters where she was. She hadn't meant to stay.

She made a grab for the letters as if she could escape unseen. Unembarrassed.

Impossible.

She bolted to her feet and her knees buckled, stiff from the couch and the fetal position she'd been lying in, and quickly ran her fingers through tangled hair. She turned to face the door.

Just explain and slink away. Hopefully he wouldn't be with anyone she knew. And she was confident that he would never cross the line with one of their guests.

The footsteps continued past the living room. To the kitchen? The bedroom.

Eve held still. No creak on the stairs. The stairs always creaked.

She glanced toward the door and the hall. No way could she make it out of the house without being seen.

"Mike," she called. "Sorry. It's me. Eve. I just had to borrow your living room for a bit. I'm leaving. Sorry." Damn, she sounded like a blithering idiot. Like someone who had no business being where she was.

A shadow appeared in the doorway. Followed by Mike and a beer.

"Who else would it be?" He came into the room. "No one else would leave all the lights on."

"Are you alone?"

He chuckled. God, she loved that about him. It was

a big rumbly sound that complemented his personality and his build.

"Just me and this microbabe." He held up a bottle from a local brewery.

Eve sank back onto the couch. "Thank God. I fell asleep. And I was afraid I might have interrupted—"

"It's Sunday night. Restock night. Order night. Ain't-got-time-for-love night."

"I forgot."

"I can see you've had other things on your mind," he said, taking in the littered table and the open wine bottle. His gaze moved up to her face and went all soft, something else she liked about him. He was jovial, but not clueless.

She didn't need a mirror to know what she looked like. She could barely open her eyes, swollen and raw from crying.

He glanced at the table. "Taking up scrapbooking?"

Eve shook her head. Held out her hand.

He came over to sit beside her. He ignored the letters, though anybody else would have at least been tempted to take a peek. They covered the surface of the coffee table. Maybe thirty in all. She'd read each one. Then read them again.

"From my mother," she said.

"Wow."

Still, he didn't move to touch them.

"She wrote to me for my whole life."

"I take it you just got them tonight?"

"This afternoon."

"Zoe bring them?"

She shook her head. She couldn't make herself say the truth. Her grandmother had confiscated each one as it had arrived, never bothering to read them, but keeping them hidden from Eve for her entire life.

She sorted through the envelopes, found one of the square ones. Handed it to him. Watched as he opened it.

" 'Happy first birthday,' " he read aloud.

The card had pink balloons on the front. "Open it."

She watched as he read the printed greeting then squinted as he reached the lines her mother had written in a neat, sloping script.

He gently slid the card back into the envelope, set it on the table, then leaned back and put his arm around her shoulders.

She leaned into him. She didn't need to hear his words; she didn't have to tell him anything. They just were. As if they knew each other so well, they could read each other by osmosis.

Of course it wasn't true. That was just her commune

upbringing talking. But they'd known each other most of their lives, and they knew each other pretty well.

"I don't think I'll ever be able to forgive her."

He pulled away to look a question at her. "Jenny?"

"Hannah. She took every one my mother sent and hid them. Henry and Floret didn't even know about them. She must have waited every day at the mailbox to intercept them."

Just to prevent what? Eve knowing that her mother had loved her even though she couldn't or wouldn't keep her? Eve had cried herself to sleep more nights than she could count. She hadn't at first. Not until she began to see other kids with mothers. Floret became her mother. Or as like a mother as she could be. She'd never had her own children. She said it wasn't in the cosmos.

Eve hadn't understood until much later what she meant.

"She thought I didn't want to know her because I never wrote back to her." Eve buried her face in Mike's shoulder. "I never knew."

Mike wrapped her up in his bear arms, and she felt safe. Safe to cry, to let her nose run, to not be in control, not be successful, not take responsibility for strangers' psyches.

"I never knew."

And Mike just held her. Occasionally he'd lean forward to reach for his beer, carrying her with him, then settled back onto the couch.

After a while, Mike took her phone. Texted someone, Noelle probably. Put the phone down. A responding ping. Mike ignored it.

"She saw me graduate, Mike. She came to see me graduate."

Chapter 14

It was barely light when Zoe left her hotel room the next morning, her tote stuffed not with the celadon urn, but with two plastic laundry bags from the hotel. She didn't think anyone would question where she was going. She doubted Mel or Noelle would be manning the desk. There had been a few frantic phone calls last night, and both of her nieces, not being able to find their mother, had deferred to Zoe to help them out.

It was an odd feeling. To have family, not strangers, depending on her. And she didn't want to look too closely at that revelation. Being the baby, she'd always been taken care of. Now it seemed it was her turn to do the caring.

"A feud, star-crossed lovers, an angry old rock star,

and a missing hotel proprietor—it's just like Shakespeare in the Park without the mosquitoes," said Chris after the third call from Eve's worried daughters.

They'd been returning to the hotel from dinner in one of the trendy bistros along Main Street.

"She's probably in the bar and can't hear her cell over the music," he added.

A quick look into the bar showed that it had closed early and only Mike was there, bent over a laptop computer and with papers spread out along the bar top.

Zoe went to bed; Chris had gone back out. He was a city boy through and through. He liked his night life. Zoe did, too, normally, but she was tired. Overwhelmed in a way that she'd never been before.

And she needed to call her other brothers, let them know about the beach. About the ashes. About not being their real sister.

She had to do it before she sent her mother's ashes into the next world.

What held her back was the fear that they would want nothing to do with her.

She didn't call, but the thought kept her up long into the night, so she was awake for the lifting of the red alert over Eve's disappearance. She'd spent the night with Mike, the bartender.

The lobby was empty this early; there was no one on duty at the reception desk.

Zoe tucked her tote under her arm and hit the streets. Her first stop was the coffee bar. A double-shot latte and she was on her way.

She didn't follow the drive all the way to the house, but cut through the edge of woods that surrounded the property. She didn't want to run into Dulcie and have her alert the household to her presence. She just needed some time to herself to clean up some of the trash from the beach—and to think. Then she would go up to the house. They'd invite her in for coffee, give her some pastries, maybe reminisce about her mother. Make her feel like family.

But first she needed to make some decisions. Alone, without everyone and their memories and advice and their opinions. Even their support. She just needed a bit of quiet. To hear the wind chimes in the breeze and try to recapture the magic she had felt in those few seconds of sound, when for that moment she'd felt as if everything made sense, would work out. Before her whole world had gone haywire.

Then she would decide once and for all what she would do with her mother's ashes and her own life.

The undergrowth was very thick in places, and she

tried to move quietly as she made her way to the path that would lead her to the beach. She was alert, waiting for the first breaths of wind, the faint tinkle of the first chime.

She'd almost reached the path when she felt it, the slight shifting in the air. She stopped to listen. Almost holding her breath for it to begin.

And was startled by the whack of a hammer.

She knew where it was coming from. She hurried along, the music forgotten until she stepped off the path into the sunlight and saw David Merrick in jeans and T-shirt, hands protected by thick work gloves. He raised a heavy sledge hammer over his head then swung it downward.

Whack. The left side of the rotten stair handrail creaked, swayed, and then a piece broke apart and dropped out of sight below the ledge. But the stairs held. He dropped the hammer to the ground and stood back, his hands fisted on his hips.

"I hope this isn't about me," she said in the sudden quiet.

Slowly, he turned around, gave her a resigned look, but didn't answer.

"Because I wouldn't think of suing."

"Floret and Henry are up at the house." He picked up the sledge hammer and turned away from her.

Zoe started down the path toward the beach.

"Where are you going?"

She stopped, turned back to him. "Well, I do want to see Henry and Floret, but first I want to clean up the debris on the beach."

"Why?"

"Because it's an eyesore."

He didn't react, which was a bit annoying, and didn't offer to help, which was more annoying, so she climbed behind the tree trunk, slid down the boulders, and jumped onto the sand.

She was surprised to see even more garbage than the last time she was here. Washed up by that brief afternoon storm?

She set the tote down next to the driftwood bench and was glad to see the glass shard of wind chime still sitting where she'd left it. She pulled out one of the plastic bags she'd brought from the inn and began to pick up pieces of garbage. Soggy cardboard that had once been a corrugated box. Two bottles of kombucha, half empty; they looked new. Maybe she wasn't the only person visiting the beach. She poured out the contents and went back for the second plastic bag. No reason not to recycle what she could.

She looked up to the ledge where David had stopped and was watching her.

"What?" she asked.

"Could you wait until I get these stairs down? I don't want you to get injured by flying debris."

"It doesn't look like they're going anywhere fast."

"When they go, they'll go without warning."

He was right, she knew. But she was driven to get this done. The thought of putting things off another minute, much less all morning and possibly the afternoon, might push her into a total meltdown.

"Thanks for the warning." She knelt down and lifted up something that looked like pillow stuffing. Holding it between two fingers, she slid it into her bag.

"Stand back, dammit." David raised the hammer.

Zoe held up her hand. "Wait a minute, there's something under there." She started toward the stairs.

"Stay away, Zoe. It's unstable."

She stopped, not because of his warning but because he had called her by name. That was a first. They must be making progress.

"I'll be careful, but there's something under here." She trod cautiously across the sand, peered into the underbelly of the stairs. Someone had made a nice little nest there. A human someone.

What appeared to be a nylon sleeping bag was crumpled up on the sand. An orange crate with a Coleman lantern. A plastic grocery bag lay on its side, a package of Oreos half concealed inside.

Someone was living rough on Wind Chime Beach. She tugged at the sleeping bag and held it up. "Hey, check this out. I don't suppose you know anything about this?"

He looked down at her. Zeroed in on the bag.

It hit her at about the same time he threw down the hammer and started down the path toward the beach.

Not a transient's hovel. A trysting place.

Damn. Mel and her boyfriend must meet here. Didn't Mel say he lived at the commune? Oh, jeez. The feud. She'd just ratted out a pair of twenty-first-century Romeo-and-Juliet lovers. She could smack herself.

This time when David reached the beach, she was ready for him.

"Look. No reason to get all—" She didn't get a chance to finish. He pushed past her and looked beneath the treads.

"Damn. So this is where they've been going."

He ducked beneath the wooden structure.

"Be careful. It might be unstable," she mimicked, but she meant it. The whole structure seemed about to fall over.

All she got in return was a growl. Followed by the orange crate, the lantern, and the grocery bag, spewing cookies across the sand.

"Is that really necessary? It's the twenty-first century. They're kids. They're in love. You did give him 'the talk,' right?"

He just glared at her and snatched the sleeping bag from her hands. He looked around the sand. Looking for a place to discard it? She shoved the plastic garbage bag behind her back.

He went after the other one.

"That's the recycling bag."

He looked as if he might be contemplating murder. Hers. More likely this would lead to the grounding of a teenager or two. Zoe had never been grounded, herself. She'd always prided herself on being too smart to get caught.

Though thinking back, she wondered if her mother had decided to just look the other way.

"I don't want to get them in trouble."

"You have no idea."

He started shoving the sleeping bag into the recycling bag.

"Oh, don't be cranky. At least don't take it out on teenagers in love." A snatch of the old fifties song meandered through her head. She sang a verse out loud. She couldn't help herself.

As if in chorus, the chimes began to sing. And she could see the woods, the beach, not as it was now, but before the stairs rotted away, before the trash took over the sand. *The perfect place to fall in love.*

She swallowed. "Do you hear them?"

"Of course I hear them, that's not the point."

"They're saying to let love be."

"God, give me patience." He snatched the garbage bag from her. "The chimes are sound in reaction to the wind, not a conversation, and they don't give a shit about love, young or otherwise."

She laughed. "You don't believe that."

He gave her a look and leaned over to pull a rusted can out of the sand. He gave it a vigorous shake. "Just because I live here doesn't mean I've lost my mind."

"Maybe not, but the photographer of *LIGHT* wouldn't be such a Neanderthal."

He shoved the can into the bag, narrowed his eyes at her.

"I saw your book in the bookstore. *LIGHT.*" She didn't think he needed to know she'd also bought it. "You don't think the chimes are just reactive sound. You think they're magic."

He stuck the bag under his arm, ran his forearm across his forehead. "You don't know what I think. And you don't know what trouble those kids will be in if anyone finds out about this."

"The feud," she intoned. Seeing his expression, she asked in her normal voice, "It's as serious as that?"

"For years."

"I won't tell if you won't."

"I'm afraid it might already be too late."

"Oh, come on. Things like that don't happen in this day and age."

"Have you been living under a rock lately? Not only do they. They're thriving."

He let the bag drop by his side and came to stand in front of her. "Look, there's a lot you don't understand. Hell, I don't understand half of it. And I know you're dealing with your own life crisis. And—"

"And you want me to stay out of it."

"Please."

"They're my family, too."

"Only since Saturday. And half of them don't want you."

He might have slapped her. She froze, tried to suck in air that refused to get to her lungs.

"Shit. I shouldn't have said that. Just forget it. Do what you want. You strike me as someone who would anyway. But don't say I didn't warn you when all hell breaks loose."

"Aren't you being a little melodramatic?"

He let out an exasperated sigh. "Come on. I'll take you up to Floret. She'll give you a cup of something and make you believe everything will work out fine."

Zoe looked around the beach, but she wasn't really seeing anything. *Half of them don't want you.* "Which half?"

"Come on. I'll come back and clean up the garbage."

"No really, which half?"

His answer was to take her elbow and steer her toward the rocks.

She pulled away. "You don't have to come. I know the way."

"I'm coming. I was rude. I spend a lot of time alone. I don't always remember my social skills. I'm sorry."

"Too late."

"Listen, there's more at stake than your injured feelings or teenage hormones." He took the lead, reached back down to help her up the boulders.

This time, she accepted his help. "Like what?" she asked when they were back on the path.

He didn't answer, just grabbed the sledge hammer and waited for her to precede him.

She looked at the hammer. Then at him.

He laughed. "Just returning it to the shed, but I'll walk in front."

So he *could* laugh.

She ran to walk beside him. "Why do you always escort me everywhere?"

He frowned down at her. "You've only been here twice."

"Why are you so surly?"

"What are you? Two?"

She laughed; she couldn't help herself. "Let's just call it inquisitive." She walked a few steps. "Besides, I'm beginning to feel a case of 'know your enemy' coming on."

"I'm not the enemy."

"Who is?"

"Here at Wind Chime House"—his voice took on a dreamy quality—"there are no enemies. Just acceptance."

"That sounded like sarcasm. I thought you liked it here."

"I do."

"Then . . ."

"It's . . . exhausting."

She stared at him. Opened her mouth to ask him . . .

"And don't say, 'Why?' "

She grinned. "Why?"

He let out an exasperated groan, walked faster, and soon they stepped into the sunlight.

Floret and Henry were talking to a man standing next to a mud-splattered SUV. He was medium height, halfway between Floret and Henry. He was smiling and gesticulating in the air; his head, which was topped by a Crocodile Dundee hat, bobbed back and forth between them. He was surrounded by a battered suitcase, a dusty frame backpack, several metal file cases, and Dulcie, who gamboled about his legs, nearly knocking him over.

"They're busy, I should come back."

"That's just the professor. He's been on vacation."

"He lives here, too?"

"For now. People are always coming to live here. Some move on after a while, some stay."

Zoe swore she heard an odd tinge in his voice and wondered if the end of that sentence was "against their will."

David strode forward. Zoe followed reluctantly behind.

David reached them first and the professor greeted him with a hug-slap-on-the-back combination that guys used for good friends they hadn't seen in a while.

Henry noticed Zoe and motioned her over. "Zoe Bascombe, come meet the professor."

Zoe stepped toward them.

The professor turned his bright eyes on her, and they widened slightly. "Indeed. A pleasure." He whipped off his hat. His hair sprang out like a ballerina's tutu from a totally bald head.

"Albert Lippincott, retired anthropologist," the professor said. "And currently hunter home from the hill." He saw Zoe's frown. "Oh, not of the animal variety, but relics of the past. I've just been in Mexico touring and studying the recent Mayan discoveries. An exciting addition to history." He smiled, nodded, reinforcing his enthusiasm. "It's lovely to meet you."

"Zoe is Eve Gordon's sister," Henry said.

"Jenny's daughter?"

Zoe's smile faded, and she looked from the professor to Henry and Floret. Did everybody know her mother? How was it possible?

"Yes, isn't it wonderful?" Floret said.

Wonderful? thought Zoe. She was here to bury her mom.

"Jenny's come home at last." Floret sighed, smiled slightly. "Sooner than we thought."

All three of them looked past David and Zoe and into the woods behind them. Zoe shivered. All that was missing was eerie movie music.

"I'll take your stuff upstairs," David said.

"If you could just take the file cases. They're rather heavy, I'm afraid. I'll take the rest of this to the laundry room." He winked at Zoe. "Less than adequate laundry facilities on the dig, I'm afraid. A pleasure my dear."

The professor pushed his hat back onto his head, hauled the backpack onto his shoulders, and rolled his suitcase after David. Dulcie trotted after him, jumping after one of the straps that trailed loosely from the pack.

Zoe, Henry, and Floret were alone.

"I wanted to talk to you," Zoe blurted, before Floret suggested tea and whatever she'd baked that day. There was much she wanted to know about her mother and the days she'd spent with them, but Zoe didn't feel it was fair to ask without Eve being present.

But she did need to get their approval for spreading her mother's ashes.

"I came here because . . ." She started again. It was hard to say the words. "My mother . . ." *Asked me? . . told me? . . . ordered?* "Requested that—" She swallowed. Blew out a long stream of air.

"Take a walk with us." Henry and Floret turned as he said the words, and Zoe could do nothing but follow.

As soon as they stepped onto the path in the trees, the chimes began to play. Henry kept them walking while the music surrounded them, sending chills up Zoe's arms and down her back. The sound ebbed away, but before the last tinkle had faded, a new wave began and then another, until the woods rang with the sound.

Zoe knew it was a coincidence, but it was hard not to think Henry—or Floret, or both—had summoned them.

And that's when she realized that they weren't on the path to Wind Chime Beach but on the other fork that led past the beach. She could feel the breeze now, more steady than it had been before, as if they were closer to the water. Ahead of them, a keyhole of light beckoned through the trees.

Henry stopped.

Floret sighed. "Lovely, isn't it?"

They both turned to Zoe, welcoming her question. And she knew it was time to begin the letting go.

"My mother sent me here to spread her ashes."

They didn't interrupt.

"In a letter she left with her lawyer." Saying it aloud stabbed at her. It sounded so impersonal. And so like her mother.

She'd wanted Zoe to meet her other family, to be the messenger to Eve. Had she been afraid to tell her in advance? Afraid that Zoe would refuse, cause a scene, hate her for lying to her all these years?

Would she have felt any of those things? Zoe didn't know. Everything was so confusing. She was glad to find Eve, her sister, but it complicated things like crazy. How would her brothers take it? Would they cast her out of the family? Was that why her mother kept her secret life a secret all these years?

She cleared her throat. "She wanted to rest here at Wind Chime Beach. If that's okay."

"We've known this day would come," Henry said. "Hoping she would want to return to us. She won't be alone, Zoe."

"She'll join the others." Floret laid her hand on Zoe's back. It was a brief gesture, but Zoe felt a warmth spread within her, a warmth that remained when Floret withdrew her hand. Zoe didn't understand.

Henry stepped beside Floret, took her hand.

Floret smiled up at him and their love for each other was palpable, so intimate it made Zoe want to pretend she didn't see.

But Floret turned toward her. Gestured to the woods. "Many lives began here, flowered here, then left to discover other things. Now they've begun to come back, the ill at ease, the displaced, the lonely, the old.

Our once-thriving commune of free love, joy, and self-discovery has become a house of memory, of refuge, of hospice." Floret walked a little away from them. Turned back. "She'll be among friends."

"Other people are buried here?" Zoe looked down at her feet. Was she stepping on the ashes of strangers?

Floret laughed. "They aren't buried. They've merely returned to the earth. They've become the earth. Supporting life. Supporting us. They celebrate us. And we celebrate them."

"Is that why the professor is here?"

Henry smiled. "That's why we're all here."

"What if—someone buys the property, bulldozes it, and builds condominiums?"

"Someone probably will," said Henry.

Hannah Gordon came to mind. Zoe's own grandmother. Surely she wouldn't.

"Everything will work out fine," Floret said. "We'll have a grand celebration for our Jenny." She darted a look at Zoe. "Unless you would rather it be private?"

Zoe shook her head. "I don't know."

"Well, there's no hurry. Take time to decide. Unless *you* have to be back somewhere."

Zoe thought about it. Shook her head. "I guess not."

"Well, then here comes Dulcie. The professor must be hungry. Let's get some lunch."

Bewildered at their *acceptance,* the word David had used, she let them lead her back toward the house while she fought the swell of "Circle of Life" in her head. But that's what it was, birth, life, death, birth, life . . .

"I'll make an omelet," she heard Floret say. "I picked some lovely mushrooms this morning."

In the circle of life.

Chapter 15

Eve wiped sweat from her forehead and brushed it off on her shorts. It wasn't that hot outside, it wasn't even that hot inside the basement laundry room, but her back hurt, her head hurt, and her eyes were still swollen and gritty from crying. She'd slept late at Mike's, had been tempted to spend the rest of the day there, but he worked at the local brewery on Mondays helping with their books, and she didn't want to be alone.

She might as well be alone now. Her children were barely speaking to each other and Mel wasn't talking to Eve at all.

She tried not to think. To just concentrate on the rhythmic folding of hotel linen as the dryers *thump-thump*ed in the background. It wasn't easy. She hadn't had to fold laundry for thirty-six rooms in a long time. She was getting soft.

Mondays were their changeover days. They'd had a full house over the weekend, and things had backed up. She'd already lost some of her summer staff to college preparation. Two of her usual laundry ladies had had family emergencies. Another was on a scheduled vacation.

Eve thought she and Mel and Noelle could handle the extra work, but it was not going well.

All machines, washing and drying, were running at capacity. She pulled a sheet out of the dryer. Noelle took the other half, both feeling around the edges of the fabric while stepping back until the sheet was taut. Noelle brought her corners to Eve, grabbed the bottom edge and handed it to Eve. Eve folded the last section while Noelle reached into the dryer and pulled out the next sheet. Eve placed her folded sheet on top of the pile on the table and reached for her half of the next sheet.

And felt like screaming.

None of them wanted to be here today. Mel was on towel duty and was going about her task as if she was the only person in the room. Eve knew she was still smarting over their morning argument.

She didn't appear to be speaking to Noelle either,

which was unusual. They fought like most sisters . . . at least, Eve imagined they did. Would she and Zoe have sister spats if Zoe stayed long enough to get to know her?

She handed her half of the sheet to Noelle, who went through the folding process, while Eve reached into the dryer for the next sheet.

This was mindless work, which she didn't always resent. It could be very Zen-like, folding laundry, but today it just made her more agitated.

She should be getting to know her sister. Trying to glue her family back together, so they could be a family and accept a new member. Hell, she could be out seeing the world. All those places she'd meant to visit.

She stuffed that thought neatly back into the recesses of her mind. She'd given up that plan decades ago and couldn't imagine why it had chosen to pop out now.

Maybe because of all the angst over Mel going to college. Really, most young women would give their eyeteeth to learn, to be able to have the wide array of experience in the world before them. Which was why she needed to make Mel understand the importance of education. Mel needed to know her options. Even if she chose to come back at the end, at least she would have had the chance.

"Mom?"

Eve snapped her head toward Noelle. The movement hurt her head.

"Do I need to put a quarter in to keep you going?"

"Sorry, I just spaced for a second." Eve straightened out her end of the sheet.

Oh, for a day off. A day of lying on her own beach without worrying about guests. A day getting to know her sister and half brother.

The price of success, she thought wryly. She had taken a neglected, dying hotel, bought by Hannah for a song, and turned it into a popular destination spa, twelve months a year. Last year they had even stayed open Christmas break. It was one of their most profitable weeks ever.

But what good were profits if two of your children weren't speaking to each other, and the other was living two thousand miles away?

Chris Bascombe stuck his head in the door. "Thought I might find you guys down here."

"Am I needed upstairs?" Eve asked. He didn't look at all like Zoe. He was blond and wiry. His personality was a lot more outgoing than Zoe's. He must take after his father, George Bascombe.

"Nope, everything's fine. The kid—" Chris slapped both hands to his head. "Oh God, anyone under thirty looks like a kid to me—the guy at the desk was playing

Words with Friends." He grinned. "He told me you were here. Seen my sister?"

None of them had.

Noelle placed a folded sheet on the stack. "Maybe she went down to Wind Chime House."

"Probably. I'm trying to get her to kick back. But she's on a mission." Chris abstractedly took a towel and began folding it. "I know she's anxious to get the whole thing over with, but . . ." He placed a perfectly folded towel on the stack.

Chris looked up to see the three women watching him. "I'm an actor. It's Monday. It must be laundry day. What can I say? It's a glamorous life."

"Are you saying she didn't want to come?" Eve asked.

"What? Well, not at first." He took another towel from the pile. "I mean, it's cool she found a whole other family we didn't know she had. Hell, I say the more, the merrier."

"Then what?" Mel asked in her first communication of the day.

He stopped midfold and looked at her, then at Noelle and Eve. "Oh, it's not you. She didn't even know you existed. She's over the moon about having a sister and nieces and stuff. So am I. It's the other family." He frowned at them. "You know. Over the ashes."

"What ashes?" Mel asked, growing pale.

Chris shot a panicked look at Eve. "Sorry, I— She didn't tell you? Not like her, she's usually very organized, like our mother."

"Like our mom," said Noelle. "But what ashes?"

"I imagine she didn't want to hit you with everything at once," Chris said. "That's how she found you. Mom designated her as the one to bring her ashes to Wind Chime Beach. None of us had ever heard of the place. Everybody at home is pretty pissed at her. That's why I came. I figured she could use the support. I didn't know I was going to find a whole other family." He clutched the towel to his chest. "Don't hold it against her. She's in a pretty unenviable position right now."

"Man," Noelle said. "Do you think we have aunts and uncles strewn across the country?"

"Our mother was not that kind of woman," Eve said.

"But Granddad was," Mel shot back. She yanked the towel from the pile and snapped it in the air.

"Stop it." Noelle snatched the towel from Mel and put it on the folding table. The two sisters glared at each other.

Chris took the towel and folded it.

Noelle turned to Eve. "How weird is that, to find

out that you'd grown up with a man who you thought was your father and then turned out not to be?"

"God," said Chris. "She hasn't even mentioned that. I wonder if she has even thought about it."

"Who? Thought about what?" Zoe walked into the room, stopped, and looked at the others, who had all stopped in a freeze-frame.

"Nothing," said Chris, and came forward to meet her. "I told them about Mom's ashes. I didn't realize they didn't know."

Zoe's eyes widened and her mouth slackened.

Eve hurried toward her. "It's okay. Just kind of a shock."

"I was going to tell you. But I thought there was so much else to say, and take in and . . . well."

"It doesn't matter. I'm glad you brought them."

"But where is she?" Mel asked.

"In my hotel room."

Noelle burst out laughing. "Sorry, but what if the maids throw her out by mistake?"

Zoe's mouth smiled against her will. It was a ludicrous possibility. But one she'd thought of before. "She's in a ceramic urn in the closet. I bring her out at night. I know that's crazy, but it seems mean-spirited to keep her in the closet. Plus, it's such a nice view."

Noelle snorted. "You're definitely our aunt. Too bad Harmony lives so far away; she'd love you."

"So, what are you going to do with her?" Mel asked.

Eve was anxious to know herself.

Zoe leaned her elbows on the folding table. "She didn't give me specific instructions. Just to take her ashes to Wind Chime Beach. At first I thought I would just come, find the beach, and when there was no one around, I'd say a few words and spread them, but things got more complicated. Floret and Henry want to do a big ceremony with you all there. If you'd want to come—or not. David Merrick said half your family doesn't want me. I guess that would be my father and grandmother. But who else?"

"Not us," Noelle said. "Right, Mel?"

Mel looked up from her folding. "Right."

Noelle made a face. "Don't mind her, she's sulking."

"Am not."

"Don't start." Eve shot a commanding look from one daughter to the other.

"It's just like being at home," Chris said. "Oh, shit. Are you going to ask the bros to come?"

Zoe pushed away from the folding table. "Ugh. I don't know. I want them to. But first I have to tell them I'm not even their whole sister. Maybe they're going to hate me."

"Nah. You're their sister." Chris's face fell. "But it may take them some time for them to get used to the new development." He turned to the others. "Very straight-laced, our brothers. Beautiful wives. Two point nine children. McMansions on cul-de-sacs. The whole nine yards. But nice people." He got an unholy gleam in his eyes. "Hey, Dil, want me to call them for you?"

"No!"

He stretched over and spun her around. "Just like Fred and Adele," he said. "We'll do it together."

She pushed him away. "I guess I have to tell them. What if they don't want me in the family anymore? And what about Dad?" Her eyes widened. "Oh my God, my dad isn't even my dad. What will I say to him?"

No one spoke. Even Mel quit folding.

"Well, you know what they say," Chris said.

Zoe shook her head. "What?"

"If it were done when 'tis done, then 'twere well it were done quickly."

Zoe groaned.

"Come on, let's text them now and schedule a conference call for ASAP." He guided her toward the door, casting a look back at Eve, Noelle, and Mel that would have been funny if the situation wasn't so dire.

Zoe stopped at the door. "Have you ever thought about using a laundry service?"

Chris gently pulled her out the door. "Come on, girl. No procrastinating."

"Do you think they'll disown her?" Mel asked, looking at the empty doorway.

Was she actually thinking about someone other than herself for a change? Eve wondered. Or was she worried about her own future with her family?

This all had to stop. Eve was sick of dissension. Her father's bitterness, her grandmother's feud and anger toward Eve and Zoe's mother. Hannah's determination to make Floret and Henry pay for something that had begun long before Zoe Bascombe had entered the scene. And Hannah, Eve had no doubt, would punish Mel if she dared enter into an alliance with Eli Merrick.

Eve shoved the sheet she'd been clutching for the past few minutes at Noelle. "I'll be back in a few."

"Wait? Where are you going?" Noelle asked.

"I don't know. I have to think."

"About hiring a laundry service?" Noelle asked.

"Among other things."

Mel ducked her head and concentrated on the stupid towel she was folding until she heard the door close behind her mother. Then she threw the towel on the folding table.

"Where are you going?" Noelle asked.

"To the bathroom."

"You better not think of skipping out and leaving me to do the rest of the folding."

"Why don't you get a job?"

"Why don't you get a life?"

"I will, and you can stuff this laundry. Zoe's right. We should hire a service."

"'We'?" Noelle gripped the sheet she was folding in front of her. "What 'we'? Do you pay for it? Do you work ten- or twelve-hour days to keep this place running? No, you don't. You sit at the reception desk streaming videos for a few hours a few times a week, and you have to fold a few towels when things get backed up."

"Well, what about you? Mom didn't pay for you to go to college just so you could come home and mooch off her. A lot of good it did you."

"At least I have options."

"Doesn't look like it to me."

"Then go. Get out and go have some fun."

"I will." Mel headed for the door. Stopped at the threshold. "You're wrinkling the towel."

"Just go."

And Mel went, but not before she saw Noelle's face start to crumple.

Mel's stomach lurched, and she turned away and ran

down the hall, her sister's expression seared into her mind. Not just anger, but something else that made Mel blush hot with shame. Her sister was scared. Of what?

Mom being angry? What was going on with Zoe Bascombe? Because Noelle couldn't get a job? Because she thought she was letting them all down?

She wasn't. Noelle was really talented, and she'd studied hard and graduated cum laude. She was just having a hard time finding a job. It wasn't her fault. She would get a good job in the end, Mel was sure of it.

She ran until she was out on the back lawn in the sun. Her steps slowed. She should go back and tell Noelle not to worry. Besides, she couldn't really leave her to finish up alone.

She turned to go back, but she really needed to talk to Eli. If she cut across their hotel beach, she could see him and come back. It would hardly take any time at all.

He'd come straight over last night to tell her that he thought he'd done well on his exam, but he didn't stay long; he said he still had to study. She could tell he was excited about going away. More excited than he was about staying with her.

Mel just wanted things to stay the same. She wasn't

smart or talented like Noelle—and look at her. All that work and she was back living at home.

Noelle had been so happy when she graduated; now she didn't think she was so great. Mel didn't want to admit it, but she was kind of glad, in a mean-girl way.

And that made her feel worse. Noelle wasn't mean. Mel was. Especially when she didn't understand what was going on. Like now. And that scared her.

She was scared. So was Noelle. Maybe her mom was scared, too.

She turned to go back, took two steps toward the inn, then turned and ran down the path to the beach.

Zoe and Chris sat on the bed in her hotel room, heads together, Zoe too upset to even cry.

"Don't worry about it, Dil. They'll come around."

"And if they don't?"

"They will." But he didn't sound totally convinced to Zoe.

"It was almost like they'd been waiting for my call," she said.

"It was the fastest text to conference call I've witnessed in years," Chris agreed. He pushed off the bed and went over to the mini fridge. Took out a bottle of wine and a can of beer.

Zoe shook her head. "I think I'll be sick if I drink that."

"Because you probably haven't eaten today. Have you?"

Zoe shrugged. "I . . . don't remember."

"Well, I'm calling room service." He picked up the phone. "And then we'll go out on the town. Catch some action. You can sit in with the local band, I'll applaud in all the right places while I'm checking out the scene. It'll be just like the good old days in Manhattan."

The good old days. She tried to smile. She'd loved making the rounds of the music clubs and bars with Chris. He'd always been supportive. Even now.

But still. Trying to talk to Errol had been hard. Maybe the hardest thing she'd ever done. Hands down the hardest phone call she'd ever made. It started out okay. They'd been concerned for her. Though she noticed no one had tried calling or texting her to see if she'd made it.

And then she hit them with the news. Her mother had sent her to Wind Chime Beach because she had another daughter there. That had been met with total silence. Then she hit them with the rest. That she was only their half sister.

"God, that was awful," she said after Chris hung up the phone.

“I thought onion rings would cheer you up,” he said.

“They do—I mean the other stuff.”

“The part where Errol refused to believe you were only a half sister, or when Robert screamed, ‘They’re after your inheritance!’ What a putz.”

She laughed. It had been rather hysterical. “I don’t know how Laura puts up with him.”

“By being a saint in public and putting it to him when they get home.”

“No.”

“He’ll be calling to apologize before the night is out. Mark my words.”

“But he’s right.”

“What? That Eve Gordon is after your measly quarter of a mil. Have you looked at this place? Gold mine.”

“No. About the inheritance.”

“Lost me.”

“I’m not a Bascombe.”

“Sure you are.”

Zoe gave him a look.

“Well, half maybe, and our dad isn’t any great shakes.” He sighed and dropped his hands and shoulders in an over-the-top reaction that always made her laugh. “I’d much rather have a father who was a rock star than a bloated, philandering lawyer who deserted us for his secretary. Unimaginative even in Long Island.”

"Maybe I should give it back."

"Your inheritance? Are you nuts? You're Mom's daughter, it's her fortune and her choice. And have you ever known our mother not to organize everything just the way she wants it?"

Except twice in her life.

"So just get that out of your head right now." His frown turned to a big smile. "Besides, if you did, I'd have to share my third with you, cause that's how we roll, sister mine."

"Oh, Chris, I do love you."

"Ditto."

"I didn't even get a chance to invite them to the ceremony."

"Well, hell, you haven't planned one yet. Have you?"

Zoe shook her head.

"Plenty of time. They'll come around. We'll leave it to the wives for that one. Just hang here with the Gordons for a bit and let things take their course. Not to be insensitive or anything, but there's really no rush." He lifted his beer can toward the dresser and the green urn. "You don't mind hanging for a while, do you, Mom?"

"Chris."

"I know. Sacrilegious, but so was she, when you think about it. And she kept you and Eve secret for so many years. I wish I had known *that* woman." He sniffed.

So did Zoe.

"Well, that's settled," he said.

"And what about you?"

"Me?" He grinned. "I'll provide moral support and handle the guest list." He walked out to the balcony and leaned over the rail.

She followed him out.

"I mean what about your life. Do you have to get back to the city right away? I love having you here, but aren't you getting antsy to get back to auditioning? Or have you decided to go to Chicago?"

"Hey, isn't that Mel out on the lawn?"

"Yeah," Zoe said, watching Mel turn in one direction then the other. "What's she doing?"

"Her slo-mo Wonder Woman act?"

Then Mel broke into a run headlong across the lawn and down the path to the beach.

"Uh-oh, trouble in Laundry City."

Zoe turned to look at him. "Think we should intervene?"

Chris gave her a look that said, Stupid question.

"What should I do?"

"What you do best. Fix things."

Zoe had already started for the door. She should probably just stay out of it, but Mel was family. So was Chris. "Then we fix you."

The last thing she heard before the door closed behind her, was Chris's voice. "Can you put a hold on that room-service order?"

Zoe took the elevator to the path that led straight down to the beach. There were a few people sunbathing, but she didn't see Mel anywhere. She walked over to where the footpath opened onto the sand. No sign of Mel. Maybe she had changed her mind and gone back.

Zoe made one last sweep of the beach. And found her. Sitting on the top of the jetty, her arms clasped tight around her knees, her head buried.

One unhappy teenager. Teenager-dom was a decade behind Zoe but she recognized Mel's "the whole world's against me" posture. The "nobody understands me" depths of despair. God knows she'd felt it all when she realized she'd lost her chance at Juilliard, and even before that. Now that she thought about it, the prom, the cheerleading squad, all the things that she hardly remembered now but had been worthy of so much angst then.

They had diminished in her mind, but that didn't mean she couldn't still sympathize with the pain they'd caused.

She took off her shoes and trudged over the sand. Climbed up the rocks and out to where her niece sat.

Maybe she just wanted to be alone.

But Zoe also remembered wishing she could talk to someone who would just listen. Her mother had listened but never really heard. Zoe would be different with her niece. Hopefully.

She sat down on the rock next to Mel. "Hey."

"Go away."

Zoe didn't move.

Mel turned her head enough to glare at her. "I wish you'd never come."

"Ouch," Zoe said, reminding herself that she was the adult here. "I know this is pretty unsettling. At least you've always known who your family was. Imagine my surprise."

Mel's head rose a little higher. "You mean you really had no idea?"

"None."

"What are you going to do?"

"Spread my mom's ashes. Look for a new job. Get on with my life. Like the rest of the world."

"You make it sound easy."

"Do I? Then don't listen to me. It isn't easy. It kind of makes me sick to think about what's going to happen next." She was here to help Mel, she reminded herself. Not let all her own insecurities make things worse.

"Really, it does?"

"Make me sick? Yeah, it kinda does."

"Me, too." Mel frowned at her. "But you know what you want to do."

"Do I? Glad I fooled somebody."

Mel straightened up and turned to face her. "You mean you don't know?"

"I know what I could do. What I might do. What I might have to do. But I'll figure it out when I have to."

"I wish I knew what to do. But it seems like even if you want to do something, it doesn't work out. Harmony wanted to be a teacher. Noelle wants to be a graphic artist. Harmony is always pregnant, and Noelle can't get a job."

"She will. What about you?"

"What do I want?"

"Yeah, what do you want?"

"I don't know. I just want to marry Eli and stay home and raise our children. A lot of people do that."

"That's cool. If you have enough money."

Mel shrugged. "I guess I would have to get a part-time job. I like working the reception desk okay. Except Mom is so set about me going to college. I know I should be grateful and I am, it's just . . . Everyone seems to know what they want to do, and I don't. I'm such a loser. Maybe there's something wrong with me."

Zoe laughed. "Sorry, not laughing at you, but at how much you sound like me."

"No, I don't. You're a successful event planner."

"I wanted to be a songwriter."

"You did? What happened?"

"My family wanted me to go into business. I blew my audition at Juilliard, so I went into business."

"That sucks."

"It turned out that I liked my job. And now that I think about it, I could have been writing music as well. You don't need an office to do that." *You just have to have the guts,* she told herself.

"I think Mom wanted to travel, but that's not a profession."

"It could be. Look at Eli's uncle. He travels for work. Do you want to travel?"

"I don't think so. Well, maybe a little. But I like being here, where everything is . . . I don't know."

"Safe?"

Mel hesitated, bit her lip, then slowly nodded.

"Home will always be here."

Mel turned to fully look at her, frowning as if that hadn't occurred to her.

"Look at the professor. He goes off to see the world. But he always comes back. One day he'll probably retire here for good."

"But what about Eli? He might go and not want to come back."

"I don't know much, but I do know better than to depend on another person for my own happiness. You kind of have to find your own place and once you've done that, other people make it better. But you have to make it for yourself first."

Mel turned away, looked out to the waves. "My family kinda sucks at doing that. Not Noelle and Mom. But Granddad never got over your mom, did he? That's why he's so bitter. And Granna has to control everybody's life . . . because she isn't happy with herself. Am I like that?"

How did Zoe answer something like that? She was so tempted to say, You'll understand when you're older. But she was older and she didn't have a clue.

"I don't think so. You don't have to be."

"Do you have a . . . a significant other?"

Zoe laughed. "I'm still a work in progress."

Mel snorted. Rolled her eyes.

Zoe stood up. "Come on."

"Where to?"

"To the nude-beach side. We're going skinny-dipping."

"No way."

"Double-dog dare you." Zoe scrambled off the jetty and ran across the sand to the private beach.

"Wait, Zoe, you can't. We'll be in so much trouble."

"Try and stop me," Zoe called over her shoulder, and started pulling her T-shirt over her head.

Mel caught up to her and grabbed the tail of Zoe's shirt. Zoe spun around and they both fell fully clothed into the surf.

Mel sputtered, and Zoe, laughing, took the opportunity to splash her. Mel splashed back. Zoe jumped up and began kicking water. Mel grabbed her ankle, and they fell together laughing in the surf.

In the end they didn't go skinny-dipping. Actually, Zoe hadn't really planned to. But they had a little fun before they finally staggered out of the water, holding on to each other and giggling.

They stood on the sand, panting, until Mel stood upright, suddenly serious again. "I left Noelle to do all the laundry by herself. I gotta go."

She took off over the sand and was soon sprinting up the path.

Zoe gathered up their shoes and her cell phone and followed more slowly, texting as she went. *Forget room service. Put on your high-heel sneakers, bro, 'cause we're going out tonight.*

Chapter 16

David and Henry sat stretched out on two chaises on the front lawn, drinking beer and watching the ocean sky go through its pyrotechnics of sunset. The smell of fresh-mowed grass mixed with salt air. David was half thinking about going to get his camera, but he had photographed thousands of sunsets from all over the world and tonight there were more important things on his mind.

He glanced back to the house and Eli's window. He was inside studying. He'd been studying for weeks whenever he wasn't with Mel. Even more since returning from taking his exam. David didn't know what that meant. Did he think he was accepted? What was he going to do about Mel? How was David going to see him through if he left before Eli got started?

"I got a gig offer today," he said into space.

Henry made a "go on" sound but kept looking at the sky.

"September through most of October."

"Where is it?"

"Patagonia."

Henry chuckled and pulled on his beer. "Had enough of civilization?"

"Not really. Well, yeah, sort of. It's a travel shoot, but there are also some interesting caves and . . . but I don't know."

"What's stopping you?"

"I don't . . ." David tapped his beer bottle with one finger, started again. "Here's the thing . . ." He wished Henry would help him out here. He wasn't sure why he was worried about leaving. He'd done it plenty of times before. But usually not for so long and not when everything was up in the air.

"First of all, there's Eli."

"I have no doubt he'll be accepted into the pre-semester program and then he'll start college. Floret and I will make sure he gets settled." Henry turned his head on the chair cushion. "I'll even wear jeans and a button-down shirt." He grinned.

David grinned back and was struck with a wave of love and trust he didn't often let loose. He'd known

Henry for most of his life; he'd been like a grandfather, uncle, mentor, and friend all rolled into one. He trusted him completely with Eli and anything else.

"I guess I'm just worried that he'll feel abandoned."

"Floret will keep him stocked with cookies. The regular kind."

"I know but . . ."

"You feel responsible."

"Yeah, even though I know you're the ones who have really raised him. And I can't tell you—"

"Then don't."

"But—"

"But nothing. You know what they say. It takes a village. Not sure who said it, but they were right. We'll be here for him until you get back."

"I know, but I'm kind of worried about him. He's been remote lately. I don't think he's even seen Mel since he got back from the exam. Do you think they broke up?"

Henry laughed, slapped his knee.

"Really. I mean, it would be for the best, but then I feel bad for thinking that way."

"Well, if you're worried about him, go talk to him."

David glanced back at the house. "He doesn't seem to want to talk to me lately."

"It's what kids do when they're making the break from their parents."

"Does he seem different to you?"

"He seems preoccupied. And he and Mel might be feeling like they're stuck between the Montagues and the Capulets."

"Nobody's against them going out together. But the sex thing."

Henry burst out laughing.

"You laugh, but look at Eve and Zoe Bascombe."

"Now you're thinking Eli and Mel are doomed to repeat history?"

"Actually. Well, hell, I was down tearing out the steps to the beach, which I didn't finish because Zoe interrupted me. Anyway, she found a sleeping bag and a bunch of stuff under the steps. They belonged to Mel and Eli."

"They're young and in love. If you think they're not using protection, say something." Henry shook his head. "That I should have come to this. Advice on birth control. But I wouldn't worry. Eli's had the talk from both of us and probably Floret, too. And I'm sure Eve has done the same with Mel."

"It isn't that."

"Then what is it? Spit it out."

"I kind of got pissed off and tossed the place and then threw the stuff in the dumpster."

"What the hell did you do that for?"

"I don't know. It was such a suck-ass thing to do. I don't know what got into me."

"Fear."

"Jeez, Henry."

"Loss of control, maybe?"

"I think it's because I'm an idiot."

"Possibly."

"It sounds stupid, but it was more of a reaction not to what they might do, but what Hannah would do. You heard her."

"Ah. We've been dealing with Hannah Gordon since before you were born. We lost her somewhere along the way. But we all live our lives in our own way."

"That would be fine if she just wasn't so intent on destroying yours. And mine and Eli's. And now she's talking about trying to buy Kelly's place just to get back at you. Because it isn't just the land she wants, is it? Why does Hannah hate you so much? I vaguely remember her and Eve living at the commune when we first came. Eve used to babysit me and Andy. Hannah wasn't so awful then, was she? Then one day they left, no one ever said why. I'm asking now. I never felt like it was my business before, but now I do, if Eli's going to be caught in the middle."

Henry drew on his beer, then sat up to face David. "We don't know. And that's the honest truth. I'm not sure even Hannah knows why she is like she is. The reason got lost in history, years ago, but she just can't seem to stop. She's attached her own disappointments to Lee's, and they're so muddled up in it that it just grows and grows whether they nurture it or not. Slaves to their own disappointment. Sad, but not for us to change. And not for you to worry about."

"She's vicious."

"David, you can't stop Hannah Gordon from being herself. It's a futile occupation." Henry smiled and leaned back in the chaise. "Do you remember when you first came here?"

"Yes, sort of. I remember being here. I don't remember before then."

"You were just a tyke. Just turned four, and Andy was six. Your parents had had some rough times. They needed a refuge. They found it here. And they went on to do good things. Some people are like that."

"And some people aren't," David said.

"And so the world goes. If you're worried, you should go tell him so."

"I'm not worried. Not exactly."

"It's best that truth come to light. . ."

"Oh hell, don't quote Shakespeare at me. I'm going." David pushed himself out of the chair.

Henry gave him a thumbs-up and took a swig of his beer.

David didn't normally hesitate talking to his nephew. They got along pretty well. But lately, everything around them seemed so volatile. They'd already had a couple of run-ins about Mel. David had nothing against the girl. He just didn't want them doing something stupid just to prove they were in love.

That thought stopped him halfway up the stairs.

Maybe Eli's silence was due to worry over the outcome of the exam, or disappointment because he hadn't done as well as he'd wanted. He hadn't come straight home to tell them. He'd parked David's old station wagon in the yard and gone straight out. Probably to meet Mel.

Had they met at Old Beach? Did they know he had tossed their "love nest." *Love nest?* Hell, he was beginning to sound like Henry and Floret.

Eli's door was open. He was sitting at his desk in the dusky room, his desk lamp shining on his bent head.

He was so engrossed in whatever he was studying that he didn't hear David coming to the door.

And David just stood in the doorway watching him, remembering.

Eli reached for a soda at the edge of the desk, which put his face in profile, and David's heart clenched a little.

He was looking more and more like his father every day.

David had always looked up to his big brother. Strong, confident, compassionate, adventurous. He traveled the world taking risks, reveled in it. Then one day he fell in love, settled down to have a family. Play it safe in the suburbs, he'd say a little ruefully. Then lost his life on the way home from the movies, some drunk driver . . .

That it was ironic made it even harder to accept. David had thought he'd never get over his grief or the panic of suddenly finding himself guardian of a ten-year-old boy.

Henry and Floret had taken them in, soothed them, given them time, kept them safe. Henry introduced the confused, angry young boy to the thing he loved most beside Floret. Science. And Eli had blossomed. David had learned to cope. Though even now he still had jolting-awake dreams, when the sheer weight of his responsibility sent his heart pounding.

He needed his time away from that, not to shirk his responsibilities but to remind himself of the internal efficiency of nature.

Zoe Bascombe had asked why there were no people in his photos. He'd taken plenty of Eli growing up, of their life with Henry and Floret at the commune. But that was recording family history for Eli when he was older, for the next generation of his family, for Henry and Floret and their life at the commune, the good times, when the remembered times grew fuzzy in their minds—and his.

His professional photos were for his sanity, where he could lose himself in the consistency of it all—where even the irregularities made a pattern. Even when he couldn't see it himself, he knew it was there. It might disrupt, disperse, disappear, even, but it merely became part of another pattern and continued on.

He'd come back renewed, grounded, his mind clear. A kind of Zen cleansing of his existence. There were days, sometimes weeks when he hardly saw or spoke to another person.

He didn't really miss people, until he came back and realized he'd forgotten how to incorporate them into his life. He had the day-to-day stuff down pretty well, the guys at the diner, at the bar where the locals hung out, with Henry and Floret, with Eli.

It had taken a long time for him to accept his role of caretaker of his nephew; he had no experience, no understanding. Eventually he'd learned to enjoy and love Eli, for himself, for both their selves, Eli's and David's.

With Henry and Floret's help of course. He couldn't have done it without them. But it had left his own—what?—personal life? This was his personal life. His private life? Photography was his private life.

His love life. He had none. He went on dates sometimes. Not often. It just seemed senseless. A good time, maybe sex, then what? He couldn't commit to a relationship. Between work and Eli and keeping the commune afloat, he had his hands full.

Now Eli would be leaving soon. He'd thought he was prepared. It was weird. He'd gone from clueless and frightened at suddenly having a kid to be responsible for, to trying to be a father while trying desperately not to replace Eli's father. Now he was feeling like a father must, wanting to send Eli equipped into the world, and yet wanting to keep him close.

With Eli gone, he really wouldn't have a reason for sticking around. Henry and Floret could manage without him. They hardly seemed to notice when he was gone. Always welcomed him back like he'd just popped out to the grocery store.

As for David, he didn't think he could settle down to this life without the other. Hoped that when his time came, it would be out in the wild and not at the hands of a drunk driver as he was coming home from the movies.

He intended to face life—and death—head-to-head.

He knocked on the doorframe. “Busy?”

“Just studying. What’s up?”

David came into the bedroom. A teenager’s room. Dirty socks on the floor, a Nerf basketball hoop suctioned to the closet door. Magazines, books, an iPad lay on the lightweight quilt on Eli’s twin bed. It could be a bedroom anywhere in the country.

“We didn’t get much of a chance to talk about your day at the exam.”

Eli glanced over his shoulder. “Yeah, we did. It was fine.” He swiveled his chair around. “I met some cool people. The exam seemed fair. I think I did okay. We’ll just have to wait and see.”

So it wasn’t that.

“How’s Mel? I haven’t seen her much lately.”

Eli shrugged. “You know.”

No, he didn’t know.

Eli turned back to his desk. It was a cue that he was finished with the conversation, but David wasn’t. If nothing else, he needed to confess his tossing of their stuff on the beach and why.

“Listen. I was down at the beach, Old Beach. I’m

tearing down the stairs, they're rotten and dangerous. I found a bunch of stuff and threw it out. I mean . . ."

"It doesn't matter."

"Hey, talk to me."

"About what?"

"Whatever's going on."

"I'm studying. I realized that I'm behind in several areas so I have to bone up to not look like a total jerkwad when, if, I get into the program. Henry got me into the Stanford library online."

"Good thinking. Everything else okay?"

"Yeah."

"Okay. I'll yell when dinner's ready."

"Okay."

David got to the door.

"Uncle David?"

"What is it?"

Eli shrugged.

David came back into the room and sat on the bed. Eli sat down next to him.

There was a long, drawn-out silence while David held still and waited for the worst.

"Don't get mad."

"I won't."

"Mel's grandfather caught us down on the beach Saturday night."

"What was he doing down there?" A stupid question—the kid was having a crisis and David was worried about some old man trespassing on the commune's property.

"He grabbed Mel. And yelled at us. Told me to get off his beach. It's not his beach. It's Floret's and Henry's.

"Mel ran away. She's afraid of him. Then he told me that if Mel got, you know, that nobody would help us. And he was going to tell Hannah all about us. I hate them both."

David glanced at the open door. "Yeah, I don't blame you. I don't really like them either, but try not to hate them for Henry's and Floret's sakes."

"Why don't they stick up for themselves? I'm not going to let the Gordons tell me what to do."

David tried to think what Andy would say if he were alive. Even after all these years, David still sometimes felt he was struggling in uncharted waters.

"What do you want to do?"

Eli grasped his hands between his knees and looked at the floor. "I don't know. I told Mel that we should cool it, until things die down."

David nodded.

"You don't think they'll hurt her, do you?"

"Of course not. This is really more about Hannah and her 'issues' than you and Mel. Hannah is overly loyal to her kin. She won't hurt Mel, but she might hurt Henry and Floret." Though David wasn't so sure about Lee.

"You think we should cool it." Eli shrugged. "I know you do."

"I just want you to follow your dream."

"Oh God. That's such a nerdy thing to say."

"Yeah, well, that's me. The all-supreme and magnificent nerd."

Eli laughed, then his expression fell. "Mel's afraid that when we go to college we won't . . . you know. Stay together. She doesn't want to go to college. I get it. There's nothing she's excited to learn. You know? Like, she'd just be going to get a general education."

"That's how most people start."

"I guess, but it's hard for her."

David nodded.

"I think she wants me to stay here."

David sat up. "Instead of going to school?"

Eli nodded.

"But you still want to go, right?"

"Yeah, but I don't want to leave her here alone."

"She's not exactly alone, and plus, she's supposed to go to college, too."

"But she feels alone. And now with Lee and Hannah threatening Floret and Henry again . . ."

"I don't think this latest outburst has anything to

do with you and Mel. I think it's because of Zoe Bascombe."

"The lady who says she's Eve's sister?"

"She is Eve's sister."

"They should be glad to have more normal family."

"Yeah," said David. "They should."

"What am I going to do?"

"You're going to catch up with your studies and leave the Gordons to me."

It was nine o'clock the next morning when Zoe's cell phone rang. She was awake but she hadn't ventured out of bed. She was pretty sure she was going to have a hangover.

She and Chris had hit several music bars the night before. She'd never been able to keep up with Chris's idea of fun. She vaguely remembered sitting in with a couple of the bands. In fact, she had written down e-mail addresses of several musicians on a napkin. She could see the napkin on the table across the room where her phone buzzed away.

She eased back the covers. Slowly sat up. Blinked. *Hmm.* Not so bad. She stood up. Definitely a little pounding on the left side of her head. She padded across the room and picked up the phone.

Chris.

"Hello?"

"Oh, man, don't tell me I woke you up?"

"No. But what are you doing up?"

"Things to do, agents to see."

Now she knew she must have a hangover, because her stomach flip-flopped.

"You got an audition?"

"Maybe, but I got something better than that."

"A part?"

"A callback for our niece."

"Huh?"

"You know, Noelle interviewed last week in the city? Well, they called her back this morning, they want her to come in again."

"That's great," Zoe said.

"And I thought, why don't I drive her down? I can check in with my agent, show her the sights, and drive her back. If I can borrow your car. You aren't using it, are you?"

Zoe eased herself down into the closest chair. *He was leaving?* "My car? No. Sure, you're welcome to take it. You're coming back?"

"Of course I'm coming back. Weren't you listening? We'll be back as soon as Noelle knows something."

"And if *you* get work?" She cringed, knowing how needy she sounded and not wanting to put pressure on her brother. "I'm just worried about my car." She laughed, or at least meant to. She'd had every intention of doing this by herself. Had never considered doing it any other way. But she'd never been so glad to see Chris in her life, and now she didn't want to lose him. She wouldn't lose him, in spite of whatever happened. Would she?

"I'm coming back for the ashes thing definitely. Anyway, you never just get a part, you know that. There will be callbacks, etcetera. I may have to do some running back and forth if something looks good. But I haven't even heard of anything that sounds interesting. Still, it's good to show your face."

He'd only been gone three days. But his show had closed several weeks before, she reminded herself.

She pulled herself together. "That's great about Noelle. When are you leaving?"

"Not until after breakfast, if you can get your slugabed body downstairs in the next few minutes."

"I'll hurry." She stood, her hangover forgotten. "They won't seat you until everyone in your party is there."

"Sure they will. I have an in with the owner."

"I'll still hurry." She hung up, jumped in the shower long enough to wet her hair, threw on some clothes, and hurried downstairs.

Four hours later, Zoe, Eve, and Mel stood outside the inn saying good-bye to Chris and Noelle.

"I know you'll ace the interview," Eve said.

"Thanks," Noelle said, and gave Eve a big hug.

"And be sure to call Joyce Redfern while you're there," Zoe said. "She's expecting you, and she heads a great graphics department and everybody says she's a love to work for. Even if nothing comes of it, just knowing that someone else is interested in you might put some pressure on them at your interview."

"Thanks, I will. Thanks so much."

Zoe gave her a quick hug.

"Drive carefully," Eve said.

"I will," Chris said, and put Noelle's suitcase in the back seat of Zoe's SUV. "Hey, I remembered this." He dragged out Zoe's old guitar.

Zoe made a desperate face at him.

He just grinned. "You may need this while you're here." He pushed it into her hands and kissed her cheek. "So wow them."

"I wouldn't dare," Zoe hissed back at him.

"Don't worry. You'll do fine. Just enjoy your sister time. We'll be back before you know it, Silly Dilly. Make sure she practices her chords." Chris gave Eve a kiss, then said, "Oh what the hell," and kissed Mel, too.

He waved when he got into the driver's side of the car. "Adieu and adieu and adieu."

"Me too," said Noelle, and got in the car.

Before she closed the door, Mel ran to her, gave her a hug. "Good luck, I know you can do it."

Noelle looked taken aback.

"Ready when you are, CB," Chris called.

"I'm ready," Noelle said, and closed the door.

"They'll be great together," Zoe said.

"Looks like it," Eve agreed. "Well, just us girls. What shall we do?"

"Don't you have to do hotel things?" Zoe asked.

"Always, but Tuesday is a slow day compared to the weekend. I can make time for my sister."

Eve smiled, but Zoe noticed that Mel didn't. "What are you up to today?" Zoe asked her.

Mel shrugged. Looked at her mom.

"You can hang with Zoe and me, or you can take the day off. I think it's time we had a little holiday. Who's on the desk today?"

"Carly."

"Great. We'll stick close and I'll keep my cell handy."

"I . . . I think I'll go out for a while."

"Fine. Maybe we'll all have dinner together later."

Mel hesitated. "I'll see what's going on."

"Sure. Let us know."

Her gaze slid past Zoe and Eve, and she hurried off.

"I didn't think our last summer together would be like this."

"Cutting those apron strings," Zoe said. "I'm not sure I ever did. I think maybe it would have been better, but water under the bridge and all."

"I wish you'd tell her that."

They walked back into the hotel.

Zoe lifted her guitar. "Let me get rid of this, before anyone sees me," said Zoe. "Then maybe you could show me around the hotel. I've hardly had a chance to see any of the programs or anything."

"You're interested?"

"Of course. I want to know everything about you and my nieces. If that's okay," she added hurriedly.

"I'd love it. We can put this in the office and I'll give you the tour."

They stowed the guitar out of sight and left instructions for the receptionist.

"You've seen the dining room and the bar. There are also two meeting rooms on this floor and a small ballroom that we use for yoga and tai chi during winter and inclement weather."

They walked down the hall and into a large room with a shining wooden floor. The ceilings were high and once again French doors let in a stream of sunlight and a view of the lawn and the ocean beyond.

"Wow," Zoe said. "It seems like every room has an ocean view."

"It was a real beauty in its day. Actually, we've only restored part of it. The whole third floor is still unfinished."

"You're kidding. Why?" Zoe clamped her mouth shut. "If I get too snoopy, just tell me. I'm used to butting in and taking over. Kind of have to in my business."

"Ask anything. You're family. And I feel stupid, but what exactly is your business?"

As they toured the second floor, Zoe explained what a project manager actually did. "You know, setting up events for clients, keeping everyone conducting the event on the same page, arranging transpo, accommodations, food for guests, coordinating vendors, managing event teams. Stuff like that."

"It sounds mind-boggling."

"You just have to be efficient and have a thick skin."

"So when you told me to hire a laundry service, you knew what you were talking about."

"No. I don't know anything about your expenses, but generally in my business, you don't use experts in one field to do the job of experts in another field.

Inefficient, costly, and with usually inferior outcomes over the long haul. Just my opinion. Like I said."

Eve had to use a key to open the elevator doors on the third floor.

"Yikes, it's a little like *The Shining*," Zoe said as they stepped out into a hallway of wall sconces and faded fleur-de-lis wallpaper. "You know that Jack Nicholson movie?"

Eve laughed. "I know it. I saw it the first time around."

Zoe looked up and down the hall. "All guest rooms?"

"Actually, no. And if I had a bigger operation . . . well, come and see." She led Zoe to the left and opened a set of double doors.

Zoe stopped in her tracks. "OMG." She stepped onto the dusty wooden floor of a huge dining room. The old tables and chairs were still stacked along the walls. Heavy brocade drapes hung from ornate, patina-covered rods.

Eve walked across the room, leaving footprints on the dusty floorboards. She pulled open a pair of drapes, releasing a cloud of dust motes and revealing the most spectacular view Zoe had ever seen.

She joined Eve at the window. "I can't believe you left this to last. It's an incredible venue."

"It is," Eve agreed. "But just a little beyond my ability. I'd need to grow the staff and it would cost a lot. We've always been pretty much a family-style business—part of the appeal. I'm not sure I could maintain everything without going corporate, which I refuse to do. We're successful because of our personalized attention and our laid-back atmosphere. The thought of taking it to the next level is just a little overwhelming."

"I get that. But still . . ."

Eve closed the drapes, and they returned to the hallway. "There's a kitchen down at the end of the hall, but it's been gutted. The equipment was totally unusable and we decided it would be safer just to get rid of it all."

Zoe nodded. All in all, Eve had done a wonderful job with the renovation and the ambiance. Had a happy, helpful staff. And, from what she'd said and Zoe could see, had made Solana a success. "You're pretty amazing," she said.

"Thanks. What do you say we walk down to the beach? I seem to never get down there. I'll show you the classes that are in session on the way."

"Sounds great."

"Maybe you could tell me about growing up with our mother. And then . . ." Eve pressed the elevator button. They stepped in and the doors closed behind them. "And then I think you should meet our father."

Chapter 17

"No."

"You can't just keep trying to avoid each other," Eve said. "It's a small town."

"He resents me. He won't even acknowledge me. It's better I just do what I have to do and leave."

"No." Tears filled Eve's eyes, and Zoe moved to her.

"We won't let him come between us. Okay? He doesn't have to accept me. It's only important that you do." Zoe gave Eve a quick hug. It felt strange. More than a girlfriend hug. A sister hug. "And since you've sorta, kinda, half taken the day off, why don't we go down to the beach and laze in the sun for a minute?"

"Okay, but you're still going to have to deal with each other before you go."

Zoe let it pass. Her father didn't want to see her,

didn't want to have anything to do with her. Would her Long Island father feel the same way? He hadn't paid much attention to any of them since he'd started a second family. He'd come to the funeral, expressed his condolences with the rest of the guests, and left.

Well, she was an adult, and she didn't need a father in her life now that she didn't have a mother.

But she did have a sister who wanted her, and at least one half brother. *Oh, Mom, how could you have screwed up so royally?*

Zoe and Eve didn't talk on their way down the beach path. They stopped at the edge of the sand. A few guests were relaxing in chaises set up beneath brightly colored umbrellas. A group class of something that looked like Pilates was taking place near the water's edge.

"You should spend more time down here," Zoe said.

"I know. Amazing, isn't it? Like all your troubles just flutter away when you're at the beach."

Zoe nodded. "But they don't really."

"No. But it's enough just to give you time to regroup."

"True."

Ahead of them, the refreshment cabana looked more like an open-front beach house. Lively blue-and-white-striped canvas curtains were pulled back from lattice columns across the front. A concession counter ran along the back. A semicircle of changing rooms and showers sat off to one side against the lawn.

"I didn't notice the other day how big the cabana is," Zoe said. "You could do dinners down here."

"We have for a few weddings. A pain. It only has a grill, not a full kitchen."

The concessioner saw them coming, put down his tablet, and waved.

Eve waved back. "At ease," she called. "Just us chickens."

Zoe stared at her. "Mom used to say that. I never knew what it meant. That's just weird."

"Not really," Eve said. "Floret used to say it all the time. We probably picked it up from her."

"Six degrees of separation," Zoe said.

"And I still don't know what *that* means. Come on." Eve struck off across the sand in the direction of Wind Chime House.

Zoe hurried after her. "You said Floret used to say it? Doesn't she anymore?"

Eve stopped. "No . . . she doesn't. At least . . ."

They both looked at the black rocks of the jetty that tumbled across the width of the beach like a poorly healed scar.

A sign posted where the rocks met the lawn read PRIVATE. KEEP OUT. And the image of Mel sitting on the jetty rose in Zoe's mind. Half in one world, half in the other, and not belonging to either. The symbolism was hard to ignore. *Just like Romeo and Juliet.*

"Isn't it ridiculous?" Eve said. "I hate that it's cut the beach in two."

"Then why does it? Does anybody on their side even go down there? Naked or not?"

"Not really. It was Hannah's doing. I was thinking about expanding the inn and asked Henry and Floret if they'd be willing to rent me their portion of the beach, with the stipulation they could use it, just not nude. After all, they have Old Beach, which I guess they used to call Wind Chime Beach. I offered decent money and all was on its way, until Hannah decided we should buy the beach and the land behind it outright, for expansion. Then things fell apart. As they always do between the three of them. Hannah threatened, they withdrew their acceptance of my offer, and the next day, trucks arrived to build the jetty. Floret and Henry were forced to put up the sign to protect themselves legally. Actually, it was David who put up the sign."

They began walking toward the jetty.

"Look, there's Floret."

Zoe looked toward Wind Chime House to where a big straw hat bobbed above the rows of beans like a sailboat.

Tacitly, they squeezed past the sign to the other side of the jetty, where another stretch of pristine sand greeted them.

"Not much of a deterrent," Zoe said.

"No," Eve agreed. "Just an eyesore."

They crossed the sand and climbed up the slope of lawn to the house.

Someone had mowed the rest of the lawn. From this angle Wind Chime House didn't look as ramshackle as it had before. Nothing close to the carefully restored old hotel behind them. And yet both were havens in their own way.

Yeah, with a big, ugly jetty—and David Merrick—to keep them apart, Zoe thought.

He was walking toward them with the same measured steps that he'd used to accompany Zoe off the property the first day they'd met. This did not bode well. Maybe he didn't recognize them and thought they were trespassing.

Eve waved, and he stopped to wait for them, feet spread, arms crossed, a colossus protecting his home. Was he conscious of how arrogant he looked? Maybe that was the point, because he obviously recognized them now.

"If Lee sent you, you can tell him to stay away

from my nephew. I'll tell him myself as soon as I can find him."

"What happened?" asked Eve. "What are you talking about?"

David's jaw tightened. He was evidently having a hard time containing his temper, and Zoe felt an overwhelming urge to remind him of peace, love, and all that jazz.

But his next words stifled her.

"Eli and Mel just broke up because your father threatened Eli if he ever saw her again. And while he isn't afraid of Lee, he is afraid for Mel."

"For Mel? Lee wouldn't hurt either of them," Eve said.

"No? Not even if he thinks history is repeating itself?"

Eve recoiled as if he'd slapped her. "She's not—she—is she pregnant?"

"She'd better not be," David said, forgetting that he was on the offensive.

Zoe saw Floret running toward them and holding her hat to her head. Dulcie trotted after her, then passed her and kept going.

Straight for David.

Zoe bit her lip and waited for impact.

David and Eve were oblivious, face-to-face in a standoff.

"So you can tell him for me—"

Anger goeth before a—

He had no warning before Dulcie, hornless head lowered, ran full tilt into his side and knocked him off balance.

He staggered to the side. "Mind your own business, you damn goat."

Dulcie was loud in her response. Zoe could only guess what she was saying, probably something along the lines of what Zoe was thinking.

Floret stood a few feet away, her hat askew. "Dulcie, leave David alone! I'll just go put on tea." She hurried into the house, followed by Henry, who had been sitting on the front porch.

"I'm sorry, David," Eve said. "Poor kids, they must be so upset. But he would never hurt them. I don't know what's wrong with him."

"Like mother, like son? Some people just can't let go."

"Ugh." Eve turned to Zoe. "I'd better go see about Mel. Do you want to come?"

"You two should have some mother-daughter time. I'll stay here. Call my cell if you need anything."

Eve nodded and hurried back the way they'd come.

Zoe turned back to David.

David stuck out his hand in a gesture of "after you."

It was a gesture she was beginning to know well and disliking more with every repetition.

"You think this is all my fault."

He didn't bother to comment.

"Don't you?"

"Not everything is about you."

"Oh, goody, that makes me feel so much better." She stalked past him.

He caught up to her. "I didn't mean it as a judgment. I just meant that this has been fomenting for a while now. You're probably just the catalyst."

"Capulet," she said.

"What?"

"It was a play on words. Not catalyst, but a Capulet. Just like Romeo and Juliet."

"Spare me the Shakespeare reference."

"Actually I was thinking of the Reflections."

"What?"

She groaned. "It's a sixties song. '(Just Like) Romeo and Juliet' sung by the Reflections."

"Never heard of them."

Zoe looked to heaven. "Tristan and Isolde? Heard of them? They're pretty famous. Brad and Angelina?"

"I give up. What the hell are you talking about?"

"Star-crossed lovers."

David groaned. "Sorry to disappoint you, but it's none of those. Just a few myopic adults, so caught up in their own pasts, they don't see the harm they're doing to a couple of kids just trying to understand life and having to feel their way through the mess."

"Whoa. You're right. It sucks."

"Yeah, it does."

They reached the house and she went inside; David didn't.

Eve stood outside Mel's bedroom listening. She expected to hear sobs or sniffs or even out-and-out wailing, not Mel lumbering around her room making noise. Was she so upset she was actually throwing things? Then she heard a drawer open, then close, then another—

She knocked. "Mel? Mellie?"

"Go away."

"Listen, I talked to David. He told me what happened."

"Go away."

"Mel, let me in." Eve waited. Finally, she heard the lock click. She didn't rush in like she wanted to. To take her daughter in a safe hug and promise her that everything would work out. Because she couldn't promise that. She wasn't even sure she didn't agree with her father about Mel and Eli, but never with his technique.

The door opened enough for her to slip inside. Mel's face was blotched and her eyes were swollen and red. All the Gordons' faces looked hideous when they cried. Except maybe Hannah's. Eve had never actually seen her grandmother cry.

"He said you and Eli broke up."

"Just because Eli is afraid of Granddad."

"I heard it was because Eli was trying to protect you from what he was afraid Lee might do to you. You know your granddad—he's rough and gruff, but he would never hurt you or Eli."

"Too late. He's wrecked everything. I hate him." Mel shoved a T-shirt into her backpack.

"Now, wait just a minute."

"It doesn't matter."

"Of course it does."

"It doesn't. Eli wants to go to college. So he can go. If he doesn't want me, I sure as heck don't want him."

Eve's heart broke a little. "I'm sure he wants you. It's just—"

Then she saw the clothes spilling out of Mel's backpack. *The opening and closing of drawers.*

"What are you doing?"

"Leaving."

"Why?"

"Everybody hates me. You don't care what I want in life."

This was the same Mel that a few hours ago had hugged her sister good-bye and wished her luck? "Of course I do." Eve tried not to feel hurt. Knew something must have happened to make Mel lash out like this. Knew that she was having a hard time adjusting to no longer being a high school student.

Eve took a deep breath and sat down on Mel's bed next to the backpack. Reminded herself to be the adult in the room. No one hurt like a teenager, unless maybe it was a teenager's mother.

"I love you. We all love you."

"And want what's best for me. But who says you know what's best for me?" Mel shoved a pair of jeans into the already stuffed backpack.

"Wait a minute. When did this turn from your grandfather to me? I haven't told you not to see Eli. I like Eli. I just want you to keep your options open. That's all I've ever said."

"But you didn't mean it."

"Of course I do."

"It doesn't matter."

Eve's blood froze. Her mind pinballed from a young

girl hitchhiking across the country to a suicide pact. She couldn't stop it.

"Mel, wait. What are you going to do? If you don't care about Eli. And you don't care about us. Where can you go?"

For the first time since Mel had unlocked the door, she slowed down, a pink striped T-shirt hanging from her hands. Her mouth worked spasmodically. "Somewhere."

"I'll be unhappy when you're gone."

Mel sniffed. "No, you won't be. You're making me leave anyway, to go to college."

"I just—"

"I know, you just don't want me to make the same mistakes you and your mother made. Well, she did fine. She dumped you and went off to have a cushy life with another family."

Eve didn't know where the slap came from. Her palm made contact with Mel's cheek before she knew what was happening.

For an eternal moment, they both froze.

"I'm sorry. Oh my God, Mel." Eve reached for her daughter, but Mel dodged away. She grabbed her backpack and ran out of the room.

Eve followed but stopped when the front door of the

cottage slammed shut. She'd done something unthinkable. She'd hit her daughter. She'd hurt her own daughter. What kind of monster was she?

But she knew. She had just proved it. She was a Gordon.

While Floret steeped tea, Zoe sat at the kitchen table watching the professor, his head bent over his work, which consisted of piling slice after slice of corned beef onto a piece of mustard-slathered rye bread.

He looked over his shoulder at Zoe, his wiry curls springing about his ears in reaction to his enthusiasm. "For weeks I've been living on masa and beans, with the occasional piece of meat that defied classification, and dreaming about Jim Kelly's corned beef."

"Which he had as soon as he deposited his suitcase inside." Henry lifted a tin down from the cabinet and set it on the table. "Jim sent him home with another pound of beef and a loaf of rye bread."

"Well, this is the last of it," the professor said, smiling down at his creation. He slathered more mustard on a second piece of bread and balanced it on top. "Ah. A masterpiece." He stood back to admire his handiwork.

"You'd better sit down and have a cup of chamomile tea with that," Floret said, bringing the pot to the table. "Aids in digestion," she explained to Zoe.

"I will, my dear, but later. After I've washed this sandwich down with a couple of beers." His head disappeared into the refrigerator. He came out with a brown bottle. "German beer and corned beef. A marriage fit for heaven. You know, no matter how much fun I have out in the world, there is no place like home." He bounced on his toes, clicked his heels together like Dorothy in Oz, and carried his sandwich and beer to the table.

Zoe smiled. The professor's energy lit up the room, in a different way from Henry and Floret, but just as important, she realized. Sometimes when you added a new person to a group, it took away from the group's spontaneity, but here the camaraderie just kept growing.

The professor sat down and pulled his chair close to the table, but instead of digging in, he laid his palms flat on each side of the plate. He inhaled, closed his eyes, and exhaled.

Zoe found herself breathing with him.

Then slowly he opened his eyes. "Ah," he said again, and dug in.

Floret poured the tea into Zoe's mug; the sweet aroma of chamomile filled the air, and Zoe relaxed a little. Floret's simple, practiced movements, Henry's calm presence, the professor's effervescence . . . They were all so different from the people she knew, how she lived.

Ordinarily she knew how to deal with people. Manipulate when necessary. It was what made her good at her job. She'd been called the ultimate VIP herder by one of the guys at work. Not totally a compliment, she realized.

But this group. They had become her VIPs. Every single one of them. They were her family, her friends, even though she had just met them.

She wanted to feel at home here. But too much was preying on her mind.

She sipped her tea even though it was too hot to enjoy. Refused the tea cakes that Henry offered. She felt as if there was something she needed to do, something that couldn't wait.

"I have to go," she said halfway through her first cup of tea.

Floret just smiled at her.

"I'm worried about Eve and Mel. And . . ."

"You don't have to explain, dear."

"Thanks for the tea." Zoe pushed her chair back from the table and headed for the door.

Henry stood. The professor bounced up from his chair.

"You don't need to see me out. Thank you."

She fled.

She didn't know whether they followed her or not,

but once she'd left the house, she faltered. She'd been so anxious to get away, but now didn't know what she'd intended to do. Why had she suddenly panicked like that? She turned back to see both Floret and Henry standing on the porch.

As if welcoming a stranger? Or saying good-bye.

Both, Zoe realized as she reached the gate and saw Mel running across the yard. Zoe opened the gate and stepped out to meet her, but she barely slowed down.

"I thought it would be better, but it's not. You were wrong. It's not." Her voice broke. "Tell Mom I'm okay."

She tore open the gate and ran past Dulcie to the porch, where she threw herself into Floret's open arms. Floret looked past her to Zoe, then took the girl inside.

Chapter 18

Eve stood in the middle of the living-room floor, surrounded by posters of the world, and wanted nothing more than to have her whole family at home with her. After twenty minutes she'd accepted that Mel wasn't coming back. She couldn't go after her. Running down Main Street begging for her forgiveness would be beyond embarrassing to both of them.

But she couldn't stand here and do nothing. She called Mike.

"Slow down and tell me what happened."

She took a breath and told him.

"Do you want me to send some of the guys out to look for her?"

"No. I don't know. I slapped her, Mike."

"I know, babe. But you'll both survive. It was just a slap."

"But what if she feels so despondent, she—"

"Will not do anything drastic. Did you check with Eli?"

"Not yet."

"She's probably gone there. Just give her some space. She'll get over it."

"Do you think so? David said they broke up because Lee had threatened them."

"Damn the man."

"I'm going to his house right now. That's one thing I can do."

"Do what you have to do. I'll stay here at the bar and keep an eye out. I'll call you if I see her. Okay?"

"Thanks." Eve rang off, stuffed her cell in her pants pocket, and cut across the back of the hotel to the mostly deserted part of town where her father lived in one of the old beach cottages.

Eve didn't like coming here. The old road was used only for delivery vans and the occasional unsuspecting visitor who took the wrong turn into town and didn't have the sense to turn back toward the highway.

An unsuspecting visitor like Zoe. Had he seen her drive through that night? Did he hail her over and give her directions, little suspecting who she was? Of course he didn't. It wasn't her father's way.

His way was bitterness and loneliness. Well, he'd gone too far when he threatened Eli and Mel.

It was cool and damp beneath the scrub oak and pines that hugged the pockmarked road. Fallen trees littered the way. In daytime, glimpses of cottages could be seen through the woods. Cottages that had once been brightly painted and rented to capacity during the summer months, before decades of storms had washed away the beaches in front of them. Now they were pitiful remnants of a better time, sagging under their own weight, just waiting for the next big storm to sweep through and finally put them out of their misery.

Zoe must have thought she'd entered the Twilight Zone when she drove this route in the dark.

Eve felt a little like that now. But her anger and her shame kept her from turning back.

Her father's cottage had been restored somewhat; Hannah had seen to that. But he might as well be living on a deserted island for all the visitors he had. She walked through the leaves up to his door, setting off the smell of damp decay that even the summer heat hadn't managed to erase.

Up the creaky steps.

She knocked. Waited. And finally the door opened.

Her father stood there in tattered jeans, and a stretched-out Grateful Dead T-shirt.

They stood eyeing each other for a few long moments. Him, wondering why she'd come, or perhaps knowing and not caring. Her anger threatening to boil over.

She wanted to beat him with both fists. Make him tell her why he had frightened and threatened his own granddaughter.

"Well?" he said, and stepped aside.

She stepped inside and shut the door to her back. Suddenly she was afraid. She was standing before a man she didn't even know, or maybe just knew too well. "You threatened Mel and Eli."

"I told them how it would be."

"You told Eli to never see her again."

"For their own good."

"To satisfy your self-imposed unhappiness."

"Bullshit. He'll get her knocked up and then go off to college and then where'll she be?"

"You don't threaten your family."

"Looks like it worked, though."

"Are you happy, then? Because Mel has run away. If something happens to her, it will be on your head." She took a shuddering breath. "And I will never, never forgive you."

She turned and groped for the wobbly doorknob. She felt like ripping it out of the wood.

"She's probably run off with that Zoe person."

Eve gripped the doorknob. "That Zoe person is your daughter."

"Get out."

"Gladly." She yanked the door open. Fury blinding her. Turned back. "And by the way. There *were* letters. Lots of them. Letters to me. From my mother. She wrote to me, loved me, wanted to know me. But I never knew because Hannah stole those letters. She's kept them hidden all these years. She never even bothered to read them. Just kept them for God knows what. Some kind of emotional blackmail that she might be able to use one day. There *are* letters. I have them."

She saw her father reach out as if to steady himself. She left him to stand or fall. Right now she didn't care which.

Zoe meant to go straight back to the inn and let Eve know that Mel was with Floret and safe. God only knew what she might be imagining. But instead she stepped into the trees looking for the glen Floret and Henry had shown her, wondering at the turn her life had taken.

She found it near the path to the beach. That day it

had seemed magical; the breeze lifting the chimes and singing a gentle lullaby in the air. Today the air was still. The chimes hung limp, not even catching the sun.

The ashes of others lay around her, or maybe not, maybe they had been blown away by a storm. Maybe no one was even here anymore.

Scattered so wide as if they'd never existed.

Would she have the courage to leave her mother here?

"Is this what you really want?" she asked out loud.

Not even a bird's call answered her.

The ocean was a diamond of blue framed by the trees, and she walked that way. Right up to the opening. A stone threshold stretched from one side to the other and she stepped over it onto a narrow ledge. And was surprised to find the beach closer than she'd imagined.

So close that she could see David Merrick sitting on the driftwood log, his legs bent, his elbows resting on his knees. She watched him for a minute, wondering what he was thinking. And then something in his hand caught the sun and reflected a quick prism of colored light.

The piece of wind chime that she'd found in the sand.

She hurried back to the path, afraid that he was about to throw it into the sea. It shouldn't matter, but suddenly it mattered more than anything else that had happened.

She thrashed through the underbrush and slid and stumbled down the rocks to the beach, frantic to stop him.

He didn't even look up when she stepped onto the sand.

Not ignoring her, she realized, but his thoughts so far away that she didn't exist. She cautioned herself not to butt in, but she walked toward him, sat on the log beside him, watched him turn the piece of glass between his fingers.

Now that she was there, she could kick herself. How could she intrude on someone like this? What was she thinking? He obviously wanted to be alone. Why had she come? And how was she going to leave without appearing totally stupid?

She couldn't. So she just sat. Next to him on the driftwood.

After a while he looked up, not at her but to the beach. "My parents used to bring my brother and me here to play in the sand. We could wade up to our knees here, because the land sheltered it on two sides. The big beach was too dangerous."

Zoe couldn't see his expression. It was impossible to tell if he was even talking to her or to someone she couldn't see.

"We had a yellow plastic pail with a chunk broken

off the top. And two big serving spoons that Floret gave us to play with."

Now she did look in time to see him smile, a fleeting reminiscent smile that softened his features before disappearing.

"We had to take them back to use for dinner. Andy would always hold my hand. I was afraid of the water. I don't remember that. Being afraid. But I remember him holding my hand."

His fingers closed around the piece of glass, and Zoe thought maybe he was finished sharing.

She was trying to think of something to say when he said, "We had nothing when we came here. I don't remember that either. But Henry and Floret took us in. Gave us a home, became our family. That's why I brought Eli here when . . . when Andy . . . when Eli's parents died."

This was where she normally would say "I'm sorry," but it hadn't worked back at the house, so she didn't attempt it here. Besides, being sorry didn't help anything. It was just something you said—even if you meant it—to transition over the awkward moment. "Sorry" was something useless to say unless you had done something wrong.

Silence descended around them. Only the waves

kept their rhythmic caesura, rolling in like the passing of time. One after the other. Like the second hand of the clock. Time was passing for all of them, for Eli and Mel, for David Merrick, for herself. Today the waves were an unrelenting march forward.

David opened his fingers. The glass sat in his palm, its edges no longer sharp enough to cut, worn down by time and the sand.

"It belongs there," she said, and pointed to the glass chime that hung unmoving from a branch of a spindly pine tree. "I have to go." Which was a stupid thing to say, since he hadn't invited her here in the first place. Before he could remind her of that, she left him. This time moving quietly, swiftly . . . like the breeze that refused to blow.

She climbed back to the path. As she passed the stairs, she glanced down to see if he was still there. He was. Still sitting on the log, looking out to sea, the piece of broken glass moving like worry beads in his hands.

It was as if she'd never been there, sitting next to him, listening as he shared a moment from his past.

Would it be like that once her duty here was over? Would she drive away, until she was out of sight and out of their minds, a dim wisp of memory, without a soul left to wonder where or what she was.

She didn't slow down or even look back at Wind

Chime House, but hurried down the drive toward town, heedless of the broken pavement, suddenly anxious to get back to Eve and let her know that Mel was with Floret. And she was safe.

She wasn't sure why she felt this urgency. It came on as quickly as the emptiness of the glen today, as her sudden empathy for David Merrick and his memories.

She hurried toward the sunlight and the bustle of the tourists on the street. Her world. Brightness and energy. Music. And she needed to get back to that. She walked faster, head down, determined to get her life back on track.

Maybe that's why she didn't see the big silver Cadillac making the turn into the drive.

Chapter 19

Zoe froze. The car was headed straight for her. And it wasn't stopping. She jumped to the side, but the car turned toward her. She could only watch, unable to breathe, unable to move. At the last second it swerved to the right, just enough so that instead of hitting her head on, it knocked her to the side.

She landed hard on the asphalt. Felt a pain flash through her shoulder. Was dimly aware that the car had pulled across the width of the drive, blocking it. The window lowered and a shriveled old woman, cheeks red with rouge, short white hair cupping her head, peered out.

And Zoe knew who it was. Through the pain and confusion and surprise, she knew. Her grandmother had just tried to run her down.

Zoe staggered to her knees, felt the sting of skinned flesh on legs, elbows, and palms.

"Get up, you're not hurt," the old woman demanded in a thin, dry voice.

Yes, she was, and not just physically. Her grandmother wanted to hurt her. Maybe kill her. One thought looped through the fog in her brain. *This is your grandmother. Your grandmother.*

Not the nice lady who lived in a colonial brick house in Long Island, who remembered every birthday, sent little notes on special days, who was kind of old-fashioned and way too conservative for Zoe's taste, but who would never, ever hurt her or her brothers.

And suddenly it was really important for this horrible woman to know about that grandmother.

Zoe staggered to her feet and limped toward the car, her knees throbbing and her shoulder and hip pounding with pain.

She wasn't sure what she planned to say or do. Dealing with demanding, demeaning clients had thickened her skin, taught her to watch her back, never to get herself backed into a corner. Placate them, but don't take shit.

But she had never had a client try to run her down with a car.

Her own grandmother had.

As she reached the Cadillac, the door swung open, forcing her back.

"I've been looking for you, girl. Get where I can see you."

Cautiously, Zoe moved away from the car. Her heart breaking. What had she ever done to this woman to make her hate her so?

Hannah scrutinized her from head to foot. It was pointedly rude and dismissive. Zoe half expected her to tell her to twirl around.

Hannah snorted. "Now I've seen you, you can go back where you came from. You won't get a thing from me or anyone in this family. I've seen you around town trying to weasel your way into this family by sucking up to Eve and her girls."

And I've seen you, stalking Mel and making everyone's lives miserable.

"You can forget it. The only thing you'll get from claiming you're my son's daughter is a heap of trouble."

The vitriol pouring from this old woman, who should love her, was staggering. And the only thing Zoe could think of to say was "You're my grandmother."

The woman raised her hand; it was bony and frail and shaking slightly, but whether from emotion or old age, Zoe couldn't tell.

"So you say. Where's your proof?"

"A letter from my mother saying so."

"Your mother. Your mother is a lying little slut."

Zoe stepped toward the open door, her fists clenched unconsciously in an effort not to strike out. "Be a horrible old woman if you must, but do not drag my mother into it. She was a well-loved, well-respected member of my family and the community. She helped others. Cared about others.

"If she ever did anything wrong, it was getting involved with your son. But I really can't complain, can I, because I'm here and I have my mother and him to thank for that. And I have—" She stopped. Better not to drag Eve into this. She would have to deal with Hannah and Lee long after Zoe had gone. "And I have perfectly good grandparents back in Long Island. I don't need you."

And she'd have to go back there. There was no place for her here. The idea shocked her, leaving her fumbling for a split second. Of course she'd have to leave. She'd always meant to leave. She couldn't stay. Why would she even want to stay?

Because she had a sister. Nieces.

Hannah shook an arthritic fist at Zoe's nose. "Show me this letter."

"I don't have it."

"Ha."

"Eve has it. My mother sent it to Floret and Henry. Ask them. I saw it for the first time three days ago."

"Floret and Henry." She spit out the names. "I might have suspected they put you up to this."

And Zoe had finally had enough. "What is wrong with you? Why are you so mean? My mother sent me here. I didn't even know about Henry or Floret or you or Eve or my father until then."

Hannah's eyes flashed, but Zoe was on a roll and she didn't let up.

"I'm sorry you're unhappy, but that's not my responsibility. If you and my 'alleged' "—she let the word slither out—"father—alleged by my mother, by the way—choose to be bitter and angry about something that happened before I was born, if you want to drag everyone in your family down with you, it's not my problem. Go be miserable, but you'll do it without me. Good day. I'm done."

This time it was both fists. Hannah was like a caricature of an evil witch from a fairy tale. Only the beauty-parlor hair and pants suit kept her rooted in reality. And made her dangerous. "What do you want?" she demanded.

"Nothing from you."

"Money? Is that it? How much?"

"I don't want your money." *I wanted your love.*

"Name it. What will it take to get rid of you?"

Zoe stepped back and turned away, all hope for a relationship, acceptance, love evaporating in a flash of pain.

"Don't you walk away from me, girl."

"She'll do as she pleases, Hannah."

Both Zoe's and Hannah's head snapped toward the new voice.

David Merrick stood at the hood of the Cadillac. "You're done here. Turn this bucket around and go home."

"I'll go where I damn well please," Hannah spat back.

"But not today." David walked slowly around the car to her door. Shut it, barely missing her outstretched hand.

Zoe swore she could hear the theme song from *The Magnificent Seven* in her head.

The Cadillac screeched as Hannah threw it into reverse, then sped off toward the street.

"Are you okay?"

Zoe nodded, though her legs were shaking almost too much to hold her weight. "Thanks. You rode in just like the cavalry."

"Hmm, I was going back to the house and saw the Caddy."

"She aimed for me," Zoe managed.

David grasped her arm. Turned it around to see a patch of broken skin. "Looks like she scored a bull's-eye."

Zoe nodded. She so didn't want to cry.

"Can you walk?"

"Of course." She hoped.

"Come back to the house. Floret's good with stuff like this."

"I just want to go home. Back to the inn. Back to Long Island. I should never have come here. I just want—"

"To come with me."

He put his arm around her waist. Lightly, more as moral support than physical aid, but she was suddenly grateful for it.

It was an excruciatingly long walk back to the house. By the time she climbed the stairs, with David's help, one knee had started to swell, her shoulder ached, and her skin burned in several places.

"What happened?" Floret asked as David steered Zoe past her and toward the kitchen. "Was it the beach steps?"

"No," said David. "Hannah Gordon just tried to run her down. The woman should have her license revoked. I'm calling the police."

"No," said Floret and Zoe at the same time.

"We should file a report. She's a menace."

"She's a sick old woman," said Henry, coming in

from the parlor. He was wearing a pair of wire-rimmed reading glasses, Zoe noted. It made him seem so normal that she wanted to hug him.

"A dangerous, hateful old bag," David said.

Something akin to a whimper escaped Zoe's lips. She sucked it back in.

Floret took her other side and she felt a calming warmth spread through her.

They sat her down at the kitchen table, and Floret went to get salve for her wounds. As soon as she withdrew her touch, Zoe felt cold. But Henry was there with a soft throw blanket, which he draped over her shoulders.

She smiled up at him and saw the understanding in his eyes. Her grandmother had just tried to run over her. Had she meant to hurt her? Or had she just meant to scare her and being old had misjudged the distance?

Did it matter? The old woman wished her ill, wanted her to leave, had no intention of accepting her as her granddaughter. Well, like she'd told Hannah, she already had grandparents who loved her. That should be enough.

Floret returned with a basket of jars and powders and several fresh flowers. She rinsed a cloth in water and sat down next to Zoe to dab at her abrasions.

Zoe braced herself, waiting for the pain, but it didn't

come. Floret's touch was like a breath, like a flutter of butterfly wings.

And while Floret worked, Zoe found herself not wincing but putting those words in her head to a vague but familiar melody.

When Floret had finished covering Zoe with herbal salves and lotions, she plied her with herbal tea and lemon-blueberry tea cakes. "You just keep using these and you'll be right as rain in a couple of days. David will drive you back to the inn."

Zoe wanted to say no. But just getting out of the chair changed her mind.

She turned to the door just in time to see Mel standing in the doorway. *I'm sorry,* Mel mouthed, before she quickly slipped out of sight.

By the time Zoe made it to the door she was already feeling better. She even managed to get down the steps without too much discomfort. Still, she was thankful when David opened the door to the dilapidated old station wagon that Zoe had mistaken for a wreck on her previous visits.

Even Dulcie kept her distance until David got Zoe stowed in the front seat. He handed her the care package Floret had packed and went around to the driver's side. Only then did Dulcie stick her nose through the window, though Zoe wasn't sure if it was really a show of sympathy or curiosity about what was in the package.

The engine started on the first try; the station wagon was loud but solid as David slowly drove toward the street, navigating the potholes, frowning at each one as if it were a personal affront.

"Why don't you have the potholes filled?" Zoe asked. "It can't be that expensive."

"It's complicated."

She gave him a look.

"Really. The first half of the drive is a right-of-way owned by the Kellys, but they let Wind Chime House use it. The second half runs perpendicular; it's an easement used by the town for sewers and power lines and stuff."

"Then shouldn't the town fill them?"

"They should, they could, but they won't."

"Why on earth not?"

"Two words. Your grandmother."

"Not my grandmother," Zoe said. "I'm disowning her."

He looked over to her and flashed a grin.

"Well, wouldn't you?" Zoe frowned. "But what does she have to do with it?"

"In case you haven't noticed, she owns half the town.

And she definitely has some of the local politicians in her pocket."

"She won't let them pave the right-of-way to Wind Chime House?"

"That's about it."

"She's crazy."

"Nah, just mean. You've probably been told all about the feud."

"Everybody mentions it. No one seems to know what it's about."

"Not even the participants, if you ask me."

"Then why not call a truce?"

"In Henry's words, 'filthy lucre.' "

"Hannah wants the Wind Chime property?"

"That goes without saying. Haven't you noticed that the emptiest people depend the most on external acquisitions?"

Zoe gave him an appraising look. It was almost worth getting sideswiped to get one more glimpse of the inner workings of David Merrick.

Is that why he was content to live in an old house with an old couple, raising his nephew while acting as a handyman instead of being off photographing the world? Was David Merrick's inner life filled with wonderful things? Like an old yellow pail.

And butterfly wings.

He pulled the station wagon into the circular drive of the inn and stopped at the front door.

"Give me your cell phone."

"What?"

"Give me your phone. I'm entering my cell in case you need anything."

"Planning on coming to the rescue again?"

"No. I'll get Henry to. But Eli and I have the only phones at Wind Chime. He never actually talks, just texts. So, call mine."

"Thanks."

He keyed in his number, handed the phone back, and got out of the car.

"Hey, Dave, whatcha doing here?" asked the valet.

"Got a delivery. I'll be right back." He came around the car where Zoe had opened the door and was about to slide onto the ground. He steadied her elbow.

"I can make it from here. Thanks."

He ignored her and escorted her up the steps. Stopped at the reception desk. "Hey, Carly, where's Eve?"

"In her quarters, I think. Is there a problem?" Carly asked, immediately concerned. "Oh, dear. What happened? Did you have a fall?"

Zoe had been in Carly's exact position before and knew that for all the sympathy she was showing, the back of her mind had raced forward to "lawsuit."

"I'm fine. It happened off-site. I'll just go up to my room."

"Call Eve and tell her we're coming." David trundled Zoe down the hall and out the side door. He knew exactly where Eve lived.

"I don't want to upset Eve. She has enough on her plate right now." Zoe tried to pull away, but too late. Eve opened the door.

"Oh my God. What happened? Bring her inside."

"I'm okay," Zoe said. "Just an accident."

"Hannah aimed the Cadillac at her," David said, still steering Zoe by the arm and depositing her in the overstuffed chair. "The old bag could have killed her."

"David!" Zoe warned, frowning at him. "It was just an accident."

"Bullshit." He turned to Eve. "When is this going to stop? It was one thing when she was just making everyone's lives miserable. Harassing Henry and Floret. Screwing up your business dealings. But now she's bullying the Kellys and sending your father to threaten my nephew and your daughter. Today she injured her own granddaughter. It was no accident. When are you people going to make her stop? When somebody gets killed?"

"Mel" escaped involuntarily from Eve's lips.

"She's with Floret," Zoe said.

"Thank God."

"Yeah, sure." David turned back to the door and stalked out.

"Thanks," Zoe called as the door closed behind him. She looked at Eve. "He seems pretty angry."

Eve nodded and bent over Zoe, checking her injuries.

"Floret precedes you," Zoe said, trying to make light of the fact she was beginning to hurt.

"I see," Eve said, studying the contents of the basket Zoe still held.

"But I wouldn't say no to some ibuprofen and a glass of wine."

Eve left and returned moments later with a glass, a bottle of Chardonnay, and a bottle of pain relievers.

"Tell me everything that happened. If you feel up to it."

"Sure. I've had worse snowboard wipeouts."

Eve sat on the couch facing Zoe. "Did she really try to hit you?"

"I think she just had an adrenaline rush, thought she'd scare me, and got too close. She's old. How's her eyesight?"

Eve sprang to her feet. "Her eyesight is fine. She had cataract surgery years ago. She sees better than I do. This has got to stop. We've all been making excuses for her for too long. She's tearing my family apart and now she's tried to hurt you."

She could have broken my fingers. The thought startled Zoe. She hadn't played the piano in months. Not even when she returned home and the baby grand sat idle.

That was a part of her past life, music, at least it had been until two nights ago when she had sat in on an old James Taylor cover that she'd learned long after his heyday. And that one little song, her fingers on the keys of a funky bar piano, had given her a draught of promise. A sense of coming home.

For a moment . . . but that couldn't happen. It was doomed to go dormant again.

"Is your hand hurting?"

Zoe realized she'd been flexing her scraped fingers. "Not much, mainly just annoying."

"Was Mel okay? We had a fight. She pushed all my buttons and I slapped her. I never hit people. I don't understand how I could do such a thing."

Zoe did. "Sometimes we all need a wake-up call."

Eve sighed. "Not like that. What did she say? I thought she was running away. I imagined the worst. Oh God. I even thought—I slapped her. Slapped my daughter. I've never done that in my life." She stood up. "I'll go tell her I'm sorry."

Zoe sucked in breath. "Not my business but . . . I think you should give her some space. Take it from someone who's been there recently. Your mother isn't always the person who will listen without prejudice. It's why strangers tell their life stories to bartenders." Why David Merrick had told her about his yellow beach pail?

"She hates me."

"No. Yesterday she actually blamed me for coming here."

"That's ridiculous."

"Perhaps, but it all seems to be coming to a head since my arrival. But mainly she thinks everyone is against her and Eli. With everyone making their opinion known about the two of them, and pushing her in different directions, it's a bit overwhelming."

Eve looked up, bit her lip, clearly torn. Zoe felt a rush of embarrassment. Who the hell was she to waltz into town and start handing out advice?

Because, she reminded herself, *you deal with strangers in groups every day.* She was good at it. Stupid, really, that even though she was currently unemployed, she was still herding relative strangers. Ha. *Relative strangers. Strange relatives.*

Yep. She had plenty of both. She took a sip of wine. Except these particular ones might stay in her life past the next weekend, the next rock concert, the next music award. And she wanted to get this right.

"You're right," Eve said. "Floret, for all her hippie, free-love ways, wouldn't help them to elope."

"Do you ever talk to David Merrick about the Mel-Eli situation?" Zoe asked.

Eve shrugged. "He doesn't really share his thoughts too much. He's only there because of Eli. And even so, he's gone for big chunks of time on assignments. I don't think he ever feels comfortable here, doesn't really get close to people beyond Floret and Henry, which is odd since he was raised in a commune.

"I always think of him as the Wind Chime bouncer. He protects Henry and Floret though they're perfectly able to help themselves. He's loyal. I know he wants Eli to go to school. He feels responsible for his future.

"He was only twenty-seven or -eight when he was called home to raise his nephew. I remember that day like it was yesterday. He showed up at Wind Chime in that old station wagon filled with kid stuff and Eli. He was devastated over his brother's death—he and Andy were inseparable growing up. And David didn't know anything about children."

"So he brought Eli to Wind Chime House," Zoe said.

Eve looked shocked. "Of course. Where else would he go?"

Zoe didn't know.

"He takes his responsibility to Eli very seriously. He's worried about Eli giving up too soon. I worry the same for Mel. I just hope we're not all putting too much pressure on them."

Zoe thought it was very likely they were.

Eve stood. "Mel didn't tell me about Dad threatening her and Eli. I went to see him when I left you. And told him to back off. I told him about the—" She broke off, realizing she hadn't told Zoe about the letters yet. And they were sitting on the table between them. "I didn't mention you."

"No problem. He's made it perfectly clear how he feels about me. I'll be gone soon enough and you guys can get back to normal."

"I was hoping you'd stay for a while."

"I do have to get a job."

"Want to play piano in a great little bar I know?"

Chapter 20

David was pissed as hell, and as somebody had said in some movie once, he wasn't going to take it anymore. He'd intended to go straight back to Wind Chime House. Let this thing play out the way all things Hannah played out, slow and painful. The town had been under her thumb for decades, and he doubted if anything would change until she died.

Most days he could do the peace-love thing. The turn-the-other-cheek thing. But there were some days when enough was enough. Today was one of those. He drove through town, forcing himself to keep to the annoyingly slow speed limit. If some old broad in a big car could deliberately run down a visitor, what was the point?

He should go to the police station and file a complaint. But Henry and Floret would hate that. And it wouldn't do any good. The chief lived in a big house in the suburbs. Rumor had it he was completely overextended. And in Hannah Gordon's pocket.

He stopped short for a red light.

Hell. The woman should be sitting at home spoiling her grandchildren instead of driving the town nuts with her obsessive greed.

As far as David was concerned, that was their problem, until she attacked his family. Henry and Floret could take care of themselves, and it was their choice to ignore Hannah. But Eli was hands-off and if she couldn't figure that out by herself, David would make it clear. He was done with ignoring the old woman.

As for Zoe Bascombe, he wished she had never come, but she had, and she didn't deserve to be bullied or injured by the old witch. David would let Hannah know that Zoe was off limits, too.

The Cadillac was parked in the driveway of her clapboard house. She was just getting out, pulling a sparsely filled yellow grocery bag out from the seat behind her.

David stopped the station wagon across the drive. Not that he thought she would try to escape. She was on her home turf.

He pulled the keys from the ignition, got out, and cut across the grass to intercept her by her front door.

She walked right past him to the door, unlocked it, and started to go inside. He reached over her and pulled the door shut.

If he was going to bully an old woman, he was going to do it where the world could see.

"Get off my property or I'll have you arrested."

"Oh, save it for the rest of this town, Hannah. I don't care what you do. If you want to carry on this ridiculous fight with Henry and Floret, be my guest. But you leave my nephew out of it. And you tell Lee to stay away from me and mine. Do you understand me?"

"I'm not deaf, boy. And I'll do as I please. So take yourself off. And take your nephew with you. And as far as Henry and Floret . . . I'll own Wind Chime and there's nothing you can do about it."

"Stop it, you ridiculous old woman. Either you stay away from us or you'll be served with a restraining order."

Her mouth twisted into some semblance of a smile. God, she was like a cartoon villain. Except her actions had real-life consequences. And he'd probably just provoked her into exacting a new revenge.

He turned while she sneered at him, got back in the station wagon, and drove away. What had he been thinking? He tried to stay out of the day-to-day machinations of small-town life. He prided himself on his objectivity, observing the changing dynamics with the same unfettered eye that captured the most honest photos. Only today, he had let his temper get the better of him, for Eli, for Henry and Floret, and strangely enough for the intrusive, annoying stranger who seemed determined to upturn their lives.

Well, it was done. Now it was up to Hannah. In a few weeks Eli would be gone, David would be back in the field, and things here would go back to the way they always were. It couldn't happen soon enough for David. He just hoped he hadn't made it worse.

Eve sat across from Zoe, watching her, noticing how the vivacious young woman who had arrived at the inn less than a week ago was looking tired. There were dark half-moons under her eyes; her features were drawn. She was scraped and bruised and in pain.

Her sister, physically attacked by her own grandmother, denied by her father. She didn't know why Zoe didn't just spread Jenny's ashes and leave. What could possibly hold her here?

Eve was afraid to believe that she might be the reason for Zoe staying this long. Her sister. It was an odd sensation. She'd never lacked for the company of sisters and brothers when they had lived at the commune. But now that she actually had a sister of her own, she was loath to let her go.

She didn't miss the irony of wanting to keep Zoe here while pushing Mel out the door. Maybe college wasn't right for Mel; if she really didn't want to go or wasn't ready to go, maybe she'd like to travel with Eve instead. They could see the world together.

Maybe Zoe would go with them. Yellowstone, the Grand Canyon. Eve had never been to either. Hell, Paris, Rome. The pyramids. They'd see the sights, she and Zoe and Mel. And Noelle, too, if she wanted. They'd visit Harmony and her family on holidays the way other families did.

She could put the inn up for sale. She'd gotten several offers for it over the years. She owned it outright; she'd paid back Hannah's down payment years ago.

And when the money ran out, she'd do something else. Far from her manipulative grandmother and her erratic father.

But would Zoe want to go? She looked across at her sister, but she seemed lost in her own world. Was she thinking about how soon she could leave? Eve wanted to ask, but she was afraid of the answer.

"What are those?" Zoe asked into the silence.

Eve looked at the stack of Jenny's letters that she'd taken out to reread. In her haste to get to the door earlier, she'd not put them away.

"I meant to tell you . . . but so much has been happening. You know how Jenny said she wrote me letters? I went to my grandmother's Sunday. God, has it only been two days?"

"I know. It seems like decades."

"I asked her about the letters. What had happened to them." Eve still couldn't wrap her mind around Hannah's reaction. "She'd kept them all these years. Together, tied up like love letters from an old war. She didn't even bother to deny it. Just said she'd known this day would come and pointed to a drawer in the sideboard. And there they were.

"Jenny really did send me letters." Eve reached out and touched them, not to keep Zoe from seeing them, but because she still couldn't believe they were real.

"You don't mind, do you?"

"No, of course not," Zoe said. "I'm just glad that Hannah, for whatever reason, kept them."

"You can read them." Eve pushed them in Zoe's direction.

"Someday, if you want. But not now. For now, they're yours, just yours. Something that belongs only to you."

"Thanks," Eve said. "I'll just put them away, then." She scooped them off the table, but pulled one off the bottom. "This one is yours. I kept it to show Dad, but you should keep it now."

Zoe took the letter that just a few short days ago had changed all their lives. It no longer had the feel of the crisp, clean sheets of paper that she'd first read. Now it was crumpled and had been folded over and over. Held by hands that had belonged to strangers then, but who were family—for better or worse—now.

"Thanks." She put it in her bag.

"Are you hungry?" Eve asked.

Hungry, thought Zoe. She should probably be hungry. But like a tightrope walker without a net, she was desperately trying to stay focused on her mission with the ashes and not on all the unexpected craziness that was bombarding her at every turn.

"I think so."

Eve popped out of her chair. "There's gazpacho in the fridge and some good bread." She started toward the kitchen, stopped. "Or I could call Mike and he'll send over whatever you want."

"Gazpacho's fine."

The soup was good, but Zoe's appetite was losing the battle to the throbbing in her elbows, knees, and shoulder.

And her mind screamed for closure. Longed for peace. She tried to conjure up the sound of the chimes in her head. So peaceful. She'd been trying to capture them in music since the first day she'd heard them; she'd come close, but close wasn't close enough.

But the attempt had set off feelings she'd pushed to the side for years. Had almost convinced herself she'd forgotten . . . until she came here. Now it was back. Music. *Like a bird in a cage.* No. That wasn't the song. *Like a rat.*

"I have to go."

"Why don't you stay here tonight? Noelle's room is pretty comfortable and she picks up her clothes."

Eve smiled tentatively, and it broke Zoe's heart. *You could be my mother,* she thought. How could she be a sister? She needed Chris. She needed to go home.

If only she'd taken the ashes to Henry and Floret the first day. Explained to them what she wanted to do. It would be over by now. And she would be home. Except where was home? Not Long Island and not here.

She didn't have a home. And she didn't have a job. What the hell was she going to do?

"Sorry. Thanks for the soup. I'll talk to you tom—I'll talk to you." She was backing toward the door. "I'm sure Henry and Floret will take care of Mel, so don't worry."

She fumbled for the doorknob, caught the look of dismay on Eve's face, and slipped out the door.

Outside, the stillness of twilight—and loneliness—

settled over Zoe, dug its way inside her, twisted and squeezed as she limped to the inn and down the hall to the elevator.

She jabbed at the button, half seeing. Took a deep breath and another as she rode to the third floor.

Her sister had her own family who needed her. Her grandmother had just tried to mow her down; her brothers were furious with her over a simple wish that might tear her family apart. It was time for her to finish what she'd come for and get out of Dodge.

She made her way slowly and painfully back to her room, where she closed the drapes, shutting out the sun and the rest of the world. But not her cell phone. As she placed it on the dresser, it rang. She ignored it and went to run a bath. It was ringing again when she came out.

She looked at the little rectangle of light in the dark. Errol. Great. He'd left a voice mail. *"Please call me."* She deleted it. Powered down the phone.

She groped her way over to the closet and took the urn out of the tote bag. Felt her way back to the dresser, placed the urn on top.

"Did you have any idea what you were about to unleash?"

She didn't wait for an answer. It didn't matter. And it wouldn't change a damn thing.

The room was dark when Zoe awoke the next morning. She knew it was morning because there was a sliver of light dancing along the wall next to the blackout curtains. Another sunny day, she guessed, before she rolled over in bed, sending shock waves radiating through her body. The ungodly events of the day before began to slowly unreel in the darkness.

She got out of bed, unleashing a few more jolts of pain. Her grandmother had hit her, then threatened her. Her brother had called. She hadn't called him back. She stumbled over to the desk. Powered up the phone. Messages and calls pinged on the screen. She scrolled through a list of calls—Errol, Errol, Robert, Chris, Errol—which she ignored. Texts—Errol, Chris, Joyce Redfern from the agency she'd recommended to Noelle. She read that one.

Loved Noelle. We could use an intern for the project division. Call me. Want to chat.

Started to put the phone down. What had she been thinking? What if there was an emergency? At least from Chris. The others had their own families. They probably just wanted to argue.

But Chris was different. Maybe Errol had gotten to him, too. Urging him to get Zoe to change her mind. It wasn't even her mind. It was just her duty.

She wouldn't put Chris in the middle of this. Her life was already screwed. No reason to wreck his, too.

She wanted coffee, but she needed to deal with Errol first. And where was Robert in all of this? He, of course, would defer to Errol; he always did. They all did. When their father had packed his suitcase and walked out the door, Errol had become head of the family. He wore the role well.

She pressed call.

Errol picked up immediately. "Why didn't you call me?"

"I went to bed early." *And I'm tired, sore, alone, and I couldn't face any more incriminations.*

"Are you still there? In whatever that town's called. Have you done it yet?"

"I— No. Not yet."

"Well, don't."

"I have to. It was her last wish."

"I don't understand you, none of us do. To throw us over for people who made her an outcast. She was obviously not in her right mind."

"Errol, don't. You're not helping."

"Don't do a thing. I'm getting a court order to stop you."

A court order? Was he nuts? "You can't do that.

These are her final wishes. She wrote them down long before she died."

"Well, it's no longer up to her. Or you. You're not even a Bascombe."

His words knocked the breath out of her lungs, the strength from her legs, and she dropped onto the edge of the unmade bed.

A court order? This was crazy.

"Do you hear me?"

"Yes. Errol. Please don't do this. It's hard enough losing her, don't do this."

"Too late. You'll be hearing from my lawyer. Until then, don't do anything with those ashes. You'll be in contempt if you do."

"Errol! No!"

He ended the call. She just held the silent phone while her stomach heaved.

And a searing anger passed through her. She turned on the urn.

"See what you've done? Forty years against a couple of summer months at a hippie commune and ten minutes of stand-up sex in a dressing room eighteen years later. You'd tear your family apart for that?

"What is this? The ultimate passive-aggressive act of a well-ordered life? Only you get to be passive and

I have to do all the aggression. What am I supposed to do?"

The urn sat silent on the dresser top. No longer beautiful in its simplicity, but as cold and sleek as a Hollywood femme fatale.

"I should have dumped you by the side of the road in New Haven. I could be back in the city looking for another job. Finding an apartment. Getting a life."

She covered her face with her hands. What was she saying? This was her mother. *You're not even a Bascombe.*

Maybe she wasn't a part of their family anymore. But she was still her mother's daughter.

And what was "contempt" anyway? Could they put her in jail if she spread the ashes? Was she willing to risk it? Would they go through a lengthy court battle over who had custody of their mother's remains? Did people do that?

The whole thing was ludicrous. She stood. Went into the bathroom where she smeared herself with Floret's mixtures, then dressed in jeans, a T-shirt, and sneakers. Not exactly funeral clothes, but she still wasn't sure what she planned to do. And if she had to run for her life on the way, she'd be prepared.

Besides, she couldn't sit here waiting for some police officer to come and wrest the urn from her hands.

Jenny Bascombe would be mortified. Though, Zoe thought wistfully, Jenny Campbell, band groupie and rock-star paramour, might be willing to fight for her right to be buried where she chose.

Where did Zoe's duty lie? *You are among my dearest friends. They will guide you through and see you safe.*

Henry and Floret. Zoe grabbed the tote and slid the urn inside. She'd come back later for the rest of her things.

Eve poured herself a cup of coffee and wandered into the living room. It seemed too quiet. Henry had called the night before to say Mel was staying at Wind Chime. Noelle was in New York with Chris Bascombe.

She wanted to call Zoe and see if she wanted to come over for coffee or meet downstairs for breakfast. But she didn't want to wake her; she'd looked like she was about to drop when she left last night.

Her phone rang.

Noelle. Eve mentally crossed her fingers. *Please be good news,* she thought, while feeling a pang of suddenly wanting to keep her close.

"Mom!"

Good news. You could always tell with Noelle.

"I got the job! They have this new project that

sounds perfect, but they want me to start in two weeks. I told them I had to clear it with my current employer."

"Wow. That soon? What current employer?"

"You, Mom. I don't want to leave you in the lurch, especially with all the stuff that's going on."

"Honey, this is just what you wanted. Go for it. But you'll have to find a place to live, pack your stuff."

"Mom, chill, I'll figure it out. And Chris said he will help."

"That's great, honey. I knew once they had time to consider . . ."

"Yeah, plus I talked with Zoe's graphics friend. She liked me, too. So I kind of threw it out that I was being considered for another position. Well, she didn't say thanks, but no thanks, so I just . . . you know . . ."

Eve laughed. "I do indeed." Of course she did. Noelle had a streak of her mom in her, Eve thought proudly. She was proud of all her girls, but she was most envious of Noelle for getting away.

"When are you coming home? We'll have a celebratory dinner."

"Tomorrow night. It'll be a quick turnaround."

She already sounded like a New Yorker.

"But dinner would be great. And maybe . . . should we invite Granddad? He hasn't really met Zoe, officially."

No, thought Eve, he hadn't, but he'd made his feelings clear. "It might be a little too early for him. But we'll see."

"Oh, and tell Zoe to call Chris. He's been trying to call her. I guess their brothers are being weird about the whole burial thing."

"Oh, dear. I'll tell her."

"Gotta run."

"Congratulations. I'm so happy for you. Love you."

"Thanks. Love you, too. This is just what I want. See you soon."

"See you soon." *Just what I want.* Eve sure hoped she was right. It was a big move. But Eve wasn't worried at all. Not about Noelle. Now, if she could just get Mel on solid ground . . .

Eve sipped her coffee and walked back into the kitchen. Maybe she'd just go upstairs to see how Zoe was feeling.

Her phone rang. Noelle again? She was excited.

"Eve, this is David. Kelly's Diner has just been shut down by the health department. This is Hannah's doing. Call her off before this gets really nasty. There are a lot of pissed-off people outside. I think they've had enough of Hannah Gordon."

Eve's mouth went dry. "I'm on my way."

Chapter 21

Zoe had barely left the hotel when she saw people hurrying down the sidewalk, all heading in the same direction. Something was going on that for once couldn't have anything to do with her. Maybe it was the farmers' market she'd heard about. Or one of the locals had a new truck.

A crowd was gathered on the sidewalk. There were so many people that they spilled into the street, and as more people joined them, Zoe got a terrible sinking feeling. They were surrounding the doorway to Kelly's Diner.

Please let it be a false fire alarm, a patron with chest pains. Anything but . . .

She crossed the street and saw the professor standing on the fringes of the group.

Zoe hurried toward him. "What happened?"

"Morning, Zoe. The health department just closed down Kelly's."

"Bullshit," said an old guy in a T-shirt with a Dinkins's Hardware logo stretched over his belly. "I've been eating there for twenty years and never had a bout of indigestion."

"Damn straight," agreed a man next to him.

A roar went up ahead of them.

Zoe pushed to the front of the crowd.

Kelly stood at the door of the diner arguing with two men, both of whom were dressed in khaki slacks, ties, and short-sleeve shirts. Summer official wear.

"You can't do this!" Jim Kelly yelled. "I know my rights. You can't just walk into a place and close it down. You didn't even identify yourselves."

The two men ignored his protestations while one of them posted a notice on the window and the other put a lockbox on the door.

"I need to get back in there, dammit. The grill is still on. You wanna burn down the town?"

A woman, his wife, Zoe guessed, clung to his arm, trying to restrain him. "Stop, Jim, you can't talk sense into them. You know who's behind this."

Zoe was pretty sure she did, too. Hadn't David said Hannah had been threatening the Kellys because they refused to sell her the right-of-way to Wind Chime House? And it was coming to a head now, because Zoe had brought her mother's ashes and Floret and Henry had given her Jenny's letter.

All this over a dead woman's wishes. She'd heard what Henry had called her. Pandora. Well, maybe she was, and she may not know how to get things back in the box, but she had to try.

"You haven't heard the last from me," Jim yelled as the two men pushed their way through the crowd that was getting louder and angrier.

"A damn shame," the professor said. "But I for one am not going to take this lying down. Jim Kelly makes the best corned beef for miles around."

"Where are we supposed to eat?"

"How long is this going to last?"

"You can't lock him out of his own establishment."

The two men looked straight ahead as if they were alone and kept walking across the street to a white Chevy with COUNTY HEALTH DEPARTMENT imprinted on the door.

"We know who put you up to this!" yelled the man in the hardware T-shirt.

"Yeah!" cried several other people.

"And we've had enough."

"Yeah!" commented a larger group of voices.

The two men got in their car and drove away.

Kelly stood at his front door, his wife clinging to him. The jovial, friendly man who'd greeted Zoe her first day in town was slumped forward. A beaten, dejected man.

David Merrick appeared out of the crowd and took Jim Kelly's elbow.

"Come on, Jim. Floret and Henry will meet you back at your house."

Jim tried to pull away. "It's all we got. This and the cottage. What will we do? She won't be satisfied until she's ruined us."

His wife burst into tears.

Zoe hurried over to David. "It's my fault," she said. "But I don't know how to fix it."

"You don't have to," David said. "It's time this bullshit came to an end." He started to lead the Kellys away.

"Wait, what are you going to do?"

David didn't answer. The crowd had broken into pockets and now they began to disperse, keeping a wide berth of one man who stood off to the side.

Lee Gordon. Their eyes met and he turned away; he was leaving. But not before she had her say.

Gripping the tote close to her side, she dodged her way between the departing patrons and stepped in front of him, barring his way.

He stepped to the side; she stepped with him. He moved the other way; she did, too. It was like a bizarre dance, two adversaries, father and daughter, strangers.

Finally, he stopped. But he looked over her head, gazing down the street as if she wasn't there.

"I know what you and your mother are doing. And I know why. I don't care for myself. But you're wrecking your family and these good people for no reason. Stop it. I'm leaving. You can go back to your hate and your greed and all the unhappiness you people spread wherever you go. I'd like to say it was nice meeting my father. But it wasn't. Go make yourself miserable. I don't care. But leave the Kellys and Floret and Henry alone."

She spun around and hurried down the street. Was he watching her? Or had he, too, turned away?

She didn't care. She never wanted to see him again. She didn't care. *She wouldn't care.* She had one thing to do and then she would go. Pack up her suitcase and leave the inn before anyone knew.

She tripped up the curb, grabbed the tote as it slipped from her arm. Damn, she couldn't. She didn't have a car. She'd rent one. They must have a car rental in a resort town this size. She'd call Chris and give him a heads-up not to return.

But what about Noelle?

Zoe would call them. She'd leave, have Chris drive Noelle back, and . . . what? Face Eve and everyone else by himself? And what about Eve? Could Zoe really walk—run—away from the sister she'd found only a few days ago?

"Shit," she said under her breath.

She reached the drive to Wind Chime and slowed down to make sure David and the Kellys had already reached the house.

She crossed to the verge and, keeping close to the seclusion of the trees, started down the drive—saw Floret and Henry hurrying toward her, going to the Kellys.

She stepped into the shadows of a tree, held still, hoping they wouldn't see her. Hoping that Dulcie had stayed back at the house. Hoping until her chest ached—probably a heart attack, the kind you got when your heart was breaking, the pieces disintegrating into shards of disappointment.

Once they'd gone into the house, she crossed the drive and cut through the woods to the glen.

The glen was dark today, as if the trees had closed over themselves, intentionally blocking out the sun. Not the faintest breeze disturbed their branches. Not one faint tinkle of a wind chime. They weren't singing today. Not for her or Jenny Bascombe. The air in the glen was dead. As dead as the ashes in that stupid green jar. Even the window of blue sea felt like a lie. A fakery. An illusion.

Fine. She'd do this and leave. She never wanted to hear another wind chime as long as she lived.

She lifted the urn out of the tote, let the bag drop to the ground. The urn felt cool in her hands. Cool and dead. She gulped back the sob that had found its way up her throat.

"I'm doing this because you asked me to. I hope you're happy. The boys hate me. Errol has disowned me and threatened to send me to jail. The feud that started with you is tearing this town apart, all because you wanted to come back. So you're here. Hope you enjoy your life in eternity." She twisted the top to the urn. It didn't budge.

"What were you thinking? That I would find my long-lost family and we'd all live happily ever after? Did you even think about me? Or the others?

"I didn't gain a family. I'm losing both. I bet you didn't think about that, did you." Damn, she couldn't get the top off.

"Did you?" she demanded. "Grrr." She dug her fingernail along the rim and broke the seal. Yanked off the top of the urn.

Dropped the top on the ground. She wouldn't be saying any inspiring words at this ceremony, words she'd meant to write to send her mother off. No song. No friends. No family, not even an old lover.

"This is what you wanted. This is what you get. Alone with the ashes of strangers. I've wrecked any chance of my other family coming together, jeopardized Henry and Floret's future because of you. Did you even think about them when you left these instructions?"

The tears dropped off her chin; her nose was running. She ran her bare arm across her face and then her shirt. It seemed a fitting end. "You left Lee and Eve and lived a lie your whole life. Then sprang the truth on your unsuspecting family after you were gone. Did you ever wonder how we would feel?"

She turned the urn over. Nothing happened. She shook it and stared incredulously. The ashes weren't free. They couldn't be tossed into the wind that wasn't there. She couldn't even dump them on the ground. They were sealed in a plastic bag.

"Did you even care? If you loved Eve so much, why didn't you tell us about her? Why didn't you tell her about us? She could have been a part of our family all this time." Her voice cracked; her throat was on fire and she realized she was screaming at someone who wasn't even there.

"Why, Mom?" She scrabbled at the plastic, dug her fingernails into it. The plastic stretched but refused to break. "Why?"

Why couldn't she get the damn thing open? It was the most ludicrous thing in the world. She was here, she was ready to let go, and she couldn't get the damn thing open. To hell with it. She raised the urn over her head.

It was snatched from her hands.

"Not in anger."

The voice was low, gravelly, not Henry's.

Not Henry, but someone she knew. Didn't know, but whose voice she recognized.

She turned on him. And stared up at the stern face of her father.

"Give that back. This is none of your business." She grabbed for the urn, but he held it out of reach.

"Don't send her into the afterlife in anger."

"What? Why do you care? She's been gone for days. And where do you get off lecturing me about anger? You're the most bitter man I've ever met. And for that matter, we haven't even met. Give me the urn back."

"You're right. I've lived most of my life in anger."

"Give me the urn."

"Once anger gets you, it won't let go. You think you've bested it, then it just rears its ugly head when you least expect it. It comes back stronger and meaner than it was before. Something out of your control just sets it off. And it's terrible."

Her arms dropped to her side. "Like the night you saw me in the doorway of the bar."

"Yeah, like that."

"Thanks for sharing." Zoe wiped her face with both hands. "Now give me the urn."

"I was angry at her, not you."

"It doesn't matter. I don't care. I thought I did, but after seeing you and Hannah in action, I don't want anything to do with you."

Lee swayed slightly.

Zoe fought the reflexive stretch of her hand. Snatched it back.

"What about Eve?" he asked, looking around as if he was going to sit down. "It will break her heart if you leave so soon."

"She managed her whole life without me, she'll manage now."

"You don't mean that."

"Don't presume to know what I mean or not. Give me the urn. You win. I'll take the ashes back to my brothers. They are going to sue me to get them back anyway. Fine. They can have her."

He turned from her, searched the ground, then leaned over to pick up the top to the urn.

Here was her chance. She could grab the urn and run. To where?

He carried the urn and top over to a fallen tree, motioned to it.

"Sit down."

Zoe shook her head.

"Please."

"It's because that girl came here. Isn't it?" Jim Kelly said. "The reason Hannah's doing this now. There are rumors all over town that she's Lee's daughter."

David shrugged and looked at Floret and Henry, who sat on either side of Jim like a pair of benevolent but useless guardian figures. Jim sat slumped on the couch between them, his head lowered.

"I'm sorry, Floret. Hannah's got me against the wall. We're about to lose everything."

Floret took his hand gently in hers.

His wife, Sheila, turned to David. "Isn't there anything you can do?" She cast a painful look toward her husband, then lowered her voice. "It will kill him to lose the diner. And the house. We'll lose it, too."

"Don't you have some, I don't know, savings?"

Jim shook his head. "I had to take out a second mortgage back in two thousand eight. We lost a bundle in the market, and I've never been able to get ahead since."

"Well, when you open back up, just hike the prices a dollar or so. It's not like you've raised them in years."

Jim shrugged. "People expect us to stay the same."

"They'll understand."

"If they let us reopen."

"They can't just close you down." David frowned. "What were the violations?"

"Damned if I know. Everything was the same as it ever was. They never complained before. They didn't even give us a chance to rectify whatever was amiss. They just came in, posted a bunch of gobbledygook on the door, and closed us down."

"They can't do that. Unless it's life-threatening, they have to give you time to fix the offenses."

"It's Hannah's doing, I tell you. She's forcing us out of our house and business."

"Where will we even go?" Sheila said, twisting her fingers in the apron she was still wearing from the diner.

"You'll not go anywhere," Henry said. "Sell her the right-of-way if you need to. We can keep the station wagon somewhere else or David can sell it. We can always walk out when we need to get to town."

"I think it's a little late for compromise," David said. "I think the old broad has gone over the brink. She tried to run down Zoe Bascombe with her car yesterday."

"Oh, heavens," said Sheila. "What did any of us ever do to her?"

Three pairs of eyes turned unconsciously toward Floret and Henry.

"We don't know," said Henry. "We've never known. One day she came home from one of her real estate conferences, said 'I know what you're up to,' told Eve to pack, and they moved out that afternoon."

"We were never up to anything," Floret said. "We've asked, guessed, racked our brains for years to no avail. It's been over thirty years and we still haven't learned why she was so upset with us. I don't even think she remembers."

Henry sighed in a way that set off alarm bells in David's head. "Perhaps . . ."

"Yes, my dear," Floret finished, as if she knew what he was going to say next.

David sure as hell didn't. This was not the time for them to go into one of their personal communion bits. Things were coming to a head.

"What?" Jim asked. "Perhaps what?"

"It's time for us to go," said Henry.

"We'll have to find a place for the professor," Floret said. "Where he'll be among friends. Among his good memories."

Both the Kellys and David stared at her in disbelief.

"Hell, no," David said. It was a pure knee-jerk reaction on his part. "Sorry, Jim, Sheila, but that's not an option."

"No, of course not," said Jim.

Sheila shook her head.

"It will not end until the source of her pain is removed," Henry said. "And we must be that source."

"Bullshit," David said.

Henry smiled. "Poor woman. One's pain is never cured by causing another."

David stood. "What the hell does that mean? If you leave, she'll just find another victim. Some people are like that. You can't fix things by always accepting whatever happens."

The others gave him their full attention. Henry nodded slightly. And David felt a sudden sinking feeling that Henry had just taught him a lesson he didn't want to learn. There were some things in life—and death—that David refused to accept.

But, hell, they weren't responsible. It was a sickness

in Hannah, one that no one had thought about trying to curtail until it was too late. Well, it wasn't too late. He didn't know what to do, exactly, other than starting a GoFundMe page to help support the Kellys until they could see their way clear. And he knew they were too proud to allow that. But he'd be damned if he'd sit by any longer and let Hannah Gordon wreck more people's lives.

"Besides, maybe it isn't about Zoe Bascombe at all. At least not totally. She's also angry about her great-granddaughter Mel seeing my nephew."

"That's crazy," Sheila said. "Eli's a lovely young man."

"Do you really think that's what it is?" Jim asked.

"Possibly. And I went to see Hannah to tell her to lay off the kids. I might have pushed her one step too far." He was grasping at straws. That didn't explain why she'd lashed out at Zoe.

"You did what anyone would do to protect their kin," Jim said.

"They're just children," Sheila said. "They shouldn't be dragged into this."

"No, they shouldn't." Henry stood. So did Floret. "I believe I may be able to end this once and for all."

"It's time," Floret agreed.

Jim pushed to his feet. "You're not going to sell because of us. I'd never be able to show my face in town again."

"Not to Hannah, no. But I have an idea."

"Don't do anything rash," David said. "I think she may have met her match this time."

"How so?"

"This town expects breakfast, lunch, and dinner at Kelly's. From the looks of things this morning, they won't stand by to see it closed down permanently."

"Yes, indeed," said Henry. "And I will attempt to take care of the rest." He walked calmly toward the door.

Floret lingered only long enough to cast her calming smile over the other three.

David bolted from his chair. "Wait, what's he going to do?"

Floret turned her smile to him. "I have no idea. But all will be fine." And she followed Henry out.

Chapter 22

Keeping her eyes on the urn, Zoe walked over to the log and sat down beside her father—not too close—and turned slightly so she could see his face, even though he was looking down at the urn he held in both hands.

He didn't say anything, so Zoe sat watching him watch the urn.

The air was still, so still that Zoe began to wonder if the chimes had been a dream and didn't really exist. She was tempted to look into the trees, catch sight of one of them, but she didn't take her eyes off her father. *Her father.*

He was a stranger. An angry man, who until a few moments ago wanted nothing to do with her. Maybe didn't even now.

"She came back for Eve's graduation."

His voice was such a surprise that Zoe started. It wasn't really a statement that required a response. So she didn't give one.

He turned sharply. "Why do you think she did that?"

Zoe frowned. "Because she loved her daughter and wanted to see her?"

"But she didn't see her. Not so as Eve would know. Not any of us saw her."

"It seems pretty clear to me that none of you wanted to see her, ever acknowledge her. And Eve didn't even know about her."

"That was wrong."

"Pretty much," Zoe said tentatively. She needed to stay prepared in case he lashed out at her in his anger. Like mother, like son. Zoe didn't trust either of them.

He fell into silence.

She waited. She wanted to get up and leave. She didn't think they would ever be anything to each other. But he had the ashes.

"Why didn't you follow your music?"

Zoe shot him a glance. "I don't know what you mean."

"You were going to be a musician."

"How do you know?"

"Your brother told me."

"Did he tell you I blew my Juilliard audition?"

"Juilliard isn't the only place to learn music; you gave up."

Of all the things they could be talking about, this was the last she'd expected, though it made sense. If ever there was going to be a conduit to Lee Gordon, it might be through music.

"Well?"

"I didn't give up. It was a deal I made with myself. If I failed, I would study something useful."

Lee carefully placed the urn beside him. The side farthest from her, Zoe noted. "Music is useful."

"I know, I just . . ."

"You got shouted down by your family, just like your mother did."

"No, I didn't." She could have stood up to her family—she could have, but she didn't. "You don't know what I'm like. You don't even know what my mother was like."

"I know she left me. She gave in to her parents. She didn't give us a chance."

"Maybe. But my mother loved order above everything. Do you really think she could have been happy sharing the life you led?"

"Why not? You only know her after the spirit was taken out of her. She wasn't like that before."

Before you got her pregnant and she gave in to the comforts she'd grown up with? For the first time, Zoe felt a pang of sympathy for this man. She had a creeping feeling that the woman Jenny had become was already firmly established in Jenny the teenage mother. "She made her choice."

"She gave up too easily."

"Maybe. Did you go after her?"

"I was on tour."

Zoe just looked at him.

"Then it was too late. Her parents wouldn't let me see her. When Hannah told me about the baby, I couldn't believe it. At least they let her bring the baby home."

He hadn't even known about Eve before Jenny left? Talk about the coward's way out. The same way her mother had left her to deal with the ashes. The same way Zoe had planned to dump the ashes and run?

Maybe Lee Gordon deserved a little more understanding than she'd thought. But she wasn't ready to let him off the hook yet. If ever.

"So you blamed her for your unhappiness and let that disappointment wreck the rest of your life. Everyone says you succumbed to drugs and alcohol and made everyone around you suffer."

He looked out into the distance, straight through the

keyhole of trees to the sea. They were perfectly positioned, as if the log had been placed there to admire the view. Maybe it had been.

"At least she knew where Eve was. I never even knew about you."

"And if you had?"

"I would have told her to send you to me."

"What? You don't even like me."

"I would have raised you right. With music."

"Oh, give me a break. You had Eve and she hasn't mentioned music once since I came." Except to jokingly offer Zoe a job playing in the bar downstairs.

"Eve can't carry a tune in a bucket. Music just isn't in her soul. That's okay. Something else is. The inn, the spa—she's a nurturer. But you . . . music is in your soul."

"You don't know me."

"I heard your song."

Zoe looked away. Afraid of the burning in her throat, the feel of tears welling up in her eyes. Those four words, *I heard your song,* they touched something hidden, something carefully protected. *I heard your song.*

She found herself being drawn to this old, gaunt, ponytailed rock 'n' roller from a decade long gone. She had to consciously pull back; to care about him would be a betrayal of the woman who had nurtured her for her entire life.

"You shouldn't have brought her back."

"I know."

From the moment Zoe had driven into town, Jenny had been causing strife and anger. What a legacy to leave. And yet there were Eve and Mel and Noelle and Harmony. Floret and Henry and David, Eli and the professor.

Would Jenny Bascombe have ever fit in here, really? Had she ever wondered what life would have been like if she'd stayed?

Did you have any idea of what havoc this would cause? Did you plan this as your revenge for a life lived in a lie? Everyone oblivious to your subterfuge, even on that rainy day when two kids discovered Sonny and Cher. What unhappiness were you living with that we never saw.

The perfect suburban mother and wife. *Until your husband betrayed you.* Was it all a lie? Except for a few minutes backstage at the Nassau Coliseum. *And me, your little secret, the product of those few minutes of relinquishing your well-practiced control. We could have lived on without ever knowing. Had you known from the beginning that this would be your final act?*

The urn appeared below her downcast eyes. The smooth celadon cradled in long, leathery fingers.

"Take her."

Zoe took the urn. Watched as Lee Gordon pushed himself slowly up from the log and walked into the woods.

Zoe sat there in the quiet, listening for the sounds of footsteps, but there was nothing. Why had he just left like that? *Take her?* Take her where? Back to Long Island? Or dump her wherever, he didn't care.

She wanted to run after him. Say, *Not so fast. You can't just unload on me and leave.* But it was just what he'd done.

She felt the breeze before she heard the first tinkle of sound. This time she didn't welcome it. It sounded like it was mocking her, every little thing, as it echoed through the trees. She stood, snatched up the tote, returned the urn inside, and got the hell out.

Mel watched as Eli nervously tore open the envelope from the university. She kind of felt like she was going to throw up. Because she was sure it was his acceptance to his big pre-semester program. She was glad for him. She would be a horrible person if she wasn't glad for him.

"Yes!" he said, and pumped the letter in the air.

She smiled. It wasn't a real smile. But it was the best she could do. "That's great. Congratulations."

He picked her up and twirled her around. "I made it. I made it." He set her down and wrapped his arms around her. She clung to him. It was such a loser thing to do. She didn't care. She just wanted things to be the same.

"Mel, be happy for me."

"I am. When do you leave?"

He let go of her abruptly. "In three weeks. But we'll see each other all the time. I'll only be in Boston. It's not so far away. Can't you be a little happy for me?"

"I said I am. I think it's great."

"It's only a couple of hours away. I'll come home every weekend. Well, not at first, but once regular term begins."

"You're already talking like a college student."

Eli's face fell. "Please be happy for me, Mel. You'll find what you want, too. We have all our life before us. We can do so many things. Learn so much stuff. Just think about it."

She wanted him. To stay. Here. She'd been thinking of nothing else for the past few months. Eli had a plan. All her friends had plans. She didn't have a clue. Much less a plan. What was wrong with her? Why couldn't they just leave her alone? Not everybody had to go off and do great things. Some people just stayed home and were normal.

"I am happy for you. I really am." She had to turn away. She was happy for him, but not for her. She looked out the window trying to keep from crying. Saw Zoe Bascombe running down the drive.

What the hell? Why was she running like somebody was chasing her? Mel leaned into the window, peered into the woods, but didn't see anything.

Eli came up behind her and put his arms around her, nestling his chin into her shoulder like he sometimes did. "I love you, Mel."

"I love you, too."

"But I don't want to get married. Not yet. We're too young. I don't even have a way to support you."

"We can both work at the inn."

"Mel—I want to be a scientist. If we're meant to be together, a few years won't matter."

"They matter to—" Mel sucked in her breath. Her grandfather stepped out of the trees, looked toward the house. Mel pulled back from the window, pushing Eli backward.

"Mel, don't."

Mel peeked around the window frame. He had turned from the house. He was going down the drive after Zoe.

"I have to go."

"Mel. Don't be like that. It's for the best. You know it is."

"It's not that. Something else." She rushed out the door, swung around the newel, and took the stairs two at a time.

"Mel, wait."

"Later." She ran outside, letting the door slam behind her. Dulcie jogged up to meet her. *Ma-a-a*'ed, and butted against her leg. "Go away." Mel pushed the goat away and ran across the yard. She didn't know what was going on, but she had to stop him from doing something awful.

Zoe wasn't sure what she planned to do, but things couldn't go on like this. Chris would be back soon and they could go home together.

She'd meant to go straight to her room, but when she reached the Solana lobby, she changed her mind. Or something changed her mind for her. Instead of going down the hall to the elevator, she turned to the right, stopped at the closed doors of the bar.

It was early still, and the bar wouldn't be open for several hours. The door was probably locked. She tried it anyway. It opened; she slipped inside.

The room was dark. The rectangle of sunlight

framed by the French doors cast everything else into shadows. Everything but the edge of the bandstand.

She didn't know why she'd come here, didn't question it. She was on autopilot; something beyond her moved her closer and closer until she was standing in the sun, staring at the shining ebony wood of the piano.

She stepped onto the bandstand, placed the tote carefully on the floor. Pulled the piano bench out and sat down.

Lifted the fallboard. The sun cast a diagonal swath of light across the keyboard, and she sat just looking at the pattern of light and dark.

There had been a time in her life, most of her life, when she would rush home from school, from a playdate, from a soccer game, wash her hands, and sit down at the piano. She dutifully practiced her scales, her études, learned her first Scarlatti, then Beethoven and Mozart, but it was her free time she cherished most. When tunes came into her head, then to her fingers—sometimes words, sometimes just a harmony.

Should she have studied more? Practiced harder? Performed more? Put herself out there, taken a chance?

She thought about what Lee Gordon had said in the glen. Had she given up too easily? What did that say about her? It was like the decisions were all black-and-white like the unplayed keys of the piano. Until they were joined in music.

Her life had been exciting, lived large with events, and travel, and the adrenaline rush of working in the entertainment business. It had been one event after another, all played out in loud music and high-def color.

But Lee was right about one thing. Her mother.

Zoe saw it now, though she hadn't recognized it before. The reason for her mother's award-winning flowers. It was the color—the underlying harmony—she was missing in her life. Two things she had probably found with Lee Gordon. Not that Zoe thought for a minute it would have lasted.

Jenny's life was ordered by black and white. Logical, no wiggle room, down to whether pearls or gold looked better with whatever outfit she wore on a particular night. She never veered from her decision. Pearls with the black de la Renta cocktail dress, and the gold mesh chain with the blue Anne Klein. Never once did the pearls make their way to the blue dress nor the gold to the black.

Because she'd made a choice and lived with that choice with precision. If someone wrote her biography, it would be called *Jennifer Bascombe's Precise Life.*

Zoe had left that painstakingly precise family and

fallen into this messy, angsty alter family. They were complicated and unreliable; they caused too much heartache, sometimes catching onlookers in the cross fire, like the Kellys. She'd left a life where she had a place, even if it wasn't exactly the place she had chosen, and now she was afraid she couldn't go back—or if she even wanted to go back.

She certainly couldn't stay here. As much as she wanted to get to know her family, it was a relationship that was rife with emotional landmines. Her career was already filled with emotional landmines; she didn't want to live that way 24/7.

But whether she stayed or not, whether the Bascombes threw her off or not, or Hannah Gordon ran her out of town, when she left, she'd take one thing with her. She wouldn't forsake it again.

She lowered her right hand, fingers curved; her index finger gently touched the keys, and a deep, unnamed current surged through her, branching out and filling every empty place inside her. She lifted her wrist, lowered another finger to the keys, the faint hint of a sound, the left hand, quietly joining the first individual notes, slowly at first, barely touching, moving closer and closer until they tumbled together. Separating, interweaving, running along the scale, then exploding in pure little bits of sound.

The song of the chimes she had been carrying in her head. Now it was all around her in the air, and she relished it, lost herself in it, and she played, alone with her music. Where she belonged.

"What are you doing?" Mel whispered, coming up behind her grandfather.

He was standing at the doorway to the Solana bar. The double doors were ajar. The bar should be closed at this time of day. She didn't see Zoe anywhere. She hoped he wasn't after the bourbon.

He glanced back at her. "Shhh. Listen." He motioned her to stand beside him.

She did, straining her ears to hear what he was talking about. Then she heard it. Someone was playing the piano.

Not their house piano player, maybe one of the guests. They weren't supposed to be in there. She started to tell him to ask them to leave, but she saw his face. It had a strange expression. She couldn't tell if he was mad or sad or what. His mouth was slightly open and his eyes seemed too bright.

It scared her. Like most everything else in her life. She started to open the door, put a stop to whatever was causing him to act this way. He grabbed her arm and held her back.

"Just listen."

She listened, watching his face, feeling the energy in him. So they stood there, grandfather, granddaughter, one rapt, the other wondering what the hell was going on and whether she should go find her mom before he did something crazy.

Eve knew things had gotten out of hand. She'd let Hannah run her life all these years, but whatever was driving Hannah, it was killing her family, and turning the town into an angry mob.

She'd missed the confrontation with the health department, but she'd been accosted more than once on her way back to the inn by friends demanding that she do something. As if she could.

She wondered if Hannah had finally gone too far by closing down Kelly's. There was no doubt that this was Hannah's doing. She had more than one local official under her thumb.

There was trouble ahead. Eve was sure of it. She'd overheard Ralph Perkins, who owned the three laundromats in town, telling a group of local store owners who had gathered on the sidewalk that it was time someone did something about Hannah's stranglehold on the town. He'd recently lost to Hannah in a bidding war for a property outside of town. A very lucrative property that was soon to be the site of high-end condominiums. He had breakfast at Kelly's every day. And he was not happy about this turn of events.

Funny if eggs and toast would be the straw that broke Hannah Gordon's empire.

Maybe it would come to nothing. And yet Eve couldn't help worrying. Would the anger spill over to her own family? The inn? She made a point of using local suppliers and services when possible. She could always go outside for the inn's needs, but at what cost? It would be less expensive but would cost her plenty in good will.

It was not something she wanted to test.

She could stand with the town if things came to a head. She already sided with them, but could she turn on her grandmother, who had given her a good life and a start in business?

But Hannah was old. Did Eve owe allegiance more to her than to her own family? They needed a secure future. And what about her new family? She had a sister, half brothers. Hannah would never acquiesce to Zoe Bascombe being a part of the Gordon clan.

Eve wandered around the empty cottage, straightened a poster of Les Deux Magots in Paris. Mel said it sounded gross, like worms, instead of a café where famous intellectuals had met to drink espresso and argue about art.

Mel would be gone soon. The last of her three girls to leave the nest. She was resisting so hard, but Eve couldn't let her stay. There was more in the world for her daughters than Eve had managed to find for herself, and she was determined that they would at least get a taste of another life.

Not that her life had been bad. She loved the inn—at least she'd learned to love the inn. And she'd grown to love Walter. A foolish teenage mistake could have ended much worse. He stuck by her, even though it was hard always being under Hannah's thumb and not able to support his family the way Hannah constantly reminded them he should. So he took off with a friend to the Alaskan oil fields. The money was good; he sent it home every month, but he rarely returned. They got used to living without him. Mel never even got to know him. Then one day, Eve received a phone call saying he had died on the job, and that was that.

And the strange thing was that she and the girls didn't really miss him, as if he was still working the Alaskan oil fields.

Would she have been happier if she had gone to college, traveled the world like she'd dreamed of? Maybe not. Especially knowing now what joy her girls would bring her? Maybe Mel wouldn't be happier either. But at least she would have the chance to find out.

And now Noelle had a job in New York City.

And Eve had a celebratory dinner to prepare. She walked over to the bookshelf, pushed aside a miniature painting of the Grand Canyon, and reached for her favorite cookbook.

She'd just opened it when there was a knock at the kitchen door. She went to answer it.

Henry Gladstone stood in the doorway. "Let's take a walk."

Chapter 23

Zoe was still playing when the lights to the bar suddenly popped on and Mike the bartender walked through the door.

She stood and hastily covered the keys.

"Hello, I thought I heard music."

"Sorry, the door was open, and I—I shouldn't have come in."

"Don't apologize. It sounded nice. And after all, you're one of the family."

"I guess everybody knows."

"Is it supposed to be a secret? You couldn't get a better sister than Eve. And her girls, too. I hope you're not upset."

"No. I've always wanted a sister. Just didn't expect to get one this way."

"Come over here. You like white wine, right?"

She nodded.

He reached under the counter to a half fridge and took out a bottle of Chardonnay. He poured a glass for Zoe.

"I keep this for Eve. Grand cru. The local house wine is good, but this . . ."

He kissed his fingers, a gesture so incongruous to his burliness that Zoe laughed.

"That's better," he said. "Have you seen Eve lately?"

"No. I saw her this morning. Kelly's got closed down. She was there but I didn't get to talk to her. I've been out."

"Yeah. It's been a long time coming. Though I'm thinking that this time Hannah may have overplayed her hand."

"What do you mean?" Zoe asked. She took a sip of wine. "Oh, that is good."

"Stick around, kid. You'll get an education in the finer wines of New England."

"So how did Hannah overplay her hand? Will Kelly's be able to open again?"

"If Kelly's regulars have anything to say about it, yes and soon. She's been jerking this town around since I can remember, but you don't get between folks and their favorite diner. They're already planning a pushback. I wouldn't want to be Hannah if they follow up on the talk I was hearing this morning."

"They won't hurt her, will they?"

"Just where it hurts her most, in her purse and her ego. She'll survive. But maybe next time she'll think twice about lashing out against people who never did her any harm."

He took out a white cloth and wiped the scrupulously clean bar.

"Mike, did I cause all this?"

"Nah, it's always festering beneath the surface. Hannah's just a mean, old, lonely woman. She doesn't have to be. It's her choice."

She watched him set up the bar, while she sipped on the delicate, crisp wine. She liked it here. She'd really like it here if things would just calm down. The inn's guests went back to their homes, refreshed and revitalized. But Zoe was wound as tight as an E string.

"There's the boss lady," Mike said, looking past Zoe.

Eve came in and sat down next to Zoe. Mike poured her a glass of wine.

"The oddest thing just happened."

Mike handed her the glass, and he and Zoe gave her their undivided attention.

"Henry just offered to sell me Wind Chime—house, grounds, beach, everything."

Her announcement was met with a minute of total silence. She was pretty gobsmacked herself. Henry and Floret were willing to give up their lifelong home to get the Kellys out of Hannah's sights. It was more than she could bear.

"You can't," Zoe said, at the same time Mike said, "It's worth a fortune. Can you afford it?"

"As it turns out, I could. He was offering it for a song, on time, the dear man. He hoped to save the Kellys from losing everything to Hannah. That's why he made the offer. He didn't see any other way. And quite frankly I don't either."

"So he's giving in to Hannah?" asked Zoe.

"Or making it so that Eve has to deal with her," Mike said. "Selling to you is not going to solve the problem. It will just roll over the problem to you."

"Would it? With Floret and Henry gone, what more could she want?"

"Gone?" Zoe blurted. "But where would they go, and what about the professor?"

"They would have to consult with the professor, but Henry suggested one of the old cottages on the old road."

Mike snorted. "Where Lee lives? They're barely standing. Talk about out of the frying pan—"

"I know. And there were certain caveats."

"For instance?" Mike asked.

"Mainly, that I'd keep the glen as a memorial garden and let others continue to be buried there."

Mike reached across the bar and put his large hand over hers. "Is this what you really want?"

"No, it's not what I want." At the moment, Eve just wanted to take her family and get far away. But she couldn't let the Kellys lose everything because her grandmother was a heartless old witch. "It's a lot of land, but I'm not sure I want to expand. Ever. I like the intimacy of the inn. I don't want a big convention center. What would be the point? Besides . . ."

She didn't want to put any more 24/7, life-sucking hours into expansion. She wanted to kick back a little. Enjoy life. See the Grand Canyon.

"I'm full to the gills already. In a few weeks I lose the last of my summer staff to college and high school. And we're already booked solid into the New Year. Totally unfeasible."

"What did you tell him?"

"I turned him down, of course."

"So the Kellys are still in danger of losing everything," Zoe said.

"Maybe not," Mike said.

Eve and Zoe both looked at him.

Mike shrugged. "Evidently, after the closure this morning, there was an impromptu meeting at the lodge house. Some of the local businessmen—and women—have called for a general boycotting of your grandmother." Mike winced. "Sorry, but they're serious. She's made a lot of enemies in this town. Closing Kelly's might have been the last straw."

"I heard some grumblings this morning, but do you think anything will come of it?" Eve asked.

"Mr. Paxton at the market already canceled her account and refused to deliver groceries."

"No. Where did you hear this?"

Mike laughed. "I'm a bartender. Actually, I was in the barbershop. The only place you hear more gossip than behind the bar. If everyone sticks to their guns, the cleaners, the landscapers, and all the other services she uses will no longer have her as a client. And while I was there, Judge Briggs came in for his weekly rearrangement of the three hairs he has left. He said his wife, who is best friends with Sheila Kelly, said Hannah is about to be blackballed out of the Woman's Club."

"Harsh, but she can't say she hasn't been asking for it," Eve said.

Zoe put down her glass. "Do you think they'll all really stand together?"

"Without losing the best, cheapest diner around as the other option? Yeah, I think they will," Mike said.

"Poor Hannah," Eve said.

"Don't start feeling sorry for her now. It will do her some good to see what it feels like being on the other side."

The bar began to fill up, and Zoe and Eve returned to Eve's cottage to make plans for Noelle's celebration dinner.

"I guess we should invite my—our—father. If that's okay," Eve said as they pored over recipes. "He probably won't come."

"It's okay. I guess. Actually, we kind of talked this morning. I'm not sure how it went."

"You met him? How did this happen?"

"It wasn't exactly planned. I sort of told him I was leaving and to call Hannah off. I'm afraid I wasn't very nice. I'm usually more diplomatic than that, but . . ." She shrugged.

Eve closed the cookbook and sat down at the table. "You want to share?"

Zoe started with the call from Errol and his threats to sue her for Jenny's ashes.

Eve got up and went to the fridge for wine.

"Then I was so angry and confused, I was going to

dump the ashes and go back to Long Island. Don't look so shocked. I'm still here. And so are they. Anyway, the damn things were enclosed in indestructible plastic, so while I was fighting to get them open, Lee sneaks up on me and grabs them out of my hands."

She looked at Eve and wasn't sure if her sister was about to laugh or cry.

"Sorry," Eve mumbled, and burst into laughter.

It was infectious. Zoe succumbed. "It was totally ridiculous, I know. Not to mention embarrassing, and humiliating. He told me I couldn't scatter her ashes in anger, then gave me a lecture on my life."

"Really? That's a start, I guess."

"A start? I'm not so sure. Then he got up and left without a word. I waited a few minutes and came back here."

"Don't feel bad about that. That's what he does when he has to think about stuff. He just leaves. Then he'll come back in a few hours, sometimes days, and give you his reaction. That's when the fun begins." Eve took a sip of wine.

"Oh, goody. I can hardly wait."

"So you're not taking the ashes back to Long Island?"

"I don't know. I'm going to wait until Chris gets back and consult with him. He's probably talked to my other brothers already. Maybe he'll have some insights.

But it's ultimately my decision. She instructed me, not them, to dispose of them."

"Then we won't worry about that now. If I invite Lee, I'll have to invite Hannah. Don't worry, she won't come unless it's to deliver some sort of threat and make an exit. Maybe we should keep it to the four of us. Or five if Mel comes back."

"She's still at Floret and Henry's?"

Eve nodded. "I've texted her. Apologized. But I've only gotten radio silence. Henry says to give her a few days, she's working through stuff." She sighed. "I hope I haven't pushed her in the wrong direction."

"Can't help you there, sis. I don't have any experience with teenagers."

Eve smiled across the table. "There's still time."

Zoe rolled her eyes and reached for the wine bottle.

Chris and Noelle rolled into the inn the next afternoon, loaded down with Noelle's suitcase and several large shopping bags.

"Presents and some updated wardrobe for me," Noelle announced, dropping everything on the cottage couch and giving Eve a big hug. "I've got a job." She hugged Zoe. "I've got a job." She danced around the room singing, "I've got a job. I've got a job."

"She has a job," Chris said drily. "In case you're wondering."

"How about you?" Zoe asked.

"Eh. Nothing in my inbox at the moment. But hey, it's the theater. These things happen."

"So you don't have to go right back?"

"No, Dilly-Do. The only thing on my dance card is brokering the 'what to do with the ashes' deal."

"I thought they might have called you."

"Not to worry. After Errol's first call, I called back and got the lovely Allison on the phone. She's tired of the whole rigmarole—her word, not mine. The lady has a short attention span, but Errol is putty in her hands. She promised to dissuade him and Robert from suing. Robert will go whichever way Errol goes. So I don't think we'll be visiting you in the slammer quite yet. You still have the ashes?"

"Yep," Zoe said, suddenly glad Lee had stopped her.

"So, where's Mel?" Noelle asked. "I have something for her." She rummaged in the bags and pulled out a mug probably bought at one of the tourist shops in Times Square. *World's Best Sister.* "Peace offering," she said. "I also brought her a great sweater for fall, compliments of Bloomingdale's. Wow, what a store."

"I take full credit—or blame—for this wacky shopping spree," Chris said. "But who can resist Bloomies?"

"We shopped the whole Upper East Side and Soho and the Village," added Noelle. "But don't worry, I didn't buy things in every one. Some of them were really expensive. You wouldn't believe. But I did need to spruce up my wardrobe. Chris insisted."

"Me?" He wobbled his head à la *H.M.S. Pinafore.* "Okay, maybe me."

"So where *is* Mel?"

"We had a bit of a scene; she's been staying at Wind Chime House."

"Ugh. She is such a head case. No wonder she hasn't been returning my texts." Noelle took a deep breath. "What's that divine smell?"

"Your favorite. Boeuf bourguignon. The kitchen is sending over lobster patties. And I have asparagus and homemade hollandaise. And . . . pineapple upside-down cake for dessert."

"Lord, I won't be able to fit into my new clothes."

"It may just be the four of us," Eve said apologetically. "I asked your grandfather. And I left a message for Hannah, but . . ."

"They're both being buttheads. It's okay. We'll have a feast. I'll call Mel and tell her she has to come." She sashayed into the other room and closed the door.

"She's a little enthusiastic," Chris said. "Plus we had a little sugar on the drive up," he added in his deadliest deadpan. He reached into one of the bags. "Compliments of Godiva, Greenberg's, and"—he rattled the bag—"a couple of chocolate chip cookies from your favorite bakery." He groaned and clutched his stomach. "There were a dozen. We're both riding a sugar-caffeine high."

"Good thing we're having lots of protein for dinner," Zoe said, and reached for the bag. "You have to try these, Eve."

Noelle came out while the two of them munched the last two cookies. "Her princess-ness has said she'll come. I invited Eli, hope you don't mind. She's feeling a little fragile. I thought Eli's presence would help."

"Of course it's fine," Eve said, wiping the crumbs off her jeans. "That was delicious, but I'd better go check the stew."

Mel and Eli arrived just as Zoe and Noelle finished setting the table. Mel was wearing a bright red baseball cap with the university's logo across the front.

Noelle gave Mel a hug, which Mel returned tentatively.

"Like the cap," Noelle said.

"It's Eli's."

"Does this mean you're going steady?"

Eli blushed.

"He's letting me break it in," Mel said, and went into the kitchen.

"Congratulations on the new job," Eli said. He held out a bouquet of flowers. "Floret sent them."

Noelle took them. "Thanks. I'll just go put them in a vase. Park it with Chris. You've met, right?"

"Yo," said Eli.

"Yo-ho," said Chris. "Try one of these cheese puffs."

Eli laughed and sat down on the couch.

Eve was serving the main course when there was a knock at the front door.

A moment passed when they all looked at each other; then Eve shrugged and went to answer it. Mel and Eli looked as if they might run for the back door.

"I'll just get some more plates," Noelle said, and slipped into the kitchen.

Eve opened the door, stepped back, and Lee Gordon stepped into the room. "Dad. Glad you could make it. We're just getting started."

"Just like Scrooge at Christmas dinner," Chris whispered to Zoe.

She nudged him in the ribs.

Lee nodded toward the people at the table.

Chris popped out of his chair. "Sit here. I'll get another chair."

Zoe watched her father walk across the floor. He was freshly shaven; his hair was pulled back in his usual ponytail, but he was wearing black jeans and a black button-down shirt. He was actually kind of handsome, something Zoe hadn't noticed in their few brief encounters.

He nodded to Chris and sat down without looking at the others. Chris trotted off to the kitchen, rolling his eyes at Noelle as they passed the doorway.

It was left to Noelle to carry on the conversation. *Thank you for all that sugar and caffeine*, Zoe thought. The rest of them seemed totally tongue-tied. Mel and Eli didn't even look at each other. Eli turned to Zoe, but she had nothing. She was too busy reconciling herself to the fact that she was sitting down to dinner with her father. Her biological father. It was weirder than she could have imagined, if she had ever imagined it, which she hadn't. She hadn't really thought he would come.

Chris and Eve returned with the last serving plates and the extra chair, and the unease was covered over by the passing of dishes, the pouring of wine—seltzer for Eli and Mel, about which neither complained.

Eve raised her glass. "To Noelle's new job and a bright future."

"Here, here," said Chris.

They all joined in and drank the toast, then dug into their meals.

Conversation gradually began again once the initial bites and compliments subsided. It did remind Zoe of the scene where Scrooge comes to dine with his nephew. She hoped their dinner tonight had as happy an outcome.

After dessert, Chris and Zoe cleared the table and Eve made coffee. When they returned from the kitchen, Mel and Eli were getting ready to leave.

"Sorry to eat and run, but I have studying to do," Eli said.

"Sure, so glad you came," Eve said, and walked them to the door.

"I'm just going to walk him home, but I thought since Noelle and all . . ." Mel trailed off.

"You're coming home?"

Zoe couldn't hear the answer, but she saw the red hat bob up and down. And then Eve gave her daughter a hug.

Zoe let out the breath she'd been holding unconsciously. She turned and caught Lee watching her. She smiled tentatively, but when Eve came back in, he stood and took her aside.

She looked startled, then nodded and took him into her bedroom. A few minutes later she came out alone.

"He apologizes, but he wants to read Jenny's letters." Eve's mouth worked. She looked at Zoe.

Suddenly, it was all happening fast, maybe too fast. Noelle's job, Mel's return home, Lee making an overture to both daughters. Now if Zoe could just resolve the problem of her mother's ashes. She immediately felt contrite. It wasn't a problem. It was an honor that her mother chose her to send her on her final journey.

And she realized with a jolt of blinding clarity that she wanted her brothers to join her for the ceremony. No matter if she had to keep the ashes in the hotel room closet for however long it took. Jenny should get her wish, but her family should be there to send her off.

"We'll leave you two alone," Zoe said, standing up. "Call if you need us."

"Where's Noelle?" Chris asked, looking around. "I'll just tell her to meet us in the bar downstairs." He pulled out his phone to text her.

Noelle stepped out of the kitchen, licking her fingers. "What's up?"

"We're going out," Chris said, and trundled both her and Zoe toward the door.

Chapter 24

Eve watched them go. When the door closed behind them, she tiptoed over to the hallway and listened for any sound coming from her bedroom. Nothing. The only thing she could hear was the hum of the dish-washer.

She went into the kitchen and turned it off.

She poured herself half a glass of wine and went back into the living room to wait. She began to wonder if he was ever coming out. She imagined dozens of things as time dragged by: That he'd managed to sneak out of the cottage while she'd been in the kitchen. Or climbed out the window, too angry—too sad, too humiliated—to face her. Destroyed all the letters while she sat here waiting. Been so shocked to read them that his heart failed and he was lying on the floor near death.

The last thought had her up and knocking on the door of her bedroom.

When she didn't get an answer, she turned the knob and peeked inside.

He was sitting on the bed, her mother's cards and letters spread out across the coverlet. His head was bent, and she saw that the hair on the top of his head had begun to thin. It was a heart-melting realization. Her father was getting older. They'd wasted too many years caught in a web of regret and blame.

It was time to reclaim him and her mother.

Eve stepped inside and closed the door.

He looked up, and she realized that his cheeks were wet with tears. "I'm sorry," he said.

She rushed to the bed and sat down beside him, wrapped her arms around him. "I'm sorry, too."

"You? You have nothing to be sorry about."

"I do. Don't be sad. I shouldn't have told you about them." She reached for them, meaning to gather them up and put them away, but he stopped her.

Picked up a card with pink and green balloons on the front. *Happy birthday, six-year-old!*

"How did she know?" he asked.

"Know what?"

"That pink and green were your favorite colors?"

"They were? I don't remember."

"They were—every cake from four to seven always had pink icing with pink roses and big green leaves."

She remembered. "I always thought that was Floret and Granna's doing."

Lee shook his head. "They made the cakes. But she knew. She was your mother."

Eve wasn't sure she believed that, but if it made Lee feel better, so be it. Would he be able to forgive Jenny now? After all those years? Would Hannah let him?

"And you really didn't know about these?" she asked.

"No. Never. I would have tried one more time. Even though I knew it was too late. She chose the life she knew, instead of giving the one with me a chance. We promised forever."

But it didn't mean the same for you. The words to his song.

"I loved your mother with all my heart, and when she left I kind of went crazy. Well, I did go on a self-destructive binge. Hannah bullied me through, and she brought me the best gift she could . . . you."

Eve's throat felt about to burst. Her dad had never opened his heart in all these years, had never shared anything with her. But how could he have, when Hannah was manipulating them all even then.

"But she didn't show you the letters. Didn't let me

know that my mother loved me. Wanted to know me. Remembered me and always thought about me. I didn't even get to know who she was while she was alive."

She felt her father's hand on her hair. A soft touch, it helped, but not much.

"Why did she do that?"

"She never approved of Jenny. She warned me against her. Said she'd never leave her comfy life for the erratic life of a musician. She was right, as it turned out."

"People split up all the time, it doesn't have to be a fight to the death."

"For your grandmother it did."

"But why? Was it because of me?"

"No. She moved heaven and earth to get you."

"To use against Jenny?" *And to keep you hostage,* she added to herself.

He sighed. "No. It was just Hannah's way. I think she did it for me at first. At least, I hope she did. But Hannah doesn't understand love. She can only love what she can own. It's how she is. It started long before you or even me."

Eve pulled away to see his face.

"I don't understand."

"She married my father when she was fourteen. She'd grown up on the poor side of town in a house full of hate, with parents who blamed others for their own failure. You know the type. I'm one of them," he added more quietly.

"No, Dad, you're not a failure. But it wasn't Jenny's fault either. Hannah manipulated you both just like she does everyone."

"It's the only way she knows how to act. She thought she escaped all the poverty and hopelessness when she married your grandfather. He was a handsome guy, a big talker. He swept her off her feet. She took what little love she'd kept alive through her childhood and placed it and all her hope in him, but he was just as bad.

"And this goes no further, not to the kids, not to anybody. He cheated on her, spent all the money she meticulously saved. They lost the house, and we had to move in with Henry and Floret and the others.

"When he died, she was determined to make her life a success. And she did. She went to night school. Learned real estate and gradually turned nothing into a lucrative business. Along the way she lost my brother and my sisters married deadbeat moochers just like our father. I pretty much screwed up the rest for her.

"That's all on me. I let myself turn into a disillusioned, bitter old man. That's what Zoe told me. That I was the most bitter person she'd ever met. I guess I am. And I'm sorry."

Eve shook her head. Everything he said about himself was true, but it didn't have to be that way. "It's because Hannah kept Jenny away from you."

He coughed out air. "Jenny could have tried harder."

"So could you."

"I guess I could have. And I could have done better by you, and I'm sorry for that."

"Don't be. Life is what it is. We'll just do better from here on out. Deal?"

"I don't know if I can. I'm old, with a lot of bad, ingrained habits. But I need you to know that I love you. Hannah at least gave me that—my most precious gift of all."

"And what about your other daughter?"

"What about her?"

"Will you love her, too?"

"I don't know if I can." Eve was shocked to see tears in his eyes. "I just don't know if I can."

Mel wasn't in a hurry to say good night to Eli, so she'd been stopping to look in shop windows of stores she never went in and would never buy anything from, just to keep what she had for as long as she could. Tonight felt all wonky. Like stuff was changing. Well, it was for Noelle, and definitely for her grandfather. She didn't like it, but she was afraid she couldn't stop it.

"That was just too weird," she said, stopping to look in a window of picture frames. She wasn't interested in picture frames. She just wanted to slow things down.

"What was?" Eli said, looking at her and probably wondering why they'd stopped for the millionth time since they'd left the inn.

"Granddad showing up like that. And everything," she added.

"Yeah, that was kinda weird. I thought he was gonna ream us in front of everybody, for sure, but he didn't even mention it. He was actually kind of nice to me."

Mel huffed out a sigh. "Definitely weird."

Eli nudged her onward, but Mel saw a silver Cadillac coming down the street and pushed him back to look at the window.

"What?"

"It's Hannah." Mel tucked her head down and looked over her shoulder. "Do you think she saw us?"

"So what?" He gave her a little shake. "Hey, don't worry. She didn't see us."

Eli put his arm around her shoulders, but Mel thought it might be just to move her faster down the street. She could tell he was anxious to get home, not just because Granna might see them, but because he wanted to read about some process they were going to work on at his science program. He made it sound like something out of *Star Wars,* but it just sounded like summer school to her.

Still, she kept her head down and her face hidden by Eli's university cap until she was sure the Cadillac had driven off down the street. They walked past the diner with its door padlocked and no lights on inside. Maybe that's why Hannah was out so late. Making sure that they hadn't reopened. Everybody in town knew that closing it down was Hannah Gordon's doing. Her grandmother could really be a douche sometimes. Still, she was her granna.

They turned down the drive to Eli's house much too soon. They passed the Kellys' house where they could see the flicker of the television through the front window.

"Poor Mr. Kelly," she said.

"It's pretty lame what happened, but David says it won't last."

"How can he be sure? You know Granna, she never backs down on anything."

"Peer pressure."

"Huh?"

Eli shrugged. "I don't know. He just said that even this town had its limits."

"That sounds scary."

"I guess."

Dulcie was waiting for them at the gate.

"How come you're still out?" Eli said. "It's past your bedtime."

"That's why," Mel said, and pointed down to the beach where a couple was standing on the sand looking out to sea. Moonlight washed down on them. "It's Henry and Floret," Mel said. "They're holding hands. It's so romantic, just like—" She broke off. She'd almost said like figures on a wedding cake. And that *would* have been lame.

At the same time, the silhouetted figures raised their arms.

"What are they—"

Fabric waved above their heads before dropping to the sand, and they walked toward the waves.

"OMG, they're skinny-dipping," Mel said, and giggled. "It's true what everybody says."

"Yeah," Eli said, and took Mel's hand.

"Wow. That's amazing. You don't think about old people . . . you know."

"Why not?"

"I don't know. It's nice. Growing old together. Like that." Mel leaned into him. "That's what I thought we would be. But it's different with us, isn't it? You know what you want. I don't know what I want or if I want anything at all."

"Come on, Mel."

"No, really. We're not like Henry and Floret. Not two halves of the same thing."

"We don't know that yet. We're teenagers. But if we do have that thing, it'll last longer than a few years at college. And if we don't . . ." He trailed off.

So she finished for him. "Maybe it's better we find it out now."

"Yeah."

Mel looked back out to where Floret and Henry floated on the waves as still as the moon itself. Two parts of one thing. *Soul mates.* "I'd better get back."

"You sure you don't want to stay here tonight?"

"Yeah. Thanks, but it's time for me to go home."

"Come sit down for a minute." He pulled her over to the steps, and they sat down.

He turned slightly toward her. Took both her hands. "You know I love you, right?"

Mel nodded. "But we have things to do before we . . . yeah, I get it."

"But things are still cool, right? With us. Friends and everything?"

"Yeah."

"You really mean it?"

"Yes, I really mean it."

"Great. And we'll text and stuff. And . . ."

"Yeah." She pulled his new cap off her head. "You'll be needing this."

"You keep it. I'll get another one." He took it from her and put it back on her head. "To remember me by."

"You're not going for another three weeks."

"I know. I just want you to wear it."

A fleeting shadow was all the warning they got before Dulcie careered out of the darkness and butted Mel backward.

"Dammit, Dulcie. Get off."

Dulcie snapped for the bill of the hat, and Mel twisted out of the way.

Laughing, Eli pulled the goat away. "Red isn't your color, Dulcie. Go find someone else's hat to eat."

"She is so lame," Mel said, standing up and holding the cap with both hands. "Gross, Dulcie. Gross."

"See you tomorrow?" Eli asked, standing up beside her.

"Yeah, probably. See ya"—she kissed him, but already it felt different—"mañana." She turned and walked quickly down to the drive. First Noelle, now Eli. Who would be next?

She felt something at her leg. Dulcie.

"How did you get out again? Go home," Mel hissed at her. "I don't want you. Go away."

A car turned into the drive. A Cadillac. She recognized it even at this distance in the growing night. Granna had seen them in town. She was probably coming to ream out Henry and Floret and then drag Mel home.

Why couldn't she just leave things alone? Hadn't she done enough damage for one day?

Mel turned back to the house, but Eli had already gone inside. She wouldn't make it inside before her granna saw her. And she didn't want to face her alone.

"Go!" She pushed Dulcie away and raced into the woods. Hid there while she waited for the Cadillac to pass and for Granna to go inside. But the car slowed down.

"I saw you, Mel! Come out and get in this car. I won't have you running around in the middle of the night."

Mel held her breath and plastered herself against a tree. She was such a coward.

"Mel!"

Mel held still, and finally the Cadillac drove on. But instead of stopping at the house, it turned and stopped at the edge of the woods.

What the—

The door opened. Hannah got out of the car and reached back in for her cane. "Mel, come out of there!"

Mel eased back and nearly fell over Dulcie.

Granna was coming down the path. She'd pass right

by Mel. Mel grabbed Dulcie around the neck and dragged her into the trees.

"Shh," she said, and held the goat close.

Hannah moved slowly past them, almost close enough to touch. "I'm not going to ask you again," she called. "You're in big enough trouble as it is."

Mel's mouth twisted, and she buried her face in Dulcie's rough coat. Even her great-grandmother hated her. *Please, just go away. Please.*

Hannah disappeared for a minute, and at first Mel thought she had given up and gone back to the car. Then she heard Hannah's voice from the opposite direction.

"I know where you're going. To meet that boy—on the beach. Just like your grandfather and that Jenny."

She wasn't going back to her car; she was going to Mel and Eli's beach. Because she thought Mel was going there. Then Mel remembered the steps. Granna didn't know they were rotten and she might try to climb down them.

"Granna, no!" Mel tried to get up, but Dulcie wanted to play. She butted her back down and nipped at the cap Eli had just given her.

"No, Dulcie." She fought to her feet and ran toward the path. "Granna, I'm back here. Behind you! Stop!"

Mel ran, crashing through the trees until she reached the path. She saw her grandmother ahead, standing at the steps looking over the caution rope at the beach below. "You can't hide from me. I know you're down there."

"Granna, I'm back here!"

She was almost there when Hannah reached out to grasp the balustrade.

"Granna! No!" Why didn't she stop? Because she couldn't hear her. She must have her hearing aids off. "Granna!" she screamed.

Hannah stepped on the first step. The frame swayed. Mel raced toward the stairs to stop her.

Just as she reached the steps, they gave way, slo-mo; Hannah swayed with the motion.

Mel threw herself at her great-grandmother and managed to grab her as the steps sagged and broke into pieces. She swung Hannah to the ground, but her own momentum carried her forward. Her feet scrabbled on the dirt but couldn't find purchase. She grabbed for the closest thing—the last standing piece of wooden support. The post teetered, groaned.

And it gave way in her hand.

The whole stairway collapsed, sweeping up Mel and carrying her downward.

She heard Hannah cry out above her, then nothing but the rumble and splintering of wood.

It only lasted seconds. But somehow, the wood ended

up on top, with Mel underneath, her ears ringing, her eyes gritty. But she was still alive.

It's less than ten feet down, dumbass.

She moved slightly, setting off a small rain of splinters and wood pieces. Not a good idea. It was really dark. She gingerly lifted her head. Saw that the whole frame and risers were crisscrossed like that game of pickup sticks, and she was on the bottom.

"Granna," she croaked. "Are you okay? Granna?"

Hannah didn't answer. Mel had pushed her out of the way before she fell, hadn't she? She tried to look around but saw only dark, jagged pieces of wood.

"Granna!" Mel pushed at the wood, but it only made the pieces shift and the whole mess settle lower on top of her.

She had to get out. Make sure her great-grandmother was okay. If she could just get out. She moved her leg, gently so she didn't pull the whole mess down any more. She tried the other leg. One arm, then the— "Ow." She grabbed the arm. That really hurt.

She turned her head, afraid to turn over completely. There was a small rectangle nearby where she could see some sand. If she could just reach it.

She tried scooting on her back toward it. *Man, her arm really hurt.*

She managed to get close enough to see out to the

beach. But the opening was way too small for her to escape through. She might bring down the whole thing.

"Granna, are you up there? Are you okay? Can you go for help? Granna. Turn on your hearing aid!"

The reply she got was the last one she expected or wanted to hear. The most irritating sound in the world. One ear-grating bleat. Dulcie stuck her head in the opening and grabbed Mel's cap in her teeth. One tug and she backed out of the opening, sending another shower of sticks and lumber down on Mel's now bare head.

"Stupid goat."

Though . . . maybe she would go home, and when Henry came out to put her in the shed for the night, he'd see the cap and wonder where it came from . . . then they would look for her and find her.

Only, what if Dulcie dropped the hat? What if she didn't go back to the house?

They'd come looking for her . . . *Please come look for me.*

Dulcie had stopped just out of reach, the hat dangling from her mouth. "Go get Henry, Dulcie. Please."

She just had to be patient. Henry or David would come looking for Dulcie before long. They never let her stay out all night. There were wild animals that might hurt her.

Or Mel's mom would call to see where she was. And then they'd look for her. Except maybe she'd think Mel had changed her mind and was staying out here tonight. Then her mom wouldn't call.

They'd see the Cadillac and wonder where Hannah was. They'd go look for her. Surely they would look for her. Or were they just too mad at her to care?

No. Henry and Floret weren't like that.

But what if Granna was hurt? What if she was hurt really bad and they came too late?

"Dulcie, you gotta go get help. Please, I'll never call you stupid again. You have to help us."

Chapter 25

David set down his beer on the table and listened. "Is that Dulcie? Why isn't she in the shed for the night?"

Eli looked up from his iPad. "Because Henry and Floret are out swimming in the raw. Mel and I saw them. Mel was kind of surprised."

David hid his smile. "Yeah, crazy old folks, having fun and getting it on."

"Ha. I know it's the brownies. Most old people are uptight and pitiful."

"The professor? He's not."

"No, but that's because he's kept his mind active. That's important."

"Thanks for the lecture. They're not so old."

"Seventies. That seems old to me."

"It won't for long. Trust me." David dragged his ancient thirty-six-year-old body from his chair.

"I'll go bed her down. Let them have their fun." While it lasts, he added to himself.

"Huh." Eli went back to his reading.

David opened the front door and trotted down the porch steps. Dulcie was standing at the bottom. She saw him, let out another lengthy bleat, and ducked her head. She came up with something in her mouth.

"What the hell have you found now? You'd better not be raiding the Daltons' laundry line again." He walked over to her and pried whatever it was out of her mouth. Eli's new university cap. That didn't take long, though it wasn't like Eli to be so careless. "Okay, it's bed for you, Dulcie."

He started toward her pen, but Dulcie didn't budge.

"If you don't go now, you'll have to wait for Henry or Floret and they're busy." They were also amazing. David had always been suspicious of the existence of that kind of long-lasting love, but no more. It was possible. He supposed.

"Come on, Dulcie." He went back to urge her toward the shed, but she danced away and took off into the woods.

"Suit yourself, but there are wild animals out there."

But not this early, he thought, and went back into the house.

"Here's your cap," he told Eli, and tossed it toward him. "Dulcie had it."

Eli picked it up. "How did she get it?"

"I dunno. Where did you leave it?"

"I gave it to Mel."

David felt a frisson of unease skitter up his spine. "You better text her and tell her you found it." He hoped they hadn't had a fight and Mel had tossed it in a moment of anger . . . Surely Eli would have said something and he hadn't seemed at all upset this evening.

Eli was already on the phone texting. They both waited, staring at the phone.

Eli fired off another text.

They waited.

"I'm calling. Mel, we found my cap, call me back. ASAP." Eli stood up. "I'm going to look for her."

"She's probably in the shower and can't hear the phone." That was the most logical explanation. On the other hand . . . "When did you last see her?" They didn't have more than the normal crime of a beach town, and it was still early. Nonetheless . . .

"She walked me home from dinner and then she left, down the drive."

Now David was on his feet. "Let's just check to make sure she didn't step in a pothole and sprain an ankle or something."

Without a word, they both headed for the front door.

They met Henry and Floret coming back from the beach, their robes clinging to wet bodies.

"What's afoot?" Henry asked.

"Dulcie found Eli's cap. Mel was wearing it when she left here a while ago and she's not answering her phone."

"Oh, dear," Floret said. "Look."

David and Henry followed her outstretched hand to where Hannah Gordon's Cadillac was parked at the edge of the woods.

"Is she inside?" Henry asked.

"Not in the house, maybe in the car," David said, running toward the car. "Eli," he called.

Eli, who was already halfway down the drive, came running back. He saw the car. "Hannah saw us together in town."

David slowed down long enough to make sure no one was in the car. "Not here. Oh, hell, the beach." He shoved his cell phone at Henry, and he and Eli ran for the path.

"Mel!" Eli called. "Mel! Mel!"

They ran headlong into Dulcie, bleating her head

off. Behind her, Hannah Gordon, bent nearly double, gripped her cane with both hands. "There." She gasped and took several pained breaths; David just managed to catch her before she collapsed.

"There." She waved her finger in the air not pointing to anything, but Dulcie let out a unearthly wail and bounded away.

Henry caught up; David transferred Hannah to him and he and Eli ran on.

Dulcie had stopped at the steps to the beach—where the steps had been. The treads, the risers, the stringers, the posts, the warning rope were gone.

"Mel!" Eli called.

"Eli? Down here," came the faint reply. "Help me."

"We're coming. Hold on. Uncle David?" Eli pleaded, before he took off to the rocks where he could climb down to the sand.

David followed him down and just managed to grab him before he ran headlong into the crumpled structure.

"You don't want it to collapse anymore." He moved Eli out of the way and crouched down to try to ascertain how severe the collapse was and how badly Mel was injured.

He found a small opening near the bottom. He should have brought a flashlight.

"Phone," he ordered Eli, and reached out behind him. The phone was pressed into his palm. He opened the flashlight app and shone it into the opening.

Mel's scared, dirty face looked back at him.

"Get me out?" she whimpered.

"Absolutely," he said, a lot more cheerily than he felt. "Are you hurt?"

"I don't think so. Just my arm. The rest of me can move."

David could have laughed with relief. "Well, don't. We're going to have to take some time to get this debris off you safely, so just be patient."

"Okay."

An answer rife with fear.

Henry appeared above them. "We called the EMTs. I left Hannah sitting on a rock with Floret. She wouldn't let us take her back to the house. Do we need beach rescue?"

"I think the three of us can manage," David called back. "Mel, if we lift the beams off, do you think you could crawl out?"

"I think so. Maybe."

"Okay. Hold still until I tell you. Cover your head. We have to go slowly. I don't want it all falling down on you."

"Okay. Is Granna okay?"

David looked over to Henry.

"I think so," Henry said. "And as ungrateful as ever."

"It was an accident."

"It's all right. You're not in trouble," David said, and moved back to figure out a tactic.

"I don't think she meant herself," Henry said under his breath.

"You think the old witch pushed her over?"

Henry gave him a look. "No. Doesn't mean she's not responsible."

It took some time and several false starts, but at last they opened a hole wide enough for Mel to wiggle through.

She sat on the ground and burst into tears. Eli sat down beside her. "You're okay. You're safe now."

Henry and David shared a relieved smile over the two teenagers' heads.

They made Mel wait where she was until the EMTs arrived. The hardest part was getting the EMTs past Dulcie, who was guarding the way to their patient. Even after Henry pulled her away, she insisted on staying close and walked beside them all the way back to the house, only occasionally butting one of the EMTs to keep him in line.

Hannah was sitting up on a gurney while an EMT monitored her blood pressure.

Floret met them in the yard. "She refuses to go to the hospital."

David rolled his eyes.

"I called Eve. I didn't want to alarm her, but I didn't think I should wait."

"Do I have to go to the hospital?" Mel asked. "I can move my fingers and everything."

Henry looked at the EMT who was wrapping her wrist and lower arm in ice packs.

"She should have an X-ray to make sure her arm isn't broken," the EMT said. "How old is she?"

"Seventeen," Mel said.

"Her mother is on her way," Henry said. "She should be here in five minutes."

"I have to talk to Granna first," Mel said.

"When your mother comes. Until then, you sit right there with the EMTs."

The squad began packing their things. Once again Hannah refused to go into the ambulance.

"Well, then you'll have to come inside," Henry said. "Until someone can drive you home."

"I can drive myself."

"No, you can't," Floret said. "You'll come in and have some tea."

Hannah licked her lips, and David noticed that she was smeared with dirt.

"As long as it isn't one of your funny-business teas."

Floret looked toward heaven and helped Hannah to stand.

David stared after them and then turned to Henry. "I don't get them. I really don't."

"Sometimes it's best not to try," Henry said.

They were interrupted by a car careering down the drive. It screeched to a halt next to the ambulance, and Eve jumped out of the passenger side and rushed to Mel's side. Lee and Noelle were right behind her.

Zoe's brother climbed out of the driver's seat, at the same moment Zoe got out of the driver's-side back seat.

The whole parade reminded David of a clown car at the circus.

Eve consulted with the EMTs. "I've promised to take her to the doctor's first thing tomorrow." She tried to lead Mel to the car, but Mel hung back.

"I have to make sure Granna is okay." Her voice sounded on its way to hysterical. "It was my fault."

David blew out air and went to assist.

"She was looking for me, she saw me, and I hid in the trees. She said she knew where I was going and by the time I figured out what she was doing, she'd gotten out of the car and was going down the path to the beach. She didn't know about the steps. I called but she didn't hear me, and then I got there and she was looking down and I startled her and she fell. I tried to pull her back up, but then I— She's not hurt, is she?"

Eve looked to David.

He shook his head. He had no idea if she was or not, but he'd be damned if he'd let the kid take the heat for an old woman's obsession.

"It wasn't your fault," David said. "I put a rope across the stairs. She had no business getting that close. And you saved her from a serious fall. So don't blame yourself."

Eli looked up at him, so grateful that it squeezed David's heart.

"That's right, Mel. You're a hero," Eli said.

"No, I'm not," Mel said, and fell into Eve's arms. Noelle joined the hug.

"We'll go see Granna and she'll tell you herself." Eve walked her up the stairs and into the house. Everyone else followed, including David, who intended to make sure Hannah Gordon exonerated her great-granddaughter if he had to sit her on his knee and move her head like a ventriloquist dummy.

He smiled—he would enjoy doing it.

"Maybe we should wait outside," Zoe told Chris as they started up after the others.

"Not on your life. I wouldn't miss this denouement

for the world." He nudged her up to where David waited at the door. "It's bound to be surprising."

They walked into the living room on Hannah's "Don't make a fuss, girl."

Mel recoiled as if she'd been slapped.

"What an old bee-otch," Chris said in Zoe's ear.

She nodded.

"Lee, take me home."

Lee just stood there with his arms crossed.

Everyone waited. Zoe couldn't have moved if she'd wanted to.

"Mother, Mel, who is in pain, wanted to make sure you were okay before she went to get treated. You could at least be grateful that she kept you from a nasty spill."

"Huh," the old woman said. "Is that what she said."

A cry was wrenched from Mel. "Why did you go after me, Granna? You frightened me. What were you going to do? Tell me I couldn't see Eli anymore? He's going to college in a few weeks. You didn't have to come after me." She glanced at her grandfather.

Lee had the good sense to look ashamed and lowered his head.

Mel shook her head slightly and buried her face in her mother's shoulder.

Zoe heard Chris growl beside her.

Lee took a step forward. "Get up. I'll drive you home."

"I can drive myself."

"She can't stay alone tonight," Floret said. "What if she has a turn during the night?"

"You'd be happy to see me go, I expect," Hannah snapped.

Floret didn't react. Maybe she'd spent so many years with Hannah's personality that it no longer bothered her.

But it bothered Noelle. She stepped forward. "Why do you have to be so mean? You both could have been killed tonight. You had no business going after my sister like that. Mel saved your life, at least you could say thank you."

"Fly, little bird, fly," Chris intoned sotto voce.

Hannah raised a finger in Noelle's direction, but the gesture was palsied. It held no fear factor for its intended victim.

"No more, Hannah," Noelle said, emphasizing her name. "No more bullying our family."

Eve sucked in her breath. David and Eli looked surprised. Only Lee and Noelle stood firm.

"Come on, Mel. We'll go home and take care of you." Noelle put her arm around Mel's shoulders. "We'll wait in the car."

They didn't get far.

Hannah tried to push herself out of the chair. Fell back with a grunt.

"What's one night," Floret continued. "We'll make up the daybed on the porch for you. It's quite comfortable."

"So you can poison me in my sleep."

"Lee can stay, too, if you'd like. To protect you."

"I won't stay here." Hannah tried to push herself out of the chair.

"Why not?" Floret asked in her sweetly modulated voice. "You made this your home for twenty years. What's one more night?"

"Why would I stay in the house of betrayers? You've turned my family and the whole town against me. The laundry returned my clothes without cleaning them. The grocers refused to deliver my groceries. This is your doing."

Henry sighed. "When will you learn, Hannah? It's *your* doing. All you. We had nothing to do with any of this. Everything that happens is because of you and your relentless greed and vendetta against Wind Chime and everything it stands for. And just so you know. I've offered to sell Wind Chime to Eve."

"No," Mel gasped.

"I turned him down, of course," Eve said. "But

maybe we can come to a compromise. My children have suddenly shown me the way."

Hannah's eyes grew glassy. "You've planned this all along. I saved her from you once and you'll do anything to get her back."

Henry for once looked shocked. "Hannah, have you lost your mind? What are you talking about?"

Hannah coughed. "You dare ask? You've tried to take everything I ever had."

There seemed to be no answer to that. Even Chris had no rejoinder for once.

Was this going to be the reveal of the terrible secret of the decades-long feud?

"Lee. Then Eve. Now you think you can subvert Mel with that boy. Well, you won't get her. And neither will he."

Henry's jaw clenched, and for a minute Zoe was afraid she might be about to witness Henry actually lose his temper.

He moved closer toward Floret; it was the first time Zoe had seen him make any kind of protective move toward any of them.

"I think it's time for you to explain," Floret said. "This has been going on for too, too long. So tell us all why, because I don't know. I never have. Henry doesn't.

I don't think you even know why you're so angry. We never tried to take Eve away from you. You left us to watch over her while you were building your business. It's what friends do."

Hannah's eyes narrowed. "You. You conniving witch."

Floret moved away from Henry as if she were afraid he might get caught in the cross fire of Hannah's venom.

"Tell me, get it all out and let's settle this."

"You and my husband."

"What?" The question was pure gut-level. And suddenly Floret was all too human and not a bit ethereal. "Your husband? What on earth does he have to do with anything? He's been dead for a good forty years."

"But not before you tried to steal him away."

Floret laughed. Clapped her hand over her mouth. "I beg your pardon, Hannah. It isn't funny. But you'll have to explain yourself."

"You seduced him."

"She did no such thing," Henry said simultaneously with Floret's "I did no such thing."

"Actually, Hannah, that's an insult," said Henry. "Stop this nonsense. We're tired to death of it. Surely you are, too."

"Don't play innocent with me, Floret. He came to

you day after day. Night after night. With your salves and your massages and your—I knew what the two of you were doing."

"Love potion number—" Chris began.

Zoe elbowed him in the ribs.

"I knew what you were doing, I hated him even then, but he was mine."

Floret smiled. "Good heavens." She made a quiet purring sound. A laugh maybe. "My dear Hannah. Free love is one thing, but I would never commit adultery in a sordid affair. Especially not with Ed Gordon. Where are your wits? He cheated on you—that was common knowledge—but not with me. He stole from you. Lost your home. Destroyed your future. He came to me because he was sick. He came for treatment for pain, and for a little understanding. You were too angry about what was happening to give him the strength he needed to die. So he came here. There was nothing else to it."

"I don't believe you."

"Believe it. He was a drunken, uneducated oaf. But he was dying and I tried to ease his way out because you were our friend. You needed our support and were too stubborn, even then, to ask for it. We never tried to steal Eve's affections. She was an affectionate child. There was plenty of her to go around. And Mel is young, with all her life before her. She has discoveries to make. We would never hold her back."

"You took in that girl, Eve's mother, and look what it did to my son."

"What *you* did to your son," Henry said.

"Everyone is welcome here," Floret staid. "Even you, Hannah. So all this has been for nothing." Floret sounded suddenly very tired. "No more. We never guessed and we tried over and over again to understand. If you'd only let down your guard once in all these years to ask, I would have told you the truth about it all. Instead you spent years building up your resentment. I think you enjoyed it. But it's over now. Eve can have Wind Chime House as long as she keeps the glen for those who wish to return for their final rest."

"No!" cried Noelle, Mel, and Eli. Zoe wanted to add her voice to theirs, but she didn't want to draw attention to herself and risk adding more flames to Hannah's furor.

It made absolutely no difference. Hannah turned on her. "And now this one shows up. Trying to take advantage. What will it take to get you to leave?"

"I don't know. What did it take to get my mother to leave?"

The room dropped into silence.

Zoe tried to swallow. Why had she said that? She didn't want anything from this horrible old woman. Not anymore. Zoe had just wanted to hurt Hannah. Her venom had missed, but she was afraid that it had hit her sister instead. How could she have been so thoughtless?

Eve stood immobile in the sudden vacuum that Zoe's words had created. And Zoe didn't dare to look up to see her face.

Zoe turned on Hannah instead. "You can't answer, can you? Because I know my mother would never have given Eve away to you. She loved her children—all her children—above everything. What did you do to her?"

"How dare you." The old woman struggled to get out of the chair.

"What *did* you do, Mother?" A voice hardly recognizable as her father's.

And Zoe suddenly didn't want to know the answer. What if she was wrong, what if her mother had left Eve willingly? It would destroy her sister.

"I merely informed her parents of her whereabouts and they did the rest. Did you honestly think they would let their precious daughter give up all they had planned for her? Marry a drugged-out musician, always on the road? Is that any life for a pampered rich girl with the whole world at her feet?"

Hannah pointed a palsied finger toward her son. "Did you think she would travel with you, her and the baby? Were you so bewitched you couldn't see that there was no future for the two of you? The Campbells had no illusions as to where that would lead. So they came and got her. And they could have her, but by God they wouldn't get my granddaughter."

Eve sucked in a raw, ragged breath that cut through the hollow silence. And then Floret was there by her side without seeming to have moved from her place across the room.

"They agreed to let me adopt her with the understanding that they would keep their daughter away from her. They were only too happy to agree. They thought they were saving their precious Jenny from a terrible future. I was saving my son." Hannah coughed out a dry, raspy laugh. "It was the best deal I ever made."

For a long moment no one moved; then Lee crossed the floor and took his mother's arm. Hauled her out of her chair. "Come on, Mother, I'll take you home. You've caused quite enough trouble for a lifetime." He steered her out of the room.

Several minutes later they heard the Cadillac drive away.

The whole room exhaled.

Henry squeezed Floret's hand. "I think some tea

would be in order, dear. Spiked with something a little stronger," he added to the others.

"That's exactly what I was thinking. Valerian for Mel, and then off to bed with her."

A half hour later, they were all piling into Zoe's car. David carried a sleeping Mel to the back seat. Eve sat in back with her, and Noelle, Zoe, and Chris squeezed into the front.

"I'll never complain about our boring Long Island family again," Chris said as Zoe turned into the drive.

Zoe smiled. "Yes, you will."

"Damn straight, I will. So, you crazy, cockamamie New Hampshire folks. Has the tempest been tamed? Do you think the drama is over yet?"

No one even bothered to answer.

Chapter 26

At nine the next morning, Eve stood across from her grandmother's house staring at the scene before her. A row of a dozen townspeople lined the sidewalk in front of the house, carrying placards. REOPEN KELLY'S. DON'T MESS WITH OUR DINER. IT WORKS BOTH WAYS.

Hannah was being picketed. Eve wondered if the backlash would also include her and her family. There was only one way to find out.

She headed across the street.

"Morning, Eve," said Bobby Pritchard, owner of the local Cadillac dealership.

"Morning, Bobby," Eve returned, and raised her eyebrows in question.

"Like we told Lee this morning when he came out to get the paper, there won't be any paper this morning, or tomorrow, or the next morning. Not until Kelly's reopens. We've had enough, Eve. Tell Hannah that until she backs off from Kelly's and the stranglehold she has on some of the inhabitants of this town—"

"And the council," broke in Rudy Larsen.

"And the council," Bobby added. "She won't get any more services from us. Nothing personal to you or yours."

Eve nodded. She didn't argue. She agreed with them; things had gotten totally out of hand. But for all her faults, Hannah was her grandmother and she wouldn't side against her. Not yet.

She walked up the path to the front door. Lee opened it as she reached for the bell.

"I was looking out for you. Wasn't sure what your reception would be."

"When did this happen?" she asked, coming inside.

"They were there when I got up this morning."

"You stayed here all night?" How could he after the things he'd learned the night before?

Lee shrugged. "I couldn't really leave her alone, could I?"

Eve sighed. "Is she okay? Is she awake yet?"

"Yep. And full of piss and vinegar. Already planning her attack. The woman's incorrigible."

"She can't go on like this, you know that."

"Yes, and I don't intend to let her. There has been enough heartache all these years. Including hers. It's got to stop."

Eve shot him a surprised look. "You mean—"

"I've enabled her behavior—no, supported her—all these years, because, well, because I'm an ass. I didn't see the harm it was doing to my own family much less the town. I saw it last night."

Eve gave him an impulsive hug. He patted her back, stiff and awkward as ever, and she loved him in spite of it, all the more for it.

"We'd best go get it over with."

Hannah was sitting in a wing chair in the parlor, fully dressed and made-up, though it didn't hide the bruises on her cheek and forehead; her pants suit probably hid a few more.

She sat up when she saw Lee and Eve.

"Well? Did you get rid of them?"

Eve hesitated. Lee stepped ahead of her and a thrill of love coursed through her.

"No, I didn't," he said. "It's no more than you deserve. This has to stop. No more. It's finished."

"So you turn against your own mother. I gave you everything." She lifted her head at Eve. "I gave you your daughter."

Lee's whole body tightened, and for a long moment

Eve didn't know whether he would back off or go for the old woman's throat. Which, to her horror, Eve certainly was considering.

"No, Mother, while I appreciate what you did, it was Jenny who gave me Eve, for which I'll ever be grateful, though I didn't always show it to my daughter, and for that I'm sorry."

Eve gulped back a cry.

Lee plowed on. "We let you run roughshod over us—over the whole town—all these years. And I turned my back on what you were doing. Told myself that it had nothing to do with me. Hell, I even benefited from it.

"But I was wrong. It took you turning on your own family for me to see how wrong I was. Well, it stops now. My God. You could have killed Zoe Bascombe." He stopped as if the words had stuck in his throat. "My daughter. And Mel, my granddaughter, your own flesh and blood could have been killed last night because you couldn't stand to let her be free. And for my sins, I abetted you in that, too. And for what? All for your wounded pride over things that you thought happened years before either was born."

Hannah glared at him, and the pieces of Eve's heart that were left crumbled.

"I gave you everything. And this is how you repay me?"

"You didn't give—you bought. Our love, our lives. And you didn't have to. We loved you, every single one of us, but that wasn't enough, was it? I looked the other way at your heavy-handedness, made excuses for your vindictiveness, because I thought you were doing it for the family, for me and my sisters and then for Eve and her children. But it wasn't about us. Not really. It was all done in revenge, wasn't it? For your upbringing, for an affair that never happened, for affection you mistook for a power play. For innocent love. You've been punishing us all for nothing—nothing.

"I'm sorry for your unhappy childhood, for your disappointment in adulthood. I admire your courage, but not how you used it. This vendetta against Henry and Floret is tearing the whole town apart. Is that what you want?"

Hannah lifted a shoulder. "I don't care about this town. They never gave me anything I didn't take."

"Maybe because you never asked."

Hannah turned hard eyes on Eve. "I suppose you feel the same way."

Eve nearly jumped out of her skin. She'd become so hypnotized by her father's emotional outburst, she'd almost forgotten Hannah was there. "Granna, you're family. We love you. We always will. But we love you too much to let you go on in this way. We won't let you destroy our family or our town."

Though, really, seeing the people outside, Eve thought maybe Hannah had met her Waterloo.

"Even though you hurt my father beyond bearing, and used me against your best friends, I still love you. How could you think that I would throw you aside for Floret and Henry? But they were a place of calm and safety against your unrelenting rage at the world, and I loved them, too. I loved you because you were my granna, I still do. But I don't like what you have done. And I won't sit idly by like I did before. Because that makes me guilty, too." She glanced at her father.

"And I'm done with that. The whole town is pretty riled up over the closing of Kelly's. You went too far by dragging them into this. We're going to appeal the condemnation of Kelly's to the council. I'll tell them you're not in your right mind if I have to. And that we'll lead a campaign to vote them out if they don't."

"Hmmph. Get out, then. Go on and do your worst."

Eve turned to leave, years of reacting automatically to Hannah's demands, but Lee grasped her elbow.

"It's over, Mother, you're finished bullying this town and your family."

Hannah grasped the chair arms and tried to push herself to her feet. She fell back and tried again.

Eve started to go to her, but Lee held her back.

"Just stay in your chair. I'll call Vicky Rogers and ask her to send someone over to help you until you're feeling back to par," he said.

"Don't bother. I can do for myself."

"I know, Mother." Lee's voice cracked on the word. "But you don't have to. You never had to."

"You ungrateful—"

Eve burst forward. "Stop it, Granna. Just stop it. We have never been ungrateful. Just the opposite. Why would you think that? Is that what your family said to you, that you were ungrateful, when they barely gave you enough to exist? You ran away from them, but you carried their sickness with you and let it grow inside you. It has to stop now."

"Go." Hannah barely croaked out the word.

Lee took Eve's arm and guided her out of the room. She was too numb to move on her own. Too numb to say good-bye.

She did glance back as Lee opened the door. Hannah sat in her chair, chin against her chest, just an old woman who had chosen anger over everything else, her life consumed with bitterness, and whose bitterness had almost consumed them all.

She stopped. "I should go back."

"No going back."

Eve looked up at him through blurry eyes. "You sounded a little like Henry."

He put an arm around her and pulled her close, and they stood on the porch looking out at the throng of people that seemed to have grown since Eve had gone inside.

"We can't leave her alone," Eve said.

"Nope, but she needs looking after and I don't find myself having the patience right now." Lee took out his phone. Keyed in a number. "Vicky. Glad I caught you . . ."

Vicky Rogers agreed to come herself until they could find a caregiver. She was on her way over.

"Hannah won't take this lying down."

"Vicky is used to ornery patients. And she's a good friend. She'll be patient but won't be bullied."

"Did we go too far?"

"Maybe, but if we hadn't waited so long, we wouldn't have had to."

Perhaps he was right. Though Eve wasn't sure that any of them could have changed Hannah's course in life. Her determination was her most effective strength and her most debilitating weakness.

They had reached this point because they had enabled her all these years. Walking that treacherous line between loyalty and revulsion. Between love and fear. And almost wrecked all their lives in the process.

"It's not your fault," Lee said as if he'd heard her thoughts.

"It isn't yours, either."

"Maybe not totally. She was a strong woman, overcame odds that would crush most people. She chose her course in life, but it is my fault that she went after Mel. I told her about catching the two of them on the beach."

He groaned. "Mel could have been seriously hurt, over what? Because she's seeing a boy that lives with Floret and Henry? Because I freaked out just finding them together at Wind Chime Beach? I have nothing against Eli. It was just . . ." He took a painful breath. "It was our place. Mine and Jenny's. We made plans, dreamed dreams. Seeing them, it all came back." Another sharp intake of breath. "I should have tried harder to get her back."

"Dad, it was fifty years ago. You have to let it go. Let her go."

"I have to apologize to Mel—and Eli. Do you think they'll forgive me?"

"I know they will. And Zoe?"

Lee closed his eyes, and Eve thought he must be reliving the pain of that second encounter and rejection all over again. "And Zoe," he said at last.

They stood arm in arm on the porch until Vicky Rogers arrived, bearing a tote bag filled with food. They explained what had happened while Vicky nodded her head, asked a few questions, then convinced them not to accompany her inside to explain her presence to Hannah.

"I know what to do. Sometimes it's better not to push the issue."

Still, they waited a few minutes more, then, with a wave to the picketers, walked back to the inn.

Zoe overslept the next morning and had to rush to get downstairs, where she'd agreed to meet Chris before going over to Eve's cottage for morning coffee. Mel was up and relishing the attention from Noelle, who seemed to have designated herself as personal assistant.

There was no sign of Eve.

"She went over to Granna's," Mel said. "I think she was worried about her." She lifted her arm, which this morning had a thick soft cast covering her wrist and most of her forearm.

"Yikes," Zoe said. "Is it broken? When did you get that?"

"This morning Mom took me over to Dr. White's. It isn't broken, just sprained." Her phone pinged. She opened it with her left thumb, read. "But it makes texting a bitch." She started a one-handed feat of holding and tapping.

"Maybe you should just call him," Zoe said.

Mel gave her a look, then smiled sheepishly. "Good idea." She went into her bedroom and closed the door.

"Young love," Chris said. "I smell coffee." He wandered off to the kitchen to help himself.

"Have you heard from your mom since she left?" Zoe asked.

"She just called and they're headed home. I told her to stop at the bakery on their way."

Zoe started to get up from the chair she'd just sat in. "They? Who? Not Hannah?"

"No. Granddad. And don't even think about escaping. It's about time this family stopped living in the past." Noelle grinned and kicked her feet in glee. "I for one am living my flight-to-Manhattan-and-a-new-job dream."

"You'll do good. Just remember to pack your thick skin."

"Not a problem. I learned from some real zingers."

Chris came back into the room carrying two mugs of coffee. He handed one to Zoe. "You good?" he asked Noelle.

"Yeah. Who needs caffeine when I'm rushing on Manhattan?" She spun around.

Chris rolled his eyes. "We need to work on your sparkle technique."

"We?" Zoe said.

Chris shrugged. "She'll need the expertise of her half uncle to show her the ropes."

"You decided to stay in the city?"

"Yep." He took a sip of coffee, savored the taste. Looked up when he realized they were both watching him.

"Timothy decided to take the job in Chicago. It's a great career opportunity. But not for me. My life is in the city. Anyway, now I have to keep an eye on my niece. And if Eve doesn't think it looks too weird for an old gay uncle to offer to share his apartment until she finds some happening young millennial to live with, I won't have to look for a roommate right away."

"She won't," Noelle said. "She was raised in a commune; she's pretty with it in the scheme of things."

The front door opened and Eve walked in. Lee followed her, carrying a big bakery bag.

Mel stuck her head out of her bedroom door. "Did you get sticky buns?"

"A whole dozen," Eve called back.

"I'll just take these things to the kitchen," Lee said, not catching anyone's eye.

Zoe licked her lips.

"How's Granna?" Noelle asked.

"Same as she always is, but we called Vicky Rogers to sit with her until we're sure she's back to normal."

"What did you say to her?"

"You don't want to know," said Eve.

"But I'm gonna tell you," Lee said, coming back into the room. "But first I got something to say. Where's Mel?"

"On the phone," Noelle said warily.

"Dad," Eve began.

"Mel," he called. "Get out here."

Eve sighed. Zoe braced herself. Couldn't the man just let it go?

Mel came out, shoving the phone in her pants pocket, but she stopped halfway into the room.

He looked down at her cast, then up to her face. Licked his lips. Swallowed. "Mel, I was wrong to go after you and Eli. You know sometimes I get a little crazy. No excuse. But just saying. That was me being crazy. I got nothing against Eli, he seems like a nice enough guy. As long as you two don't do anything stupid. But I apologize. To both of you."

Mel's eyes widened. "That's okay, Granddad. I understand."

And Zoe thought that Mel more than any of them might understand exactly what he was going through.

He turned toward Zoe.

She braced herself.

Chris, who had just sat on the arm of Noelle's chair, stood.

"Zoe." Lee shrugged, opened his hands.

In surrender? she wondered. She shook her head. "It's okay. You don't have to accept me. It was not your fault or your responsibility. I get it. It's cool." But she felt the cold ache of disappointment anyway. A week ago she hadn't even known of his existence, of any of them, but now she did, and she wanted more than anything to be accepted by them.

She turned to Chris. "Maybe we should go."

"No," said Lee. "I'm not easy. But I loved your mother. I was a fool then. I'm gonna try to be a little less of a fool from now on. So we play it by ear." His voice rose a halftone on the last sentence.

"Sure," Zoe said, her stomach rebounding back

from defeat. "That's fine. I was always pretty good at improv."

Eve chose that minute to return with a tray of pastries. "I've got a fresh pot brewing."

"Everything okay, Mom?" Noelle asked.

Eve exchanged a look with Lee.

"Well, there's a picket line in front of Hannah's house."

Noelle snorted. "What?"

"More like a protest movement," Lee said.

"Over Kelly's?" Zoe asked.

Eve nodded. "They're not going to let her off easy. Already the cleaners, grocers, the local paper, and the Cadillac dealer are boycotting her. Others are bound to follow."

"Shows you what can happen when you get between a man and his eggs and bacon," Chris quipped.

Eve sighed. "I feel a little sorry for her."

"Well, I don't," Mel said.

"Maybe if she gets a taste of her own medicine, she'll lay off everyone else," said Noelle. "Oh, BTW, Uncle Chris said I could live with him until I find a place."

Lee opened his mouth.

Zoe jumped in. "I can vouch for him. He's very responsible."

"Thanks, Dil." Chris beamed at her in his most angelic impersonation. He reached for a sticky bun, put it on a plate, and handed it to her. "You can come visit whenever you want. You too, Lee."

Lee started like he'd been goosed. "Uh, thanks, but right now, I need to go."

"Dad, sit down and have some coffee and a pastry," Eve said.

"Thanks, but there are things that need to be done, and it's time I did them."

"Later then," she said.

"Later." He nodded to the room and walked out the front door.

They all watched him go until the door shut behind him. Even then no one moved.

"Now that's an exit," Chris said. "What are those flaky things with the jelly oozing out?"

Chapter 27

"Now, for our afternoon entertainment," Chris announced when they'd boxed up the leftover pastries and the last mug had been squeezed into a filled-to-capacity dishwasher, "we're all going to the beach. The hotel beach. No naysayers."

There was immediately a round of excuses. "I can't get my hand wet." "I have to pack." "I have to do next week's schedule." "I—I . . ." Zoe was the only one who couldn't think of a reason not to go.

"Not good enough," Chris said. "We'll put a plastic bag on Mel's cast. Noelle, you can wait a couple of hours to come to more indecisions on what not to wear. Zoe can help with next week's schedule. Hell, she can probably schedule you into the next century."

"What about—?" Zoe began.

"Mom?" he finished. "Well, heaven can wait. Get your stuff, everybody. I can't believe you have this beautiful beach and never enjoy it. Though I must say . . ." He patted his stomach. "I shouldn't have eaten that last pastry. I'm not sure I can fit today's stomach into yesterday's swimsuit. Now chop, chop."

"You're right," Eve said. "Let's all go."

"That's the ticket. We're going to relax, dammit. Have drinks with little umbrellas in them. You *do* have little umbrellas?"

"Of course we do," said Mel. "We're a full-service establishment. And they're made of paper and wood, so they're eco-friendly."

Eve smiled at her and Mel blushed.

"We'll make a day of it," Eve added. "I'll have Mike hand over the bar to whoever is on duty and tell him to join us. Noelle, call your grandfather and tell him to come down to the beach when he gets back. We'll have a family picnic. I have an announcement to make."

After that, there was no naysaying. They all agreed to change into beachwear and meet again a half hour later.

"I just wish Errol would call," Zoe said as she and Chris went to change.

"Really, Dil, there's nothing to do but wait. And it's

not every day you have this beautiful beach and these wholesome cabana boys at your beck and call."

It was a family affair. At first they just lazed and swam and watched the beach yoga class twist themselves into one asana after another.

"I should try that someday soon," Zoe said.

"You should," Eve said.

Getting into shape and getting to know her sister—not a bad way to spend a couple of weeks of summer. But first there was the situation with her brothers and the ashes. Zoe was determined not to obsess about them today.

And her resolve lasted all afternoon. Mike arrived accompanied by two busboys carrying two large coolers and a picnic basket.

"I figured since the beach officially closes for the evening soon . . ." Mike opened the lid of one of the coolers to reveal several wine bottles, beers, gin, vodka, and mixers.

Chris peered in. "S'all right. S'all right." He grinned at Mike.

The busboys went off to store the food in the cabana, then returned to the inn. Mike sat down in the sand next to Eve's chair, his arm stretched comfortably along her bare leg.

Noelle and Chris volunteered to make the drinks. They drank, they swam. They did cartwheels on the sand. The day grew long and the sun began to arc toward the horizon. They were all back in their chairs, sighing over fruit and wine when Chris said, "Damn, he makes great entrances, too."

They all turned to see Lee walking toward them, silhouetted by the setting sun and surrounded by a blaze of red and orange.

"He does," Zoe said.

"You said to meet you here," he said as if maybe they'd forgotten.

"Yes, Dad. Sit down. Noelle, get your granddad a beer."

Noelle reached into the cooler and handed him a bottle.

When everyone was settled, they all turned expectantly to Eve and her announcement.

"Now that everybody's here, I have something I want to say." Eve took a breath. "I want to travel."

The statement was met with silence.

"That's your big announcement?" Lee said.

"Yes."

"Well, hell. Nobody's stopping you."

Mel stood up, dumping her paper plate of chips on the sand. "But what about the inn?"

"I have a capable staff that can run things while I'm away. I'd just need to start looking for a manager who could run things while I'm gone."

"But why?" Mel's question was almost a wail.

"Don't be dense," Noelle said. "She's always wanted to travel. Haven't you, Mom?"

"Yes. Since I was a little girl. But I never went anywhere. So much has changed this summer. I don't want to wait any longer."

"You're not going to sell the inn," Mel said.

"No, Mel, I'm just thinking about taking a few weeks off to see someplace I've never seen before. Gradually turn over the day-to-day running of the inn to give me more free time."

"But for how long?" Mel asked. "Where would you go?"

Eve smiled. She sat up in her chaise and dropped her feet onto the ground.

Zoe wondered if Eve was preparing for a quick getaway. Not everyone around her seemed happy with the announcement. Zoe knew she herself was having mixed feelings. She'd just learned about having a sister. She certainly didn't want to lose her this soon. But it was not her place to say so.

"Well, to start with, the Grand Canyon, or maybe Paris, then Easter Island, London, the Redwood

Forest. China. Hell, I've never even seen the Statue of Liberty. I've never been anywhere."

Noelle clapped her hands together. "Good for you, Mom. I think it's great."

"Thank you." She turned to Mel. "What about you, Mel?"

Mel shrugged. "I guess. I mean, you should go if you want to."

"I was thinking that maybe you'd like to go with me."

"Instead of going to college?"

Eve shrugged. "Well, you could postpone until second semester."

Mel ran her toes across the sand. Back and forth, back and forth. It was mesmerizing.

"You can even study hotel management in school, and when you graduate you can come back to run the inn if that's what you want. But only if it's what *you* want. I lived my life right here. I made some mistakes. I hope I did some good. But I've always dreamed of traveling. What I got in return is so much better than what I wanted, but now I would still like to travel."

"What did you get?" asked Mel, who looked like she was about to cry.

"You and Noelle and Harmony. So it's just something to think about. But I will be taking a few weeks off. As soon as I find someone to keep things going."

"That won't be easy," Mike said. "I can try, but needless to say I don't have your charm."

The girls laughed, and Eve hugged him. "You dear, dear man. You don't, but you could be the point man for whoever comes in. It's a family business. It would have to be someone special who knows how we do things; who understands that the inn's soul is what keeps it safe from becoming some corporate octopus."

"I think I recognize a quote," Chris broke in.

"It's a Mom original," Noelle said. "You have to give her a pass—she was raised in a commune," she said in an aside loud enough to incur laughs.

"Well, you can count on me," Mike said.

"I always have, my dear."

He slipped his arm around her.

"So now we have to go about finding the perfect replacement. Any suggestions?"

There weren't any. Silence ensued while Mike, Lee, Noelle, and Mel considered. And Chris made ticking motions with his finger that only Zoe could see.

"I could."

Everyone turned to look at Zoe.

She swallowed. What was she thinking? She'd just gotten here and everybody was leaving. "Not take over. But I bet I could run front end for a few weeks while you were gone.

"Think about it. I know how to move people, organize their trips, book flights and hotels, synchronize transport and meals. It would be a learning curve. And I'd need help. I can't do orders for a restaurant or stock a bar, but I can schedule work shifts and events. And I'd hire a laundry service—doing it in-house is a big time suck and doesn't save that much money.

"I mean, if that's okay with you. If you think I can do it until you get back. You are coming back, right?"

"Of course," Eve said. "That would be perfect. I could take a few weeks to show you the ropes. Then I could take off for a few weeks and you'd still be here when I got back. And at Thanksgiving and Christmas we could all—" She broke off.

"Let's just get through summer first," said Zoe.

"I could show you the reception things," Mel volunteered. She shrugged. "If you think I could help."

"Of course I do," Zoe said. "I checked out your hospitality skills the first time I met you." Zoe laughed. "Occupational hazard. And let me tell you, girl, you crushed it."

Mel beamed. "And, Mom, maybe if you schedule your vacations around school breaks I could come and help Zoe out then, too."

"Wait!" Zoe said. "I can juggle front end for a few

weeks. I don't know anything about long-term management."

"Ahem," Chris said. "Not to mention this in the midst of all this exuberance, but, Mel, does this mean you're going to college?"

Mel picked up a chip off the sand and flicked it at him. "Maybe." She looked over at Eve. "I've kind of been thinking."

"About?"

"Just stuff. But Eli always says that in science you have to have more than one option to make an informed hypothesis. That if there's only one, it doesn't prove anything."

"Whoa, Eli," said Noelle.

"Well, he's right, isn't he?"

Zoe realized Mel's question was not her being defensive, but her seeking affirmation.

Zoe wasn't the only person on the beach having a lightbulb moment. She let out a long breath. "Why don't we take a test run and see if it will work? If you're up for it. Just say no if you're not."

"I think it would be great," Eve said.

Noelle and Mel nodded their agreement.

"And I could come up on Mondays and give your beach an air of a certain je ne sais quoi," Chris said.

Zoe gave him a look, and Noelle pushed him off his chair.

"Hey, don't mess up the talent." He brushed off sand and climbed back onto his chaise.

Leave it to Chris to add a little levity to a life-churning situation.

"I think it would be perfect," Eve said. "But are you sure you want to?"

Was she? Or was she crazy? "It's like Eli said, you need more than one choice. I could put my experience to work in a different field and I . . ." She hesitated. "I'd get to know my new family."

"For a couple of weeks before they all split on you," Chris said.

"No!" they all yelled in chorus. "There are weekends and holidays and—"

"And me," said Chris, putting up his hands to fend off imaginary assaults.

"And . . . I could learn music somewhere besides Juilliard." Zoe risked a tentative look at Lee.

He looked blank, then slowly his expression changed. Pointed to his chest.

She nodded.

He frowned for a bit, then stood. Zoe's heart slipped. She shouldn't have given way to the hubris around her. She'd pushed him too fast.

"Dad, where are you going?" Eve said, alarmed.

He patted her on the shoulder. "You girls work it out. I'm just gonna make sure the piano's tuned."

The next day David, Henry, and a group of volunteers showed up at Kelly's to begin the minor cosmetic and organizational changes that would put the diner in line with the HD complaints. Eve and Lee had called each of the commissioners personally and evidently made them an offer they couldn't refuse. Zoe guessed it had something to do with their reelection.

Whatever the cause, two men showed up on Monday morning, did a cursory inspection, and declared Kelly's back up to code. There was general celebration and free coffee while diners waited in line for a place inside.

And Eve knew what she had to do. That afternoon, she drew up a formal agreement and took it to Wind Chime. Henry and Floret read it over, and all three of them signed a lease agreement for the inn to use Wind Chime House's adjacent beach. Henry and Floret agreed to restrict nude sunbathing to the secluded beach on the opposite side of the property during the day. What happened after dark was left to the occupants. Eve promised that no further attempts to cut off the right-of-way to the house would be made by her family. She'd have to get Hannah to sign off on it. She had every intention of making that happen.

She headed straight to Hannah's house and with some trepidation told her of the arrangement. But Hannah didn't seem interested. She was more concerned that the cleaners had twice returned her dry cleaning uncleaned.

"They're doing this on purpose."

Yes, they most likely were, thought Eve, but at least it would give Hannah something to keep her mind off Kelly's and Wind Chime House. And the Zukowskis, who owned the only dry cleaners in town, also owned almost as much real estate as Hannah. Maybe at last Hannah had met her match.

Hannah signed the contract with "Who cares about them anyway? But if that lowdown Sam Zukowski thinks he can give me the cold shoulder . . ."

Eve, amazed at how easily she'd acquiesced, left with Hannah mumbling about the nerve of some people.

She'd been afraid that with her grandmother thwarted on all sides, it would drain the life out of her. But Hannah had merely shifted to another arena. She must enjoy the constant confrontation, the chaos it created. She could have it. All to herself.

But Eve didn't think she would be as successful as she had been in the past. It was funny that the thing that had finally led to her downfall was the local diner and a dilapidated house on the edge of the sea.

Two days later, they all watched as a dump truck and backhoe arrived to tear down and cart away the jetty that had separated them for several years.

And Errol still hadn't called.

Zoe still hadn't made a decision about what to do with her mother's ashes. She left Chris and Noelle arguing over how much stuff she really needed for the first weeks of work in Manhattan. She ran back to the hotel and up to her room, to use her phone in private.

She keyed in her brother's landline, so he wouldn't be distracted, and listened to it ring while her nerves warred between hoping he didn't answer and wanting to just get it over with.

On the fourth ring, she was about to hang up when he picked up.

"Hi. It's Zoe."

"Zoe," he began.

"Please, Errol, just let me have my say, then you get the rebuttal." She heard him sigh and she hurried on. "I want to have a ceremony here. Nothing extravagant, just a few friends and family." She crossed her fingers. "I understand how you feel, I really do. I wasn't happy about this either, not until I got here.

She was happy here. She was happy with us, but she's no longer with us. This is what she wanted. She had a whole other life that she gave up for us. I think we owe her this much."

"Well, I can't say I blame her totally," Errol said. "Not after what our father did. But who's going to look after the grave, put flowers on it?"

Zoe heard a click and for a second she was afraid he'd hung up.

"Honey, there's not going to be a grave."

He hadn't hung up; someone had picked up. Allison was on the other line. "We talked about this."

"It's just . . . She'll just be floating around out there."

"She'll be in good company," Zoe said.

"What?"

She had to move the phone from her ear. "It's a memorial garden. There are others here. Not really a garden but a glen with a window through the trees where you can see the ocean. It's really beautiful."

"And there's someone to take care of her?"

"Yes. Her friends who, um, take care of the garden."

She heard a strange sound and realized that her brother was sobbing.

Tears filled her own eyes. She couldn't remember seeing him cry, not even at the funeral.

"I want you all to come to the ceremony, if you

think you would like to. Rob and Laura, too. I think we should all be together."

"Of course we will. When is it?" Allison asked.

"Whenever you can make it. I was hoping next weekend or the next. Does that give you enough time?"

"I'll check with Laura and get back to you, but we'll be free one of those weekends. The sooner the better, I say."

"Me, too. Thanks, Allison. Oh, and, Allison. Am I still one of the family?"

"Of course you are. What a thing to say. I'm guessing we're not wearing black?"

"I'm thinking it's going to be a colorful, very celebratory affair."

"Excellent. I'll call you when I know. And don't worry about Errol. He'll come around."

Zoe hung up. Dropped the phone on the bed. Whew. Now to consult with Floret and Henry about what to do.

She pulled herself together and walked down to Wind Chime House.

Henry and Floret didn't appear to be at home, but she heard hammering from the woods. Now what was he doing?

She walked down the path until she saw David standing between two new posts sticking out of the earth where the old stairs had been.

"Déjà vu," she said, walking up behind him.

He nodded in her direction. "I should have finished tearing these down the day I started. I just got busy and—"

"Stop. You cordoned them off. It was an accident. Everyone's okay." She frowned. "So you're building them back?"

"Yeah, Henry and Floret said the commune will be using this beach, since they're leasing Eve the other beach, so I decided to make life easy for them."

"You take care of them."

"More the other way around. But I need to do this before I leave."

"You're leaving?"

"As soon as I get Eli off to college. An assignment in Patagonia."

"Sounds exciting."

He cocked his head as if considering. "It is sometimes. Mainly it's just waiting for the right shot. I like it."

"You're coming back?" She was beginning to sound like Mel.

"Yeah, but I'll have more freedom to take more work; for a while anyway."

Until Henry and Floret need you again, she thought.

"Listen." He stopped.

Zoe listened but she didn't hear the chimes.

He breathed out a laugh. “I didn’t mean that kind of listen. I meant . . . Well, I just wanted to say that we got off to a rocky start. I’m sorry I didn’t get to know you better.”

Zoe tried not to smile. “Thanks. But don’t worry. If you’re only going to be gone a couple of months, I’ll probably still be here when you get back.”

“You’re staying?”

“At least to help run the inn while Eve is gone.”

“Eve? Where is she going?”

“She, like you, wants to travel. I told her I’d keep the home fires burning while she’s away.” She laughed. “It’s funny. I just got here and everybody’s leaving.”

Her eyes narrowed. “Did you just groan? You did, didn’t you? I know you did.”

“I didn’t. Not exactly. Do you have any idea how to run an inn?”

“Not really, but I know how to deal with people at major music festivals. How hard can it be? Anyway, Mike said he’d help.”

This time he really did groan.

Chapter 28

The celebration of the life of Jenny Bascombe was held the following weekend. It was a clear morning. The sky was blue, the clouds were high, and the day was hot. They'd decided on a simple gathering, with a few short prayers in deference to the Long Island family.

There would be a feast afterward at Wind Chime House where food and drink and music and whatever else would abound.

Errol and Robert and their wives drove up the night before. They arrived late, with only time for a nightcap at the bar before going off to bed in the two rooms Eve had reserved for them.

The next morning, they got back in their car, this time with Zoe and the ashes squeezed into the back seat between Laura and Allison, and they drove to Wind Chime House.

The others—Eve and Mike, and Noelle and Mel—had walked ahead. Chris had chosen to walk with them, arguing that there wasn't enough room in the car. They were all dressed for a celebration, even Allison and Laura, in a Manhattan-design kind of way. Errol and Robert insisted on wearing summer suits, but they were there, and that's all that counted.

Zoe thought Errol gritted his teeth when he saw the state of the house, and she prayed that he wouldn't change his mind before she could discharge her duty.

But Allison said, "Oh, how charming." Laura agreed, and the crisis passed. Zoe had never appreciated Allison as she deserved. Not just a trophy wife, she had managed to get both brothers on board. And Zoe was grateful.

They parked at the house, and Zoe was glad to see David and Eli and the professor had joined with Henry and Floret, both dressed in full robes and flowers, in greeting the Bascombes. Floret held the wind chimes they would hang in the woods, wrapped in a prayer shawl of brilliant colors.

Zoe carried the urn, her fingers molding to the cool ceramic, suddenly reluctant to let go. Henry gave her a calming smile and patted the side of his robe and the pocket that held the penknife that would cut the ashes free, unlike the day she had come to throw them away and had been stopped by plastic and her father.

Lee wasn't there. She'd invited him but hadn't pushed him to attend. She didn't know how her brothers would take him as a stand-in for their own father, whom they had decided not to invite.

Zoe began the procession down the path, feeling a little queasy and hoping she wouldn't embarrass herself by bursting into tears.

They reached the glen and formed a semicircle facing the keyhole in the trees, where the brilliant blue of the sea shone through to the glen like a pathway to the sky.

In her head Zoe could hear Chris saying, "Great lighting effect." But today even her theatrical brother was quiet.

Henry stepped forward and faced the group, his robes outlined by the sea. "We are here today to welcome our dear friend Jenny home. We promise to love her and keep her soul safe."

He looked to Errol and then Robert, who both lowered their heads. Zoe knew they wouldn't say anything, but she also knew that beneath their stoic demeanor they were saying good-bye in their own way.

She handed the urn to Chris, who held it while Henry

cut the plastic. That was when she saw Lee standing in the trees, near the group but not a part of it.

She was glad he'd come. Henry cut the ashes free, and she began to sprinkle the ashes in an arc until she completed a full circle.

And then it was done. Henry took the bag from the urn and held it in the air until the last vestiges of Jenny Bascombe were set free. Together he and Floret hung the wind chime Jenny had sent to them for safekeeping.

"Welcome home, dear friend," said Floret, and the two of them started toward the house. Everyone else followed. Zoe lingered, but only to let the professor, flanked by David and Eli, get a head start. The professor seemed to be walking slower today than he had the day she'd met him.

As she stepped out of the trees, the breeze lifted the leaves behind her and the first faint tinkle of the chimes teased her ears. She stopped to listen as it swept gently through the woods, knowing today her mother's chime would join the others. And as the clear sound grew, another voice rose above it. Another melody wove in counterpoint to the chimes. A melody she knew well, and a voice she was growing to love. *Lavender's blue, dilly dilly. Lavender's green . . .*

Zoe smiled, knowing her mother was at peace and she would never be alone.

David was waiting for her at the gate. "Are you okay?"

She huffed out a breath. "Yes, yes, I am."

In the yard, a flute and drums had struck up a lively rhythm.

"I'm glad that the professor could come today," she said.

"I am, too."

"I haven't seen him the last few days."

"He had to go up to Boston for his great-granddaughter's birthday party. Something he didn't want to miss."

"Of course not. He travels a lot, doesn't he?"

"Yep. Kind of a pre-bucket list."

"He's lucky that he has Wind Chime to come home to."

"We all are."

She tried to catch a glimpse of his face, but he was looking out to sea.

"He'll be traveling less soon, make shorter trips, spend more time here."

"Until he spends all his time here," Zoe said, catching his mood.

He nodded. "For eternity."

The Long Island family left about an hour later, pleading a five-hour drive and wanting to miss the

Sunday-night exodus from the beach. When Eve and Zoe left about an hour later, the music had changed to reggae, friends and townspeople and maybe just strangers passing through had joined the party, and things were rocking. A perfect end to a day that could have been steeped in sorrow.

Zoe and Eve were walking back to town when a car turned into the drive and came to a stop. The window lowered and a young woman with curly red hair stuck her head out.

"I'm sorry to bother you, but our family is vacationing nearby, and I'm out with my grandmother today. She wants to go to this place where she had seen some wind chimes, I think. Not to buy, but, I'm not sure. I think it was a long time ago. It might not even be here still." She looked over to the older woman seated in the passenger seat, who looked straight ahead. "She thought it might be down this road."

She smiled apologetically. "She doesn't remember things so well, and she may be confused, but I feel like I should try, you know."

"Of course," said Eve. She leaned in toward the old woman. "And you're perfectly right. Wind Chime House is straight down at the end of the drive."

The old lady turned, smiled. "Wind Chime House," she whispered, and looked ahead in anticipation.

"Oh, thank you. Thank you. Do you think the owners would mind if we just drove by? We'll try not to bother them. It's just, it would mean so much."

"Not at all," said Zoe. "They'd be delighted to see you. In fact, I think they're expecting you."

Acknowledgments

Once again my sincerest thanks to my agent, Kevan Lyon; my editor, Tessa Woodward; Elle Keck, and my whole William Morrow team for your enthusiasm, your expertise, your patience, and for all the wonderful work you do.

Many more thanks to my writerly and not so writerly friends, Gail, Lois, Carolyn, and Pearl, who willingly volunteer as sounding boards and Dutch uncles while I ruminate, hypothesize, act out, and pace over the pieces that go into making up a story.

You all make writing an exciting and fulfilling adventure.

About the Author

SHELLEY NOBLE is the *New York Times* and *USA Today* bestselling author of *Whisper Beach* and *Beach Colors.* Her other books include *Stargazey Point, Breakwater Bay, Forever Beach, The Beach at Painter's Cove, Lighthouse Beach,* and four spin-off novellas. A former professional dancer and choreographer, she lives on the Jersey shore and loves to discover new beaches and indulge in her passion for lighthouses and vintage carousels. Shelley is a member of Sisters in Crime, Mystery Writers of America, and Women's Fiction Writers Association.

About the Author